Good
Cop

Bad
Cop

Sallie Moppert

Good

Cop

Bad

Cop

SALLIE MOPPERT

ZIMBELL HOUSE
PUBLISHING
UNION LAKE, MICHIGAN

Sallie Moppert

For permission requests, write to the publisher at the address below:
"Attention: Permissions Coordinator"
Zimbell House Publishing, LLC
PO Box 1172
Union Lake, Michigan 48387
mail to: info@zimbellhousepublishing.com

© 2017 Sallie Moppert

Published in the United States by Zimbell House Publishing
http://www.ZimbellHousePublishing.com
All Rights Reserved

Print ISBN: 978-1-947210-01-1
Kindle ISBN: 978-1947210-02-8
Digital ISBN: 978-1947210-03-5
Library of Congress Control Number: 2017958491

First Edition: December/2017
10 9 8 7 6 5 4 3 2 1

Zimbell House Publishing
Union Lake

Dedication

This book is dedicated to my Aunt Dar. Even as a writer, I don't have the words to describe how much you were loved and your importance in our lives. The line of people out the door of the funeral home during the visitation was a good indicator of just how much you meant to so many. You brought so much joy and laughter and left us with so many truly wonderful memories (some PG-rated, some not so PG rated–though those tended to be the best stories!).

I know you were looking forward to this book and I hope you have a chance to read it up in some heavenly bookstore.

Acknowledgements

It is with sincere and heartfelt appreciation that I say thank you to my family for the never-ending support and encouragement given to me to follow my dreams of becoming a writer since I first knew that's what I wanted to do with my life when I was a child.

An extra special thank you goes to my mom, Patty, and my sister, Stacy, for always being willing to read over draft after draft, even if the changes were only a few words and some updated punctuation. Thank you to my dad, Paul, for always listening to my stories as my mom read them out loud time and again.

Stacy, thanks for always being the springboard I bounced most—if not all—of my story and character ideas off of—and got a lot of great ideas and feedback in return.

Thank you to Bernice for helping me to get my writing career started. You gave me some of my first writing credits and those will always hold a special place in my work as an author.

Thank you to Zimbell House Publishing for believing in my abilities and giving me the opportunity of a lifetime, the thing I have wanted more than anything else in my life. And Jeanne, my editor, thank you for all of your help; your suggestions and guidance allowed me to not only improve my stories and make them better but my skills as a writer too.

To all of my friends and family members-thank you. Truly, deeply and sincerely, thank you. You have my utmost gratitude for always having my back and supporting my literary endeavors. It's been a long road, but we've ALL finally made it.

Contents

SECOND CHANCES

Throwing open the door to his tattered apartment, Seth Tucker stumbled inside. He was drunk again, having consumed enough alcohol to put a frat boy party to shame, and wanted nothing more than to collapse on the lumpy sofa with the deflated cushions. Instead, he found Charlotte Marlowe seated there, directly in his spot. Arms folded across her chest, Prussian blue eyes glared sternly at him, shooting daggers of loathing across the room.

"Nice of you to come home," she said.

Her words dripped with disdain. She craned her neck to look behind Seth's chubby six-foot frame.

"Where's Sam?" Charlotte asked. "Seth Tucker! You were supposed to pick him up from practice!"

Seth grunted in response. The weather had taken a turn for the worse on his way home, going from a chilly night drizzle to a raging downpour. Seth pressed a hand against the nearby wall to keep himself from wobbling as he kicked off his muddy work boots and removed his dripping black jacket, leaving both in a pile on the dirty burgundy carpet.

"Seriously, Seth?" Charlotte let out a breath and brought a hand up to her temple.

"You want this shit moved?" Seth slurred out. "Do it yourself."

"I don't care about the clothes; I only care about my son," Charlotte replied.

She stuck her hand out toward Seth, sliding forward to the edge of the couch cushion.

"Give me the keys."

Seth made it halfway to the armchair located a few feet away from his couch before pausing.

"He's got feet that ain't broken."

"Dammit, Seth!" Charlotte slammed her hands down on either side of her.

Courtesy of the alcohol coursing through his veins, Seth's already short fuse was shorter than normal. He rolled his eyes as Charlotte continued yammering on and on and on.

"I've learned to deal with your drunkenness, your cheating and whatever the hell else you do when you decide to not come home, but I draw the line when it comes to my son," she said. "Did you miss the freakin' monsoon outside? There is no way I am going to let my son walk all the way home at this time of night, in the dark and in the rain! He could get sick, get lost or hurt or killed!"

"So what?" Seth grumbled. "A kid from the projects ain't ever gonna amount to anything, so who the hell cares?"

Collapsing in the armchair, Seth was now facing Charlotte. Her eyes narrowed until they were barely more than slits. The blue orbs were dark and full of rage, mirroring the storm outside. Popping up from the couch, Charlotte stomped over to the armchair.

"Who the hell cares?" she repeated. "He's my son, you jackass! We could be living in the biggest, fanciest mansion and it wouldn't change the fact that he's my child and I would do anything for him!"

Once again, Charlotte stuck her hand out, putting it inches away from Seth's face. It tremored, the movement messing with Seth's already fuzzy double vision.

"Give me the keys so I can go get him," Charlotte said. "Now."

"I ain't giving you the keys," Seth replied, nostrils flaring.

She had done it again. Seth clenched his jaw, his hands on the armrests curling into fists. Fifteen years ago, Charlotte had chosen Sam's biological father over him. Every time she chose Sam over him, it was another slap in the face to Seth; it was that rejection over and over again but in the form of a fourteen-year-old boy. Anger bubbling up inside of his chest, he was tired of always coming in second place in the race for her affections.

Seth's wandering thoughts were yanked back to the present by a tiny hand slapping him across the face, the sound of flesh colliding with flesh echoing through the silent room. Charlotte recoiled as Seth turned his head toward her. Her oversized gray sweater brushed past her knees as she folded in on herself like a folding lawn chair, dwarfing her tiny body even more.

"Seth, I–I'm sorry … I–I didn't mean it," Charlotte said as she backed away.

Her words became lost in the alcoholic haze in Seth's brain; he hadn't heard anything she had said. Seth became the bull and Charlotte, the matador with the red cape. She had awakened the jealous, possessive beast from deep within him. Seth charged at her and swung his fists wildly, pummeling her with all his might. Charlotte raised her arms to defend herself when she couldn't slip away, Seth using his size and strength to his advantage to keep her in her place.

It could have been minutes, or it could have been hours, Seth wasn't sure. He saw red, and the powder keg of rage, inadequacy, and jealousy had exploded in a flurry of fists. Seth continued swinging away as Charlotte's body went limp.

★★★

Stuffing his hands into his jeans pockets, fourteen-year-old Samuel Marlowe gave up waiting for his stepfather to show up at the Odette Ice Rink to pick him up from practice, instead forcing his exhausted body to begin the long walk home to his apartment. He slung his hockey bag up and over his shoulder and then made his way across the deserted parking lot and out to the main road. Sam wasn't all that surprised that he had to walk home by himself; Seth wasn't reliable. The only reason Sam even agreed to let that slouch pick him up after practice was to make his mother happy, something he strove to do. The jerk was lazy, a drunk and a waste of space. Even worse, Seth put his hands on his mother. The mere thought of that slime hurting his mom ignited a fire inside of Sam.

At least Seth usually didn't beat his mother when he was around. It was probably because Seth knew Sam wasn't afraid to stand up to him and defend his mom. The teenager considered his mom his best friend and would do anything to protect her, even if he had to take a beating for her from the guy who was supposed to love her and her kid. It was easier for Sam to explain away his cuts and bruises; he could blame a fight in hockey for them. His mom didn't have an excuse like that, which made it hard to hide the bumps and scrapes from neighbors and the people at her waitressing job.

Mom didn't deserve any of what Seth did to her over the last six years. She was a hardworking lady who did so much for him.

Adjusting the strap on his hockey bag to sit more comfortably on his shoulder, Sam recalled how his mother had pawned a couple pieces of her jewelry and took on extra shifts at the restaurant to purchase the hockey equipment he still needed after the business that sponsored the team got them most of the stuff. He said she didn't have to do all that, but she insisted.

"I'm your mom, Sammie," she had told him. "You want to play hockey? I'll make it happen. You are my world, Sammie, and I'll do anything for you. We may not have much, but we'll make the best of what we do have, okay, love?"

They'd always been close. It had been the two of them for most of Sam's life until Seth showed up. His mom was a spitfire and a ball of sunshine all wrapped up into one tiny body. She could illuminate any darkness through the warm smile that spread across her entire face and reached her shimmering blue eyes and brightened her already sunny golden-brown hair.

Sam cringed as some raindrops plopped down on his head. His mother was bound to give Seth hell for making him walk home in the rain. As much as he wanted to enjoy his stepfather getting punished for being a neglectful asshole, Sam worried about his mother. Seth didn't like it when he or his mom stood up to him, and if that's what she was doing right now, she was probably in deep trouble. He swallowed hard and pushed his fatigued body to move faster, desperate to make it back to the apartment before Seth did.

After walking a mile in the drizzle, it began to pour. Sam held his hockey bag over his head to try and keep the worst of it off him. He shivered as an icy gust of wind greeted him as he rounded the corner to continue his way up the main road to go home, his breath appearing in pale puffs before dissipating into darkness. Of all the nights for it to downpour, it had to be tonight.

A little way behind him, Sam could hear the splash of tires as they drove through the puddles that were beginning to form in the holes and dips in the road. He stepped off to the side of the street to avoid being hit. Noticing the pops of red and blue reflecting in the water, Sam glanced over his shoulder to find a police car casually cruising down the street, its lights silently flashing. Despite his mom instilling in him that the police were good people who could be trusted to help in an emergency, the other kids (and some adults, too) in his apartment complex always stressed that cops were the enemy. Not sure whether to duck into some nearby trees to avoid being seen by the police or to keep walking, Sam remembered that he couldn't waste any time in getting home, so he kept going. As he continued his trek home, Sam expected the cruiser to drive right past him, but it slowed down before pulling over to the side of the road in front of him.

"Hey, young man," the cop called out.

Sam stopped walking and turned to face the cruiser.

"What are you doing out here so late?" the cop asked.

His firm eye contact and gruff voice made Sam shift uncomfortably where he stood.

"You don't have a ride?"

Sam shook his head.

"No. My stepfather kinda forgot to come and get me," he replied, kicking a pebble with his shoe.

The teen felt like a bug under a microscope in science class as the cop eyed him from the cruiser. Sam wasn't entirely sure what the cop found so fascinating about him that caused him to stare for so long. His red long-sleeved shirt was soaked and sticking to his body, the same with his tawny hair. Honestly, Sam figured he looked pretty pathetic.

"Where are you coming from?" the cop asked.

"Hockey practice," Sam nodded back toward the direction in which he came. "We were practicing at the ice rink."

The cop's eyes darted to the area Sam had indicated before returning to his face.

"What's your team name?" he asked Sam.

"We're the Wolves."

Sam could have sworn that there was a smile that flashed across the gruff cop's face for an instant.

"You're part of the Odette High Wolf Pack, huh?" the cop said. "That's my old high school too, kid. My girls go there now—"

The cop's statement was interrupted by a resounding boom of thunder and a flash of lightning off in the distance. The storm was getting worse.

"Say, let me give you a ride home," the cop offered. "You're going to kill your shoulders carrying that bag over your head. Hard to hold a hockey stick if you can't move your arms, right?"

Sam didn't move. The cop must have sensed his reluctance. He left the cruiser and approached Sam. The towering officer plucked the sports bag out of the boy's hands and placed one hand on his back to guide him toward the cruiser. Sam gave a little resistance at first, forcing the cop to actually push him forward to move toward his vehicle, but ultimately gave in, figuring that he would be able to get home to his mom faster this way. The corners of his mouth turned upward in a small smile as he imagined the look on his mother's face when he was dropped off at the apartment by a cop. She'd probably have a heart attack.

The cop brought Sam around to the passenger's side of the car, opening the door and instructing Sam to sit. Sam watched silently as the cop took his hockey bag to the trunk of the car and peeked through the open zipper to check its contents before stowing it away. When the cop returned to Sam, he slipped out of his jacket and held it out to him.

"Here," he said. "You must be freezing in those wet clothes."

With a shaky hand, Sam accepted the jacket and draped it over his shoulders.

"Thanks."

Sam hated asking for help. Seth said that people would pity them because they were poor and those people thought they were better than them. But that didn't feel like what this was. There was something about the cop that Sam liked, even though the hulking man seemed like he would be kind of scary to deal with. He was older, probably older than his mom, maybe in his early fifties. His hair, though it was wet from the rain, was salt and pepper colored and his eyes were gray. The cop had a big frame, which, combined with his height, made him intimidating, which was probably a good thing for a police officer. He reminded Sam of a grizzly bear, but there was a warmth and fatherly compassion that radiated out and made Sam think he was not quite a grizzly bear, but a giant teddy bear in a grizzly bear's body.

The cop returned to the driver's seat.

"So, where to?" he asked.

"The Englewood Apartments."

"Buckle up, kid," the cop said as he put the car in drive. "If I'm going to let you sit in the front seat, you are going to follow the safety rules. You don't want to sit in the back seat, believe me. It's not comfortable."

Heading down the road, Sam had to admit it was much better to be in a warm, dry car than walking in the rainstorm outside. The windshield wipers were flailing back and forth as they tried to keep up with the downpour. Sam pretended to keep his eyes locked on the road ahead, but would occasionally sneak a glance over at the policeman next to him. The cop caught him looking at one point and smiled.

"What's your name, kid?"

Sam jumped, surprised at the sudden rough voice addressing him. "Um, Sam."

"Nice to meet you, Sam. I'm Officer Edwin Hill," the cop said. "Why don't you tell me a little bit about yourself?"

Sam shrugged, causing Edwin to chuckle.

"How about I start, then?" he said. "I've been on the force for about twenty-five years now. I have a lovely wife named Gloria and two beautiful little girls-well, they're not little anymore, but they always will be my little girls-Clarice, she likes to be called 'Claire,' is a senior in high school and Nina is in her freshman year."

"Nina Hill?" Sam asked. "I know her. She's in my math class."

"Hey, how about that?" Edwin said with a smile. "Perks of living in a small town, eh? Some way or another, everyone knows each other."

As the cruiser stopped at a red light, Sam's eyes were drawn to the lighted sign of a fast food joint across the way. Much to his embarrassment, his stomach growled, reminding him that it had been quite a while since he'd last eaten.

"I don't know about you, but I could use a snack," Edwin said. "Up for some burgers? My treat."

"I'll be okay."

"Well, I'm stopping at the drive-thru anyway, 'cause I could use a warm cup of coffee. If I happen to order an extra burger and fries, so be it."

The red light changed to green and Edwin continued forward, making a right into the restaurant parking lot. After a quick trip to the drive-thru, ordering a coffee and a burger, fries and soft drink, Edwin pulled the cruiser back onto the highway while Sam hungrily wolfed down his meal. Before the teen knew it, they were pulling into the parking lot of the Englewood Apartments.

"Thanks," Sam said as Edwin parked the cruiser in the complex's decrepit parking lot.

"No problem, Sam," Edwin stuck his hand out for a handshake. "It was great to meet you."

As the cop spoke, Sam noticed that his eyes had left his face and were now focused on the apartments behind him, which were an eyesore.

"Hey, if you ever need anything, give me a call, okay? Day or night, I'll answer."

Edwin grabbed one of his business cards from out of the glove compartment and handed it to Sam. Edwin's contact information in hand, Sam hopped out of the cruiser, meeting the cop at the trunk to grab his hockey bag. The cop followed a little way behind Sam as the teen made his way to his apartment, fishing his apartment key out of his bag as he walked. Once he was at his door, Sam turned and gave Edwin a little wave before sliding the key into the lock, opening up the door and heading inside.

★★★

Waiting until Sam was safely at his apartment door to leave, Edwin turned and began his walk back to the cruiser, thinking over the events of the past half hour. The last thing he expected was to come across a kid in need while out on patrol. Edwin took a liking to Sam. There was something about the scraggly, rain-soaked teen that played his heartstrings like a big ol' fiddle. A veteran of the police force, he had seen countless troubled youths from broken families over the years pass through the police department. Edwin hoped that, maybe, by showing the boy a little kindness and giving him someone to turn to, he could keep the boy on the straight and narrow and not let him fall prey to his circumstances as many other kids in his position had.

Edwin stopped mid-step as he heard footsteps racing toward him on the concrete. Whirling around, he found Sam booking it away from his apartment.

"Sam, what's wrong?" Edwin immediately asked.

The boy looked as though he'd taken a 100 mph slap shot to the gut. He could barely catch his breath and tears were streaming down his face.

"Dead," Sam said. "My mom ... I think she's dead."

Shit! What the hell happened?

"All right, Sam, let's try to stay calm," Edwin said. "I'm going to call an ambulance and then see what I can do to help your mom, okay?

He saw Sam couldn't respond due to his heaving breaths and trembling lip.

"We'll get through this," Edwin placed a hand on the teen's shoulder before snagging the radio receiver from his police cruiser.

He radioed for an ambulance before following Sam back to his apartment to do what he could for the boy's mother while waiting for the paramedics to arrive. They raced behind the ambulance all the way to the hospital, sirens blaring and lights flashing. Sam's mom, Charlotte, was rushed into emergency surgery to try and save her life. It was countless hours later that the attending physician stuck his head into the waiting room to update Edwin and Sam. The boy, who had finally succumbed to his exhaustion, was asleep on the floor of the waiting room, the sympathetic nurses having provided him with a fresh pillow and blanket. Edwin carefully tiptoed around the sleeping teen to meet the doctor in the waiting room doorway.

"What's the prognosis, doc?" he asked, motioning to the doctor to step outside into the hallway to avoid waking Sam.

The physician's face was grim. Edwin's heart dropped to his feet.

"It's not good," the doctor said. "We managed to stop the bleeding, and she's stable, but she took a hell of a beating. Honestly? It's a miracle she's alive."

"Do you think she's going to make it?"

"That I don't know. We have her alive and stable, but she's in a coma. With the extreme amount of blunt force trauma to her face and head, I'm not sure that she'll ever wake up, and even if she did, if she would be the same. Her brain was severely damaged. The neurologist on duty is going to review her brain activity and give us a more definitive diagnosis as soon as she can, though the outlook is not promising."

Edwin exhaled slowly, dreading breaking the news to Sam. The poor kid; hadn't he already been through enough?

"Thanks, Doc."

The doctor gave the cop a sympathetic pat on the shoulder before heading down the hallway. Edwin stepped back into the doorway and watched the sleeping figure for a few moments. He had informed people of tragedies numerous times over the course of his career. Hell, he was the one to have to break the news to the Knapp family that their teenage son had wrapped his car around a tree after drag racing with his friends on a deserted dirt road on the outskirts of town last year. But this was quickly becoming the most difficult thing he'd ever done.

Edwin took a seat near where Sam was sleeping. The boy began to stir, his slate gray eyes fluttering open and focusing on the cop.

"How's my mom?" he asked, rubbing his eyes.

Edwin forced himself to swallow the tennis ball sized lump in his throat. Words failed him at the worst possible moment. Delicately and with as much compassion as he could muster, he relayed the news to Sam. The boy did not react at first. He sat still, the white blanket covering him from the waist down, his hair a matted mess from the pillow on the floor behind him. Edwin could see a flicker of emotion on Sam's face, and it was only a matter of moments before it bubbled over, and he erupted.

The boy threw back the blanket and popped up to his feet. His zombie-like catatonia had changed to one of rage and despair. Sam flipped the waiting room chairs as he thrashed about the room. Edwin dodged the flying furniture and took hold of the teen. Sam struggled to break free from the cop's grip, swinging wildly and angrily. Edwin didn't budge; he stood firm and let Sam writhe about in his arms. After a few minutes, the flailing slowed and was replaced by heartbroken sobs. Edwin pulled Sam to him again and held him even tighter than before.

★★★

Once Sam had been calmed down enough, Edwin figured it would be best to take him out of the hospital since there was nothing more that could be done for the boy's mother for the time being. Checking his watch and seeing that it was rapidly approaching midnight, he put Sam in the cruiser and then made a quick call to one of his friends in the criminal justice field. Judge Wiseman was able to get in contact with a family court judge who whipped up an emergency order of protection for Edwin, granting him care of Sam while the boy's messy family situation was sorted out.

Leaving the hospital, Edwin drove them out to Chamberlaine Court, a modest middle-class neighborhood about twenty minutes away from Odette General Hospital. He pulled into the driveway of a bright yellow two-story residence. After parking the cruiser, Edwin got out and hurried over to the passenger's side to help an exhausted Sam up the driveway and to the front door. Fumbling around with his keys while still holding Sam upright, his wife must have heard the cruiser pull in as the porch light flicked on and the white front door with the cheery welcome sign opened, revealing a sleepy looking woman in a furry pink bathrobe, pajama pants, and slippers.

"Edwin, what's going on?" she asked, fighting off a yawn.

"I'll explain in a bit, Glorie," Edwin said. "But, right now, we need to help this young man."

Gloria stepped aside to allow Edwin and Sam inside. While Edwin helped the rag doll of a teen up the stairs, Gloria threw together the guest bedroom. No longer supported by the firm grip of the cop, Sam instantly collapsed onto the twin bed.

"Daddy? Is everything okay?" Eighteen-year-old Clarice poked her head out of her room as Edwin and Gloria exited the guest room.

"It's all right, Claire-Bear," Edwin said to his daughter. "You go back to bed. And you too, Nina."

The bedroom door next to Clarice's was ajar. Nina, having been caught listening in to the conversation, peeked out into the hallway. She gave her father a little wave before disappearing back into her room. Edwin turned back to his wife, taking her hand and leading her into their bedroom at the end of the hallway. He closed the door behind them.

"Long story short is that the kid's mother was beaten half to death by his stepfather. Neighbors heard an argument between the victim and her husband—a common occurrence apparently, so no one thought anything about it—so we're searching for the husband to bring him into custody. I had Judge Wiseman put me in touch with someone from the family courts to let us take care of the kid while the family situation is figured out."

"Be careful, honey," Gloria said.

Edwin gave his wife a quick peck on the cheek before heading out of the bedroom and out of the house. It was time to find Seth Tucker.

★★★

Odette was already swarming with police officers when Edwin joined in the search for Sam's stepfather. Driving around downtown, he pulled his cruiser over to the side of the road to answer a call from his wife.

"Edwin, we have a problem," Gloria said, barely allowing her husband to say 'hello.' "He's gone-"

"What?" Edwin sputtered.

"I'm sorry, Ed. The girls were worried and wanted to know what was going on, so I took them into the kitchen to talk. When I went to go check in on Sam a little while later, he was gone. He sneaked out through the window."

Edwin cursed under his breath. That's what he had been afraid of, Sam doing something reckless.

"It's all right, Glorie," Edwin rubbed his temples. "I'll find him."

Ending his phone call, Edwin radioed this news to his fellow officers. No more than ten minutes later, he had an answer.

"Attention all units," dispatch said over the police radio. "Two individuals matching the descriptions of the suspects have been located at Wolfgang's Bar on Arbor Road downtown."

"Roger," Edwin replied into the receiver.

"Be advised, one suspect is armed."

"Shit," Edwin released the receiver button as he cursed to himself, so dispatch didn't hear him.

Pressing the button, he said:

"En route, dispatch."

Edwin flipped on the cruiser's lights and sirens and gunned it to Wolfgang's Bar. Already having been in the vicinity, Edwin made it to the bar in a matter of minutes. He made sure his gun was locked and loaded; he wanted to avoid having to use his weapon but, if it came down to it, Edwin had no reservations about putting a scumbag like Seth Tucker down.

Hand hovering over his gun holster, Edwin weaved his way through the evacuated patrons and staff huddling outside the establishment and headed inside the bar. To his left, there were four police officers, guns drawn and pointed at a middle-aged man and teenage boy. As expected, it was Seth and Sam. What was unexpected was that Sam was the one pointing the gun at Seth.

"Sam," Edwin said. "What are you doing? Where did you get that gun?"

Gun still trained on his stepfather, Sam turned around enough to face Edwin. Despite the tears streaming down the boy's face, a twisted smile remained fixed on his lips.

"It's Seth's," Sam replied in an eerie, nonchalant tone. "I got it from the apartment. He has to pay for what he did to my mom."

"He will pay," Edwin said. "But this isn't the way to do it."

"Go ahead, you little bastard," Seth spat, his hands in the air as Sam held the gun on him. "You're a loser from the ghetto. You're never going to amount to anything. Go ahead and shoot me. If I'm going to hell, I'm takin' you with me."

"Don't listen to him, Sam," Edwin raised his voice to talk over Seth. "Don't be stupid."

Taking a step forward, he motioned to his fellow officers to take a step back and let him handle the situation. They reluctantly obeyed.

"C'mon, kid, where are your balls?" Seth said, still taunting his stepson. "You are weak and worthless! You'll never amount to anything except a street rat!"

"Sam, don't listen to him," Edwin's voice grew louder again. "Don't be stupid, Sam!"

"Do it!" Seth shouted.

Sam clenched his eyes closed. The gun in his hand wobbled slightly, and Edwin could see more tears forming in the corners of his eyes. He and Seth were using Sam as their rope in a life or death game of tug-of-war. Edwin, though, believed he had an ace up his sleeve.

"Would your mom want you to do this?" Edwin asked.

Sam's breath hitched, and the hand that held the gun shook. Edwin stepped forward again, prepared to make his pleas. He wasn't going to let this kid throw his future away over someone like Seth Tucker. He was the no-good street rat with no future, not Sam.

"Think about your mom, Sam," the cop said. "Would your mom want you to do something like this? You're not a killer. You're not just a kid from the projects. You're a good kid, Sam. I know your mom believed in you, and so do I. I believe in you, Sam."

Edwin held his hand out to the boy.

"I believe in you."

Sam's hand went limp, causing the gun to tumble from his grasp and land on the floor with a thud. The officers rushed forward to arrest Seth while Edwin pulled Sam to him and tightly embraced the boy.

★★★

Leaving the courtroom, Edwin waited in the hallway as the crowd dispersed around him. Sam, hair slicked back and dressed in a brown suit that Gloria had purchased for him, slipped through the crowd to find Edwin. The cop smiled.

"You did it, kid," Edwin said to the boy, slinging his arm around his shoulders.

Smiling back at him, Sam shook his head.

"No, you were the reason my stepfather got convicted for what he did to my mom," he replied.

"Okay, fine. We did it," Edwin compromised.

Sam slipped out from under the cop's arm and stuck his hand out.

"Thanks, Mr. Hill," he said, sounding far more mature than his years. "I probably would have done something stupid if you didn't stop me. If my mom woke up and heard that I'm in juvie for doing something like that, it probably would have killed her. Thanks for not letting me do that."

Edwin put his hands on Sam's shoulders.

"All I did was tell you the truth," he said. "You made the decision on your own. You stuck it to your stepfather by staying strong and testifying against him. Now he's going to prison for hurting your mom. I know she's proud of you because I am. And don't worry about your own sentence; Gloria, the girls and I are going to help you with your community service and whatever else you need to get back on track, kid."

Sam let his hand fall to his side, forgetting the handshake. Instead, he gave Edwin a hug. The cop happily embraced him back.

★★★

That evening, Sam joined Edwin and his family at a local restaurant to celebrate the conviction of Seth Tucker. The celebration soon expanded with an announcement from Gloria and Edwin. Upon hearing the news, Sam was beyond grateful to learn that the Hills were working with the family court to take him in as a foster child while his mom was still in a coma. Edwin and Gloria ordered a dessert each for Clarice, Nina and Sam to celebrate, along with a bottle of champagne for themselves, the family toasting its newest addition with smiles and the occasional happy tear. Sam felt that he had been given a second chance to do something good with his life. Embracing his new foster parents, Sam silently pledged to become a cop like Edwin to pay back his good fortune someday and give a kid like him a second chance at life. Digging into his dessert with his spoon, Sam couldn't recall strawberry shortcake ever tasting as sweet as it did at this moment.

JUST DESSERTS

It was only a few weeks into the new school year and the weather in Odette, Colorado was still pretty reasonable for the beginning of fall. The sunshine made it warm enough to sneak in a few more days of shorts and sandals before the inevitable jeans and hoodie climate reared its chilly head and the summer days were officially over for another year. A slight breeze whisked through fifteen-year-old Sam's fawn-colored hair as he stepped outside into the high school courtyard. The area was teeming with life, with some students having lunch while others took advantage of a free period or study hall to slip outside and enjoy the sunshine.

Sam found an empty picnic table and claimed it for himself, dropping his school books and lunch bag on the wooden table. Sliding onto the bench, he opened up his brown paper bag and smiled. Pulling out a slip of paper, Sam read over the note from his foster mother, Gloria. Although it was only a simple "Have a good day at school," to Sam, it was a bright spot in the dark year since his mom was beaten by his stepfather and left in a coma.

The Hills were doing everything they could to keep him in their custody, jumping through any and every hoop the Department of Family Services told them to like they were a bunch of trained circus monkeys. Even when dealing with all of the stress and the giant headache that officially becoming his foster parents entailed, Gloria still found time to do little things like leaving notes in his lunch. Sam knew his mom would probably love the Hills, especially with the way Edwin and Gloria were treating him like he was their own son. If—or when, as Edwin always reminded him—she woke up from her coma, he was definitely going to introduce Edwin and Gloria to her. That was going to be a great day if and when it happened.

"Can I sit with you?" a girl asked.

Sam's slate gray eyes darted upward and met the laurel green eyes of his foster sister, Nina.

"Hi Nina," he said, his face and ears suddenly burning as the brunette gave him a small smile. "Uh, sure, you can. I mean, if you want to."

Nina giggled, her sun-freckled nose wrinkling, as she slid onto the bench across from Sam.

"It still surprises you that Clarice and I want to hang out with you sometimes, doesn't it?" Nina asked.

Sam turned his attention to the sandwich he pulled out from his lunch bag. His peanut butter and jelly sandwich was pretty fascinating.

"Kind of, yeah," he said, picking at the crust of his rye bread.

It was no use denying anything from his foster sisters; they had inherited their deductive skills from their father, Edwin, who was a cop at the Odette Police Department. Proving his point, Sam saw Nina's eyes settle on something going on behind him.

"Geez," she said with a frown. "What's Scott doing now?"

Sam turned to follow her gaze. At the far end of the courtyard, he could see two larger boys in matching blue letterman sports jackets standing over a smaller boy in a black t-shirt and blue jeans.

"Isn't that Wade Dorchik with him?" Nina asked.

"Yeah," Sam said. "That's him. He lives in my old apartment building. Wade isn't the kind of guy I'd picture Scott being friends with, though."

"I think you're right because it doesn't look like anything good is about to happen between them."

"Wade, you frickin' dumbass!" Scott Farrow shouted. "You think that's funny? Well, do ya?"

"I'm s-s-sorry, Scott!" Wade said as he clutched his school books to his chest. "My computer died, and my Dad had the car, so I couldn't get to the library before it closed to do the research for your project—"

"You shoulda run," Scott's friend chimed in.

"Yeah," Scott said in agreement. "If you really cared about the star of the football team playing this season you woulda run all the way there! But I guess you don't care, do you?"

"No, no, Scott," Wade said. "T-that's not it at all ..."

His back against the brick wall of the courtyard fence, he inched his way toward the school building. "I-I want you to play football this year, honest!"

Scott cracked his knuckles as he stepped toward Wade.

"Really? 'Cause I don't believe you," he said. "I'm not going to let you screw up my chances of playing football this year. Scouts are coming to the games, so I need to play, and that means I gotta have the grades so Coach will let me play. Now, how are we gonna fix this problem, Wade?"

Wade tried to talk, but all that came out of his mouth was a pathetic little cry.

"I need that paper done," Scott said. "If you don't get that paper to me by last period, we're going to have a little meeting after school to make sure you don't forget again, got it?"

"Scott just threatened Wade," Nina said. "I'm going to get a teacher. I'm afraid he'll hurt him!"

"There's not enough time," Sam replied.

He got up from the bench and jogged over toward the three boys.

"No, Sam, don't," Nina said, catching up with him and putting a hand on his arm to stop him. "They'll beat you up!"

"Maybe," Sam replied. "But your Dad told me that protecting others was a part of being a cop. I want to be a cop one day too, so I need to start acting like one. If anyone needs protecting, I'd say it's Wade."

"Be careful, Sammie!" Nina said before she ran off to fetch a teacher.

Sam stepped in front of Wade to intercept Scott before he could get to the other boy.

"Yo, Farrow," he said. "Leave Wade alone."

"It's none of your business, Marlowe," Scott replied. "Go back to having lunch with your girlfriend."

"If you lay a hand on this kid, it's my business,"

Beneath his black-rimmed glasses, Wade's dark brown eyes darted back and forth from Sam to Scott and back again. Trembling, he slipped a shaking hand into his pants pocket and pulled out his inhaler and sank further behind his school books, using the medication to calm his errant breathing.

"Sam," Wade whispered. "You don't have to do this."

"Hey, kids from our neighborhood gotta stick together, right?" Sam said, glancing over his shoulder at his classmate.

Wade said nothing.

"Move, Marlowe," Scott said.

He tried to move around Sam, but Sam stayed put. Glaring at Sam, Scott tried to get past him again, but Sam still wouldn't let him get to Wade.

"Fine," Scott said, shrugging off his jacket and tossing it over to his buddy. "Two ass-kickings for the price of one; must be my lucky day."

Scott lunged at Sam, who shoved Wade out of the way in enough time to avoid getting hit. Scott wasn't so lucky, though; missing his target, he smacked his fist against the brick wall of the courtyard fence, hissing as the brick and mortar scraped the skin off his knuckles.

"Get out of here," Sam said to Wade, lightly pushing his shoulder to get the other boy to move.

Frozen in place, Wade stared back at him, mouth agape.

"If my hand's broken, you're dead, Marlowe!" Scott yelled, grasping his bruised hand with his good one.

"Let's test it and find out," Sam said, bringing his fists up, challenging him.

Fists up, Sam and Scott began to tussle. The fight drew a crowd, with most of the other kids in the courtyard hurrying over to where the action was. A chant of "fight, fight, fight!" started from somewhere in the crowd and grew louder and louder as more kids joined in, watching as more punches landed on both sides.

Scott threw a hook punch toward Sam, who ducked. Before he could strike again, Sam threw a quick uppercut into Scott's gut. Scott coughed and sputtered as the wind was knocked out of him and Sam seized this opportunity to tackle Scott and take him down to the grass to try and pin him to the ground. The jock was still resisting, swinging his arms and legs wildly as Sam straddled him to keep him from getting back up again and continuing the fight.

Scott continued struggling beneath Sam, deciding to spit at the boy on top of him. Sam jerked to the side to avoid being hit, which gave Scott enough leverage to push Sam off him. Sam rolled onto his back, landing on the grass near the brick courtyard fence. Pushing himself up on his knees, Scott cocked his fist back. Before he could strike, Sam whipped his leg toward Scott's knees, knocking the jock off balance. Scott landed on his back on the grass again.

Before Sam and Scott could get back at each other, an ear-piercing whistle caused everyone to freeze and cover their ears. Mr. Egan, the gym teacher, shoved his way through the crowd to get to the two combatants, his whistle still in his mouth.

"Knock it off!" he roared as he stepped in between the two boys.

Gasping, the boys obeyed. Sam and Scott pushed themselves onto their knees, putting their hands on the grass, which was matted down from all the activity, as they tried to catch their breaths. Scott wiped his nose with the back of his hand, his eyebrows jumping up in surprise when he found blood on his hand that was still trickling from his nose. He glared at Sam, who ignored him.

"You okay, Wade?" Sam asked as he looked up at the boy in the black shirt.

"Y-yes."

Gripping each boy's arm, Mr. Egan hauled Sam and Scott inside the school to the principal's office. Nina grabbed all of her and Sam's things and followed them.

Principal Porter instructed Sam and Scott to take a seat in the hallway outside her office, with Mr. Egan keeping a watch over the two of them.

"Nina, in my office, please," Mrs. Porter said, as she held the office door open for Nina.

Her head down, her chin tucked into her chest, Nina headed inside the office, looking like she was the one in trouble, not the two boys sitting outside. The school nurse tended to Scott and Sam while Nina told the principal what happened out in the courtyard. Scott's right hand was wrapped up with enough bandages to make it look like part of a mummy costume he'd wear on Halloween. His free hand held a ball of tissues up to his nose, the nurse instructing him to tilt his head back, to help stop the bleeding. The nurse tended to Scott first, having decided the jock got the worse end of the beating, before heading over to Sam. He got some bandages for his cuts and an ice pack for his eye, which was already becoming puffy and sore.

"Thanks," Sam said to the nurse, wincing as he pressed the ice to his face.

The door to the office opened, causing Sam and Scott to jump at the sudden sound in the otherwise quiet hallway. Sam watched as

Nina hurried out of the office, her head still down and trying to avoid any eye contact with him. He swallowed hard. What did she say to Principal Porter? Did Mrs. Porter not believe her? Was Principal Porter going to kick him out of school for fighting?

Sam leaned forward, resting his elbows on his knees. He felt dizzy and sick, tasting his peanut butter and jelly sandwich again. If he got in trouble at school, the Department of Family Services might find out, and they might not let him stay with the Hills. Grimacing, Sam's thoughts raced at the possible outcomes of whatever Principal Porter had to say. Was he going to be ripped apart from his new family? He couldn't, not now, not ever.

Moments later, Miss Chase, a math teacher, came down the hallway with Wade in tow. He hid his face in his books, but Sam could still see his eyes. The redness and swelling of Wade's eyes were made worse when magnified by his glasses.

Scott muttered to himself as Miss Chase followed Wade into the office, closing the door behind her, but Sam ignored him. He let out a soft groan as he slumped down in his chair, his head against the cold tiles on the wall behind him. Waiting for Mrs. Porter was killing him; he wanted to get this over with before he passed out or puked.

Miss Chase, helping to keep Wade upright, brought the boy straight to the nurse's office after a few minutes with the principal. Mrs. Porter stood in the doorway.

"Samuel, Scott, in my office, please," she said.

Sam's mouth went dry at the sight of Mrs. Porter's glare of death as she stared at Scott and him from over the glasses perched at the end of her nose. *I'm dead. I'm one-hundred percent dead. Edwin's gonna kill me.*

"Want me to keep an eye on these two while you talk to them?" Mr. Egan asked.

"No, thank you. I trust these two young men will not give me any trouble. Right, boys?"

Sam and Scott, heads hung low as they shuffled toward the office, agreed.

"Yes, ma'am."

Mr. Egan didn't argue and closed the door behind them.

★★★

That evening, Sam sat on a stool at the kitchen counter, slumped forward, his chin resting on his folded arms as he watched Gloria unpack the Chinese takeout. He hadn't said more than a dozen or so words to her since she picked him up after the first day of the week of detentions Principal Porter assigned him as punishment for his role in the fight. Scott, on the other hand, had gotten suspended from school for a few days and he was also suspended from playing in a couple of football games. Anything he did say to Gloria usually consisted of the words "I'm sorry," in some way, shape or form.

Gloria pulled out a container of General Tso's chicken and removed the lid, flooding the kitchen with the spicy, warm smell of the sauce. Sam inhaled deeply, his stomach growling. He didn't get to eat much for lunch beside a couple bites of his sandwich before the whole incident with Scott and Wade happened. As appealing as it smelled, Sam wasn't sure he'd be able to stomach the food. His eyes drifted over to the clock hanging on the cream-colored wall above the sink. Each tick of the hands reminded him that Edwin would be coming home from work at any moment and Gloria was going to tell him what happened at school today, and he was going to kill him.

"He's not going to kill you, Sam," Gloria said.

Her back to him, she turned and came over to where he was seated. He lost count of how many times she had told him that since she picked him up from school. Handing him a fortune cookie and something to drink, Gloria gave him a small smile. She gave his hand a reassuring squeeze before returning to the counter to finish getting the food ready. Sam grabbed the fortune cookie Gloria left for him and opened it.

Happiness is not the absence of conflict, but the ability to cope with it.

He frowned. *Gee, thanks for the reminder, fortune cookie.*

Clarice, Sam's older foster sister, strolled into the kitchen, dumping her college books on the counter near him.

"Hey, Mom. Hey, Sam," the blonde paused, her silver eyes roaming up and down Sam's face as she examined him. "Sammie! Your eye! What happened?"

"I'd like to know that too," a gruff voice spoke up from behind Clarice.

Sam jumped at the sight of Edwin appearing behind his foster sister. For a tall, well-built man, Edwin could be as stealthy as a ninja when he wanted to. In a panic, Sam turned to Gloria, silently pleading with his foster mother for help.

"It's all right, Sam," she said. "Come on, let's give them some space, Clarice."

Clarice gave Sam a weak smile and nudged him lightly with her elbow as she grabbed her things from the counter and followed Gloria out of the kitchen. Edwin placed his briefcase on the kitchen table before coming over to the counter. Sam shrank back on the stool. Standing in front of him with his hands resting on the counter, Edwin looked pretty menacing. Sam could only imagine how real criminals felt when they saw Edwin like this on the opposite side of the table in the interrogation room. It had to be a miserable experience if the way he felt now was any indication.

Edwin's face was calm, his breathing steady. Sam's leg began to bounce on the bar of the stool as he shifted under Edwin's unblinking gaze. *If he's gonna kill me, I'd rather he just do it and get it over with,* the teen thought. *This is pure torture. I don't know how much more of this I can take!*

"So, Samuel, what do you have to tell me?" Edwin asked.

"Um, well, I kinda, sorta, got into a fight at school," Sam whispered.

"A fight, huh? Yeah, I figured that's probably what happened based on that nice shiner you have coming in there."

Sam brought a hand up to his eye and winced. It was still pretty painful, even after icing it a few times throughout the day.

"Care to tell me why you were in a fight?"

Sam recounted the situation to Edwin, who listened quietly to his story. After he was done talking, Sam watched Edwin, waiting for his foster father to react. Edwin said nothing, and he hadn't moved the entire time Sam spoke.

"Please say something," Sam said, shifting uncomfortably on the stool. "I did it 'cause I thought it was the right thing to do."

The longer Edwin stayed quiet, the more lightheaded Sam felt. If he kept it up much longer, Sam figured he might pass out and conk his head on the counter. At least he'd have matching black eyes if that happened.

"You didn't start the fight?" Edwin asked.

Sam shook his head.

"No."

It was another moment before Edwin spoke again. Drumming his fingers on the counter, Sam noticed Edwin's gaze drift down to his digits, with an eyebrow raised and a sliver of a smile tugging at the corner of his lips. Sam instantly stopped, grabbing the cup Gloria had given him and locking his hands around it to keep himself from fidgeting again.

"Hey, at least you didn't start the fight because, if you did, you and I would be going round two right now."

Sam let out a breath he hadn't realized he had been holding in.

"You're not angry?" he asked.

"Hold your horses, there, kiddo," Edwin said. "Am I angry? No. Mad and worried? Yes."

"Oh."

"I get why you did what you did, Sam. I think it was brave of you to stand up for your classmate like that. Plus, wasn't Scott the kid that was involved in hazing some of the freshmen football players last year? Someone had to stand up to a bully like that. That being said, I would have preferred it not to come down to a brawl, especially since we're dealing with DFS to keep you in the family right now. A week of detentions on your record isn't going to look good. Gloria and I will do what we can to explain the situation, but I don't know how they'll view that kind of thing."

"I'm really, really sorry, Edwin," Sam said. "I only wanted to help."

"I know, kid. I know."

Sam put his head down, burying his face in his arms. He felt a hand on his shoulder.

"Hey, we'll get through this, Sam," Edwin said. "We've already been through some pretty serious shit; what's one more thing?"

"Yeah," Sam said, mumbling, his head still buried in his arms. "I hope so."

★★★

Around two in the morning, Sam slipped out of bed and sleepily wandered downstairs to grab a few pain relievers, as the ones he took when he came home from detention had worn off and his black eye was starting to ache again. Shuffling into the kitchen to get a drink, he was startled to find Edwin awake and dressed in his police uniform.

"What's up, Edwin?" Sam asked, stifling a yawn.

Standing at the counter, fixing himself a travel mug of hot coffee, Edwin looked over his shoulder at him.

"Sorry, kiddo," he said. "Did I wake you?"

Sam shook his head.

"No. I feel like I got hit by a bus, so I came downstairs to get some aspirin to make my head stop hurting."

Edwin laughed.

"I can only imagine how you feel right now," he said. "Well, I gotta run; there's been a report of a break-in, and I have to go check it out."

Sam grabbed a bottle of orange juice from the fridge. He popped some aspirin in his mouth and washed them down with the juice.

"Good luck, Edwin," Sam said, before leaving the kitchen to head back to bed.

★★★

The next morning, still in bed, Sam yawned and brought his hand up to his face. He winced, his eye still tender to the touch. Rolling over, he checked the clock on the nightstand. He was late. Shit. Shit. Shit.

Throwing the covers back, Sam dashed out of his room and rushed down the stairs to the kitchen.

"Nina?" he called out at the sight of the brown ponytail poking over the top of the sofa in the adjacent living room.

"Hey, Sam," Nina waved him over. "Don't panic; school's canceled today. Mom figured you could probably use the extra sleep, so she didn't wake you up to tell you."

"School's canceled? That's great, but why?"

"I don't know the whole story," Nina said. "C'mon. The news is on; Dad texted us and said a news van showed up at school, so it'll probably be on there."

Sam plopped on the couch next to Nina after heating up some toaster pastries. He handed her one as the morning news program, A.M. Odette, started.

"And our top story this morning is the discovery a body in a burning vehicle on the Odette Senior High School campus. Police were called to the scene early this morning to respond to reports of a break-in and found the burning car behind the building. Firefighters were brought in to combat the blaze. A body was found in the wreckage. When asked for a comment, the detectives on scene said that this was an ongoing investigation and they could not reveal any details at this time. Stay tuned as we will follow this story as more information becomes available ..."

Sam and Nina both stared at the television. No wonder school was canceled.

The news anchor continued speaking, but neither Sam nor Nina heard what was being said.

★★★

"Are you sure he won't see us?" Nina whispered to Sam.

"It was *your* idea that we should come and check it out," Sam said, reminding her of her plan.

The two teenagers got Clarice to drive them to the public library on her way to college, saying something about wanting to work on a research project for school. Sam and Nina weren't entirely sure if Clarice actually believed them, but she dropped them off anyway at the two-story brick building with ivy scaling the walls. Once she was out of sight, Sam and Nina ran down to the high school the next block over.

"There's probably going to be a crowd of people hanging out, trying to see what's going on, especially since it was on the news this morning," Sam said. "We can slip into the crowd and hide from your Dad in there while we try to figure out what happened."

As he figured, a group of spectators had gathered and were standing shoulder to shoulder in the parking lot of the high school. The yellow crime scene tape set up by the police kept them from getting any closer to where the cops were processing the scene. Sam and Nina ducked and weaved through the crowd to make their way toward the front to spy on Edwin and the other cops.

"Is that ... a skeleton?" Nina asked.

The burned-up car was parked by the edge of the parking lot near the school's baseball diamond. Sam squinted as he tried to focus on the car in between all the different cops and crime scene techs walking back and forth in front of it. He was able to catch a glimpse and found that Nina was right; there was a skeleton in the car.

"That seems weird," Sam said. "I mean, the lady on the news made it seem like your Dad, and the other cops found the car on fire as soon as they got to the school, but the body is just a skeleton. I've been reading through the books from the police department your Dad brought home for me; in this one chapter on arson that I read, it said it takes a lot longer than a few minutes for all the skin, muscle and fat to burn away. Look at the car, it's burnt, but it's not that bad."

"What do you think it means?" Nina asked. "Do you think it was a setup?"

"I don't know–"

"Detective Hill!"

Sam and Nina ducked down into the crowd to avoid being spotted as a young police officer ran toward Edwin.

"Officer Robinson," Edwin said, acknowledging the other cop.

"We received an anonymous tip," Robinson said. "You need to hear this."

Edwin followed Robinson to the patrol car that was parked near where the crowd of spectators was gathered. Sam and Nina did their best to hide in the crowd as they approached so Edwin wouldn't see them.

"Hold on," Edwin said, holding a hand up as he looked at the crowd.

"He saw us, didn't he?" Sam whispered to Nina.

"Yep."

"Samuel Chance and Nina Rose," Edwin said. "Out here. Now."

Both teens flinched at the sound of Edwin using their full names; it was equivalent to a "go to jail" card in Monopoly. "Do not pass GO. Do not collect $200." Go straight to jail.

Caught red-handed, Sam and Nina crawled out from the crowd and slipped beneath the crime scene tape.

"Hi Daddy," Nina said, in a sweet tone to try and charm her father.

"And exactly what are you two doing here?" Edwin asked, folding his arms against his chest.

Nina looked at Sam. He stared down at his sneakers.

"Um, we, uh, thought we might be able to help," Sam said.

"Help, huh?"

"Yeah."

Sam turned to Nina.

"Tell him what you told me, Sammie," she said.

"Sam?" Edwin asked. "Care to share with the rest of the class?"

The teen let out a breath before speaking.

"I think this was a setup," he said. "I haven't seen the body up close, but something seems wrong with the skeleton. Shouldn't it have bits of muscle and skin and stuff? Plus, aren't the bones and muscles supposed to contract, and the body looks like a boxer with his hands up to guard his face?"

"The pugilistic posture? Very good, Sam; I see you've been studying," Edwin said, causing Sam to smile. "And, yes, you're right. The skeleton looks like one that someone might have bought from the costume store or borrowed from the science room."

"Um, Detective Hill?" Robinson said, after clearing her throat.

Edwin turned from the two teenagers to face the blonde officer.

"Oh, right, the tip," he said. "Robinson, keep an eye on these two while I listen to the message."

"Yes, Sir," Robison said, before ushering Sam and Nina to the back of the patrol car.

Sam and Nina leaned back against the trunk.

"Well, he didn't kill us," Sam said.

"Nope," Nina nudged Sam with her elbow. "And, hey, my Dad seemed impressed with your knowledge about arson and stuff."

Sam grinned.

"Thanks, Nin."

"Well," Edwin said, as he stepped out of the driver's side of the car. "That's not what I was expecting to hear. Robinson, you and the team finish up here. I'm going to take these two juvenile delinquents, here, back home, so they don't get into any deeper trouble."

Robinson saluted Edwin.

"Yes, Sir."

"C'mon, you two," Edwin said, as he motioned to Sam and Nina to follow him.

★★★

Edwin dropped Sam and Nina off at the house, with a strict warning to stay put, before returning to the police department to follow up on the anonymous tip: **The body in the car is Wade Dorchik. He was killed by Scott Farrow.**

At his desk in the bullpen, Edwin dug up the addresses for both the Dorchiks and Farrows. The first stop was the Farrows.

"What is the meaning of this?" Rhonda Farrow, Scott's mother, yelled.

Edwin barely managed to explain the reason for his visit before the woman started making a scene. The elderly man next door to the Farrow house had his window open, and he waddled over to watch his neighbor rant and rave at the cop standing on the front porch.

"How dare you come to my house and accuse my son like he's a common criminal!" Rhonda said. "What the hell is wrong with you people?"

Edwin sighed.

"Ma'am, I haven't accused your son of anything," he said. "I only wanted to ask him a couple of questions, if that's all right with you."

While Rhonda continued her tirade, Edwin tilted his head to the side, spying Scott hiding behind his mother in her shadow, looking terrified and on the verge of tears. He pulled his notebook out of his pocket and stared down at it to hide his impish grin; the boy had quite a few bruises and cuts, not to mention a bandaged hand. Sam had done a number on Scott. If the boy was anything like his mother, Edwin figured the kid probably had it coming to him.

"Ma'am, again," Edwin said, interrupting Rhonda. "We're not charging Scott with anything, at least, not yet. We only have some questions for him concerning one of his classmates."

"If you want to ask my son anything, you talk to my lawyer," Rhonda said.

"Of course," Edwin said, his tone pleasant to try and annoy the woman for the hell she was giving him. "If you'd kindly provide me with his name and number, I'll contact him and set something up."

Rhonda grumbled before leaving the front door for a moment to get Edwin her attorney's information. Scott, no longer hidden behind his mother, darted out of the cop's sight, nearly tripping over his own feet in the process. Edwin chuckled but swallowed his laughter as Ms. Farrow returned.

"Here," she threw a piece of paper at Edwin. "Now get out of here."

The door was slammed shut in his face, so Edwin left the Farrow house to return to his squad car.

"No wonder the kid's an asshole," he said to himself as he fished his cell phone from out of his pocket.

"Vandenburg."

"It's Detective Hill," Edwin said to his fellow officer. "I met with the Farrows. Mom gave me the name and number of her attorney. Can you call him and set up something? They won't talk otherwise."

"Go figure," Vandenburg said. "Sure thing, Ed. Oh, by the way, the school principal and the science teacher took inventory and figured out what was taken from the science lab."

Edwin listened in surprise at the missing items.

"That's it?" he asked. "The model skeleton and a couple Bunsen burners?"

"That's it."

"Great. That answers one question but brings up a bunch of others."

Edwin paused, rubbing a hand over the stubble on his chin.

"Okay, Vandenburg. Call the Farrows' attorney and get that squared away. I'm going to go visit the Dorchiks and see what's going on there."

"Roger, Ed."

After he ended his phone call, Edwin drove out to the Englewood Apartments, an apartment complex with a name that made it sound far more appealing than it actually was. The 'projects' or 'ghetto' area was a part of Odette Edwin was familiar with, especially since it was where Sam lived before he came to live with him and the family. Sam and Wade had lived on different floors, but the run-down appearance of the apartments was consistent across the entire building. Arriving at the Dorchik apartment, Edwin knocked on the scratched-up wooden door and announced himself, but received no response. He repeated the gesture, a little louder this time, but he still did not receive an answer.

Edwin pulled his cell phone out again.

"Hello?" Sam answered the phone.

"Oh, good, you're still at the house," Edwin said, poking fun at the boy.

"Yeah, we're still here. We're not going anywhere, I promise."

"It's fine, Sam. Actually, I need a favor."

"Sure, what is it?" Sam asked.

"I'm at Wade's apartment; can you try calling there?"

"Wade? Uh, sure, hold on a sec ..."

Edwin heard the phone hit the counter as Sam went to grab his cell phone to call Wade's apartment. From inside the apartment, Edwin could hear the phone ring, but heard no movement.

"I got the answering machine," Sam said when he picked up the house phone again.

"Who lives with Wade?" Edwin asked.

"Last I knew it was Wade and his dad," Sam said. "But his dad would sometimes have to make deliveries to Denver and other places out of town, so Wade would spend some days by himself. We'd hang out in the basement together sometimes when his dad was gone, and my Mom and stepfather were fighting."

"You wouldn't happen to know if Mr. Dorchik was out of town at the moment, would you, Sam?"

"Um, I think he got back yesterday or something. I know Wade mentioned something about his dad being away when Scott was all in his face, but someone had to pick him up from school yesterday after the nurse sent him home 'cause he nearly passed out after meeting with Mrs. Porter."

Edwin exhaled slowly. If Wade's father were back in town, he would presumably have information on when, or if, Wade left the apartment and went to the high school campus. Now the question was, where was Wade's dad?

"All right," Edwin said. "Thanks, Sam."

Leaving the apartments, Edwin drove out to the trucking company Wade's father worked at, Ramsey Trucking, Co. Speaking with the receptionist at the front desk, he was put in touch with the owner, Wilson Ramsey, who radioed Jeff Dorchik in his rig.

"What do you mean he's not at home?" Jeff asked.

Edwin could hear the worry in the man's voice through the static and crackling of the truck radio.

"I just came from your apartment, Mr. Dorchik," he said. "There was no response."

"Shit. Shit. Shit. Hang on, let me pull over, so I don't crash," Jeff said.

After a moment or two, the concerned father came back on the radio.

"Wade said he wasn't feeling well after the whole incident at school yesterday. I had to come home with the big rig to pick him up since I was on the road when the nurse called me. He asked me if he could stay home from school today and I agreed, figuring he could probably use the day off to recuperate."

"When was the last time you saw Wade?" Edwin asked.

"I had to get back on the road right after I dropped Wade off at home. He's a good kid, so I thought he'd be okay ..." Jeff paused. "Detective, you gotta find my boy! Please!"

"We're doing everything we can, Mr. Dorchik."

★★★

Sitting on the living room floor, video game controllers in their laps, Nina and Sam paused the game they were playing when they heard the front door opening. The two teens heard Edwin call out to them.

"Nina? Sam?"

"In here, Dad!" Nina said.

Sam popped up from the floor to meet Edwin in the kitchen.

"What's going on, Edwin?" he asked.

He didn't like the look on the cop's face.

"We have a problem," Edwin said. "Wade is missing."

"He's missing? What the hell?"

"Sam, can you think of any place that Wade may go if he was in trouble? A safe haven kind of thing?"

Sam ran a hand through his hair.

"Uh ..." he said as he thought things over. "We'd hang out sometimes in the basement of the apartments."

"Any place else?" Edwin asked.

"I'm not sure. He stopped hanging around the basement sometime last year though, so I haven't talked to him all that much, except in school. You know? I wonder if he stopped talking to people 'cause he was dealing with Scott bullying him."

"That would make sense," Nina said when she joined them in the kitchen. "Sammie, if Wade stopped hanging out with people so they wouldn't find out about Scott, where would he go?"

"Probably the library," Sam said. "He goes to the library basement a lot, or, at least, he used to."

"The basement?" Nina asked. "I thought that was closed off."

"It is but I think Wade found a way in. I think the window by the staircase is loose but, since no one is allowed down in the basement, the library never bothered to fix it. That's my guess."

"Let's go find out," Edwin said.

★★★

With a history dating back to the gold rush of the 1800's, some of the older buildings in Odette were constructed with secret rooms or storage areas that prospectors could use to hide their gold. The Odette Public Library was one of these places, with the basement of the building being nothing more than a big hole in the ground with a few wooden beams for support. Not the safest place, it was closed off to the public years ago.

Edwin drove Sam out to the library and followed the teen to the back of the building. The sun was already setting, so the library was closed for the night. Sam got down on his knees in front of the window near the staircase that led to the basement. He rocked one of the panels back and forth for a few seconds before it began to move, allowing him to remove the window from the wall.

"Well, how about that?" Edwin said, fists on his hips.

"This is the entrance," Sam said, pointing to the hole in the brick wall.

Edwin squatted down next to him.

"Yeah, there's no way I'm going to be able to fit in there," he said. "Sam, you'll have to go in there to wait for Wade. If I go down there, you're going to have to call the fire department to get me back out."

Sam chuckled. Placing the window on the ground next to him, he stuck his feet into the opening and slid down inside, landing on a box that Wade had probably put there previously. Once inside, he moved the window back into position. Sam waved to Edwin, who gave him a thumbs up before walking away to hide so Wade wouldn't see him if he got Sam's message to meet him there and showed up.

Sam sat in the basement for a little over a half hour. He played on his cell phone to help pass the time, occasionally glancing up over his shoulder at the window to see if anyone was coming, specifically, Wade. Sam considered calling Edwin and telling him that Wade probably wasn't going to show up but stopped when he heard the window panel squeak as it was being moved. Moments later, Wade poked his head into the basement.

"Sam?"

Sam popped up from where he had been sitting on the dirt floor. "In here, Wade."

He watched as Wade slipped down into the basement and replaced the window.

"Sorry I'm late," Wade said. "I couldn't leave until it got dark."

"Why? 'Cause you're supposed to be dead?" Sam said. "It's all over the news, Wade. Plus, Edwin was called to investigate what happened to you."

Wade looked down at his scuffed-up sneakers as he kicked some of the dirt with his foot.

"Sorry, Sam," he said. "I-I only wanted to punish Scott for what he did."

"How?"

Wade let out a breath.

"I got tired of having to deal with Scott. He threatened me that if I didn't do his homework to help keep his grades up, he'd make my life a living hell at school. And he said that he'd find where I live, and well, he didn't say what he'd do, but I get the gist. My dad's on the road quite a bit, so I'm by myself a lot and have to deal with Scott and his friends on my own. Look at what he did to the other freshman on the football team last year. He hazed them pretty badly, and they're guys he's supposed to like. What's he gonna do to a guy he doesn't like?"

"Okay, so what did you do?"

"I was pissed at what Scott did yesterday at lunch. He was gonna pummel me if you hadn't stepped in to stop him, Sam, but then he went after you. You were being a good friend and look what happened. You got a black eye, and I heard you got a bunch of detentions, too. That's not fair," Wade said. "Plus, Nina must have said something about what she heard about Scott making me do his homework to Mrs. Porter. Now the whole school's gonna think I'm a snitch and if Scott's hand is broken and he can't play football, well, I'm as good as dead."

"So, you faked your own death?" Sam asked.

Wade took a seat on the box beneath the window.

"Yeah. I … I was going to maybe kill myself, but I chickened out," he said, elbows on his knees and chin in his hands. "I couldn't do it, so I came up with this plan instead. I broke into the science lab and stole the skeleton from Miss Lynes' room. My dad drove his truck home to pick me up from school, so I knew his car would be at work. After he got back on the road, I took his car from the parking lot and drove it to school and put the skeleton in the driver's seat. I set it on fire with the Bunsen burners I took from the lab. When the cops were looking around the school for the break-in, I called in the anonymous tip saying that Scott killed me. I wanted to make sure he got in trouble."

"Why didn't you tell anyone about what was happening?" Sam asked. "I'm sure someone could have helped you before you had to do something like this."

Wade shrugged.

"It was embarrassing, having to do Scott's homework and projects like that 'cause he's too stupid to do it himself," he said. "I mean, it was easier than dragging the teachers and Mrs. Porter into it too. They probably would have made the situation worse, even though they were only trying to help. It was easier to deal with it on my own."

"Dude, don't you realize how much trouble you caused?" Sam said.

"I know. I didn't want to hurt or bother anyone, but I didn't want to let Scott keep getting away with everything. All he ever got was to be the cool kid at school, the hottest girlfriends and the scouts were gonna watch him play football, and he'd probably get a scholarship to play college football and maybe be in the NFL one day. He can throw a football; so what? He's still a jerk. No matter how many times he gets in trouble, he still keeps doing stuff like what he did to me. It's time he got his just desserts."

"I get it; Scott's a dick and needs to get his ass kicked, but you committed a crime, Wade. A serious one."

Wade looked at him.

"So … what does that mean?"

"You're going to get in trouble," Sam said. "A lot of trouble."

"But, Scott … he's the bad guy …"

"I know, dude, I know, but, like I said, you broke the law and all."

Wade jolted up from his seat. Sam turned to watch as he paced back and forth for a few moments before stopping.

"I guess I'll have to go with my original plan," he pinched the bridge of his nose and closed his eyes.

Original plan? Thinking over what Wade had said, Sam figured out what that meant, and he didn't like the answer.

"Wade, come on, man, you don't need to do that," Sam said.

"What other choice do I have?"

"Let Edwin and me help you, please."

"You can't help me, Sam. Like you said, I committed a crime," Wade turned away from him. "What's my dad gonna do? I made a huge mess of things. He said I was a good kid and that he could trust me, but I screwed up. My dad didn't do anything to deserve a loser like me ..."

"Wade, what's your dad gonna do if you try to do something to yourself?" Sam asked.

He did his best to swallow down the giant lump that had formed in his throat. What the hell was he supposed to say and do in this kind of situation?

"When Edwin called your dad to try and find you, he was so worried, Wade. I mean, your dad came all the way from Denver in his truck to come and pick you up from the nurse's office yesterday. It's been the two of you since your mom died, right?"

"Yeah ..."

"It was horrible when my stepfather beat my mom. I miss her so much, but I have Edwin and Gloria now, and Clarice and Nina too. They're making dealing with my mom's injury so much easier than having to deal with it alone. If you die, who's your dad going to have?"

Wade did not say anything. After a moment, his shoulders started shaking, and he started to cry. Sam came up behind him.

"C'mon, Wade, let's go. Edwin can call your dad, and we can get this all figured out, okay?" he said. "Please?"

Wade was a sobbing mess, so Sam guided him to the window. He popped out the window pane and helped Wade up and out of the basement. After replacing the window, Sam led Wade over to Edwin, who was waiting by his police car a little way down the street.

"I've called your dad, Wade," Edwin said. "We're going to get this whole situation figured out, okay?"

Wade sniffled, wiping his nose with his shirt sleeve. Edwin handcuffed the boy and sat him in the back seat of the cruiser. Sam watched the other boy be loaded into the cop car from his spot on the steps at the back of the library. Edwin came to join him after Wade was securely in the car.

"You okay, kid?" he asked.

"I don't know, Edwin," Sam said, chin in his hand.

"What are you thinking?"

"Wade's a good kid that's been through some tough times. I hate that he has to get in trouble because he was tired of dealing with an asshole like Scott. That's not fair."

"I know, Sam. Scott put him through a lot, but Wade did do some stupid stuff instead of getting help for his problem. Cases like this, Sam, fall into a gray area of what justice is. In this case, it should probably be the other way around, and Scott should be the one in trouble, not Wade. But I don't make the rules, kid. I wish I did, sometimes, though, so people could get their just desserts," Edwin said. "But, you know, you did a good job, Sam. You're a natural at this cop stuff. You are going to make an awesome policeman one day. I'm proud of you."

Sam began to smile. He caught sight of Wade sitting slumped back against the seat in the back of the cruiser and his smile faded.

MONSTER

Sam's cheeks were on fire, and his ears burned just as much as he fidgeted under the maternal gushing of his foster mother, Gloria. He was sure his face was as red as the rose in his lapel.

"You look wonderful, Samuel," she told him for the umpteenth time.

Gloria smoothed a stray strand of Sam's amber brown hair back into his neatly parted and slicked back hairdo. She straightened his suit coat and adjusted the deep red flower in his lapel.

"Is Nina almost ready?" Sam asked.

Gloria glanced at her wristwatch before rushing out of the room to find Nina. It was the senior prom and Sam and his foster sister, Nina, were going together.

"So, are you and Nina in the running for prom king and queen?" Edwin asked as he grinned at Sam.

"We're going as friends, Edwin!" Sam said.

His voice cracked, so he cleared his throat.

"Okay, fine," Edwin said. "How about the cutest couple, then?"

"Edwin!"

Edwin chuckled in response.

"Seriously, Sam," the cop said as he fiddled with the settings on his camera to take tons of pictures of the two teens. "I need to ask you something. I overheard Nina talking to her sister the other day. When the two girls start whispering and giggling, I know something's up. It turns out there's some sort of 'afterparty' going on after prom; know anything about it?"

"Afterparty? Yeah, I know about it," Sam said. "Robby Gauthier's parents have a cabin up at Lake Odette, and they're letting him use it. He invited everyone up there for a cookout, campfire, games and some other stuff."

"Will there be drinking?"

"Probably. I think Robbie's parents gave him permission to drink up at the cabin since they own it," Sam said. "But I swear, Edwin, I'm not gonna touch any of it."

He stopped talking when Edwin waved him off.

"It's not you I'm worried about," the cop said. "Nina can be a little too, let's say, outgoing and fun for her own good sometimes. Remember how the two of you sneaked out of the house and showed up at the scene at the high school your friend Wade set up to fake his death? I have no doubt that it was Nina's idea to do some snooping. She's a good kid, but, Sam, I need you to keep an eye on her, okay? Make sure she doesn't get into too much trouble?"

Edwin trusted him enough to watch over his daughter? Sam could feel a grin breaking out on his face. His shoulders back, chin up and looking the veteran cop in the eye, he said:

"I will. You can trust me, Edwin."

Edwin put a hand on the teen's shoulder.

"I know I can, kid."

Before Sam could say anything else, he was rendered speechless when Nina royally descended the staircase and waltzed into the living room.

"Hi, Dad. Hi Sammie," Nina said.

Sam's breath hitched in his throat, and he could feel his cheeks and ears beginning to burn again. He was sure he was going to look like he had a horrible sunburn in all of his prom photos if he didn't stop blushing soon.

"You look beautiful, honey," Edwin said, giving his daughter a quick hug and kiss.

She did look lovely and regal like a Disney princess, wearing an elegant cobalt blue full-length dress with her chocolate brown hair pulled off to the side, the curls cascading down her shoulder like a waterfall. Gloria came down the stairs a few moments later, carrying a small box, which she gave to Sam. He opened up the little gift box he'd given to his foster mother for safekeeping and presented the corsage he'd bought to Nina. She smiled as Sam placed it on her wrist.

"Ready, Sammie?" Nina asked, a glimmer of excitement in her moss green eyes.

"Ready."

★★★

Sam and Nina pulled up to the Gauthier cabin, which was decorated with brightly colored and festive lights and had loud music coming from inside.

"Looks like the whole senior class showed up," Nina said, looking out the passenger's window.

"Seems like it," Sam said.

Before Sam had his seatbelt unbuckled, Nina was out of the car and heading up the porch steps of the A-frame cabin. He hurried to follow her.

"Hey! Sam and Nina are here!" someone shouted when the two entered the cabin.

Of course, it was difficult to hear the announcement over the cacophony of music and chatter, but some students turned around and waved before returning to their conversations, food, or games.

"Hey, guys, glad you could make it," Robbie said with a brilliant grin that stretched from ear to ear.

He made his way into the living room from the connected kitchen, weaving his way through his classmates. Robbie was clearly enjoying the attention and admiration he was receiving from hosting the cabin party. He was decked out in a flashy designer blue tuxedo. His matching tie had been discarded into a pile with several others as the kids prepared to party down.

"It's prom, guys, have fun!" Rob's declaration was echoed by cheers from the other kids.

Sam and Nina found their group of mutual friends up in the loft, playing a game of foosball. They played games, danced a few more dances and savored some campfire roasted s'mores under a clear, starry night sky. Sitting next to each other on a wooden bench outside the cabin, with Sam's suit jacket draped over her shoulders, Nina and Sam popped some fresh marshmallows on to their roasting sticks.

"Sam, I have something for you," Nina said.

Sam stuck his marshmallow into the fire. He looked over at Nina. She pulled out a gift-wrapped box with a curly blue ribbon tied around it from her clutch and handed it to him. Sam handed her his roasting stick to hold while he opened it. He smiled when he saw the gift. It was a framed picture of the two of them with a group of their friends from the senior breakfast last week at school.

"This is awesome, Nina," Sam said. "Thanks."

"I thought it might be a nice thing to put in your mom's hospital room," Nina said. "We can visit her this weekend, if you want, to give it to her."

"That sounds great. Thanks, Nin. This means a lot to me."

Nina gave him a peck on the cheek before getting up from the bench.

"I'll be right back, Sammie. I need to run to the girls' room," she said, before heading into the cabin.

Tony and Rita, two of Sam and Nina's friends, joined him around the campfire.

"Ready for college, Sam?" Rita asked Sam as she pulled some graham crackers out of the box on the bench next to her.

"Yeah," Sam said. "I'm looking forward to it. As soon as I get my degree, I'm going to the police academy. What about you guys?"

"I can't wait for college either. I get to finally start learning important stuff instead of this high school crap I'll never use."

The group laughed.

"How about you, Tony?" Sam asked.

Tony's reply was interrupted by the crash of the cabin door behind them. The teens whirled around to see Freddy Bourne stumble out of the cabin, looking deathly pale and clutching at his stomach. Already quite unsteady, he lost his footing on the first porch step and crashed to the ground. Sam threw his stick down into the fire and rushed over to Freddy.

"Dude, you okay?" he asked, alarmed.

Freddy's only response was to upchuck the entire contents of his stomach. Sam jumped out of the way in enough time to avoid the spray of booze and food. Rita and Tony hurried over.

"Shit, he's in bad shape," Tony said, as he rolled up his dress shirt sleeves and knelt next to Freddy.

Training to become a paramedic to help with his future career as a doctor, the blond carefully examined his sick classmate.

"His breathing is shallow," Tony said. "Help me turn him so he won't choke on his vomit if he throws up again."

Rita whipped her cell phone out of her purse and called 911 while Sam assisted Tony in moving Freddy onto his side. With Freddy barely settled, Sam and Tony jumped when they heard a shriek. Sam darted inside the cabin. Several other kids were sick. This night had gone from fun to frightening. *What the hell happened?*

★★★

Hands shaking, Sam stared at his cell phone. What was he going to tell Edwin? Whatever it was, the cop wasn't going to like it.

"Detective Hill."

"Edwin," Sam said, struggling to find the words. "We, um, have a bit of a problem up at the cabin ..."

"Problem? What's going on, Sam?"

"A bunch of kids got sick. Rita called an ambulance, and they picked up Freddy, who got sick first, but now, like, thirteen other kids are sick too. The ambulance is gonna come back after they take Freddy to the hospital, but some of the other kids are being driven there by their friends."

"I'll be right there."

True to his word, Sam saw Edwin pulling up in his car no more than a half hour later.

"Any news?" the cop asked, as Sam ran up to the car.

"Yeah. Two more people got sick," Sam said. "Tony's with them right now, trying to take care of them until the ambulance comes back with more paramedics."

"Take me to Tony."

Sam ran to where Tony was, Edwin right behind him.

"Tony, what's going on?" the cop asked.

"Everyone's got similar symptoms," Tony said. "Some are worse than others, though. Freddy and a few others were lucky, only getting nausea, vomiting, and respiratory issues."

"Lucky ones?"

"Yeah. Some of the other kids had bad respiratory problems. The ambulance picked up Jessica, who had a seizure. Before they left, I was helping the paramedics with her, and I think they said she was almost in a coma-like state."

"Shit," Edwin let out a breath.

"What do we do, Edwin?" Sam asked.

"Okay, as of right now, this is a crime scene," Edwin said. "We need to figure out what is causing this illness and fast so we can get the proper remedy. I'm going to call in backup and get some crime scene techs to start looking over the cabin. Sam, I need you to help me start to clear the cabin."

"On it," Sam said.

He pulled Edwin aside to talk to him privately.

"What do you think is going on here, Ed? Do you think it's a poisoning or something?"

"It's too early to tell, but I'm not going to rule it out yet," Edwin said. "Where's Nina? I want to make sure she's all right."

Sam could feel his heart skip a beat. Shit! Where was Nina? He hadn't seen her since before everyone started getting sick.

"She, uh, went to the bathroom a few minutes ago."

"Go find her and then the two of you need to start clearing out the cabin," Edwin said. "As soon as backup arrives, they're going to need to search the place to find out what's causing this."

"Will do."

Sam ran into the cabin and found Rita.

"Have you seen Nina?" he asked.

"Sorry, Sam," Rita said. "It's been hard keeping track of everyone since Freddy got sick. Last I saw she left the campfire to go to the bathroom or something like that."

Shit. Shit. Shit. Now was not the time to lose Nina. Edwin was going to kill him if he didn't find her.

"Rita, can you start moving everyone out of the cabin? Edwin's here, and he's called for backup so we can figure out what the hell is going on here," Sam said. "I'm going to find Nina."

He got some more of his friends to help usher everyone out of the house. Weaving his way through the people, Sam found Robbie sitting on the floor in the kitchen next to the fridge.

"Robbie! Have you seen Nina?"

Robbie had a wide-eyed zombie-like stare, and his skin was ghostly pale. Sam squatted down and shook his shoulder.

"Robbie!"

The other teen blinked a few times before looking at Sam.

"Have you seen Nina?" he said again.

"Nina? No, I haven't," Robbie said.

Sam grabbed Robbie's hands and started to pull him up.

"Listen dude, now's not the time to do this. I need you to come outside with me and talk to Edwin. He's gonna help us figure out what's going on, okay?"

"Okay," Robbie sniffled.

Heading outside, Sam dragged Robbie over to Edwin, who was on the phone.

"Backup's on the way and so is the health department," Edwin said to Sam, after ending his call. "Who's this?"

"This is Robbie," Sam said. "I thought he might be able to help us figure out what's going on."

"Good call. Robert, I need to know what food and drinks were served tonight," Edwin said.

"We-we had hot dogs, h-hamburgers, and some veggie b-burgers," Robbie said, stammering as he spoke. "And to drink ... I'm so sorry! We had beer! I mean, there was soda pop too, but we had beer and wine! My parents said it was okay! I'm so sorry! Please don't arrest me!"

"We'll worry about that later," Edwin said, ignoring the boy's frantic pleas. "Do you have the packages for all the food and drinks?"

Robbie didn't move, so Sam went to the trashcans near the grilling area. He returned with various packages and handed them to Edwin to look at.

"When did you purchase these?" Edwin asked as he looked at the different packages.

"This morning," Robbie said. "I stopped at the grocery store after the early dismissal for seniors; I wanted to make sure the stuff was fresh, you know?"

"I don't think it was the food, Edwin," Sam said. "Nina, Tony, Rita and I all had some of it, and we're okay."

"How about the drinks?" Edwin asked Robbie.

"Same thing. I bought, like, ten cases of soda pop and fruit juice this morning."

"And the alcohol?"

Robbie looked down at the dirt and gravel beneath his feet.

"My sister's boyfriend and his family have a liquor store downtown," he said. "He got some cases for us, and I paid him for them ..."

"Again, we'll worry about that later," Edwin said. "What kind of alcohol did you get?"

"Uh, mostly beer-beggars can't be choosers, right? But there were also some boxes of wine and some other stuff that we mixed the fruit juice with."

"We only drank soda pop," Sam said, making sure to reassure his foster father.

Edwin gave him a quick pat on the shoulder.

"How about the hospitalized kids?" he asked Robbie.

"I'm pretty sure that some of them had beer, but some didn't," Robbie said. "Brenda and Jessica, I'm almost positive they didn't have any beer, but they still got sick."

"Hey, Edwin," Sam said. "I'm not sure if this is anything, but I swore I heard someone say the fruit punch, I think it was, tasted like someone poured a gallon of salt in it, so they threw it in the sink."

"Salt?" Edwin repeated. "Robbie, who had the fruit punch?"

"Um, a bunch of people did," Robbie said. "We mixed some fruit juice with the wine and alcohol to kind of mask the strong taste of the booze, but I don't remember hearing anyone say anything about a weird taste, though."

"The punch is still in the cabin, right?" Sam asked.

"Yeah."

Sam and Edwin immediately headed into the cabin and straight into the kitchen. A large clear crystal bowl full of a fruity smelling red liquid sat on the kitchen counter.

"Tony, has anyone else had the punch?" Edwin asked.

Tending to some queasy looking kids seated on the couch next to the stairwell leading to the loft, Tony looked over his shoulder.

"I haven't been paying attention," he said. "I've been trying to help out with anyone who's been feeling sick."

A brunette with pink highlights to match her frilly pink dress meekly raised her hand.

"Um, Dora and Glenn had some punch a little while ago," she said. "Tony was helping the EMTs load someone into the ambulance, and they said they didn't feel so great, so Dora and Glenn grabbed some more punch."

Everyone in the cabin turned their attention toward the two individuals seated on the couch. Both of them had turned a shade of green that matched Dora's lime green dress.

"Is something wrong with the punch?" someone asked.

Sam looked to Edwin to see how to respond. He could see that the cop was completely focused on Tony and the two sick kids, Dora and Glenn. Flashing red lights filtered into the cabin through the window, signaling the return of the ambulance to pick up more patients.

"Sam, keep an eye on things," Edwin said. "Tony, you come with me to help the paramedics."

Tony helped Edwin with getting Dora and Glenn off the couch and out to the ambulance. Sam stood guard in front of the fruit punch. He eyed the bowl, various questions as to the cause of the mysterious illness bursting in his mind like fireworks. When he told Edwin someone said the punch tasted salty, it seemed to strike a chord with the cop. Sam wondered how it was connected to everyone getting sick.

"Sam!" the girl in the pink frilly dress whispered, sliding through the crowd to the kitchen.

"What's up, Hayleigh?" he asked.

"I'm not sure what it was," she said. "But I swear I saw someone putting something into the punch."

A heavy feeling settled in Sam's stomach.

"I need you to tell me everything, Hayleigh."

Hayleigh's sapphire colored eyes shimmered, and she nibbled on her bottom lip, removing some of her bubblegum pink lip gloss. She let out a breath.

"I saw Connor Babcock-I'm pretty sure that's who it was-sprinkling something into the punch bowl. I couldn't see what it was, but I thought it was sugar or something. Then, a little while later, Freddy got sick."

"What kind of container was it in?"

"It was in a little blue shaker-thing," Hayleigh said. "It looked like a plastic salt or sugar shaker, which is why I didn't think much about it when I saw him do it. I think he tossed it in the garbage can under the sink."

Sam ripped some paper towels from the roll on the nearby counter and began carefully rummaging through the trash. After throwing out several plates, cups, and other utensils, Sam recovered the blue cylindrical container Hayleigh described. Popping the top off, Sam sniffed the leftover bits of white powder inside, but it didn't have a scent.

"Where is Connor now?" Sam asked.

He looked up at Hayleigh, who had been watching him closely.

"Um, last I saw he was hanging out with Scott by one of the other cabins."

"Scott Farrow?"

Shit. Not good. Sam stepped back into the living room.

"Rita!" he called out to the ebony haired girl in the ivory colored dress.

Nina's friend raced over to him.

"Rita, I need you to guard this punch bowl and make sure absolutely no one drinks it," Sam said.

He grabbed a plastic bag from next to the counter where the punch bowl was to put the container in for safekeeping.

"Hayleigh, can you help Rita to make sure no one drinks the punch?"

"Sure, Sam," she said.

Sam left the cabin, standing on the porch as he looked around the campgrounds for Edwin. He hopped off the porch and hurried toward Tony when he found his friend.

"Where's Edwin?" he asked.

"He said the cops and the health department people are almost here, so he's down by the lake waiting to flag them down," Tony said.

Sam didn't reply. Instead, he handed the plastic bag to Tony and pulled his car keys out of his pocket.

"I need you to put this in the trunk of my car and make sure no one touches it," Sam said.

"Where are you going?" Tony asked, calling to Sam as Sam began to walk away.

Walking toward an empty cabin that had a dull light peeking out from one of the windows, Sam heard Tony but refused to stop.

"I'm going to get some answers," he said, as he rolled up his cobalt blue dress shirt sleeves.

At the sunflower yellow cabin, Sam slipped up to the window where the pale light made it glow and looked around the interior. Not much was visible, but his eyes were drawn to a door inside the cabin that was slightly ajar. If the setup of this cottage was the same as the Gauthier's, then the door led to the master bedroom.

Stepping away from the window, Sam tried the front door but found it locked. He hopped off the porch and went around to the back to try the door by the kitchen. At the back of the cabin, on the benches near the fire pit, Sam stumbled across Connor Babcock, who was making out with a girl in a red prom dress pushed up above her knees.

"Connor!" Sam pulled the teen up off the bench. "What the hell did you put in the punch?"

Connor's eyebrows furrowed.

"What the hell are you talking about, Marlowe?"

Sam held him by the lapels of his red suit coat.

"You spiked the punch with something! What the hell was it?"

"Spiked? Whoa, whoa, whoa!" Connor said.

He held his hands up.

"I swear, Marlowe, I didn't spike the punch with anything!"

"You were seen pouring something into the punch bowl!" Sam said.

"Oh, that? I got it from Scott," Connor said. "He said it was sugar, you know, to make the punch taste better!"

"And you believed him? How stupid are you?"

Sam let go of Connor and shoved him to the side.

"Marlowe, what's going on?" he asked, reaching out to stop Sam.

Sam whirled around.

"Your so-called friend Scott got you to poison the whole senior class!"

"He ... w-what?" Connor said, breath hitching in his throat.

"Yeah. While you've been fooling around out here, everyone's been getting sick! Edwin had to call the cops to investigate! He also had to call poison control because of whatever you put in the punch for Scott!"

Connor stood there for a moment before swaying side to side and passing out. Sam managed to catch him before he fell to the ground.

"Go get Tony," he said to Connor's girlfriend, Michelle. "He can take care of him."

Michelle, in tears, ran off to find Tony. Sam eased the unconscious teen to the ground before heading up to the back door of the cabin. He found it had been forced open, so he let himself inside. Kicking off his shoes to remain silent as he tip-toed through the cabin, Sam made his way over to the door of the master bedroom and carefully glanced into the room.

He could see the back of a man who was kneeling on the bed next to the limp body of a girl in a blue prom dress, which had been hiked up above her knees. Nina! No! His heart was pounding loud enough that it echoed in his ears. Sam gasped for breath as he balled his hands into fists, his fingernails digging into his palms. The moment he processed what was happening, Sam burst into the room and yanked the guy off the bed and rammed him up against the nearest wall.

"Scott, what the hell are you doing?"

"Fuck off, Marlowe!" Scott snarled. "It's none of your business!"

"You hurt Nina, so it is my business!"

Scott smirked, putting his predatory smile on display. A few inches taller than Sam, he pushed back, but Sam did not relent and shoved the bigger boy back against the wall again. Sam pressed his arm against Scott's throat as he held him there, causing Scott to cough and wheeze from the pressure on his windpipe.

"I knew that would get you here," Scott said, his voice hoarse and scratchy.

"What the hell are you talking about?"

"Your precious Nina. I knew that if I took her, you'd come find her and you'd be forced to see how I ruined her life like you ruined mine!"

"Ruined your life?"

"You got me kicked off the football team, you bastard! After that fight sophomore year!" Scott yelled. "Do you think it's fair that you all get to go on and live fairytale lives? I was supposed to go to college to play football on a scholarship, but now I can't! Someone ratted me out to the cops for using drugs, which I only started doing 'cause I was so messed up after you ruined my life and now I can't even get a decent job! And then I hear that Robbie is going to host this big, fancy party after prom with alcohol and yet not a single one of you bastards was going to get in trouble for it! It's not fucking fair!"

"Your revenge was to try and poison your classmates?" Sam sputtered.

"My life is over! I don't get to do anything I wanted to, and it's all because of you, Marlowe! It's all your fault, and I wanted you to suffer for what you did to me!"

"You can't blame this on me! You fucked up your own life, not me. Now, tell me what you did to Nina and the others!"

"I ain't telling you shit!" Scott scoffed.

"Tell me before I beat your fucking face in!"

"Go ahead, Marlowe, do it, beat my face in!" Scott taunted him. "I'm sure the police would love to hire a monster with an assault charge on his record!"

"A monster?" Sam repeated, stunned. "I'm not the one who tried to kill my classmates! Tell me what you did! Now!"

Scott refused to give up any answers, so Sam made good on his promise and began punching the other teen. His opponent fought back, but Sam, enraged by the knowledge that Scott was responsible for so much destruction and going after Nina simply to get back at him, gained the upper hand and soon had Scott in a headlock.

"If you don't tell me what the hell is in that punch," Sam growled. "I will drag you to the other cabin and force it down your fucking throat!"

"All right!" Scott coughed, sputtering under Sam's iron grip. "It's GHB!"

Sam froze. That all made sense; when the street drug/date rape drug-which was dangerous on its own-was mixed with alcohol, the effects could be severe and even fatal. Studying all aspects of law enforcement before he got to college, Sam remembered reading about the drug; the vomiting and nausea, respiratory distress, seizures and comatose state were all due to Scott tricking Connor into spiking the punch with GHB.

Scott took advantage of Sam's split-second delay and slipped out of his loosened grasp. The barrage of punches Sam had delivered moments ago was returned full force.

Sam jolted upright, the back of his head colliding with Scott's nose and mouth, temporarily incapacitating him. While the bigger boy recoiled in pain from the sudden strike, Sam rammed Scott's head into the wall, knocking him unconscious.

Breathing heavily, Sam took a moment to compose himself. He leaned forward with his head down, hands resting on his knees. Nina was almost hurt because Scott decided to punish Sam and the rest of his graduating class for his own stupid behavior. If Hayleigh hadn't told him what she saw, would he have gotten to Nina in time? He could feel the rage coursing through his veins at the thought of what could have happened to Nina ... how it would have crushed Edwin, Gloria, and Clarice. After all the Hills did for him, that's how he repays them? By letting Nina almost get raped and possibly killed from a drug overdose?

Sam shoved those thoughts from his mind for the moment as he directed his focus to Nina. He gathered the unconscious Nina from the bed and carried her out to the couch in the living room. He figured she had been drugged by Scott when she went into the cabin alone to use the bathroom. Sam closed the door to the bedroom, wedging a chair beneath the doorknob to lock Scott inside, before running out of the cabin to find Edwin. The moment he saw his foster father, he could no longer keep it together, and the tears came streaming down his face.

★★★

Sam's eyes were growing heavy as he sat in the fluffy blue armchair next to Nina's hospital bed. He hadn't moved from her side since she had been rushed to the emergency room hours ago and it was well into the early hours of the morning. The other students were also being monitored by the hospital staff as the GHB ran its course, but, unless complications arose, they were all expected to recover, including Nina.

Slowly nodding off to sleep, Sam jumped when he felt a hand on his shoulder.

"How you doing, Sam?"

He looked up to find Edwin standing next to him.

"Okay, I guess."

"Bullshit."

"You're right," Sam said. "I'm miserable."

He closed his eyes to avoid looking at Edwin, who took a seat on the edge of Nina's hospital bed.

"I'm so sorry, Edwin," Sam said. "I screwed up. You asked me to watch over Nina and take care of her and look at what happened. I failed miserably. I am so, so sorry, Edwin—"

"Samuel, look at me," Edwin said.

Eyes still closed, Sam turned his head. He felt Edwin's hand on his chin, turning his head back toward him.

"Samuel, open your eyes and look at me."

"I-I can't—"

"Open your damn eyes!"

Sam did as Edwin instructed and opened his eyes. Immediately, he could feel tears stinging and burning his eyes.

"Listen to me, Samuel," Edwin said. "You didn't fail me. Yeah, I'm pissed about what happened to my daughter, but do I blame you? No. You didn't go with Nina to the afterparty with the intent of having Scott go after her. If you did, this would be a very different conversation, believe me."

Sam gave a small laugh followed by a sniffle.

"You and Tony," Edwin handed the boy a tissue. "You two handled yourselves amazingly well. Without you kids staying calm and collected like you did, who knows how many of your classmates would have had the laced punch? Plus, if you guys hadn't reacted in time like you did, who knows if they would have recovered? There was no way any of you knew what was going to happen. Didn't you say Connor, Scott's friend, didn't even know what he was putting in the punch? This was all because some fucked up kid was angry and wanted to take other people down with him."

This was all because some fucked up kid was angry and wanted to take other people down with him.' Edwin's words resonated in Sam. He was angry. He was fucked up. *Is this my future? Lashing out at people because I'm so hurt and screwed up? Was Scott right when he called me a monster?*

"Hey, Edwin," Sam asked, rubbing his sweaty hands on his pant leg. "Am I ... a monster?"

Edwin frowned.

"Why the hell would you ask something like that?"

Sam shrugged. He didn't want to tell him what Scott said.

"Did Scott say something to you?" Edwin asked.

Of course, he'd figure out what happened.

"Listen, Sam, you are not a monster; do you think I would have moved you into my house with my family if you were?" Edwin said, using the same fatherly voice he did with Clarice and Nina. "Sure, you've gotten angry and have had some outbursts and gotten into a fight or two—but usually defending someone—so we can let that slide for now. Life's dealt you a crappy hand on occasion, sometimes sticking you with more shit than a kid your age should have to deal with. That's bound to make anyone a little frustrated. Does that make you a bad kid or a monster for reacting to it that way? No way."

"But, when Scott told me what he did, how he tried to hurt everyone, including Nina-especially, Nina-I ... I could have killed him," Sam said.

He looked down at his bruised knuckles.

"My mom told me that she didn't ever want me to know my real dad because he wasn't a good guy; what if he's some sort of killer or criminal? What if I turn out to be a monster like him?"

"Who cares about him?" Edwin asked. "Maybe your mom's right, and he's a scumbag. That doesn't matter because *I'm* your father now, Samuel. I'll be your conscience, like that cricket in Pinocchio, and I'll keep you on the straight and narrow. Even if I have to kick you in the ass."

Sam laughed out loud at that image. Edwin did too.

"And don't worry kid," he said. "I'll be keeping you a squeaky clean little boy scout for years to come because I am not going anywhere for a long, long time."

Edwin pulled Sam to him, giving the teen a much-needed hug.

"I know it's no use telling you to come home and get some rest," he said after he let Sam go. "I'm going to go run to the nurse's station and get you a blanket and a pillow, okay?"

"Thanks, Edwin."

While Edwin was gone, Sam looked at Nina, who was sedated. He sighed. Normally, he wouldn't question Edwin. He knew the veteran cop was smart and good at what he did. But, in this case, Sam wondered if Edwin was wrong.

HOLDING ON

Twenty-one-year-old Samuel Marlowe strolled into the Odette Long Term Care Facility, smiling as he caught his reflection in the glass doors. Dressed in his navy police uniform with golden brown hair neatly parted to the side and bright silvery eyes, the image of the person staring back at him was surreal. The badge pinned to his chest glittered in the sun's reflection. Seeing himself this way, as the thing he dreamed of becoming for years, as a cop, Sam felt as though he was ready to take on the world and that things were finally as they should be. His chest swelled up with pride and joy, puffed out so much that he wouldn't have been surprised if some of the buttons from his uniform top would pop off. But that was fine with him. He was a cop, and nothing was going to dampen his mood.

Graduating from the police academy a little over a month ago, Sam was beyond excited and thrilled to be starting his first day as a member of the Odette Police Department. The best part was that the police Captain, Captain Buchanan, assigned Sam's foster father, Edwin Hill, to be his partner and supervise and train him while he was completing his probationary period. Working alongside Edwin to help others was all Sam could dream of doing ever since the veteran cop rescued him from his family turmoil seven years ago. He was ready to pay that good fortune forward.

His first assignment was to join his fellow officers patrolling the Odette City Carnival. Thousands of families, including some from nearby big cities such as Colorado Springs or Denver, would pack the boardwalk to capacity every summer to attend the annual carnival. Located on the Lake Odette boardwalk on the lake's shore, the miles long wooden walkway full of shops and food vendors or restaurants, filled up for one week each year with carnival rides, games, and performers of all kinds.

Of course, the carnival wasn't without its hiccups, which was why Sam and the other officers were assigned to patrol the boardwalk throughout the carnival's week-long tenure. Teenagers with too much time on their hands could cause mischief. Being out in the hot summer heat could cause tempers to flare, creating a ruckus between some people in the beer tent. Or, some jerk might try to cheat at a carnival game and cause a scene when caught, resulting in needing to be escorted out of the carnival. Having been to the fair himself before, Sam knew that it wasn't always fun and games.

He left the department a few minutes early to make a special stop before meeting up with the other officers at the boardwalk. Rounding the corner of the west wing of the facility, Sam slipped quietly into Room 523. A soft, steady beep greeted him, the heart monitor the only sign of life in the room. Sam took a seat in the burgundy armchair next to the hospital bed, which the doctors and nurses called "Sam's chair" because of all the time he spent sitting in it over the years. He took his mother's hand in his.

Charlotte had been in a coma since she was beaten by Sam's stepfather, Seth Tucker, a little over seven years ago. A persistent vegetative state, the doctors called it; she was essentially only being kept alive by the countless machines attached to her through various wires and tubes. They told him she most likely wasn't ever going to wake up; the injuries to her head and brain from the attack were too severe. Sam didn't want to admit his mother was gone. He didn't want to let go.

"Hey, Mom," Sam said. "Guess what? Today's my first day as a cop. I can't believe I finally did it, Mom. I got my degree and completed the academy. Edwin and Gloria were so happy at the academy graduation. It was a great day. The only thing that would have made it better was if you could have been there."

Sam reached into his breast pocket with his free hand and pulled out a picture his foster sister's boyfriend, Raymond, had taken of him with Edwin, Gloria, Clarice, and Nina at the academy graduation. He set it down on the table next to the hospital bed, alongside the other photos he'd brought to her over the years. Sam figured he'd have to get a frame for the newest picture; maybe he could pick one up at the carnival from one of the art vendors. Thinking about the fair, Sam glanced up at the clock on the wall above the dry-erase board the nurses used to keep track of patient information from shift to shift.

"Looks like I have to get going, but I'll be back to tell you about my first day," he said, with a smile. "My first day as a cop; I still can't believe it's finally here. Remember how we used to go and walk the boardwalk during the carnival every year, Mom? Well, now I get to do it again, but as a cop this time. I know it's gonna be great."

Placing a gentle kiss on his mother's forehead, Sam got up from his chair and headed out of the room.

★★★

Sam enjoyed his time patrolling the boardwalk. The sun was shining, children were laughing and the smell of all sorts of sugar-laden snacks hung in the air over the carnival. Cheery music came from speakers sitting on the platforms of the different carnival rides, from the merry-go-round to the Ferris wheel to the fun house. About an hour into his shift, Sam ran into Clarice and Raymond. His sister bought him some freshly squeezed ice-cold lemonade and shared some of her pink fluffy cotton candy as the three strolled the boardwalk together.

"Officer!" A group of teenage girls ran up to Sam. "These two dudes are arguing! They look like they're gonna fight each other!"

Sam followed the girls, Clarice and Raymond running behind him. They rounded the corner near the duck pond game, dodging people as they turned from the ice cream stand with cones in their hands. As the girls said, two men were arguing; Sam heard their heated words before he even saw the two of them.

"You here to steal another kid, Pennington?"

"Steal? Seriously, Gerald! Let it go! I didn't do anything to you or your kid!"

"Bullshit!"

Reaching the ring toss game, Sam found that the two men moved from shouting at each other to pushing and shoving. He radioed in the incident to the other officers on duty before stepping in to stop the shoving before it evolved into full-blown punches.

"Whoa, whoa, whoa," Sam said. "That's enough, you two. The carnival is for families, not for a WWE Smackdown."

Raymond, a firefighter, also stepped in and assisted Sam in putting distance between the two men until the other officers could arrive. The man Sam had a hold of still wanted to go after the other, as he tried to push past him.

"Hold your horses, there, bud," Sam said. "What's your name?"

The man didn't seem to hear him.

"His name is Gerald," Raymond's man said. "My name is Mitch."

"Pennington, you bastard," Gerald growled. "You destroyed my family!"

His hand shook as he pointed at Mitch and he clenched his teeth. Gerald tried to struggle against Sam's grip, but Sam held firm. Mitch threw his hands up as much as Raymond's hold would allow.

"I've told you a million times, Gerald!" he said. "I didn't do anything! I'm sorry for what happened to you and your family, but I swear I didn't have anything to do with it! Why can't you get that in your head and leave me alone?"

"I will never leave you alone, you monster! As long as I am on the face of this earth, I will do whatever I can to make you pay, you stupid son of a b-"

"All right, potty mouth, that's enough," Sam said. "You're scaring the children."

"Daddy?" a little girl asked.

The voice of the sweet child with bleach blond pigtails and a tear stained face clinging on to a stuffed elephant pulled Gerald out of his haze. He blinked a few times before he looked behind him at the ring toss game. The grandfatherly game operator held the girl close to him, patting her back to soothe her.

"Lizzy, sweetie ... I'm so sorry."

★★★

With the assistance of some of the other officers on patrol, Sam escorted the two men from the boardwalk. Mitch was asked to leave the carnival, and Sam brought Gerald to the police department. Clarice and Raymond volunteered to keep an eye on Lizzy while things were sorted out.

"Sam!"

He looked up from the file in his hand to see Edwin heading down the hallway toward him.

"I heard there was a throw down at the carnival. What happened?" Edwin asked.

"That's Gerald White. He was with his daughter at the ring toss game when he bumped into another guy named Mitch Pennington. Gerald flew off the handle, and they started arguing. Some kids recognized things were getting heated between the two and came and got me."

"Pressing charges?"

"No, Mitch didn't want to," Sam said. "I'm going to let Gerald go in a little bit. I brought him in mainly to let him cool down and maybe give him a wakeup call to remind him not to do that kind of stuff in front of his kid."

"Good call," Edwin said.

He looked at the file in Sam's hands.

"I thought you said the other guy wasn't filing charges?"

"He's not."

"Then what's all that?"

Sam handed Edwin the file folder.

"Gerald said some interesting things when he was shouting at Mitch," he said.

"Like what?"

"He was saying stuff like 'Are you here to steal another kid?' and 'You destroyed my family.'" Sam said. "That's not the kind of stuff people normally yell at each other during a fight, so I decided to look into it. I checked the records and found a neat little connection between the two. About five years ago, Gerald's kid vanished. His four-year-old son completely disappeared from the yard of his house. No struggle, no screams, no crying, nothing."

"How does Mitch fit into all of this?" Edwin asked as he skimmed through the information Sam had collected.

"It seems like a neighbor saw Mitch coming in and out of people's yards that day and suggested he might have been involved somehow. He worked for the electric company, so he was probably only doing his job. There was never any evidence to prove that Mitch had anything to do with what happened to Gerald's kid, but that didn't seem to matter to Gerald. Based on some of the things he was shouting at Mitch, it seems like Gerald is convinced he's guilty."

"Was the kid ever found?"

"Unfortunately, no," Sam said with a grimace.

Edwin looked into the interrogation room where Gerald was through the one-way window.

"So, this is a cold case," he said. "Do you want to take a stab at it?"

Sam's heart began pounding so loudly that it echoed in his ears.

"Me?" he asked.

"No, the guy who runs the coffee stand across the street. Yeah, you, Sam," Edwin said with a laugh. "I'm your supervising officer, right? I'll help you. Sometimes a fresh pair of eyes can find something that might have been overlooked or bring a new perspective to the evidence that no one thought of before and that could be the key to solving the mystery."

"Are you sure?" Sam asked. "I mean, I just started here, and I don't want to step on anyone's toes …"

"I'll tell you what," Edwin slung an arm around Sam's shoulders. "If it makes you feel better, talk to the detective who investigated the case and see what he or she thinks about you looking into it. If they give you the okay, we'll talk to the Cap about reopening it."

"All right."

The detective in charge of the investigation of the missing child was Senior Detective Rusty Caldwell, Sam discovered. He located the veteran cop in the break room, fixing himself a fresh cup of coffee.

"Excuse me, Detective Caldwell?" Sam asked.

He stood in the doorway of the break room, the file folder from the White case in his hands.

"Who's asking?" Rusty glanced over his shoulder at Sam. "You're Edwin's boy."

"Yeah, Sam Marlowe."

Rusty turned and rested his ample back against the counter.

"What's up, kid?" he asked before taking a sip of his coffee.

Sam opened the case file, nearly dropping the papers. He caught them before they could slide out of the folder and replaced them. Sam locked his eyes down on the documents inside, gripping the edges of the folder securely.

"Sir, there was an incident down at the carnival between Mitch Pennington and Gerald White," he said. "They were both involved in the investigation you led from five years ago when Gerald's son went missing."

"I remember," Rusty said, not sounding all too pleased. "Gerald's still gunning for Mitch, I take it?"

"Yes, Sir," Sam said. "That's actually what the confrontation was about. Um, Detective Caldwell, I'd like to, maybe, if it's okay with you, look into the case and see if I can–"

"See if you can what?" Rusty asked, interrupting him. "Solve it? I hate to break it to you, kid, but the chances of finding that boy are slim, none and forget it. The first twenty-four hours in any missing persons case are critical; as the hours go by, the likelihood of finding that person keeps going down and down and down until it's pretty much a lost cause."

"What do you mean lost cause?" Sam asked. "Finding the boy alive or do you mean finding the boy in general?"

"Both. Listen, kid, it's been five years. The odds of finding the boy are practically zero."

"But if there's still a chance, I'd like to take it," Sam said.

Rusty let out a huff. He picked up his coffee mug and started for the door.

"Give it up, kid."

Sam turned and watched Rusty head toward the break room door. Was that it? Was there no hope for Gerald for finding his missing son? Sure, five years was a long time, but that didn't mean that the child was gone forever, did it? It couldn't.

"Wait!" Sam said.

Rusty stopped, the hand that wasn't holding the coffee mug clenching into a fist for a brief moment. He turned back to Sam.

"What?"

"What if," Sam said, his mind racing as he tried to come up with a reason to convince Rusty to give him the case. "What if … what if I find new evidence? Would you let me take over the case, then?"

"Fine. If you find something groundbreaking, and it better be impressive, kid, then you can reopen the case," Rusty said. "Otherwise, drop it. Got it?"

"Yes, Sir. Understood, Sir."

Rusty shook his head and continued forward. He muttered to himself as he walked away, Sam catching the veteran detective's words:

"Damn rookie."

Sam avoided eye contact with Edwin when he returned to the hallway outside the interrogation rooms.

"How'd it go with Rusty?" Edwin asked.

Sam didn't respond.

"He gave you a hard time, didn't he?"

"Kind of."

"That doesn't surprise me," Edwin said. "Giving up a case isn't easy for a cop, Sam, so don't take it too personally. When you spend hours and hours, day in and day out, month after month, and sometimes, year after year, working on a case, it goes from merely doing your job to a personal challenge. You need to solve that case. You have to solve that case. Sometimes you can, sometimes you can't. When you can't, the case goes cold, and it's put on the back burner for another day. Maybe you'll get a new lead, maybe you won't. When someone new comes in and looks into that case, your case, and finds something, you take it personally. How did I miss that clue? I'm a shit cop and other nonsense like that. You forget the reason why the case came across your desk in the first place: to get justice for the victim."

Sam took in all that Edwin said.

"He said that I have to find some 'groundbreaking' piece of evidence," he said. "Or else I can't have the case."

"Well," Edwin motioned toward the interrogation room where Gerald was. "Then get going, kid. That evidence isn't going to find itself."

Stuck in place, Sam finally moved forward with a helpful little shove from Edwin. Hand hovering over the doorknob of the interrogation room door, he let out a breath before heading inside. Gerald White sat at the gray metal table with his head with honey-colored hair in his hands and several bunched-up tissues next to him. He remained motionless as Sam and Edwin entered the room.

"Mr. White," Sam said. "I'd like to talk about what happened to your son."

Gerald's head whipped up.

"My son?" he repeated. "You're going to reopen the search for my son? Oh, thank you, Officer Marlowe! Thank you, thank you, thank you!"

Sam gave Edwin a wide-eyed look. Shit. He didn't want to get Gerald's hopes up about the case.

"Hold on, there," Sam said, as he took a seat at the table across from Gerald. "I can't promise anything. I'd like to reopen your son's case, but there are certain rules and procedures I have to follow."

"Oh," the disappointment in Gerald's voice was unmistakable.

"But, I did talk to Detective Caldwell, and he agreed to let me take over the case if I can find a new lead. To do that, I need your help. You can start by telling me about the case."

"It was five years ago on July 12th," he said to Gerald. "My son, my little boy, William, wanted to play outside in our backyard since it was summer and the weather was nice and warm. My daughter, Lizzy, was only a year old at the time. She started coming down with a little cold or something, so I was inside taking care of her. Will, being an energetic little boy, got impatient and slipped out through the doggy door we had installed in the kitchen door at the back of the house. I had just made a bottle for Lizzy and was standing at the sink while I checked the temperature when I saw Will outside. We had a fenced-in yard, so I figured Will would be okay for a few minutes while I went upstairs to get his sister. Plus, it was easier to let him stay outside while I tended to his sick sister than making him come inside and then having two grumpy toddlers to deal with. Anyway, Lizzy was cranky since she wasn't feeling good and getting her up from her nap took a little longer than expected. By the time I got her up, changed and brought her downstairs with me, William was gone."

"Did you see or hear anything unusual before William vanished?" Sam asked.

"No, nothing," Gerald shook his head. "William just vanished. All his toys were still in the backyard, right where he had them when I saw him outside through the kitchen window a few minutes before."

"You saw he wasn't in the yard, then what?"

"I called my neighbors and asked them if Will had somehow ended up in their yards, but they hadn't seen them either. My one neighbor volunteered to watch over Lizzy while I went to look for William. I called my wife at work and told her what happened as I started going up and down the streets looking for him."

"How did Mitch Pennington get involved?" Sam asked.

"That jerk was supposedly a meter reader with the electric company. It seems awfully funny that he's going in and out of people's yards all day when my son goes missing," Gerald said. "I didn't know he was in the neighborhood until someone down the street told me about it."

"Who told you about him?"

"Her name's Audrey Tallman. Nice lady; kind of a hermit, though. Never saw her that much, so, when she came to talk to me out of the blue, I figured it had to be important."

"What's her address?"

Sam had his pen poised to write but paused when he saw Gerald's look of disappointment.

"Did something happen to her?" he asked.

"It was shortly after the … incident … that Audrey moved away," Gerald said. "I have no idea where she went. Hell, I didn't realize that she was gone until a 'for sale' sign popped up on her front lawn. She was gone before the house was even sold. My wife and I were getting divorced around that time, and well, we were otherwise occupied."

Sam excused himself from the room, and Edwin followed him out.

"Nothing," he flipped through the case file. "Nothing at all about it."

"About what?" Edwin asked.

"About the neighbor up and leaving like that," Sam said. "When I lived in the projects, anytime someone moved out in a hurry like that, it was because they either had something to hide or wanted to avoid something or someone. It doesn't seem like Detective Caldwell followed up with Audrey Tallman after the initial investigation. Does that mean he couldn't find her?"

"Rusty's a good cop, so it'd be easy for someone with his experience to track her down through her driver's license or something like that. There's got to be another reason why Audrey wasn't involved any further in the investigation, especially if she was a key witness in the case," Edwin said.

"We need to find her."

"Sam, I think you found your lead."

Sam did his best to fight the smile that was tugging at his lips but figured he failed when Edwin smiled back at him.

★★★

Staring at his computer screen at his desk in the bullpen, Sam didn't know what to make of his discovery. This had to be a fluke or some system error at the very least.

"Hey, Ed," Sam waved to his foster father as he entered the bullpen. "Can you come take a look at this?"

"Sure, what's up, kid?"

Sam pointed to his computer screen as Edwin came to stand behind him.

"Okay, this is a picture of Audrey Tallman from her driver's license," he pulled up two additional photos and moved them next to the original. "Who would you say these pictures are of?"

"Those two look exactly like the one from the driver's license," Edwin said. "Actually, I'd say that those are all the same picture. All three are the same skinny woman with dirty blond hair. She kind of looks like a scared little mouse, in my opinion."

"Yeah, I thought that too but, amazingly enough, all three women have different names," Sam said. "The first one is Audrey Tallman. The next one is Janet Somerville, and the third is Norma Humphrey."

Sam looked over his shoulder at Edwin. "What are the odds that they're identical triplets?" he asked, more as a joke than an actual explanation.

"Unless this is *Ripley's Believe it or Not!,* and they *are* identical triplets, then I think it's more likely that two of those, or maybe all three, are fakes," Edwin said.

"But how do I tell which one is the real one?" Sam asked.

"You're a cop now, Sam," Edwin said. "You figure it out."

Before Sam could protest, Edwin headed off. Sam turned back to his computer screen and let out a breath. He pulled up all three of the driver's license photos and information, arranging them to be side by side. All three were issued at different times and in various cities in Colorado. The first, Audrey Tallman, was from Odette. Janet Somerville's was issued second in Denver. The most recent one was issued in Boulder to Norma Humphrey. Sam reached out to both the Denver and Boulder police departments to have them check in on Janet and Norma respectively.

While waiting to hear back from the two neighboring cities, Sam returned to the interrogation room to release Gerald.

"Officer Marlowe!" Gerald, who had been standing by the window, whirled around to face Sam the moment he entered the room. "How's my little Lizzy doing? Is she okay? When can I see her?"

"One thing at a time," Sam replied. "The first thing is that you are free to go, Gerald; Mitch isn't pressing charges."

"He's not? Oh, thank god."

"Secondly, but most importantly, my sister and her boyfriend are keeping Lizzy occupied," Sam said. "They got her snacks from the cafeteria, and they're keeping her busy with some coloring pages."

"Thank you."

"No problem. Just promise me one thing—"

"Of course. For all your help, I'd do anything."

"Stop going after Mitch Pennington. Until we find out for sure whether or not he's involved in your son's disappearance, you gotta promise me not to do something stupid. If you go after him and we have to put your ass in jail, what's Lizzy going to do? She doesn't need to lose a brother and a father, too."

Gerald fell back against the wall. He closed his eyes and laid his head back, letting out a long, slow breath.

"I'm sorry about all this, Officer. I-I-I get so enraged when I think that someone took my son. I would lose sight of the world around me," he said. "Including my daughter ..."

"Next time you want to punch the guy's lights out, stop and think about Lizzy first, okay?"

Gerald lifted his head and rubbed the back of his neck.

"I'll do my best," he paused. "Thanks, Officer Marlowe."

Sam led Gerald from the interrogation room downstairs to the police department cafeteria, where Clarice and Raymond were waiting with Lizzy. The moment the little girl saw her father, she popped off her chair and ran over to him.

"Daddy!" Lizzy giggled as Gerald picked her up and swung her around.

"Thanks for your help, guys," Sam said to Clarice and Raymond.

"No problem, Sammie," Clarice said. "Lizzy is a sweetie; she was no trouble."

With Gerald and Lizzy reunited, Sam escorted the two to the door. As they prepared to part ways, Sam was beckoned over by another police officer.

"Marlowe, got a phone call for you from Denver PD," the officer said.

Hurrying back to his desk, Sam had the other officer transfer the call to him. Sam found that Janet Somerville had pulled a similar disappearing act to the one Audrey did.

"She's not there?" he asked the officer.

"No," Officer Reid said. "I'm with the homeowners right now, and I can confirm that this is not the Somerville residence."

There was some brief mumbling and shuffling on the other end of the line.

"Mr. Cochrane said that he and his wife retired here to be closer to their kids. They said they bought the house and moved in about six months ago. I looked over the paperwork and deeds, and all that checks out."

"Well, shit," Sam said. "All right, thanks."

Almost as soon as he hung up the phone, it was ringing again.

"Marlowe," he answered.

"There's a call for you from Boulder PD," the caller said.

"Great. Put them through," Sam said, waiting as the call was transferred to him. "Marlowe."

"Officer Marlowe, this is Leah Graeber from Boulder PD. I got a hit on the information you requested."

"Good news, I hope."

"Yes, Sir. We've located Ms. Humphrey."

"You have?" Sam said, rising from his seat. "Great. Please keep an eye on her. I'll make my way to Bolder as soon as I can."

"Roger, that."

★★★

It was a little over an hour and a half trek from Odette to Boulder. Sam drove out to the Boulder Police Department to meet with Detective Graeber, who led him to Norma Humphrey's apartment complex. It was a decent enough looking apartment building, with a nicely manicured lawn and a well-maintained sidewalk leading up to the front doors. Some of the windows had planter boxes with boldly colored flowers sprouting out of them. Sam headed inside and checked-in with the front desk of the apartment complex.

"Yeah, she's here," the attendant said. "Good luck getting a hold of her, though."

"What's that supposed to mean?" Sam asked.

"Norma's about as chatty as a corpse. Seriously. I think we've said maybe, like, ten words to each other in the year that she's lived here."

"Thanks for the warning," Sam thanked the attendant before heading up to the second floor and locating apartment seven.

Knocking on the door, it opened as far as the chain door lock would allow, and a fearful hazel eye peeked out at Sam.

Sam frowned. Gerald described Audrey as a hermit, and if this Norma was, in fact, Audrey, then that seemed to be a pretty accurate description.

"Norma Humphrey?" Sam asked.

"What do you want?" Norma asked.

"I'm Officer Samuel Marlowe from the Odette Police Department-"

"Odette?" Norma's eye twitched, and her voice pitch rose. "I have no business in Odette. You've got the wrong person."

She pushed the door as if to shut it, but Sam wedged his foot between the door and the frame before she had a chance to close it.

"Ma'am, I'm looking into a disappearance, and you might have some important information to help with the case."

"I don't."

"Do you know an 'Audrey Tallman?'"

Norma froze upon hearing the name.

"How do you know that name?" she asked.

"How do *you* know that name?"

Norma opened the door and stuck her head outside, nervously looking up and down the hallway before pulling Sam inside her apartment. She immediately shut and locked the door afterward.

"Don't say that name out loud," Norma said. "No one can hear that name. No one. Understand? No one."

"My mistake," Sam held his hands up in surrender. "I just really need your help."

Nervous and jittery, Sam watched Norma twitch her fingers. She abruptly darted from the door over to the couch, where she started cleaning up some toys that were laying there.

"What do you want?" Norma asked. "Why do you need to know about ... *her?*"

"Five years ago, a little boy went missing from his home in Odette. We're trying to find new leads in the investigation, and we believe 'she' might have information."

"I can't help you."

Sam folded his arms across his chest.

"You're refusing to help a grieving father find his missing son?" he asked. "If something happened to your child, wouldn't you want answers?"

Norma picked up a stuffed rabbit whose fur was dingy and gray, presumably having logged numerous hours of playtime with children over the years. She petted its ears and held it close to her.

Sam watched her for a moment before giving up and looking around the apartment instead. There were several framed photos hanging on the north wall, most of which contained pictures of a blond boy and a dark-haired girl. There was one photograph in the center of the whole arrangement of a newborn baby with a stuffed animal, a new, white bunny rabbit. *I wonder if that's the rabbit that was on the couch,* Sam wondered. *It's sure as hell taken a beating even though the kids don't seem to be old enough to have put in that many years' worth of damage.*

"Those your kids?" Sam asked as he walked over to the pictures.

He jumped when Norma appeared next to him.

"These are my babies," Norma said. "I rescued them."

"You adopted them?" Sam asked, noting the distinct lack of familial resemblance between the two children and their mother.

"I rescued them," Norma said, more to herself than to Sam.

Rescued? What the hell was that supposed to mean? Sam tried to fish for more information.

"I was rescued too, you know," he said.

Norma looked up at him with wide eyes.

"You ... were rescued?"

"Yep. My mom was badly injured when I was fourteen, and my foster family rescued me. They pretty much saved my life and made me who I am today."

Norma grabbed Sam's hands.

"You understand," she said, tears welling up in her eyes.

Sam played along.

"Of course, I do," he said.

He hoped he sounded more confident than he felt.

"That's what I do," Norma had a vice grip on Sam's hands. "I rescue children."

"You can rescue another child now," Sam said. "You can help rescue William; bring that little boy back to his father."

"That man," Norma said, eyes narrowing and pointing a talon-like finger at Sam. "It was that man's fault—"

"What man? C'mon, Norma, you gotta help me out. What man are you talking about?"

"From the electric company—"

"That's what Audrey said," Sam got the confirmation he was looking for. "I knew it. You *are* Audrey. Norma is a new identity! Like Janet from Denver!"

Norma began ushering Sam toward the door.

"I've already said too much," she said. "If you found me, they might too. You need to leave. Now."

Before he realized what was happening, Sam was out in the hallway with the apartment door closing in his face with a solid bang. He blinked, still unsure of what had happened. But at least he got part of what he came for, confirmation that Norma, Janet, and Audrey were all one in the same.

★★★

Sam returned to his unmarked police car. The sun had set, and the street lamps were lit up across the parking lot. He called Edwin.

"How's it going out there?" Edwin asked.

"Oh, I was able to find Norma all right," Sam said. "But I don't know if I'd necessarily consider that lucky."

"Why's that?"

"That woman is completely bonkers."

Edwin laughed.

"Glad it was you and not me, then," he said. "So, what makes you question her sanity?"

Sam relayed the details of his encounter with Audrey, aka Norma, to Edwin.

"Good work, kid. We now know that Audrey has two alter egos, Janet Somerville and Norma Humphrey. Now we need to see what Audrey knows about what happened to William."

"That might be a bit of an issue," Sam said. "She kind of kicked me out ..."

"I'd say that's a pretty big issue, there, Sam," Edwin said in agreement. "Well, it's getting late. Why don't you see if you can stay the night at a motel or something instead of having to drive all the way back to Odette? Plus, you can check with Audrey bright and early tomorrow morning to see if she's willing to tell you anything else."

"Sure thing, Edwin," Sam said.

★★★

Sam was able to find a motel room with a vacancy where he could spend the night. It wasn't the most luxurious of places, but it was pretty good for renting a room on short notice. The following morning, Sam returned to Audrey's apartment.

"Aud–I mean, Norma?" he pounded on the door. "This is Officer Marlowe. I have a few more questions for you."

He waited for a response but heard nothing. Sam continued knocking, a little louder and with more force this time.

"Norma? Open up!"

"Can you keep it down?" a sleepy looking man in his twenties poked his head out of the apartment next to Audrey's. "I just got back from third shift and want to sleep, thank you very much."

"Sorry, Sir," Sam said. "Have you heard from your neighbor today?"

"No. She left last night."

"She what?"

"Yeah," he said with a yawn. "I was leaving for work at, like, nine last night and I saw Norma pack up her two kiddos and drive off. I asked her where she was headed off to at this time of night, you know, trying to be neighborly and all that, but she didn't say anything; she just drove off."

"And you're sure it was Norma," Sam asked.

"Positive. She's a weird one. Can't mistake her."

"Shit," Sam cursed under his breath.

He tried the door handle of Audrey's apartment after the neighbor shut his door. It was locked, so he took a few steps back before kicking open the door. Checking all of the rooms, Sam discovered that Audrey's apartment was vacant like the neighbor said. He hurried out of the room, calling the Boulder Police Department.

"Detective Graeber," he said. "I need a BOLO put out for Norma Humphrey. If anyone sees her, I need her to be taken into custody immediately. She is a potential witness in a case and is a flight risk. Be advised she may have two children with her."

"Roger that, Marlowe," Graeber replied. "I'll put the alert out."

Working alongside the Boulder Police Department, Sam scoured the city looking for Audrey. His phone rang, so he pulled over to the side of the road to answer it.

"Marlowe."

"Marlowe, it's Graeber. I got word of a vehicle matching one registered to Norma Humphrey. I'm sending you the location now."

Graeber sent the details to Sam, who punched the information into his GPS and sped off. Arriving at a hospital, Sam spied a black sedan parked haphazardly in the ambulance bay. The license plate matched the one Graeber sent him.

As he was checking off the license plate number, Edwin called him.

"What's going on, Sam?"

"Audrey ran," Sam said. "She upped and left last night. Boulder PD got a hit on her possible location. I'm checking it out now."

"We've got to be on to something for her to try to run like that," Edwin said. "She moved from Odette shortly after William's disappearance, and she did something similar in Denver, landing her in Boulder. Why did she relocate again?"

Edwin's words were drowned out as Sam's eyes settled on Audrey, who emerged from the hospital carrying a sleeping toddler. A little boy and girl clung to either leg.

"Because she doesn't 'rescue' children," Sam put the puzzle pieces together. "She steals them!"

He stuffed his phone into his pocket.

"Audrey Tallman!" Sam called out.

He put his hands up and slowed his movements, so he didn't frighten the children. Audrey froze, clutching the toddler to her chest.

"You," she said. "What are you doing? What do you want?"

"I could ask you the same thing," Sam said.

He took a step forward but immediately stopped.

"Don't move!" Audrey commanded. "If you move, I'll—I'll …"

Sam prayed his gut feeling was right and that Audrey wouldn't hurt a child.

"If I move, you'll what?" Sam asked.

Audrey did not respond.

"Mama? I'm scared," the little girl whispered, tugging on Audrey's pant leg.

"Audrey, we don't have to do this," Sam said. "We don't need to upset the children. Let's work together, okay?"

"You," Audrey said. "I ... I thought you understood ... you ... were rescued too ..."

"Yes, Audrey, you're right; I do understand. My foster family rescued me, but this isn't the way they did it."

Sam took a step closer, his movement slow and lithe.

"You took William, didn't you?" he said. "That's why you moved to Denver; you were afraid 'they' would find you and take William back."

Audrey said nothing. She kept her eyes locked on Sam.

"You found your little girl in Denver, right?" Sam inched closer as he spoke. "That's why you moved to Boulder. But, now that you have this little one, here, you're going to have to move again, aren't you?"

"I have to ... I-I can't stay here ..." Audrey said. "They'll take my babies again ..."

Stepping forward this time caused Audrey to recoil, so Sam immediately stopped. He couldn't let her flee with the children or worse, hurt them in any way. Sam's mind was racing as he tried to figure out how to appease the fugitive woman.

Detective Graeber and some other officers pulled up behind them in a patrol car, Sam spotting their reflection in the sliding glass doors.

"Norma Humphrey!" Graeber said to Audrey as she stepped out of the cruiser.

Now's my chance, Sam thought.

"Her name's Audrey Tallman," he said.

Sam watched as the fear of her secret getting out caused Audrey's eyes to grow wide like beach balls.

"Those two children, they're not hers," he said. "She kidnapped them. The boy is from Odette, the girl is from Denver. The baby she's carrying is from inside the hospital here, no doubt with parents frantically trying to figure out what the heck happened to him."

"My darlings," Audrey addressed her kids. "Remember what I told you to do if we ever got in trouble?"

"Uh, Graeber?" Sam motioned for the detective to come closer, not liking what he was hearing from the woman with the children.

"Yes, Mama," the boy and the girl said.

"It's time," Audrey said. "Go, my darlings, go!"

The two kids hopped off the steps and started running as fast as their young legs could carry them.

"Get those children!" Graeber commanded the two Boulder officers.

Sam and the detective focused their attention on Audrey and the baby while the other officers caught up with the children. He could hear them screaming "no!" and "let me go!" as the two cops got a hold of them.

"Audrey, it's over," Sam said. "We've got the children. They're going to go back to their families, where they belong. No more running. It's over."

"No," Audrey shook her head and stepped back, away from Sam and Detective Graeber. "It will never be over ... not until I get my baby back ..."

"There she is!" someone shouted.

A young woman, a young man right behind her, followed by two nurses, ran through the ambulance bay doors.

"She's the one who took my son!" the woman cried, pointing at Audrey.

Sam took advantage of this distraction, running up to Audrey and snatching the child from her arms before she could react. The baby began to cry. Graeber raced over to Audrey and handcuffed her while Sam reunited the baby with his parents.

★★★

The two children were handed off to Social Services while the families of the two children were notified of the situation.

"You found him? You found William? You found my little boy?" Gerald ran up to Sam when he and Edwin arrived at the Boulder Police Department that night.

Sam allowed Gerald to look into one of the interrogation rooms where a nine-year-old William was sitting and playing a handheld video game. Gerald instantly broke down into tears.

"My little boy," he gasped through his sobs. "I can't believe it! You found my William!"

Gerald turned and hugged Sam, who stood rigid and motionless.

"Thank you, a million times, thank you. When can I finally see my little boy?"

"He's got to remain in protective custody while this is all sorted out," Sam said.

"Besides that, you're going to have to take things slow anyway," Edwin placed a hand on the father's shoulder. "Officer Marlowe was updating me on the case before I came to get you. William's been gone for five years; Audrey is the closest thing he remembers to a parent."

Gerald's face fell.

"You mean, he doesn't remember his mother or me?" he asked.

"The social worker and psychologist said he recalls bits and pieces of his life before he was taken," Sam said. "But it's going to take a bit of time until he comes to terms with the fact that his mother and sister were actually his abductor and another missing kid."

"Why?" Gerald asked. "Why did Audrey take those children?"

"Detective Graeber and I did some digging while we were waiting for you guys to arrive, and I think we might know what happened," Sam said. "At the hospital, Audrey said something about 'it won't be over until I get my baby back.' Not babies, but a baby. Graeber and I found out that Audrey had a child as a teenager, but her son was taken away by Social Services because she couldn't care for him. It seems like Audrey was in and out of some treatment facilities after that happened, but each stint didn't last that long, so she probably didn't get the help she needed."

"But why William? Why my son?"

"Opportunity. She's desperately wanted to get her son back for years. I saw a little stuffed bunny rabbit in her apartment. It looked similar to one in a picture I saw of her real son hanging on the wall in her living room. The photo was older than the rest, and based on the condition of that stuffed rabbit, I figured it had to be her son because there was no way the toy could be that dirty and dingy after only a couple of years. She kept that toy, even after all this time. If she couldn't get her own son back, she was going to get a child in a different way. William was alone in the backyard. All she had to do was go into your yard and scoop him up. Then, poof, she had a baby."

"What about the girl?" Gerald asked.

"Again, opportunity. Graeber got in touch with Denver PD. She matches the description of a little girl named Allison that was at the playground in the city with her grandparents and siblings. After Allison was taken, Audrey magically shows up here in Boulder, where we caught her red-handed trying to snatch another child."

Gerald stared silently at his son through the window, a single tear slipping down his cheek.

"What's going to happen to Audrey?" he asked.

"She'll be brought up on charges," Edwin said. "If she's deemed sane, she'll go to prison. If she's deemed unfit to stand trial or mentally incompetent, she may be remanded to a psychiatric center. There are a lot of variables at play, so it's hard to say for sure what will happen to her."

"Please," Gerald turned around to face Sam and Edwin. "Don't let Audrey go to jail. She needs help, not prison. I know how desperate I felt and how my world fell apart after I lost William. I had Elizabeth to keep me grounded; I held on for her. My son and those other two children are safe, and that's all I ever wanted, for my son to come home safely. She went about it the wrong way, but, like you said, Officer Marlowe, that's all that Audrey ever wanted too, to get her child back."

"We don't have much pull out here in Boulder, or in Denver, for that matter," Edwin said. "But if Officer Marlowe or I can do anything to help Audrey get the treatment she needs, we'll do it."

The social worker stepped out of the room where William was to invite Gerald in to see his son. Sam and Edwin watched with smiles as father and son were reunited.

★★★

Seated once again in "his" chair, Sam smiled as he held his mother's hand. He'd grown accustomed to its limp, dry and cold feel, so it didn't bother him anymore. Besides, Sam learned that if he held his mother's hand long enough, it started to grow warm, which always gave him a little glimmer of hope that she could wake up one day.

"I solved my first case," he said. "I still can't believe it. Even Detective Caldwell, who wasn't too happy with me taking over his case, was impressed. I mean, he challenged me to find a new lead, and with help from the Denver and Boulder police, we found Audrey and the kids. All of the kids were safe and sound. How cool is that?"

Looking down at his mother's serene but unmoving face, Sam sighed. Did she hear him? Did she know what he was saying? Did she know what he accomplished and how he made sure to come and tell her about it?

Brushing some of his mother's hair back, Sam briefly wondered if it was time for him to let go or if he should keep holding on. But that was a decision for another day.

FIGHT OR FLIGHT

Stephen Rochecourt did his best to swallow, a task made far more difficult on account of his desert-dry mouth. He'd just started a job at the Odette Penitentiary, located in Colorado. If Stephen was honest with himself, he was completely and utterly terrified of being around so many dangerous and violent criminals.

"They're like animals," Warden Chandler had said at roll call that morning. "They can sense your fear."

Yeah, that nugget of wisdom was going to make him feel better. Instead, it only served to make him feel even more anxious and want to reconsider his life choices. Hell, a six-figure salary wouldn't be enough for this shit.

Stephen let out a breath and straightened his posture in an attempt to portray an air of confidence before entering the cell block. The instant he stepped into Cell Block C, the row of jail cells transformed into a zoo, as the caged prisoners began hooting and hollering in an attempt to rattle the rookie guard.

"Hey there, cutie!" one prisoner shouted. "Damn, you got a tight ass!"

Stephen shuddered. He never knew innocent phrases like that could sound so menacing.

"Yo, guard," a cue ball prisoner with various gang tattoos and an unpleasant demeanor beckoned Stephen over with his finger. "Hey, you! Come here."

Stephen ignored him, not wanting to instigate any further bad behavior, instead locking his eyes on the door at the other end of the hall. The cue ball, however, did not appreciate being slighted. He banged violently on his cell door and unleashed a litany of profanity.

Stephen tugged at the collar of his uniform, beads of sweat popping up on his forehead and at the nape of his neck. "When did it get so hot in here?" Stephen mumbled to himself. "I can see the door at the end of the hall. If I can reach the door, I can get the hell away from these guys. I can make it. I can make it."

He picked up the pace, fumbling around in his pockets for his keys. Stephen managed to locate his keys and gripped the one for the door tightly, figuring he'd probably have a permanent indentation in his palm in the shape of the key from the death grip he had on it. But that didn't matter; the door was in sight.

The keys in his hand jingled against each other as Stephen brought them up to the door with a shaking hand. As he did, a loud buzzer sounded, and the cell doors slammed open with a clang.

"All prisoners report to C Yard for exercise," a guard commanded over the PA system.

Stephen slunk into a corner to avoid the Cue Ball, but the prisoner had other ideas.

"Hey, when I tell you to come, you come," he growled, shoving Stephen. "You may have the badge, but I rule this place."

"Knock it off, Dantes!" one of Stephen's coworkers, Clinton, yelled.

The other guard hurried over to Stephen and got between Dantes and him.

"Don't mind him," Clinton said. "Dantes has been kind of cranky ever since he found out that the Warden broke up his little gang, putting his little friends in different Cell Blocks and transferring some to other prisons. Now he has no one to boss around; poor baby!"

Stephen glanced back over his shoulder, his fingers and toes tingling as he took a look at the prisoner; Dantes didn't appear to be too pleased with the guard's comments.

"Ay!" the prisoner grabbed the guard's shoulder and spun him around. "Us prisoners run this bitch, not you screws!"

"Back off, Dantes," Clinton said, throwing the prisoner's hand off his shoulder. "I'm warning you."

"Warning me?" Dantes got in Clinton's face. "Oh yeah? Whaddya gonna do?"

Clinton's hand hovered over the can of pepper spray in his utility belt as Dantes towered over him. Stephen rushed forward to assist his coworker but, by this time, Dantes' fellow prisoners had gathered behind their leader as backup and stopped him in his tracks. One of the other prisoners seemed to notice Clinton's hand hovering over the pepper spray and decided to strike first. He put Clinton in a headlock from behind while some of the other prisoners held Stephen back.

A sinister grin appeared on Dantes' lips. Stephen heard about him during training; the undisputed leader of C Block, Dantes' word was law.

"It's time these guards see what it's like on the other side of the bars!"

Dantes' declaration was followed by a chorus of cheers, hooting, and hollering. Stephen closed his eyes as he wished he had reconsidered his life choices while chants of "riot" echoed throughout the cell block.

★★★

Seated at his desk in the bullpen of the Odette Police Department, Sam was dutifully filling out the paperwork from his latest closed case-a high profile case that garnered a lot of media attention when the son of a wealthy retired athlete was arrested for the rape of one of his co-eds at his prestigious college. He'd quickly risen to the rank of Junior Detective over the course of his few years at the police department due to his success in cases like that and his potential, according to Captain Buchanan, showed no signs of stopping. Signing his name on the paper he was currently filling out, Sam felt something small collide with the side of his head. Running a hand through his tawny-colored hair, he noticed a paper airplane on the cherry oak wooden floor next to his feet. Sam picked it up, unfolded the paper and read the note inside: "Hey!"

Sam chuckled and glanced over at the desk a few feet away on his right. His mentor, foster father, and partner on the force, veteran cop Edwin Hill, sat reclined in his chair, an impish smirk on his face. Beyond those three crucial roles, Edwin was also Sam's best friend.

Grabbing a scrap piece of paper from his desk, Sam crumpled it up and managed to hit Edwin dead center in the forehead. Edwin let out a hearty laugh as the paper bounced off his head.

"Challenge accepted, Marlowe!" Edwin said.

"Bring it, old man!"

Their playful banter was put on hold when an alert was broadcast over the bullpen speakers.

"Attention all units," the Captain's voice filled the room. "A riot has broken out at Odette Penitentiary. Multiple guards and prisoners injured, with three confirmed dead. Inmates reportedly have several guards hostage. All available units are to grab their tactical gear and report to the prison immediately to assist in the tactical strike."

Sam and Edwin's cheerful expressions instantly sobered up.

★★★

The officers donned their protective riot gear and raced over to the Odette Penitentiary. Sam and the other officers stood in the prison courtyard surrounded by a barbed wire chain link fence that towered over the brick building at thirty feet high. They joined the Warden at the command post set up on the grass outside, listening as she discussed the situation with the corrections officers, members of the FBI's Critical Incident Response Group and available officers from the Odette Highway Patrol.

"Warden Chandler," Captain Buchanan said, addressing the blonde woman at the head of the command post table. "What's the status of the riot? Any new developments since we last spoke?"

Warden Chandler looked up from the blueprint of the penitentiary that was laid out on the table.

"I've received word from the officers that are in lockdown in the kitchen," she said. "The disturbance began in Cell Block C and has now spread to Cell Block B. Cell Block A does not appear to be involved yet, so it is crucial to get a team in there to secure the area before it can be captured by the inmates. There are reports that they are moving west through the prison complex. Cell Block D has been locked down by the guards since the beginning of the disturbance; it's our specialty housing unit, which contains our solitary confinement cells for disciplinary purposes."

"Have we identified where the hostages are being held?"

"The inmates have taken some of the guards up into the Central Guard Control Room in the center of the facility. Other guards are confined throughout the prison, those locations we're not completely sure of yet. From the Central Guard Control Room the inmates can control all of the doors throughout the prison. There is access to the CCTV cameras and the alarms so the inmates in there can guide their cohorts across the facility to find the ideal location to hold the other hostages."

"Basically, they've got control over the prison," the Captain said, summarizing what the Warden explained.

"As of right now, yes. We've reached out to the inmates in the Control Room to attempt negotiations, but we haven't heard back yet," the Warden said. "That being said, I believe I know what this whole incident is about. A few weeks ago, we broke up a gang in the prison that was smuggling drugs in and out of the facility. I had some of the gang members transferred to different correctional facilities, and others were moved to a separate wing. The leader of this gang, a man named Dantes, has been giving my officers trouble ever since. We've been monitoring him, but most of his retaliation up to this point has been harmless. If he's the one responsible for starting this incident, as my officers have said, then his retaliation escalated far quicker than we estimated."

The phone on the command post table chimed.

"This is Warden Chandler," the Warden said, putting the phone on speaker so the Captain and the other officers could hear.

"Warden, glad you're here; you're just the person I wanted to speak to," the prisoner said.

"Dantes," the Warden said, confirming the identity of the prisoner.

"Bet you're regretting sticking your pretty little nose into our business, eh, sweetheart? Now, because of you, everyone's going to pay."

"I'm not here to argue with you, Dantes. I want to end this peacefully and without anyone else, inmate or guard, getting hurt. What do you want?"

"Negotiate? With you? Ha!" the prisoner laughed. "You'd screw us over again, you dumb bitch! No; I want someone else."

Everyone listened with bated breath as there was some shuffling and whispering on the other end of the line. Dantes returned after a moment.

"Where's that old cop?" he asked. "The one that was on the news for getting that rich kid locked up for rape?"

Sam nudged Edwin.

"Is he talking about you?" he whispered. "You know, the Mackay case?"

"Maybe," Edwin said, with a shrug.

"Do you mean Sergeant Edwin Hill?" Captain Buchanan asked Dantes. "From the Odette Police Department?"

There was more whispering and shuffling.

"Yeah, him," Dantes said. "We want him to do the negotiations; he didn't take no shit from that rich brat, so we know he won't take no shit from you state pussies."

The Captain turned to Edwin.

"Sergeant Hill?" he said.

"I'll do whatever I can to help this end without any further injuries or casualties," Edwin said, stepping forward.

"Thank you, Sergeant," the Warden said.

She addressed the prisoners over the phone.

"Sergeant Hill is here, and he has agreed to act as your liaison."

"Excellent," Dantes said. "Send him inside. We'll give you a guard in exchange. He's bleedin' pretty bad and needs to be patched up ASAP."

"Where would you like to make the exchange, Dantes?"

"The C Block stairwell. Once we get Hill, we'll give you the guard."

"Understood. We'll prepare Sergeant Hill for entry right away."

Before Edwin could join the Warden and the Captain at the command post table, Sam grabbed hold of his arm.

"Edwin, wait," he said. "You can't go in there with all those dangerous criminals!"

Edwin stopped and looked over his shoulder at Sam.

"I work with criminals every day, kid, and so do you, in case you forgot," he said. "The only difference is that, in this situation, they're all conveniently located in one building."

"But, Edwin—"

"Butts are for ashtrays," Edwin said. "Listen, kid, I am going in there because it's what I need to do. Don't forget that I'm a cop, kid. I don't want to hear another peep out of you about this, and that's an order, Samuel."

Sam had already opened his mouth to respond but closed it upon hearing Edwin's command. His hand fell to his side as Edwin headed over to the Warden and Captain Buchanan. He couldn't let Edwin go in there alone. He had to do something, anything.

Slipping through the crowd of officers, Sam stood behind Officer Therrien, using the man's towering height as a shield to hide behind while he listened in to the conversation between Edwin, the Warden, and Captain Buchanan.

"The best option is to enter through the truck loading bays," the Warden pointed to the map on the table. "The C Block stairwell is located here, in the U-shaped hallway between the cafeteria and laundry room."

"Understood," Edwin said.

"If possible," the Warden turned to Edwin. "Try to get confirmation that the hostages are alive. If Dantes is releasing one of them to receive medical attention, then it's likely that they are still alive but, at the same time, it could be a ruse in an attempt to get us to listen to their demands."

"I'll do what I can, Warden."

The Warden briefed her officers and the members of the FBI special unit. They would accompany Edwin to make the exchange for the injured hostage. Following two corrections officers, Edwin and two of the Critical Incident Response Group agents headed toward the back of the prison building. The Captain addressed Sam and the other police officers, but Sam hardly heard a word that was spoken.

"At ease, everyone," Captain Buchanan said.

At ease? Sam let out a small puff of air from his nose in annoyance. *How the hell am I supposed to be at ease when Edwin is practically a lamb being delivered to the slaughterhouse? There has to be something I can do. Something, anything. How can I stay put and let Edwin go straight into the layer of the beast on his own? I don't doubt his abilities as an officer of the law, but there are hundreds of desperate prisoners with nothing to lose. I don't doubt for a moment that Dantes and the others will do anything to get their way, though the Warden doesn't seem like she's going to budge an inch and give in to their demands. Shit!*

Sam managed to slip through the crowd and make it to the back of the building. Taking refuge against the giant chain link fences of the exercise yards, Sam watched as Edwin and the other officers made their way toward the loading bays.

"Hey! What the hell do you think you're doing?"

Sam's head whirled around, and he found Detective Rusty Caldwell a few feet behind him.

"Oh, Detective Caldwell, Sir," Sam struggled to find the words. "I was ... um ... you know—"

"You were trying to get into the prison," Rusty said.

The older, pudgy cop was smoking a cigarette. He took a drag and then shook his fingers at Sam as he spoke, ash sprinkling from the cigarette between them.

"Listen, kid," Rusty said. "I know what you're thinking about doing. You may have been able to slip past everyone else in all this confusion and worry, but I saw you. I get why you want to go in there after Sergeant Hill but *do not*, I repeat, *do not do it*. Right now, things are under control, and the prisoners seem like they're willing to talk with Ed to get this shit resolved without any more bloodshed. If you go in there unannounced, you could screw up the whole thing and jeopardize the lives of the hostages and Ed."

Sam clenched his eyes closed as he listened to Rusty. *Dammit! Why does the old cop have to be right?* As Sam turned around to go back to the command post, he heard footsteps thundering down the hallway toward the exit. Two of the officers that had accompanied Edwin ran out of the prison, carrying a bloody, unconscious corrections officer.

"Where's Edwin?" he called out to the officers.

"Wi-th Dan-tes," an officer said, his words breathy and broken as he helped carry the freed hostage to the awaiting medical personnel.

"You left him alone?" Sam gasped.

He bolted toward the prison before Rusty had a chance to scold him for what he knew he needed to do.

"Marlowe! Get your ass back here!" Rusty shouted.

Sam ignored him. *I can't let Edwin go in alone. If Rusty rats me out to the Captain, so be it. I can find another job, but I can't replace Edwin.*

Inside the loading bays, Sam slowed to a walk. He reached the connecting laundry room and looked around. The Warden had said that the laundry room connected to a hallway that had the stairwells leading to the cell blocks, which were on the second floor of the prison. The exchange of Edwin for the injured guard took place in the C Block stairwell; Sam headed out of the laundry room to find the stairway in question.

The C Block stairwell was to his left. Sam opened the heavy metal door to the stairway. It closed behind him with a resounding thud. He winced and held his breath as he waited to make sure that he wasn't about to be attacked by a gang of inmates who'd been alerted by the slamming door. Not hearing anyone approaching, Sam continued up the stairs.

The entrance to Cell Block C was a large barred gate that extended across the hallway. Sam arrived at the gate and paused, ducking around the corner and using the wall to avoid being seen. Peering around the corner into the cell block, he found it crawling with prisoners. The guards that he could see were clearly at the mercy of the free-roaming inmates, either handcuffed to a piece of furniture like a table or cell door or lying unconscious or injured on the floor. Sam did a quick count of the guards; he overheard the Warden talking to the FBI agents before slipping into the prison, and the number of hostages was estimated to be eleven. There were only three guards in the cell block. Where had the inmates stashed the others?

"Hey!"

Sam jumped as some inmates in orange jumpsuits rushed toward the barred gate. They caught a hold of him before he could escape.

"Yo, Tuck, whaddya wanna do with the poor little piggy, here?" one inmate asked as he held Sam in an iron grip.

Tuck? Sam wondered. Any and all thoughts about who "Tuck" was were squashed when something sharp pressed up against his throat.

"Let me see 'im," another inmate said.

Sam was turned around by his captor to face the inmate walking out of the cell block. If it wasn't for the shiv at his throat, preventing him from speaking, Sam was sure he would have been swearing when he figured out who "Tuck" was. It was Seth Tucker, his stepfather. He was in prison for the brutal assault of his mother, Charlotte, which had left her in a coma from the time Sam was only fourteen.

Seth gave no indication that he recognized Sam as he strolled up to him. He snapped his fingers and the inmate holding Sam let him go, Sam coughing as he fell to the floor.

"This guy ain't no threat," Seth said to the inmates. "He's a kid pretending to be a man, but he ain't foolin' anyone. I bet he's got on little cartoon boxers underneath that big, scary cop outfit."

The inmates laughed. Seth, standing over Sam, motioned to the prisoners to return to the cell block, which they did. Seth grabbed Sam by the shoulders and hoisted him up.

"If you're lookin' for Dantes and the hostages, they ain't here," Seth whispered.

Sam opened his mouth to say something, but the prisoner interrupted him.

"Shut your trap, kid, unless you want to become a hostage too, or worse. Dantes' got some guards holed up in the central guard station downstairs, and I think he's got some of his gang members holdin' up the other hostages and movin' them around to make it harder on the Warden and you cops."

"Why are you telling me this?" Sam asked.

"It doesn't matter why," Seth shoved Sam forward. "Go."

Taking a couple steps back toward the stairwell, Sam watched as Seth headed back to the cell block.

"Look at that little bitch runnin'!" he called to the inmates, causing them to hoot and holler in animalistic laughter.

Seth glanced over his shoulder and mouthed the word: "go." Nearly tripping over his own feet, Sam did as Seth instructed and ran back down the stairwell and out into the hallway between the cafeteria and laundry room. He looked around. *Seth said Dantes was in the Central Guard Control Room, which is most likely where Edwin is since he's helping with the negotiations. But how can I know for sure that Seth is telling the truth and sending me to the Control Room wasn't another trap? He could have let the inmates kill me,* Sam considered. *Instead, he gets them to let me go and tells me what's going on with Dantes. He had no way of knowing that I was coming up there to his cell block for him to come up with a trap like that. It has to be the truth.*

Sam, keeping his back against the wall, crept through the hallway and past the cafeteria. Closing his eyes and envisioning the map of the prison the Warden had on the table outside, he recalled the position of the Central Guard Control Room. In the main hallway, the control room was easy to spot, as it was the focal point of the space.

Sam raced up the stairs to the Central Guard Control Room. His chest burned as he breathed heavily, the pressure only increasing when he laid eyes on Edwin inside the control room. Dantes, who had a hold on a corrections officer and held a knife against the man's jugular, was right next to the veteran cop. Sam stood with his back flush against the wall, watching through the glass doors as Edwin and Dantes talked to each other, chatting it up like they were old buddies. His breath hitched in his throat when a hand gripped his shoulder.

"We've been waitin' for you, little rat," the owner of the hand said. "We saw you comin'."

Shit. I forgot about the cameras.

The inmate poked Sam in the back with a sharp weapon. Sam put his hands up in surrender.

"Let's move," the inmate said, shoving Sam forward.

The inmate behind him, Sam walked forward through the glass doors and into the Central Guard Control Room.

"Ah, there's the little rat that's been wanderin' around my prison," Dantes grinned, his sharp teeth looking more like a wolf's fangs. "Glad you could join us."

Sam's eyes drifted over to Edwin, who was sitting in one of the chairs in front of the wall of monitors. Based on the expression on his foster father's face, Sam was actually more scared of Edwin than Dantes. If they made it out of the prison alive, Edwin would probably end up killing him. Either way, he was probably a dead man.

"Dantes," Edwin said to the prisoner. "I know that I'm supposed to be here listening to your demands, but I have one of my own. Can you please let this guy go? If you let him go, I'll do whatever I can to help get your gang mates back to Odette Pen-"

Dantes put a hand up.

"I have a better idea," he said.

Dantes shoved the guard down and out of the way. The guard, whose nametag read "Stephen," crawled as quickly as he could on his hands and knees over to the corner of the room, looking like bugs under a rock that scattered when the rock was lifted. Dantes made his way over to Sam, towering over him as he looked him over.

"You see, copper," he said to Edwin. "If you want me to let this kid go, promising to do whatever you can to get my gang mates back, it tells me that this little rat must mean something to you. This your kid or something?"

Sam swallowed hard as Edwin clenched his jaw.

"Yes, he's my son," he said. "Please, Dantes, don't hurt him. His heart can be bigger than his brain sometimes, which is probably why he's here, to try and protect me."

Dantes let out a small snort.

"Ain't that touching?" he said. "What's your name, kid?"

"Sam."

The inmate took hold of Sam, gripping his arm in a steel vice-like grasp as he pulled him over to stand in front of Edwin.

"New game plan," Dantes said. "You're going to get the Warden to agree to all my commands or little Sammy, here, is going to pay the price."

Edwin immediately raised his hands up.

"I'm at your mercy, Dantes," he said. "Tell me what you want, and I'll do anything I can to make it happen."

"Get on the phone. Call the Warden and tell her I want my boys back. Now."

Edwin turned and grabbed the phone.

"Hello, Warden Chandler, this is Sergeant Hill ... Yes, we're okay ... I have the demands. Dantes would like to have the gang members that were transferred out of the facility to be brought back to Odette Pen. Immediately ... Please, Warden, it's urgent ... Yes, I'll let him know," he hung up the phone. "The Warden said she'll reach out to the other prison facilities and see if they'd be willing to transfer them back."

Dantes put the knife up to Sam's throat, the pressure the bigger man was putting on his windpipe making it difficult to breathe.

"That's not good enough!" he said. "I need my gang! I promised them I'd take care of them! It's my duty! I can't bail on 'em!"

"Because your gang is your family, right?" Edwin said.

Dantes did not respond. Sam hissed as the grip on his arm tightened. Edwin must have hit a nerve.

"The Warden took your family away; that's why you're doing this," Edwin said. "You're the leader; the other members look up to you for protection and guidance, but you feel like you failed them because they got transferred. Who knows what'll happen to them in another prison, outside of your protection?"

"Enough!" Dantes shouted, the hand that held the knife banged against the desk.

His roar reverberated throughout the control room. Shoving Sam forward, causing him to fall to the ground, Dantes turned away from Edwin. Sam tried to scramble to his feet but ended up falling again as he saw the inmate walk over to Stephen, who was huddled in a ball against the end of the desk and plunge the knife into the side of his neck. Stephen let out a squeal and collapsed to the ground in pain.

"Jesus, Dantes!" Edwin jerked forward as if to rush over to help the bleeding guard, but gripped the arms of the chair to keep himself in place. "What the hell was that for?"

The prisoner, however, didn't respond. Sam tried to get up from the ground to go over to tend to Stephen, but Dantes stopped him.

"Unless you want to end up like him, I suggest you don't move," he said, his back to the two cops.

Sam froze in place.

"Listen, Dantes," Edwin said, doing his best to keep his voice even. "I'm sorry I talked about your gang members like that. I get it; you're like the dad to your gang. You'd do anything to protect them, like I want to protect my fellow men and women in law enforcement. Please, let us get Stephen some medical attention."

"Hmm, let me think," Dantes said. "Uh, no."

"Please, Dantes," Sam joined in. "Do you need to take this man away from his family simply because he showed up to work today?"

"Family?" Dantes repeated, turning around to face Sam and Edwin. "Family? Why should any of you ungrateful bastards get to go home to your families? If I ain't got my family, ain't no one gonna have their families either!"

"The Warden is working on reaching out to the other prisons-" Edwin tried to explain.

"Shut it, old man!" Dantes snapped. "I thought you were different, but you're just like every other cop out there; you don't give a shit about guys like me."

"That's not true!" Sam said. "Edwin cares about the people who are in trouble. I was in trouble years ago, and he saved my life. Now I'm a cop and trying to help other people too."

A devilish smirk appeared on Dantes' lips.

"In trouble?" he repeated. "I ain't in trouble, kid. I am trouble. You know why I'm in here? I killed a man's family. I killed his mama, his old lady, and his little baby. Shot 'em all. Pow, dead. Pow, dead. Pow, dead. You know why? 'Cause he was in a rival gang and

I needed to send them a message. Don't think I ain't afraid to send a message to the Warden with you two."

Dantes walked toward the doors to the Central Guard Control Room.

"You got an hour to start makin' arrangements to get my boys back," he said. "If you fail, we'll start killin' the hostages. Every hour, we'll pull one of their names from a pillowcase and kill them. One hostage every hour; they die, their blood's on your hands."

Dantes left the Central Guard Control Room, leaving several inmates behind to watch over Sam and Edwin. The inmates stood outside, some lighting up smokes, others injecting some of the confiscated drugs they "liberated" from the control room before they could be disposed of. Once he was gone, Edwin immediately addressed Sam.

"What the fuck were you thinking?" he slammed the arms of the chair with his fists.

Sam winced.

"I'm sorry, Edwin," he said. "I ... I couldn't let you go in here by yourself, unarmed, with all these prisoners."

"Yeah, I get that, but I had things under control."

"Edwin—"

The veteran cop ignored him, instead grabbing a jacket hanging up on the coat rack by the door. He balled up the coat and pressed it against Stephen's neck in an attempt to slow the bleeding.

"Sam, get over here and hold this," Edwin said. "I need to call the Warden and let her know what's going on."

Sam exchanged places with Edwin, who called the Warden.

"Yeah, one hour ... No, I'm not kidding ... Why the change? Well, I'll say that Dantes decided to change up the rules in the middle of the game ... Where are the hostages? ... I don't know. We're in the control room ... We'll check the monitors to see if we can find them and report back ... No, I can't access anything in the system. Dantes changed the passwords, so we only can watch what's happening on the monitors ... Right, we'll let you know."

Hanging up the phone, Edwin looked at Sam.

"We need to find the hostages. The Warden doesn't want to take any chances with their lives. The Critical Incident Response Team can storm the prison to get to the captives, but they need a location first."

The two cops watched the monitors, searching the various feeds for any sign of Dantes or the hostages. They spotted Dantes and some inmates walking through the main hallway.

"Where are they going?" Sam looked at the map on the wall. "Hey, Ed, based on the map, it looks like Dantes is going to the barbershop."

"Shit, that's not good," Edwin said. "They might be going to get things they can use as more weapons, like razors and scissors."

As Edwin predicted, Dantes and the other inmates returned from the barbershop armed head to toe with new weapons. They headed out into the hallway by the laundry room to use the B Block stairwell.

In Cell Block B, Dantes headed down to the end of the row to the last cell. Some of the other inmates opened up the cell and pulled out four corrections officers.

"Four guards, plus Stephen, that's five," Edwin said. "Warden said there were eleven hostages; we're missing six. We need to find them before our hour is up."

"Let me go look for them–" Sam started to say, but Edwin cut him off.

"No way in hell. You are going to stay here and not move a fucking muscle. That's an order, got it?"

"But, Edwin—"

"That's an order!"

"Yes, Sir."

Keeping one eye on the clock and one eye on the monitor, Sam and Edwin scanned the facility, trying to locate the missing hostages.

Thirty minutes remaining. Edwin reached out to the Warden again for any updates, to which she replied that she was still working out transfers with the other prison facilities.

Twenty-five minutes remaining. Dantes and the inmates moved the hostages from Cell Block B downstairs into the cafeteria. They were positioned on their knees in front of the inmates, execution style.

Twenty minutes remaining. Stephen passed out from blood loss.

"Dantes, I got word from the Warden," Edwin said, speaking to the prisoner over the control tower phone. "She can get two of your buddies transferred back to Odette Pen in a few days."

"Close but no cigar," Dantes said. "I need results now, old man. You got fifteen minutes."

Ten minutes remaining.

"Any update?" Warden Chandler asked.

"No dice, Warden," Edwin said. "Dantes wants the rest of his gang members transferred back to the prison as soon as possible. A few days won't cut it."

"These things take time!" the Warden said. "All right. That's it. I'm sending in the Critical Incident Response Team to get you and the other hostages out of there. Stand by."

Five minutes remaining.

Dantes paced back and forth behind the hostages. One guard was visibly trembling with fear. Another vomited, and the inmates forced his face down into it.

Four minutes remaining.

"All righty, boys," Dantes said. "Time to pick the lucky winner."

Dantes drew a name out of the pillowcase-the first hostage to be executed. He showed the name to an inmate, who departed from the cafeteria. Sam and Edwin followed his movements across the monitors.

Three minutes remaining. The inmate arrived in the A and B Block showers/facilities. He left the same area with a corrections officer in his grasp.

Two minutes remaining.

"The Critical Incident Response Team is on its way," the Warden said.

"Send them to the showers in the A and B Blocks," Edwin said. "The hostages are stashed there!"

"Roger that, I'll alert them right now."

One minute remaining. The Critical Incident Response Team busted into the cafeteria as Dantes held a knife to the throat of one of the hostages. Dantes was shot by rubber bullets, knocking him off of the hostage.

"They saved them!" Sam gasped, a smile breaking out on his face as he watched the hostages be rescued.

"Now all they need to do is get to the others in the-" Edwin yelped.

Sam whirled around and found one of the inmates keeping watch over them had slipped into the control room and stabbed Edwin in the arm. The other inmates had run for the hills when they saw the Critical Incident Response Team swarm the cafeteria and capture Dantes and the others, but one remained behind and attacked Edwin.

"Edwin!" Sam shouted, his heart freezing mid-beat and his blood running cold.

The very thing he wanted to prevent by disobeying orders and heading inside the prison happened before his eyes. He didn't know what he'd do if anything happened to Edwin. The man was his best friend, his mentor, the only father he ever knew and loved, and his lifeline.

Fire in his eyes and rage coursing through his veins, Sam rushed at the prisoner, tackling him to the ground in the control room. They tumbled across the floor, Sam managing to push the inmate over and beneath him. In a white-hot fury, he began pounding away at the prisoner.

Time seemed to stand still as fist after fist connected with the inmate's face. Sam was unsure at what point the prisoner had been knocked unconscious, only noticing the catatonic body after being pulled off of him by another police officer.

"Samuel!" someone called out to him.

Sam, restrained by multiple agents from the Critical Incident Response Team, blinked a few times. The red he saw gradually dissipated, and rational thought slowly returned to his mind.

"Samuel," his eyes focused on Edwin. "It's over kid. We won."

★★★

Days later, Sam headed up to the Odette General Hospital to visit Edwin. He had visited the veteran cop every day whenever time allowed. On his lunch break, Sam picked up food from Edwin's favorite sandwich shop and then made his way up to the cop's hospital room.

"Hey there, kiddo," Edwin greeted his foster son with a smile.

"Brought some lunch," Sam said, holding up the bag of takeout.

"Nice! I hope that's a big juicy burger in there," Edwin said, eyeing the grease-stained bag. "This hospital food tastes like cardboard. Plus, they've been monitoring my cholesterol and shit since they did blood work on me while I was in surgery; I need some decent food before I go on a hunger strike!"

"I got your favorite jalapeno burger."

"Perfect. Hand it over."

Sam prepared lunch for Edwin and himself, cutting his foster father's burger in half to make it easier to hold since Edwin had only one good arm at the moment.

"Captain Buchanan stopped in here yesterday night," Edwin said.

Sam swallowed his bite of food, suddenly finding the juicy burger bitter and dry. He sipped his pop to try to flush the lump in his throat down.

"Oh," he played with the bendy straw in the bottle. "What did he have to say?"

"Do you know how idiotic and foolish your actions were?" Edwin asked. "Seriously, Samuel, you could have gotten yourself killed. You could have gotten the hostages killed. You could have gotten me killed."

"Edwin, I—"

"I'm not finished, Samuel. What concerned me is when you went after that prisoner. Yeah, I know you did it to protect me, but you went way overboard. If that would have been on the street and not in the prison with dangerous criminals, you probably would have been suspended for police brutality and possibly brought up on charges."

"But he was a prisoner, Edwin, and it was a riot. He attacked you; what else was I supposed to do?" Sam asked.

"How about stay outside with the rest of the people instead of barging in and risking our lives?" Edwin said. "Sam, I need you to listen to me. As cops, we're held to a higher standard than any other regular ol' guy. Yes, the guy who attacked me was a prisoner; I get that you had to do whatever you could at that moment to defend yourself. I was sure to tell that to the Captain and to the Warden in my incident report."

"Thanks, Edwin."

"Don't thank me yet. I'm covering for you this time, Sam, because of the circumstances. We all have the fight or flight reaction, and you happen to be more inclined to fight. Next time, though, you're going to have to deal with the consequences. Do you understand me?"

Sam looked down at the burger on his plate.

"Yes, Sir."

"Now, come here," Edwin motioned him over.

Sam did as Edwin requested, first putting his plate on the portable bedside table before coming to his foster father's bedside. Before he realized what Edwin called him over for, Sam felt the veteran cop smack him upside the back of the head.

"Enough of that bullshit," he said. "Prisoner or not, I never want to see you do anything like that again, got it?"

"Yes, Sir," Sam said.

"Good," Edwin said. "Now hide that burger; the nurse should be making her rounds and coming in to check on me in a few minutes, and she'll give me hell about making my bad cholesterol worse!"

Despite the reprimand, Sam smiled as he grabbed all the wrappers and packages from the table to hide the evidence of their meal from the incoming medical staff.

VICTIMS OF
CIRCUMSTANCE

Albert Trousdale, with his cane in hand, shuffled his way down his driveway to his mailbox to fetch his morning newspaper. The lilies were finally starting to bloom, he noted with pride as he looked over the fragrant orange flowers that lined the edges of his property. He wasn't the only one who appreciated his gardening efforts, apparently; Albert swatted at a bee that buzzed a little too close to him for his liking.

Speaking of bugs, he noticed a man in a black shirt with piercings and tattoos leaving the house next door. Why kids today insisted on putting holes all over their faces and having pictures permanently inked on their skin, only have it distorted by sagging skin into some weird Picasso style drawing when they got to his age, was beyond him. This guy was the same one that showed up sometime last night. That wasn't anything unusual, though.

The people next door bugged him. Well, not all of them did, only the mom, Kendra. The kids, well, not that he got to see them all that much, were fine. Albert considered himself lucky that he had two boys. If he had a daughter and she acted anything like Kendra Wilksford did, he probably would have locked her in her room until she was forty. "People today," Albert muttered with a shake of the head.

★★★

Junior Detective Samuel Marlowe raced forward toward the back door of Quincy's Pizza and Wings, the entryway to the establishment's banquet/party rooms. His partner, mentor, and foster father, Edwin Hill, barely had the police cruiser in park before the fawn haired twenty-something popped out of the car and started for the building. The boy had a tangible sense of urgency that concerned the veteran cop. Sam said the call was only a burglary, yet he seemed hyped up over the matter. Perhaps the suspect was still on the premises?

"In here," Sam whispered to Edwin, nodding toward a closed oak door off of the banquet/party room entrance hallway.

"Ready," Edwin said.

Sam opened the door, and Edwin stepped inside the darkened room. Feeling along the wall for a light switch, Edwin flicked on the overhead lights.

"Surprise!"

A giant group of Edwin's family, friends, and co-workers stood before him with a 'Happy Retirement' banner hanging above them. Edwin immediately turned toward Sam.

"Sam, you little shit!" he laughed.

"It's your retirement party," Sam replied, a brilliant smile on his face. "I know you're not leaving the force until the end of the month, but everyone here wanted to give you a big send-off."

Edwin was touched. He smiled at everyone as he rubbed the back of his neck with his hand.

"Thank you, everyone," he said. "I've had a great career with the Odette Police Department. I consider myself very fortunate to have had the opportunity to work alongside and for so many great people, especially my 'son,' Sam. But, even though I'm hanging up my holster and badge, I'm looking forward to spending time with the four most important people in my life, my wife, Gloria, my two amazing daughters, Clarice and Nina, and of course, Sam."

The three Hill women came forward to embrace Edwin. Afterward, the guest of honor looked up at everyone and smiled.

"Let's eat!"

★★★

Albert sat, though it was more like falling, into his favorite maroon armchair in his living room. Tossing aside the orange plastic bag the newspaper came in, he checked the day's headlines. In a place like Odette, Colorado, a small and relatively unexciting place, the newspaper headlines were typically nice and cheerful ones, not like the ones found in those gossip or celebrity tabloids Albert saw at the grocery store. Some starlet girl was going into rehab this week. Some actor was cheating on his wife with the nanny. That new actress, Tamsen whatever-her-name-was, was hooking up with Xander what's-his-face. Who cares?

That wasn't news. It was all gossip! Bologna! Balderdash! 'Loose lips sink ships,' his mother always said. People today.

Why can't they have good stories anymore?

Decorated police officer set to retire, Albert read. "Now *that's* a story!" Albert continued reading through the article, Sergeant Edwin Hill, a thirty-five-year plus veteran of the force is set to retire at the end of spring.

Despite old age diminishing his hearing, Albert clearly heard a shriek coming from next door. It took him a few tries to get out of the chair and shuffle over to the window. Peering through the window blinds, Albert looked out at the Wilksford house. He didn't see anything or anyone. With a shrug, he dropped the blinds and made his way back over to his chair.

That damned Kendra. She was always causing problems. Why couldn't she be nice and quiet like everyone else on the street? Her house was a mess, with the chipping paint and the wilting plants, and now she was going to interrupt his newspaper reading time? That lady had been nothing but trouble since she moved in a year and a half ago. People today.

★★★

Following the party at the pizza place, Sam and Edwin returned to the Odette Police Department. They brought the leftovers back with them and left them in the break room for the officers that couldn't slip away to make it to the party to enjoy. Heading into the bullpen, Edwin flopped down into his desk chair.

"I don't know about you, kid, but I'm all for getting into the back of the patrol car and going into a food coma," he said to Sam.

Sam laughed.

"Yeah, that does sound pretty good," he said.

Edwin eyed his foster son for a moment. Sam was pretending to busy himself with paperwork, but the veteran cop knew it was a ruse. Edwin knew that Sam was sad he was retiring from the force. In a way, he was sad about it too. He'd been a member of the police department for over three and a half decades. Edwin was on the force when he and Gloria got married. He was on the force when Clarice and Nina were born. He was on the force when he met Sam. He was a cop, plain and simple.

Of course, even though he was hanging up his badge and holster, it didn't mean that he was going to be idle. Edwin and Gloria had plans to travel. Clarice and Raymond were very serious about their relationship; Edwin was looking forward to the day when he could walk her down the aisle. Plus, Ruth Porter, the principal at his alma mater, Odette High, said she'd love to have him at the school as a part-time security guard. Edwin figured it wouldn't hurt to have a little extra spending money so he could spoil his family rotten.

The one thing he was going to miss about being a police officer, though, was working side by side with Sam.

"You know, Sam," Edwin said. "Since I'm going to be retiring at the end of this month, the Captain and I have been putting our heads together on who might be a good candidate to be promoted to detective to fill my position."

Sam looked up from his paperwork.

"Officer Robinson is a great candidate," he said. "She headed up that Sutherland case, which was a big deal."

Edwin gave his foster son a smile.

"Yeah, Grace is a great cop," he said. "But I wasn't talking about Robinson. I was talking about you, kid."

The pen in Sam's hand faltered against the paper.

"M-me?"

"No, my other son named Sam."

"Wow," Sam said. "Wow. That's all I can think to say, Edwin. Wow."

Edwin laughed.

"You're a man of many words, there, Sam," he said.

Sam gave Edwin a small smile.

"D-do you really think I'm ready for something like that?"

"Of course I do, kid. I wouldn't have brought it up to the Captain if I didn't think so," Edwin said. "I'll tell you what: if you're still unsure about your qualifications to be promoted, then let's tackle one last case together, except, this time, you take the lead. You can decide if you feel up to it once we close the case, okay? Deal?"

"Deal."

★★★

The raccoons were at it again. Albert pulled the blankets of his bed up to his chin and turned onto his side. From outside, he could hear the sound of his trashcans being rummaged through. He'd have to talk to his sons about doing something about these pesky raccoons. But that was something he could do the next morning because he was too warm and too comfortable to leave his bed right now.

★★★

Another day, another man at the Wilksford house. Albert always shook his head when he saw another stranger arrive at his neighbor's house. "Kids today. They have no sense of loyalty or morality. They think it's okay to go from bed to bed all willy-nilly and not think about the consequences. People today," he muttered.

After finishing his breakfast, Albert grabbed the phone from its cradle on the wall and started to dial his son's number to see if he had any ideas on what to do about those irksome raccoons. He punched in a few numbers before dropping the phone when he heard a man scream. Albert waddled over to his kitchen window. The man who stopped next door a few minutes ago was running out of the house. He barely made it off the front porch steps before falling onto his hands and knees and vomiting on the green and brown patchy lawn.

Albert pushed up the window.

"You okay, there, sonny?" he called to the man.

The man lifted his head to look at him. With a shaky hand, he pointed at the house.

"Can't you speak?" Albert yelled.

"Call the cops!" the man yelled back.

He got up from the lawn and ran toward his car, hopping into the vehicle and speeding off. Call the cops? What the hell was going on? It was his neighborhood, so Albert was going to find out.

★★★

"Sergeant Hill, Officer Marlowe, thank you both for coming," Officer Grace Robinson shook hands with Sam and Edwin when they arrived at the Wilksford house. "This case is a real doozy."

"What's up, Robinson?" Edwin asked. "Dispatch said a witness was asking for us?"

"Yes, Sir," Robinson said. "I was leaving court when I responded to an emergency call from a man named Albert Trousdale. He lives next door. Albert called authorities after he saw a man run out of the

Wilksford residence and vomit. The man told Albert to call 911 before he fled the scene. Albert said he was concerned for the welfare of his neighbors, so he went into the house using the key stowed away under a rock near the front porch for emergencies. Inside, he found the body of the neighbor, Kendra Wilksford."

"Cause of death?" Sam asked.

Normally a calm and collected police officer, Robinson's cheeks lost their color.

"The victim suffered several stab wounds, but it's not certain if they were fatal," she said. "Even if they weren't, the victim had no chance; she was decapitated."

"You're shittin' me," Edwin said.

"I wish."

Decapitation? That kind of brutality only happened in television shows, movies, and books, not places like Odette.

Edwin turned to Sam.

"Well, kid, you picked a hell of a case to lead," he said.

Sam ran a hand through his hair.

"No shit."

"Did the neighbor say why he requested Sam and me?" Edwin asked.

"Not really," Robinson said. "Dispatch said he kept saying 'send that cop from the paper!'"

"Good to know that people read that article about me in the paper," Edwin looked over at Sam. "Shall we?"

Robinson turned over control of the crime scene to Edwin and Sam before leaving the scene to return to her duties. They stepped into the house; moving from the untouched front hallway into the kitchen was like walking into an entirely different world. The kitchen had been showered with blood as if someone had filled a paintball gun with the viscous liquid and danced around the room as they fired it.

"I am so glad we ate before this," Edwin said.

Despite being a seasoned veteran of the police force, the extreme violence and blood in the room made Edwin's full stomach do some vigorous acrobatics. He wouldn't have had those Greek fries if he knew this was where he was going to end up. Silently wishing for antacids, Edwin put on a fresh pair of latex gloves, and Sam did the same. They began to investigate the crime scene.

Edwin crouched down to examine the body.

"Nineteen ... twenty ... twenty-one ..." he began counting the stab wounds. "The ME will confirm upon the autopsy, but I'm counting at least twenty-one stab wounds."

"Twenty-one stab wounds and the head was cut off?" Sam repeated. "Damn, that's a lot of rage—"

He paused, craning his head to the side like he was trying to listen to something. Edwin watched him with curiosity.

"What is it?" he asked.

"I swear I hear someone talking," Sam said, looking around the room. "It's real quiet, though, kind of like a whisper ..."

Sam's statement drifted off. He headed over to an air vent on the south wall of the kitchen, located a few inches off of the ground. Sam carefully got down on his hands and knees and put his ear up to it.

"There it is again," he said. "Do you hear that Edwin?"

"No, I don't hear anything," Edwin said.

Sam motioned him over to listen to the vent.

"Hey, I do hear something. What the hell is that sound? It's like mice or something."

"Yeah, but not quite," Sam shook his head. "I swear it sounds like words ..."

He looked around for a moment before popping up to his feet. Sam pointed to a plain white door to the left of the vent, past the front hallway.

"Does that door lead to a basement?" he asked.

Edwin came up behind him.

"I would assume so, but there's only one way to find out," he said.

Sam opened up the door, and the two cops found a wooden staircase descending into a soft orange-hued light. Pulling their guns from their holsters, Sam began heading down the stairs, Edwin right behind him. The stairs creaked as they made their descent into the basement. The cellar was dimly lit, the only light coming from a single flickering light bulb hanging overhead. The walls were a bland shade of beige, the floors, cheap gray concrete. Reaching the final step, Edwin and Sam paused, listening for the sound they heard upstairs.

The basement was empty, save for some boxes scattered around the room. A rundown washer and dryer stood up against the wall opposite the stairwell.

"There's nothing here," Sam said. "And there's no way there's a talking cat or something in the vent … right?"

Edwin glanced over his shoulder at his foster son.

"Did you seriously ask if there was a talking cat in the vent?"

"I'm kidding, Ed."

"Good. For a minute there, I thought you lost what little marbles you already had left."

"Hardy-har," Sam said.

Both cops fell silent when they heard a noise. They looked around, searching for the origin of the sound.

"Was that coming from in the walls?" Sam asked.

Edwin headed over to the washer and dryer, peeking over the appliances to look at the wiring behind it. Or, rather, lack thereof.

"Granted it's been a while since the last time I hooked up a washer and dryer," Edwin said. "But, last time I checked, for a washer and dryer to be usable, they need to actually be hooked up."

Sam came over to where Edwin was standing and looked over the appliances too.

"What do you think it means?" he asked.

"What do *you* think it means?" Edwin asked back. "Don't forget, kid, this is your case. I'll help in any way I can, but I want you to take the lead."

"I figured you were going to say that," Sam said with a sigh.

Edwin watched over Sam as the younger cop squatted down to take a closer look at the wires and pipes behind the washer and dryer. Sam ran a hand along the wall.

"There's no piping, faucets, vents or anything like that on this wall," he said. "And, another thing that's odd is the floor; doesn't it look like the concrete beneath the washer and dryer is scuffed up and scratched?"

"You mean like something's been moved?" Edwin asked.

"Yeah. Most places would use a dolly to wheel in the appliances to avoid this type of thing happening, wouldn't they?"

"Typically, unless the vic installed them herself or had someone else do it for her."

"Or if they're attached to the wall," Sam said.

He pointed to the scuff marks on the floor.

"Look at the marks," he said. "They start right here, right where the washer and dryer are. They move right in a straight line, but stop a few feet away."

Edwin rolled up his shirt sleeves.

"Looks like we're going to get our workout today, kid," he said.

Sam stood up and helped Edwin push the washer and dryer. The two appliances scraped the concrete floor with a sharp scratchy sound as the two cops shoved them forward. Reaching the end of the scuff marks, the washer and dryer wouldn't move any further. Edwin and Sam looked at the area of the wall where the appliances had been; a section of the wall had moved along with the washer and dryer, revealing a solid steel door behind it.

"What the hell?" Sam examined the door.

He tried the door handle, but the door didn't seem to budge.

"Locked?" Edwin asked.

"Actually, it feels like something's … pulling the door … trying to keep it closed," Sam said, still working on the handle.

Edwin helped Sam in prying the door open. They pulled the door, and in doing so, three children tumbled out.

"Please don't hurt us!" a blonde teenage girl cried.

The other two children, a boy and a girl, clung to each other, their grasping knuckles turning white.

"It's okay, kids," Sam got down on his knees. "I'm a police officer. I'm here to help the three of you."

"But," the blonde girl said. "It's … not just us …"

Sam and Edwin peeked deeper into the room the steel door guarded. Inside, they discovered three more emaciated children huddled together. All three were under the age of ten.

★★★

Sam stood on one side of the hallway of Odette General Hospital while Edwin stood on the opposite side, his back to his foster son. Both were keeping watch over three hospital rooms on their respective sides of the hallway. They had rescued six children from the basement of the Wilksford house, all of whom were immediately rushed to the hospital. The eldest were teenagers while the youngest was no more than a year old. Regardless of age, it was apparent to both Sam and Edwin that these children had been mistreated.

"Excuse me, detectives?" a woman in her early forties with shoulder length mahogany hair pulled back into a messy bun and wearing teal scrubs approached Sam and Edwin.

Both cops turned to her.

"How are they?" Edwin asked.

They weren't his kids, but the worried father in him didn't care.

"I'm Dr. Briggs," she shook Edwin's hand. "The children have a long road to recovery ahead of them. All six were extremely malnourished and have a severe vitamin deficiency; honestly, it wouldn't surprise me if they had been locked away in the dark for weeks at a time with their state of ill health. The children have a multitude of bruises, scratches, and contusions all over each of their bodies, as well as a couple of them having broken or fractured bones that are in various stages of healing."

Edwin's breath hitched, the anger bubbling up inside of him at hearing the terrors the children had suffered.

"But," Dr. Briggs' face was pale and stoic. "That's not even the worst part. Four of the children, the fifteen-year-old, the thirteen-year-old, the ten-year-old and the eight-year-old, have been sexually abused."

Edwin's jaw clenched tighter than before, and he closed his eyes and shook his head slowly. He heard Sam cursing under his breath.

"Recent abuse?" Edwin asked, his voice low and quiet.

"The ten and eight-year-olds, no," the doctor said. "They have some old tearing and lacerations that have since healed."

"How about the older two?"

Dr. Briggs let out a reluctant and sorrowful sigh.

"Both were recently victimized," she said. "Detectives, during our examinations, we discovered something else; the fifteen-year-old has given birth before."

Edwin had no words.

"May we speak to the kids?" Sam asked.

"The younger children are currently sedated, but the eldest two may be able to speak to you," Dr. Briggs said. "I've contacted the Department of Family and Child Services, and they're sending an agent down here to investigate the case."

The doctor escorted Sam and Edwin into the eldest child's room. Her dirty blonde hair was limp and dull, with the rest of her body in a similar state. The large hospital bed looked like it could swallow her up whole like a Venus Fly Trap with a fly. Fifteen-year-old Isabel looked up at Sam, Edwin and Dr. Briggs as they entered her hospital room. She had steel blue eyes that, under different circumstances, would have been bright and serene but were cold and glossy as they regarded the two cops with a mixture of suspicion and unease.

"Isabel, this is Detective Hill, and this is Officer Marlowe," Dr. Briggs said. "Are you feeling well enough to speak to them?"

The girl shrugged her shoulders.

"Sure, I guess."

The doctor's pager beeped, so she excused herself from the room. Sam and Edwin moved to stand at the foot of Isabel's bed.

"I guess you probably want to know who killed my mom," Isabel said.

Edwin and Sam exchanged a quick glance.

"That would be a good place to start, yes," Sam said.

"Well, I can't tell you," Isabel said.

"Can't or won't?" Edwin asked.

Isabel examined her chipped fingernails. Edwin got the feeling the teen knew or at least had suspicions of who killed her mother, but refused to identify him or her for some reason.

"Okay, we can come back to that," Edwin said. "How about you tell us about how the six of you ended up in that basement dungeon instead?"

"Kendra kept us down there when she didn't feel like dealing with us," Isabel said. "Which was the majority of the time."

"Kendra?" Sam repeated.

"Yeah, Kendra. Sorry if I don't call her 'mom' or anything like that; she wasn't anything like a mom should be, so we all called her Kendra."

"I get it. My stepfather was a jackass, so I called him by his first name. He didn't deserve to be called 'dad' or anything like that," Sam said.

It appeared to Edwin that the teen appreciated Sam's understanding of her plight, as Isabel's intense gaze softened.

"All six of you were in that basement together?" Edwin asked. "Are all six of you siblings?"

"Sort of …" Isabel's sentence trailed off, and she looked away from the two cops.

Sam nudged Edwin. The veteran cop looked at his foster son, the latter mouthing the word: "baby."

"Can you tell us about the other kids?" he asked Isabel.

"Sure, I guess. Josiah is thirteen, Gavin is ten, Faith is eight, Leslie is six and Eli is one," Isabel said.

"Okay, we get that Kendra wasn't really a mom to you kids," Edwin said. "How about anyone else? Is there a dad in the picture somewhere?"

"Nope," Isabel shook her head. "None of us know who our dads are."

There was a knock on the hospital door, which Sam went to answer.

"Hayleigh. Hey, it's been a while," Sam said.

"Nice to see you again, Sam," Hayleigh, a former classmate of Sam's, stepped into the hospital room. "Being a cop suits you."

"Thanks."

Edwin looked at the girl as she approached.

"I remember you," he said. "You went to school with Sam and my daughter, Nina."

"That's right," Hayleigh said. "Now I work for the Department of Family and Child Services; what happened at prom a few years ago made me want to dedicate my life to helping people."

She turned to Isabel.

"My name is Hayleigh," she said to the teen. "I'm going to do whatever I can to help you, okay?"

Isabel said nothing, instead pulling her knees up to her chest and resting her chin on them.

Sam and Edwin sat in the waiting room nearest Isabel's room while Hayleigh conducted an interview with her about the possible abuse. The DFS worker stepped out of the hospital room and joined Sam and Edwin in the waiting room.

"Well?" Sam asked.

"It's not good," Hayleigh took a seat next to Sam. "I recorded our conversation. I'll get a copy over to you as soon as I can, but the gist is this: the kids have been sexually assaulted multiple times. Isabel claims that her mother, Kendra, used them as a kind of currency to get money and drugs from people. She stated that she has been raped multiple times and so has one of her siblings, Josiah. Isabel told me that Kendra was grooming the two younger siblings, Gavin and

Faith, to be, essentially, prostituted out, but Isabel and Josiah tried to intervene and protect the younger children by taking the brunt of the assaults."

"Christ, Hayleigh," Sam said.

Edwin ran a hand over the gray stubble on his chin. The poor kids. He couldn't wait to find the bastard who did this to them and drag his ass to jail where he belonged.

"Hayleigh, did Isabel say anything about possibly being pregnant at some point?" he asked. "When the Doc was examining her, she said she saw signs that Isabel had likely given birth."

"Not specifically," Hayleigh said. "But, when she was telling me about an incident that occurred a little less than two years ago, Isabel actually became very distraught and emotional. She was calm and collected throughout most of what she told me, except for that one incident. I tried to get more information out of her about this specific assault, but I have to be careful with my questioning, so I don't ask any leading or suggestive questions. I plan on doing a follow-up interview with her after I meet with the other children."

"Nearly two years ago, huh?" Edwin tapped his chin. "Hayleigh, before you arrived, Isabel told us that she and her siblings don't have any idea of who their fathers are. Do you think you could get in touch with the courts to get an order for a DNA test? Between the three of us, we might be able to get some answers."

"I'll put the word out immediately," Hayleigh said, pulling her phone out of her purse.

★★★

While Hayleigh worked with the children, Edwin and Sam left the hospital to return to the crime scene.

"Isabel told Hayleigh that the vic was essentially pimping her and the others out for money and drugs," Sam said. "Could one of Kendra's 'clients,' perhaps, suddenly have grown a conscience and decided to take that miserable piece of shit out of existence?"

"It's possible," Edwin said. "Let's continue looking around to see if we can find any names, addresses or anything else that might point to any of these child molesters."

Searching the Wilksford house only succeeded in making Edwin more infuriated than before. A pig pen was cleaner than the Wilksford house; even a landfill was in better condition. There were empty beer cans and bottles scattered throughout the house, and some used roaches and pipes were left on various counters and tables. It wasn't uncommon to find a used condom wrapper alongside them either.

"Quite frankly, whoever killed Kendra did the world a service," Sam grimaced as he came across yet another torn and discarded condom wrapper. "This guy should be given a medal of honor instead of a jail sentence. People like Kendra don't deserve justice."

"Normally I'd disagree with you and say that everyone deserves justice of some sort," Edwin said. "But I think people like Kendra are the exception to the view that 'all life is sacred.' There's a special place in hell for people who hurt children."

"Hey, even prisoners don't like child molesters and people who hurt kids," Sam said. "Why should we?"

"Yeah, can't argue with that logic."

He turned away from the government check issued to Kendra that he found lying on the kitchen table next to a couple of empty beer cans. She received thousands of dollars of government assistance to aid in raising her children but, by simply looking at the squalor the children resided in versus the comforts and luxuries the victim enjoyed, it was apparent very little of that money was spent on the children.

"Do you think she kept her kids simply because she could get money from the state?" Sam asked.

"Honestly, it wouldn't surprise me," Edwin said. "All of the kids look different from each other, so it's safe to assume they all have different fathers. It's likely that Kendra accidentally got pregnant each time and kept the kid for the money. It's absolutely disgusting. There are families all across the country, good families, great people, who would have loved to have adopted any or all of the kids. No, instead she keeps popping out kids like a freakin' Pez dispenser."

Sam started heading toward the basement door.

"I want to check out the basement again," he said. "I didn't get a good look at things because we were too concerned with the welfare of the children."

Edwin motioned for him to lead the way. They headed back downstairs to the basement where they found the children. The room the children had been locked in was not roomy enough to comfortably fit two children, let alone six. There were six sleeping bags of various colors and designs sprawled out on the floor, along with toys that were crudely put together, presumably by Isabel or Josiah for their younger siblings with the few materials they had at their disposal. The only light in the room came from a light bulb hanging overhead that buzzed steadily as it bathed the room in a yellowish light.

Edwin's heart dropped to his feet at the sight of the living conditions the Wilksford children had been forced to reside in. He glanced back over his shoulder at Sam, who was inspecting the steel door to the chamber.

"Hey, Edwin," Sam said. "Check this out. Look at the screws on the handle; they look like someone took a screwdriver to them."

The two cops began searching the room for any tools. They were surprised to find one sewn into a secret compartment in one of the sleeping bags.

"We'll have to take this door back to the lab for a tool mark comparison," Edwin said. "But I have a feeling these marks are going to match the screwdriver we found."

"And it's likely the kids used the screwdriver to remove the handle and sneak out of the room," Sam finished Edwin's thought.

★★★

While Sam finished up at the crime scene, Edwin headed next door to meet with the neighbor, Albert Trousdale, who had reported the crime to the police and specifically requested to speak to Edwin.

"I read about you in the paper," Albert said, waving the folded-up newspaper around as he spoke. "Thirty-some years on the force, eh? That's why I asked for you, sonny; I figured you'd know what you're doing!"

"Well, thanks for the vote of confidence," Edwin said. "So, Albert, I'm all ears. What have you got for me?"

The veteran cop followed the elderly man into the living room.

"That Kendra's a bad egg," Albert said. "I'm not surprised that someone went after her like that."

"What makes you say that?"

"She's always got men coming and going from the house. Women, sometimes, too. They're always drinking and partying and making noise and being a real thorn in my side! Not to mention that they can sometimes get really loud when they're having se—"

"I get it," Edwin held a hand up to stop Albert from getting too far off topic. "Albert, you told Officer Robinson that there was a man who ran out of the Wilksford house this morning; can you tell me about him?"

"It's hard to keep track of all the men that come to the house, you see, sonny," Albert said.

The elderly man paused, his face brightening.

"You know, my sons worry about me living out here alone," he said. "I told them I'd be fine, but the boys wouldn't listen! They said they wanted to keep an eye on me to know that I was safe, especially after Kendra moved in and started causing problems in the neighborhood, so they installed some security cameras."

"Security cameras? Albert, you're my hero," Edwin said. "Can I see the recordings?"

"Sure. As long as you know how to run that damned computer gizmo, be my guest."

Albert directed Edwin into his spare bedroom where a relatively new computer sat on an oak desk. It had a fine layer of dust on it, a testament to Albert's amount of use of the machine. Poking around the computer, Edwin loaded up the security program. He began at midnight and fast forwarded until he saw the man Albert witnessed run from the house appear on the screen.

"That's him!" Albert pointed a bony finger at the computer screen.

Edwin let the recording play. The man arrived in a dark blue four-door sedan with a Colorado plate (and a loud muffler, which Albert was sure to point out to Edwin), the number to which Edwin scribbled down in his notepad. It was hard to discern the man's height from the angle of the camera, but Edwin was able to see that the man was bald, built like a weight-lifter and had a couple of tattoos on his right arm.

Albert watched with interest as Edwin printed out a still image of the man and of the man's vehicle.

"I'll never understand how all this new-fangled stuff works," he said.

"You're a smart man, Albert, I'm sure you could manage," Edwin said. "I also know that you're protective over your neighborhood, right?"

Albert's skinny chest puffed out as much as it could, and he attempted to straighten his back but couldn't get much more vertical than he already was.

"You got that right, sonny!" he said. "I keep a watch over my neighborhood like I watched over my boys in the army!"

"Like I figured," Edwin said. "Albert, I want you to think about what's happened in the neighborhood over the past few days, see if there was anything odd or unusual that happened. I can count on you, right?"

"Of course, sonny. It's my job," Albert said. "Oh, and another thing—"

"What's that?"

"Do you think you could do something about those damned raccoons that keep digging through my trash?"

Edwin fought back a laugh.

"Albert, I'll make you a deal," he said. "If your information helps us get whoever did this, I'll help you get rid of those pesky raccoons."

★★★

After looking over the text Edwin sent him about his meeting with the neighbor, Albert, Sam headed to the hospital and stepped into the room of thirteen-year-old Josiah. Tall and lanky, the brunet was skinny and sickly like his siblings. He was instantly stricken with fear upon Sam questioning him about the screwdriver.

"Jo, it's all right," Sam tried to reassure the teen. "Kendra's gone. She can't hurt you anymore. You don't have to hide anything from anyone."

Josiah, who had brought the bed sheets up to nearly cover his eyes, leaving his feet uncovered, cautiously lowered them. His face was ashen, and his lips trembled, his eyes were bulging from their sockets.

"It's ... my screwdriver," he whispered. "I s-stole it from the g-guys who installed the d-door in the basement when we moved here. We needed food and water ... Isabel and I would sneak out when Kendra was passed out or ... doing 'other stuff' with those people ... and steal food from the kitchen ... I'm so sorry!"

"There's no need to be sorry."

"We *stole*. That's a crime!"

"True," Sam said. "But, based on the circumstances, Josiah, you did what you had to do. I get it; my stepfather was a ghoul, too. He would sometimes deliberately not feed me because my mom wasn't there to make him take care of me. He lived by the idea that if he gave anything to me, it meant that he had less. I'd sneak out and steal something to eat or sometimes drink, too."

Josiah relaxed ever so slightly, though Sam could still see that he was visibly tense and frightened.

"Josiah, did you and Isabel sneak out yesterday?" he asked.

"Y-yes," the boy kneaded the sheets between his fingers. "Eli was hungry, so Isabel and I went upstairs to get food for him."

"What time was this?"

"I don't know. There's no clock downstairs," Josiah said. "But I think it was before, like, ten, because Kendra would usually go to the salon to get her hair and nails done around ten-thirty or something like that."

"Where was Kendra when you two slipped out of the basement?" Sam asked.

"Kendra had been drinking, and she probably did drugs, too, so she was passed out at the kitchen table," Josiah said. "Isabel and I used that chance and grabbed some food and went back downstairs."

"Did you see or hear anything odd or unusual recently?"

"What do you mean?"

"You know, weird stuff," Sam thought for a moment. "Were there any guys hanging around the house? Were any of Kendra's … friends, we'll call them, rough with her? Was there any yelling or screaming?"

Josiah shook his head. Sam let out a breath. This was getting him nowhere fast. He decided to switch tactics.

"Hey, Josiah, you and Isabel are close, right? Can you tell me if your sister had a baby, by any chance?"

"Josiah!"

Both Sam and Josiah turned their heads toward the doorway and found Isabel standing there. She was carrying Eli on her hip and held little Leslie's hand.

"I think you need your rest now, Jo," Isabel said.

Josiah stared at his sister, his caramel eyes wide.

"Right," he said, sliding down in his hospital bed.

★★★

Having a couple of offenses on his criminal record made it easier for Sam and Edwin to track down Lee Fernandez, the man who Albert saw running from the house on the morning that Kendra's body was discovered.

"I didn't do anything," Lee said, trying to shut the door to his trailer on Sam and Edwin.

Edwin wedged his foot in the door before Lee could completely close it.

"We have you on video, Lee," Sam said, showing the man the picture on his phone. "We know you were there the day Kendra Wilksford was found dead. We also have a witness who said he saw you there yesterday morning."

"The old man? Shit, he's a nosey bastard!"

"Yeah, but a nosey bastard who got you on camera," Edwin said with a small grin of victory on his lips. "Why don't you tell us what you were doing at the house that day?"

"Why don't you go and fuck off?"

Edwin looked at Sam.

"People today can be so rude," he said.

"No kidding," Sam said. "Maybe we should bring Lee to the station for a little time out."

"Fine!" Lee said with a huff. "I was there that morning, all right?"

"It's a start. Tell us everything about that morning."

"Fine. I went over there to meet with Kendra. We were gonna do some blow together before she went to go get her hair done. I got there, but she didn't answer the door, so I let myself inside. I didn't see Kendra, so I went into the kitchen to grab a beer and wait for her," Lee's face became ashen. "I found her in the kitchen. She was dead ... her body was by the table, and her head ... was near the sink—"

"You saw the body, what then?" Sam asked.

"I got the fuck out of there!" Lee said. "I ain't gonna wait around in a house with a headless body! Seriously, you said you got me on tape, right? Check the tape; I was only there for, like, ten minutes! I couldn't have done *that* to Kendra in that amount of time."

Sam and Edwin exchanged a look. Lee was probably right; that didn't seem like enough time to kill and decapitate Kendra. Plus, the findings from the initial autopsy report indicated that Kendra had likely been killed the day before her body was found. Perhaps, Edwin considered, it was time to visit Albert again and check through what else his security cameras found.

★★★

Sam and Edwin checked in with Hayleigh at the Department of Family and Child Services before heading out to visit with Albert again.

"I talked to the judge in Family Court, and she agreed to order DNA tests for all of the children," Hayleigh said. "In the meantime, they'll be put in to foster care once they're released from the hospital. I'm doing whatever I can to make sure those kids stick together. It's apparent from my conversations with them that it would be traumatic for them to be separated."

"They only had each other to rely on, so it kind of makes sense that they'd be afraid to be separated," Sam said.

"Any updates on the investigation?"

"We're searching through the list of contacts the victim had in her phone and throughout the house. She got around, so the suspect list is pretty large."

"Plus, we've reached out to other departments across the state from previous cities Kendra, and the kids lived in for assistance in tracking down these persons of interest," Edwin said.

"The people responsible for the atrocities to these kids need to be punished," Hayleigh clenched the pen in her hand, her hand shaking from the intense pressure. "The poor kids … when they were being examined, the poor children were so scared and in pain. It was heart-wrenching. They all suffered so much and are still suffering."

Edwin's phone buzzed.

"Gotta run, kids," he said. "My new friend Albert just returned from his doctor's appointment, and I need to go visit him."

★★★

"How are you doing, Albert?" Edwin asked as the older man let him inside.

"Fit as a fiddle!" Albert said.

"Glad to hear it."

Returning to the spare bedroom, Edwin fired up the computer once again. Albert pulled up a chair and sat next to him, watching the veteran cop as he navigated the computer. Edwin skimmed through the footage, stopping at midnight on the day of the murder. He let the recording play.

"Heard any more raccoons?" Edwin asked Albert.

"No," Albert said, sounding pretty happy about the fact. "I've been a light sleeper since my days in the army, and I haven't heard a peep. It's been great!"

Watching the recording, Edwin found a man arrive at the Wilksford house shortly after one in the morning. A motion activated light on Albert's house lit up as the man made his way up toward the Wilkford's.

"Wait a minute," Edwin frowned. "I think I've seen this guy before."

"He's probably a criminal," Albert said. "Look at all those piercings and tattoos-he's a hoodlum!"

Edwin opened his mouth to correct Albert but, after taking another look at the man on the video, he fell silent. The old man might have been right.

★★★

"I think Albert deserves a medal," Sam said.

Edwin gave his foster son a laugh as he made his way back to his desk in the bullpen.

"What makes you say that?" he asked.

"The guy on the recording on the day of the murder is Wesley Allan," Sam said. "He was released from prison about a year ago for, get this, sexual abuse of a child."

"You're shittin' me."

"I wish I were, but the tattoos and piercings on the guy in the security footage match up with those of Allan from his mugshots and arrest photos."

"What about his victim?"

"Kid was young," Sam paused. "Under the age of seven."

"Jesus H. Christ," the hand Edwin had resting on his desk balled into a fist. "Sick fuck-"

"If Allan was visiting Kendra, it probably means that he was looking to secure a new victim. We should talk to the kids and see if they recognize him."

"Good idea. I'll go pay a visit to Allan while you check in with Hayleigh and the kids."

★★★

Josiah started tearing up the moment Sam showed him the photo of Wesley Allan.

"Do you recognize this man?" Sam asked.

"Y-yeah," Josiah sniffed and wiped his eyes. "Kendra was gonna let him hurt—"

"Hurt who?" Hayleigh asked.

"Josiah!" Isabel appeared behind Sam and Hayleigh.

The teen looked over at his sister as he sniveled and sniffed.

"Izzy, they found the guy who wanted to hurt Eli," he whispered. "He should go to prison."

"Y-you ... found him? The man Kendra was going to let abuse Eli?" Isabel looked between Sam and Hayleigh.

"Yes, Isabel, we found him. You remember Detective Hill? Well, he's bringing Wesley Allan in as we speak to question him about what happened with Kendra and about abusing Eli."

"He didn't abuse Eli," Isabel was adamant. "I wouldn't let Kendra do that to him! I couldn't! How could she do that to her own grandch—"

She stopped abruptly, bringing a hand up to cover her mouth. Sam and Hayleigh exchanged a look.

"Isabel, what were you going to say?" Hayleigh asked. "It sounded like you were going to say Eli was Kendra's grandson."

"You're Eli's mom, aren't you?" Sam asked softly. "That's why talking about the incident that happened about two years ago deeply upset you; that's when you got pregnant."

Isabel said nothing.

"Izzy, please," Josiah pleaded with his sister. "I don't want to hide this anymore. I'm tired. I want to get this over with."

"Isabel, we have DNA tests," Sam bluffed. "We know the truth already, but we'd like to hear it from you."

Isabel folded her arms across her chest and turned her head away from Sam and Hayleigh. Her bottom lip was trembling.

"So what if he's my son? That doesn't change anything," she said, before turning and walking out of Josiah's hospital room.

Sam watched Isabel leave before looking back at Josiah.

"We had to protect Eli," he whispered. "He's only a baby ..."

Sam let out a breath. Edwin wasn't going to believe this.

★★★

The pen Edwin had been tapping against his desk in the bullpen as Sam explained what had happened with Hayleigh at the hospital was suddenly snapped in half when he heard the latest development in the case.

"Kendra was going to let a known child abuser come in and assault a one-year-old?" Edwin looked down at the pen in his hands, which was now in two pieces. "Not only a one-year-old but her own grandson?"

"Yeah. I got Isabel to confirm that Eli is actually her child and not her brother, but we'll know for sure when the court ordered DNA tests come back," Sam said. "What scares me though, is what Josiah said: 'We had to protect Eli, he's only a baby.'"

Edwin tossed the broken pen into the garbage can beneath his desk.

"Yeah, that's not something I want to hear, either," he said. "But we have no evidence linking them to Kendra's death. As far as we know, they were locked downstairs in the basement at the time Kendra died."

"But Josiah confirmed that he and Isabel would sneak out to get food and water. Based on the fact that they're not dead, starving, but alive, it must be true," Sam said. "You talked to Wesley, right? What did he say about Kendra? Any chance that he is the one who killed her?"

"I wish. Wesley, even though he's a piece of shit, is at least pretty upfront about everything," Edwin said. "Essentially, the slimeball told me he's not interested in older women, not that Kendra was that old, but he likes them young, really young. He didn't admit to planning anything with Kendra, but he didn't deny anything either. Thankfully, being so close to children violated the conditions of his parole, so I was able to throw his ass back in jail."

"That's a plus, at least. But we need to find more evidence to get a definitive answer on who killed Kendra, preferably something that doesn't point to the children."

"Right, but we can't ignore evidence that points to them," Edwin said. "It's not our job to choose who we think deserves to go to prison for a crime and who doesn't; we have to do our jobs according to what the evidence tells us."

"But, Edwin, Isabel, and Josiah don't deserve to go to prison. Look at all that Kendra did to them!"

"Do I want to send them to prison if they're guilty? No. Not one bit. Quite frankly, if they did kill Kendra, they did the world a service. But we're cops, Sam. We don't get paid to decide who's prison-worthy and who's not."

"Yeah, well, in some cases, I think we should be," Sam said.

★★★

It was back to Albert's house once again to review the security camera footage.

"I managed to turn on that computer-thing," Albert announced to Edwin as they took their customary seating arrangements in the spare bedroom.

"See, Albert? I knew you could do it," Edwin said. "Next thing you know, you'll be sending emails and posting updates on social media."

"Social media? Did you make that up, sonny?"

"Never mind."

"What are you looking for today?" Albert asked.

"We may have a lead on who killed your neighbor," Edwin said. "Now, we need evidence to prove it. Speaking of which, did you think of anything that could help us out?"

"There was no one in or out of the house after that tattooed and pierced up man. The only thing that was a little strange was a scream."

"A scream?"

"Yeah, while I was trying to read my newspaper!" Albert said. "Can't a man read his paper in peace?"

"Albert, when did you hear this scream?" Edwin asked.

"When I got my paper. The paperboy usually brings it around eight, before he goes to school, I think. I got it around eight-thirty and was going to read the paper after I had breakfast."

Accessing the security program, Edwin fast-forwarded to the day before the murder, stopping at around eight in the morning, the time when the newspaper should have been delivered. As Albert said, a pre-teen boy drove by on his bike, tossing a paper into the driveway as he whizzed by a little after eight in the morning. Around eight-thirty, Albert appeared on screen, making his way down the driveway to retrieve his newspaper. He disappeared into the house shortly afterward. A little after nine, Edwin heard the scream that Albert told him about.

"Hot damn, there it is," Edwin said, jotting down the time stamp in his notes. "Okay, Wesley left the house already when the scream was heard. Shit. That's not good."

"What's that sonny?" Albert cupped his ear to hear what Edwin was muttering to himself.

"Nothing to worry about," Edwin said. "Let's see what else happened a few days ago."

The remainder of the day before the murder was uneventful, with no one coming or going from the house, except for the mailman to drop off the mail in the mailbox at the end of the Wilkford's driveway. As day turned to night, all was still around the Wilkford residence.

"See? No one in or out of the house," Albert said.

"No visitors in or out of the house, you mean," Edwin rewound the recording, replaying a specific portion of the video that caught his eye.

The section in question showed an individual at the bottom of the screen, being caught on camera after the motion-activated light on Albert's house lit up. The individual was throwing something into Albert's trash cans.

"What's that?" Albert squinted, trying to discern what was being discarded in the trash cans.

"I think that's your raccoon, Albert," Edwin said. "Let's see what they were doing over there."

Heading outside, Edwin began searching through the elderly man's garbage cans. Albert joined him outside as the veteran cop retrieved what had been thrown away.

"Jackpot," Edwin said.

★★★

A few days later, Sam and Edwin stopped into the Odette General Hospital to check in on the six children. They brought in balloons and tiny stuffed animals for the children. The youngest two, Leslie and baby Eli, quickly adapted to their gifts, thrilled to have a toy to play with. Faith and Gavin were thankful and snuggled into their beds with their new toys and watched some cartoons, a luxury they were becoming accustomed to. Isabel and Josiah, however, seemed reluctant to accept the gifts from the two detectives.

"I can't accept these," Isabel said, her eyes locked on her bed sheets.

"Why not?" Edwin asked.

"It's not right."

"Why isn't it right?"

Isabel began tearing up.

"Because—"

"Because we killed Kendra," Josiah said from the doorway of his sister's hospital room.

"We know," Sam said.

Josiah and Isabel exchanged a look.

"How?" she asked with a sniffle.

"We have a video of you, Isabel, slipping out of the house and discarding knives in your neighbor's trash cans after wrapping them in your bloody clothing," Edwin said. "Mr. Trousdale's sons installed security cameras to keep an eye on their dear old pop, and the electric eye caught you. Plus, whenever you'd sneak out and rummage through the garbage cans looking for food, he heard you. Albert thought you kids were raccoons."

"Oh," Isabel looked down.

"The knives we found were tested for fingerprints and blood, as well as the clothing you tossed away," Sam said. "Kendra's blood was found on the knives and so were your fingerprints. Her blood is also all over the clothes."

"We did it," Josiah said. "We killed her."

He turned to Isabel.

"I'm sorry, Izzy. I know you said we couldn't tell anyone, but I can't keep it inside anymore. When Detective Hill and Officer Marlowe gave me those presents, I felt horrible. I don't deserve any presents; I deserve to go to jail."

Isabel reached her hand out to take Josiah's in hers.

"I know," she said.

"Can you tell us what happened?" Sam asked.

Isabel let out a slow breath before speaking.

"Kendra was talking with that guy, Wesley. Josiah and I sneaked out one night and saw some text messages she'd been sending back and forth with him. Apparently, he was gonna pay Kendra a lot of money to ... hurt Eli. I know what people have done to Josiah and me; I couldn't let that happen to my baby," she said. "Kendra came downstairs to get Josiah for ... a client ... I begged her not to let Wesley hurt Eli. She laughed and said that the money meant more to her than any of us. That's when I knew she wasn't gonna listen to anything Josiah and I had to say.

"That night, I was trying to make Josiah feel better. I went upstairs and got him an ice pack and a pillow to sit on. Kendra was passed out. She did the drugs the guy who hurt Josiah must have brought her. I got so angry ... I saw the knives on the counter, and I grabbed them. I brought them downstairs and showed them to Josiah. He and I agreed that the only way to stop Kendra was to kill her."

"We didn't know what else to do," Josiah said. "We had to stop her."

"Kendra didn't care about any of us. That's why she stuck us in the basement. I saw her when she got pregnant with Gavin and Faith, and Leslie ... she drank, did drugs and didn't care about the baby. I didn't want to have a baby at fifteen, but I didn't do anything like that. I love Eli. I love him so much. That's why ..."

"That's why we killed her."

"How did it happen?" Sam asked.

"It was after Wesley left. He had come over to the house and stayed the night. They did drugs together, and he left the next morning. I knew that Kendra must have gone ahead with setting up Wesley to do stuff to Eli, so I had to stop her. Josiah and I slipped out of the basement and headed upstairs. Kendra was coming from upstairs. She didn't even know we were there."

"We stabbed her, and she screamed," Josiah said. "She screamed real loud, and I kinda panicked and kept stabbing her. Izzy and I both kept stabbing her."

"Why did you cut off the head?" Edwin asked.

"We wanted to make sure that she was dead and that there was no way she could come back," Isabel said.

She looked up at Sam and Edwin, eyes steady and unblinking.

"Please, let my brothers and sisters stay together. They need each other. Plus, I know they'll take care of Eli. My brothers, sisters and my baby, they mean everything to me. I killed Kendra to stop her from hurting them. I deserve to go to prison for what I did."

"Me too," Josiah took his sister's hand.

Sam's hand hovered over his handcuffs. Could he do it? Could he really arrest these two kids after all they'd been through? They weren't cold-blooded killers. Isabel and Josiah were victims of their circumstances; they did what they had to do to survive and stop Kendra from hurting them and the others ever again. How the hell was he supposed to arrest them for that?

"Hey," Edwin whispered to him. "We'll talk to Hayleigh. Maybe between the three of us, we can work with the family court to get these kids the help they need instead of going to prison."

"They better," Sam replied. "Or else I might have to make some evidence disappear."

Edwin started to question Sam about his last comment, but Sam ignored him, instead stepping forward to arrest Isabel and Josiah.

★★★

Sam closed the drawer of the filing cabinet and turned around to head back to his desk. He looked down at Edwin's empty desk and sighed. With the Wilksford case wrapped up, it was officially Edwin's last day on the force. He was going to miss his partner and best friend working with him but knew that Edwin was looking forward to enjoying his retirement with his family, himself included.

"Hey, kiddo," Edwin said as he strolled into the bullpen. "I heard back from the family court judge taking on the Wilksford case. The DA is going to work out a deal with the kids. They're finally going to get the help they need."

"Edwin, that's awesome," Sam said. "Now, maybe, they can finally start to work toward having a normal life."

"Speaking of normal life," he said. "I'm looking forward to going into retirement and having a regular, run-of-the-mill life. I can leave the force in good faith, knowing the safety of Odette will be in good hands with you, Detective."

Sam stared at his foster father.

"Detective?" he repeated.

"Congrats, Sam. The Captain was impressed with your work on the case. You've been selected as the newest Detective," Edwin said. "I'm proud of you, kid."

Sam was at a loss for words. He got promoted to Detective because he arrested Isabel and Josiah and closed the case. Was that really grounds for a promotion?

Sam wanted to say something to Edwin, but some of the other detectives and officers who overheard the news came over to him to congratulate him on a "well-deserved promotion." A well-deserved promotion, indeed.

INTO THE FIRE

Coffee in one hand and the daily newspaper in the other, Edwin Hill leaned back in the black office chair at his desk in the front foyer of Odette Senior High School. After retiring from the police force a few months ago, Edwin quickly became restless and realized he needed something to keep himself occupied when his family was out of the house. His wife, Gloria, was still working. His older daughter, Clarice, had moved out and was now living in an apartment with her boyfriend, Raymond. Having recently been promoted to Junior Partner at her law firm, Clarice was spending long hours at the office. His younger daughter, Nina, had also moved out and was working on her degree. And Sam, of course, was now a detective with the Odette Police Department, so his hours varied depending on his caseload, though he would always make sure to stop by for the family pizza night on Fridays before heading home to his own apartment.

Sleeping late, watching television and puttering around the house had been fun at first, but Edwin wasn't one for idleness. Mrs. Porter, the principal, offered him a job as a part-time security job when the new school year began and the retired cop jumped at the opportunity. It was a great gig; he got to sit at the security desk near the front doors and enjoy his coffee and newspaper while keeping an eye on the kids currently attending his alma mater.

"Hey, Mr. Hill," Gym teacher Brian Egan said, as he headed toward the front doors, a mesh bag full of sports supplies slung over his shoulder.

"Morning, Brian," Edwin said. "Looks like you've got some fun stuff planned for the kids today."

"Can't let a warm day in autumn go to waste, right?" Egan said. "Oh, I heard there was almost a fight the other day; what happened?"

"Yeah. The Jennings boy wanted to fight the Taylor kid. It seems both boys wanted to take little Miss Medina to the homecoming dance and found out that the other wanted to do the same. They agreed to meet up in the back parking lot after school and fight but the rumors made their way to me, so I decided to pay them a little visit. The three of us had a nice little chat together, and well, let's say they're going to think twice before trying something stupid like that again."

"Scared the daylights out of them, huh?" Egan said with a laugh. "It's probably for the best, though. I heard from Mila that Melanie Medina was asked to the homecoming dance by one of the boys in her second-period history class."

"Young love can be so fickle sometimes," Edwin said.

The first-period bell rang overhead. Egan said goodbye to Edwin and headed outside to set up for his upcoming physical education classes. Even though classes were officially now in session for the day, Edwin made sure to keep one eye on the paper and one eye on the front doors for the occasional straggler that tried to sneak in after the first-period bell rang. As a cop, Edwin thought he'd heard practically every excuse in the book, but these kids nowadays were undoubtedly a creative bunch. They came up with explanations that Edwin had never heard of in his fifty-plus years on Earth.

He kept a notebook on him to write down the especially good ones. Edwin was told the usual excuses for coming in late, like "my car broke down," and "my alarm didn't go off," or "I missed the bus." He appreciated the kids that were brutally honest and said, "The line at Starbucks was long." Edwin's favorites, though, had to be the sarcastic, joking kids. "I'm not late; you're early," was a good one. "The whole getting-up-early thing wasn't working, so I decided to come in when it was more convenient," gave him a good chuckle. His personal favorite, however, was the kid who quoted Van Halen's "Hot for Teacher" by explaining, "I don't feel tardy."

Edwin chuckled to himself as he recalled the various excuses as he read over the recap of the girls' softball game from last night. They were off to a good start this year. It wouldn't surprise him if they made the playoffs. One of the two sets of doors opened, followed by the thud-thud-thud of footsteps. He tipped his newspaper down so he could see the arriving individual as he pulled one of the second set of doors open and entered the school foyer. The kid was carrying a large camouflage duffel bag that was big enough that the kid himself could hide away in it if he wanted to skip gym class or something. He was dressed in black from head to toe, like Neo or Morpheus from "The Matrix."

Edwin cleared his throat as the kid walked past him. The kid paused, looking over his shoulder at him.

"You're late, Dillon," Edwin said, pointing to the clock on the wall above the front doors.

Dillon Harris's eyes flicked from Edwin's face to the clock, and back again. He didn't seem to care that he was late. The boy turned his head and continued walking.

"Whoa, whoa, whoa," Edwin said, tossing his newspaper aside.

His tone was louder and sterner than earlier, using his "cop voice," as Gloria called it.

"Pump the brakes, there, pal. You need to march straight to Mrs. Porter's office and sit there until she comes back, got it?"

Again, Dillon stayed silent, and he turned to continue walking toward his destination. Edwin jumped up from his desk and caught the kid by the arm as he passed by him. Edwin's height and meaty build usually intimidated the troublemaking kids, but the boy was unimpressed.

Edwin's years on the force afforded him a glimpse into the dark side of human nature that he was glad to put behind him when he hung up his badge and holster for good. But staring into the ice blue eyes of this young boy, Edwin's pulse raced, his legs turned to jelly, and a bolt of ice slithered down his spine.

Dillon reached into his black trench coat.

A flash of silver.

Three deafening pops.

A sudden, sharp, searing pain.

Edwin fell back onto his chair, a hand clutching at his chest. He watched blood spilling out between his fingers like a burst dam. As his eyesight faded, the young mechanical soldier returned the gun to his trench coat before walking off.

★★★

"Attention all units. Reports of an active shooter at Odette Senior High School. All units to respond immediately."

★★★

Detective Samuel Marlowe blinked, uncertain of what he had just heard. *Wait, did dispatch really say what I thought it said?* Driving his police cruiser back from the local courthouse, Sam pulled off to the side of the road and grabbed the radio receiver from its cradle.

"10-9, Dispatch. Please repeat," he said.

"Reports of an active shooter at Odette Senior High School," dispatch repeated. "All units to respond immediately."

A lightning bolt of horror jolted through Sam's body. He tried to swallow, but his mouth was too dry. His heartbeat pounded in his ears, drowning out the repeated calls and updates from dispatch. *Edwin.*

Not only was Odette High his alma mater and full of children, but Edwin was there. His beloved foster father, mentor and best friend worked there as a security guard for a few hours each day. *Fuck! I know Edwin. He'll do anything and everything to keep those kids and teachers from getting hurt ... even if that means putting himself in danger. Fuck!* Sam shuddered from head to toe.

Sam flipped on the lights and sirens on his cruiser and shot out back onto the road, his tires squealing over the blaring horn of the red sedan he cut off. Pedal down to the floor, Sam sped off to the school.

★★★

A few other police officers arrived at the school before him, and with screaming sirens in the background, more were on the way. His car barely in park, Sam hopped out of the vehicle and hurried toward Denomy, Madison, and Robinson.

"What's going on? Dispatch said there were reports of an active shooter," he asked.

"Yes, Sir," Officer Denomy said. "The principal, Mrs. Porter, is in contact with Captain Buchanan. The school is on lockdown, and all of the teachers and staff are following the protocols mandated by the school for this situation."

"Good. Do we have any reports of injuries or—" It had to be asked. "Casualties?"

"We're not sure yet, Sir. Mrs. Porter has everyone sheltering in place, so she hasn't been able to—"

Denomy's sentence was interrupted by the sound of a pop coming from the school building. It was followed by another. And another. And another. And another. Sam and the other officers flinched with each sound. Denomy's face paled, Madison turned green, and Robinson shivered.

Additional police cruisers pulled into the parking lot, and their drivers hurried over to Sam and Denomy.

"Officer Therrien and Officer Kelley, reporting, Sir," two officers said as they raced over to Sam and the others.

As the highest-ranking officer present, Sam took charge.

"We heard shots fired. The shooter is active and moving. We need to get inside and neutralize the threat ASAP. Gear up and let's go."

Sam and the other officers suited up in their bullet-proof vests and checked and loaded their guns.

"Therrien, Kelley, stay here and be ready to barricade parents, reporters and whoever else may show up. Once word gets out about what's happening, everyone and their mother is going to come down here," he said. "Get the other officers that are on their way to help you out when they get here. If any new developments come through, send word immediately. Make sure the fire department and paramedics are on the way and ready for anyone who's injured."

"Yes, Sir."

Sam and the other officers made their way to the front doors of the school. Trying the doors, he found them locked as a part of the lockdown procedure. Sam peered inside, looking for the shooter. All was still; a pair of feet pointed at the ceiling.

"Shit," Sam's blood began to boil at the sight. "We have one down."

Sam motioned to two officers to bring up the battering ram. It took a couple tries to break through the locks, but the doors ultimately gave way and the cops headed inside. Sam rushed over to the person on the floor.

"No, no, no! Shit! No! Edwin!"

Sam collapsed onto his knees, falling forward as if he had been struck in the back with the battering ram.

Edwin lay in a pool of blood resulting from several bullet wounds to the chest. Sam grabbed Edwin's jacket from the back of the chair and used it to help apply pressure to his wounds. He checked the gray-haired man's pulse and was relieved to feel he still had one.

"Edwin, hey," Sam said. "It's Sam. Hey, come on, Ed, wake up."

There was another pop of gunfire overhead.

"S-S-Sam?" Edwin's voice was weak and hoarse.

Sam repeatedly blinked, trying to keep the tears at bay.

"I'm here, Edwin," he said, one hand applying pressure to Edwin's wounds, the other grabbing hold of the ex-cop's hand. "I'm here. We're going to get you out of here-"

Edwin shook his head in a slow, robotic movement.

"Get the shooter," he said. "Leave me here."

"I can't leave you, Edwin."

Edwin gripped Sam's arm.

"Leave me, Sam!" he repeated. "Do your job!"

"Edwin-"

"Fucking go, Sam! Don't let any kids die for me! Do your job! That's an order!"

The tears stung his eyes. Sam clenched his jaw tight enough he thought it might shatter his teeth. Another gunshot rang overhead. Edwin was right; the shooter needed to be stopped immediately.

"I won't let him get away with this," Sam whispered.

Edwin placed one of his hands on top of Sam's before Sam stood up to continue searching for the shooter.

"Detective Marlowe," one of the other officers said. "That last gunshot sounded like it came from the second or third floor."

Sam let out a breath, taking a second to compose himself.

"Right, let's go," he said.

Sam headed up to the second floor via the nearest stairwell. Reaching the second-floor landing, Sam cautiously stepped out of the stairwell, his gun drawn. Looking around, he found the floor completely empty, except for what appeared to be puddles of water all across the hall.

"What the—" he started to say. "Is that ... gasoline?"

He was interrupted by some tiny noises as a small object was tossed onto the floor from the other end of the hallway.

CLINK

CLINK

Silence.

BOOM

The floors buckled like an earthquake was tearing through them. Sam and the other officers were knocked back. He hissed as he skittered back against a row of lockers, his shoulder crashing into the wall with a thud. Like a hockey puck rebounding off of the glass surrounding the ice, Sam popped up from the ground, shaking off the shock of the impact and flexing the arm that had smashed into the wall moments ago.

Sam was shocked to find a sea of flames.

"Shit! That was a pipe bomb!" he gasped.

The water all over the floors ... it was gasoline, and mixed with the explosion, started the fire. Squinting and peering through the flames to the other side, Sam's heart skipped a beat when he discerned a petite figure standing there. *Is it a student? A teacher? The shooter?* As his eyes focused, Sam discovered the figure had a gun. It was the shooter.

"He's got a gun!" Sam shouted to the other officers behind him.

He trained his gun on the figure. As the fire continued to burn, the sensors in the alarm system were activated and set off the fire alarms throughout the building. Moments later, Sam could hear the stampede of students on the floor above him.

Shit! Everyone is supposed to be sheltering in place! The fucking fire alarm—they were supposed to ignore everything until word was given that it was safe to resume normal activity! Fuck!

There was no stopping the people from the third floor now that they were already on the move. *Maybe I can at least warn them about what's going on.*

"Fire on the second floor; repeat, fire on the second floor," Sam shouted into his radio in an attempt to be heard over the blaring fire alarms. "Do not use the east or north staircases; repeat, east and north staircases should not be used."

As he spoke, Sam saw the figure turn and make his way toward the north stairwell. *Shit! The shooter's going to go after the students and staff coming down that stairwell.*

Sam's grip on his gun tightened as the shooter rounded the corner and out of his sight. He couldn't reach the killer from here. There was only one way to the other side that would be quick enough to get to the shooter without risking too many lives, besides his own.

"Go downstairs and head up the north stairwell!" Sam yelled at the officers behind him. "The shooter is heading that way."

"Detective Marlowe!" one of the officers started to say.

"Go!"

Letting out a breath and bracing himself, Sam holstered his gun and then darted through the flames.

He felt nothing.

No pain.

No burning.

Nothing.

Every sense, every fiber, was focused on the shooter right around the corner.

The shooter's angelic halo of golden hair disappeared around the corner of the north stairwell. Sam propelled his aching body forward, praying for another surge of adrenaline to help him overcome the pain flooding his system. Pulling his gun out again, he used his arm to wipe the sweat dripping from his forehead into his eyes.

Sam reached the stairwell entrance as the boy's arm jerked up in the air. It was another pipe bomb. Sam and the boy were slammed backward into the seizing floor by the bomb's shockwaves. Gritting his teeth, Sam pushed himself up and lunged for the shooter.

They wrestled for control of the gun the boy had in his hand. Sam was gaining the upper hand, twisting and yanking the weapon out of his grip, until the boy kneed him in the groin with considerable force. Sam recoiled from the burst of pain, granting the boy enough time to worm out of the cop's grasp.

The boy hopped to his feet and pointed the gun at Sam.

"D-Dillon?" Sam sputtered upon discovering he recognized the teenager.

The boy's icy blue eyes locked onto Sam's gray ones for a split second, but that was more than enough time to understand that this boy was only a shell of the kid he knew from the projects. The child standing in front of him, pointing a gun at him, was Dillon Harris. Sam remembered little Dillon when they both lived in the slums named the Englewood Apartments. Barely more than a few months ago, Sam had tried to reach out to the deeply troubled teen through the mentorship program he and Edwin had started with the police department. Sam felt like he had been making progress until Dillon's mom got involved and pulled him from the program.

The boy must have snapped. But why today? Why now? Why this way?

"Dillon," Sam said. "You can stop this. You don't have to hurt anyone else."

Dillon's face remained stoic.

"The Superintendent is here today," he said, his face impassive and words robotic. "He hurt me, so I'm going to hurt him."

"Please, Dillon. You can stop this now. You've made your point. No one else has to get hurt."

"I shot Edwin."

Any words Sam wanted to say to convince Dillon to stop what he was doing died in his throat. It crushed him to know that the kid he and Edwin tried to save from this very path ended up putting a bunch of bullets into Edwin. It was disgusting, painful.

Sam scrambled forward toward Dillon, but the boy, his eyes closed tightly together, fired a shot. Sam rolled away. When he tried to stand, his right leg buckled under him. Blood gushed down his leg and onto the floor. He got the adrenaline boost he needed, but it was only because of the bullet that had penetrated his flesh.

Gritting his teeth, Sam forced himself up and limped forward to chase after Dillon. The boy was poised at the top of the railing of the staircase, aiming down at the occupants of the stairwell. The other officers had arrived in the stairwell by this point, as Sam heard the orders the other officers were shouting as they worked to evacuate the staircase before shooting up at Dillon. With each shot and each scream heard, Sam pushed forward until he was a mere foot away from Dillon.

'I shot Edwin,' the words echoed in Sam's mind as he raised and aimed his gun at Dillon. An iron grip on his gun, Sam pulled the trigger. Dillon's body lurched forward from the impact of the bullet striking his body, tumbled over the railing, and landed on the stairs below.

★★★

Bandaged leg resting on a pillow on the coffee table in the living room of his apartment, Sam took a long swig of his beer as he flipped through the channels on the television. He groaned when he heard a knock at his door.

The two weeks since the school shooting had been the longest in his life. Not a day went by that someone tried to say thank you for his 'heroics.' He'd been sent gifts. Some of the students, teachers, and administrators from the school came to visit him in the hospital while he was being treated for his gunshot wound, bringing flowers, chocolates, balloons and all sorts of goodies for him to express their appreciation for saving them. Hell, the police department gave him a medal of valor and courage. Another knock at the door probably meant another person trying to give him something to show his or her appreciation for what he did at Odette High.

"It's open," Sam called.

The door opened and his older foster sister, Clarice, came inside the apartment.

"Hi Sam," she said.

Clarice looked tired, Sam noted. Ordinarily neat and nicely dressed, her blonde hair was messily pulled back by a clip, and she had sunglasses resting atop her head. The sunny yellow tee-shirt she wore only seemed to draw attention to the dark circles under her usually bright hazel eyes. Clarice was carrying a large and heavily stuffed gift basket.

"One of the partners at the office has a kid at Odette High," she said, Sam figured she must have caught him staring at the basket. "Everyone wanted to chip in to get you a little something to say thank you."

"A little something?" Sam repeated. "It looks more like a lot of something."

Clarice placed the basket on the coffee table next to Sam's leg.

"Well, everyone at the law office was thankful for what you did," she said with a shrug. "Plus, they know about Dad ..."

"Oh," Sam looked away from his sister, turning his attention back to the television. He scowled in disgust. He wasn't sure why he was still attempting to watch it at this point.

Practically every station on tv touched upon the shooting in some way over the past two weeks; it even made the national news. As a result, Sam's picture was plastered across the screen continuously, typically with the caption, 'Detective Samuel Marlowe, hero.'

Sam reached over to the end table to his right and grabbed the bottle of pain medication that the doctor at the emergency room prescribed to him to help him combat the pain from the gunshot wound. He ignored the fact that Clarice watched him as he popped in a few pills and washed them down with his beer. He was going to have to get a refill soon. He was only two weeks into his recuperation, and he was already almost out of pills. The doctor wasn't going to like that. But who cares what the doctor thought?

He was a cop; he had plenty of access to all sorts of drugs. If the doctor wouldn't give him more pain meds, he could always get them on his own by swiping some from evidence or by shaking down some criminals.

"Sam!"

Sam shook his head and looked at Clarice, who was staring at him, hands on her hips and a frown on her face.

"Sorry, I zoned out for a second there," he said.

"Yes, I noticed. As I was saying, Sam, you shouldn't be mixing alcohol and pills. It's dangerous."

Sam tossed the empty pill bottle aside, joining the rest of the clutter gathering in his apartment from his lack of caring over the past two weeks. He blamed it on his injury but, in all honesty, it was because he didn't give a damn.

"I know, Clarice," Sam said. "I slipped up once or twice. I won't do it again."

He changed the subject.

"How are you holding up?"

Clarice had headed into the kitchen, returning to the living room a few moments later with a garbage bag to start picking up the empty beer cans, food wrappers and other trash Sam hadn't bothered with scattered around the room.

"All right, I guess," she said with a sigh. "Sam, if you need anything or anyone, you know you can come to Ray and me, right?"

"I know," Sam said. "Thanks for the offer, but I'm fine."

Clarice put the bag aside. She walked over to the coffee table where Sam had his leg propped up and sat down.

"Sam, I can't even imagine what you're going through," Clarice said. "I know you think you have to be strong for everyone, but you can come to Ray and me, Nina and Mom, too. We're all here for you."

Sam stared down at the bandage wrapped around his calf. The wound seemed to be throbbing in pain.

"I failed, Clarice," he said. "I failed."

"Failed? What are you talking about? You're a hero, Sam."

Sam let out a laugh.

"A hero?" he repeated. "I killed a kid. I shot and killed a fucking kid."

"But you stopped Dillon before he could hurt anyone else," Clarice said.

"Before Dillon even entered the school building that morning with his arsenal of weapons, I failed. Did you know that Dillon was a part of that mentoring program Edwin and I started?"

Clarice shook her head.

"Yeah. I tried to reach out to him and help him like your dad helped me. You know what happened? His mother stopped us. She prevented us from talking to him, seeing him and anything like that. She refused to work with DFS when we sent them out to check on them; DFS couldn't do anything because they couldn't substantiate any of the claims. Because of that, Dillon had no one."

"That's horrible," Clarice whispered.

"But that's not the worst of it," Sam said. "You know how the school had some budget cuts? It turns out one of the programs cut was the art program. Dillon was a big artist. I did some research into the Board of Education meetings over the past few days since I've had nothing to do other than sit on my ass all day; Dillon actually went and addressed the board members to try and get the art program reinstated. They didn't do it. Apparently, it was more important to fund some sports programs. That's two strikes against him: no art and no one to talk to. The final piece of the puzzle came together with Dillon's autopsy. His left arm had been broken and was in the process of healing; the ME thinks it was a break caused by someone twisting his arm until it snapped like a pencil. Know what I think did it? His mom. It's a hunch, but I'm pretty sure it's the right one."

Clarice brought her hand up to her mouth, shocked.

"She … broke his arm?" she gasped.

"That's my guess," Sam said. "It would explain why he put a bullet in her brain before he went to shoot up the school."

He sighed.

"I failed him, Clarice, and because of that, everyone paid the price for it … Edwin paid the price for it …"

Edwin Hill. His mentor, his friend and the man who saved his life. Edwin had survived thirty years on the police force but died by the hand of some stupid kid. The paramedics did all they could to save Edwin when they arrived, but it was too late. Edwin died, according to the medical examiner, shortly after he made Sam leave him behind.

Sam could feel the bile bubbling up in his throat. *Leave me, Sam,* Edwin had told him. He made Sam choose between staying with him in the foyer or going forward and shooting Dillon. Either choice resulted in death. How the hell was he supposed to live with that decision? By doing his job, Edwin died. Not only him but others, too. Four students, two teachers, and Edwin.

Sam ran a hand over his face.

"You know, I'm kind of tired. Can I call you and Ray later?"

Clarice sat silently for a moment before standing up from the coffee table.

"All right," she sighed. "Please, please, please call me, Sam. I'm worried about you. We all are."

"I'll be fine, Clarice. I'm the man of the house now, right? I've got to take care of my Hill women."

Clarice gave him a small smile. She kissed his cheek before heading toward the door, pausing for a brief moment to look back at him. Sam forced himself to smile at her. Once she left, his smile instantly faded, and he dropped his head back against the couch.

He was almost that kid. Sam knew he was almost the kid who threw away his life doing something stupid until Edwin intervened and kept him from going after his stepfather when he attacked his mother. Edwin kept him from ruining his life on several occasions. What did Edwin get as a reward? Three bullets to the chest.

It was unfair. Edwin was the good guy. He deserved better. Sam mulled over this fact as he finished the rest of his beer, tossed the can aside and then opened up a new one from the six-pack resting on the couch next to him. If that's what good people like Edwin got for doing good deeds, then why the hell should he try to be a decent human being?

Being a good little police officer who listened to the rules obviously didn't get anyone anywhere, at least as far as he was concerned. It didn't get Edwin anything except a one-way ticket into the Odette cemetery in a black box. Taking the law into his own hands was a far better option. Maybe if he had done something like that with Dillon's mom a few months ago, Edwin would still be alive today and so would the students and teachers that died in the shooting.

He'd go it alone, though. No getting close to anyone or allowing anyone in. Sam knew he'd have to distance himself from the few people that he truly loved, his foster mother, Gloria, and his two foster sisters, Clarice and Nina. Anyone who got close to him could be in danger. He'd already lost his mother. He'd already lost Edwin. He wasn't going to lose anyone else.

Maybe by doing so, he could prevent future tragedies like what happened at Odette High School from happening again … or it could turn him into the very monster he was trying to destroy …

Sam frowned as he pushed that last thought back into the dark recesses of his mind. He'd already been through the fire, so he might as well continue his venture down into the Dark Side.

It was more fun over there, anyway.

RISEN FROM THE ASHES

With a groan, Sam reached one hand out from beneath the covers of his bed to smack the snooze button on his alarm yet again. Still face down in his pillow, he opened one pewter gray eye to peek at the time on the clock on the nightstand next to his bed. Shit. He was going to be late.

Eventually convincing himself to get up, Sam threw back the covers and sat up on the edge of his bed. He rubbed a hand over his weary face and then ran it through his disheveled tawny hair. It was probably only a matter of time until the police captain called asking where the hell he was, so Sam figured he should probably get moving. He quickly showered, shaved and dressed, the latter of which was quite a feat considering his bedroom looked as though it had recently hosted a frat party and its unkempt state made it difficult to distinguish the clean clothes from those in need of washing.

Slipping on the freshest looking and smelling turquoise dress shirt and navy slacks, Sam stopped in his kitchen to grab a bite to eat before leaving his apartment. His meal of choice over the past month, though, wasn't food, per se, but a mixture of booze and painkillers. The breakfast of champions, Sam mused as he popped a handful of pills into his mouth. Bracing himself against the sink, he closed his eyes and waited for the wave of nausea and the pounding headache to subside. Once the room stopped spinning, Sam grabbed a couple of breath mints and stuffed them in his mouth before making his way out the door. Smelling of alcohol wasn't going to help his chances of returning to full duty.

Within a few minutes, Sam was pulling into the Odette Police Department parking lot. Entering the brick building, he was not surprised the find Captain Buchanan in the bullpen waiting for him.

"There you are, Sam," the Captain said, visibly relieved at the detective's arrival. "Nice of you to show up."

"Yeah, I thought so too," Sam said, plopping down in his chair at his desk.

He glanced up at Captain Buchanan, who had his arms folded across his chest.

"What? My alarm didn't go off."

"That's the third time this week, and it's only Wednesday; either you need to get a new alarm, Sam, or we have a problem."

"There's no problem. Actually, scratch that; there is a problem. This 'light duty' bullshit," Sam said. "I'm going to tear my freakin' hair out if I have to sit here one more day and do paperwork while everyone else gets to do their job. I need to get back out in the field, Cap."

The Captain did not respond. Instead, he motioned for Sam to follow him, which, with a groan-like sigh, the detective did. They ended up in the Captain's office.

"Have a seat, Sam," Captain Buchanan said, closing the office door.

Sam took a seat in one of the chairs opposite the Captain's desk. Sliding down in the chair, he had a flashback to a time in high school when he was sent to the principal's office after his fight with bully Scott Farrow during his sophomore year. Being called into the Captain's office felt just like that.

"I'm going to be honest with you, Sam," the Captain said. "Based on the recommendation of the department psychologist, we moved you to light duty. In her notes, she said that it would be helpful for you to keep busy because idleness wouldn't be good for someone like you. In your Fitness for Duty evaluation, your return to full duty was conditional upon your completion of treatment and all-around recovery. As of right now, Sam, you haven't done either. I've seen the psychologist come looking for you time and again since your initial required session together, which leads me to believe you haven't been participating."

"Ding-ding-ding, we have a winner," Sam said, his fist resting against his cheek.

The Captain ignored his comment.

"Sam, you know that there's no shame or guilt in getting help after a traumatic incident, right?"

"Cap, is there a point to this conversation?"

"Yes, there is. Your behavior, quite frankly, sucks. We're all worried about you, Sam. I don't want to have to keep you on light duty when I know there's so much good you could be doing for the people of Odette, let alone be forced to deem you 'unfit for duty' on your next evaluation-"

Unfit for duty? No way in hell was that going to happen.

"You can't do that to me, Cap!" Sam said. "You have to put me back on duty. You have to! Seriously; let me prove I'm ready, Cap. C'mon!"

The Captain let out a breath.

"If you were anyone else, Sam, we probably wouldn't be having this conversation," he said. "All right; here's what we'll do. Cooke is on vacation for a few days, so his rookie partner will need someone to monitor him. The next case that comes in here will go to the two of you. Depending on how that goes, we'll discuss your fitness to return to full duty. Deal?"

"Deal," Sam said.

He wasn't going to turn down this opportunity. It was his chance to get back on full duty instead of slaving away at his desk over a pile of enough paperwork to have killed an entire forest.

The Captain reached for his desk phone. A few minutes after the Captain finished his phone call, there was a knock on the office door.

"Come in," Captain Buchanan said.

A young officer opened the door and stepped inside the office.

"You wanted to see me, Sir?" he asked the Captain.

"Yes. Since Cooke is on vacation for a few days, I'd like to have another officer supervise you, so it does not interfere with your probationary period, Officer Marsden," the Captain said. "For the next few days, you'll be working with Detective Samuel Marlowe."

The polished young officer, whom Sam figured was probably fresh out of the academy, stuck his hand out to Sam.

"Officer Peter Marsden," he said. "I'm looking forward to working with you, Detective Marlowe."

"Nice to meet you," Sam said.

While the Captain rambled on about something Sam didn't give a shit about, he took the opportunity to look over his temporary protégé. Peter was a few inches taller than him, probably putting him around six-foot-two. His brown, almost black, hair was neatly slicked back and parted, reminding Sam of a businessman from the 1960's or a character straight out of Mad Men. Peter's ocean blue eyes were similar to the color of the waters up at Lake Odette, someplace he hadn't been since that nearly-tragic party after his senior prom seven years ago. The boardwalk, while patrolling the carnival during his first day on the job, was the closest he'd gone to the campgrounds, and quite frankly, that was as far as he cared to go.

"All right, Marsden, Marlowe," the Captain finished his speech. "You're dismissed."

Sam gave the Captain a lackluster salute before heading out of the office, Peter right behind him. He took a seat at his desk in the bullpen. Peter went to sit at the empty desk to the right of his.

"That desk is actually occupied," Sam said.

Well, not anymore, he considered. *Edwin can't use it ever again.* Sam dug his nails into his palm and did his best to shove that thought from his mind.

"Sorry, Detective," Peter said.

Sam waved him off.

"It's fine," he said. "All right, Marsden, let's get to work. We need a case."

"Right," Peter said. "On my way into the Captain's office, I saw a woman come in. Robinson put her in an interrogation room. The woman said she needed to report a crime, but Robinson was on her way out to respond to a call for a new development in a case she's working on. If no one's taken that case yet, it might be something to look in to."

Sam shrugged.

"Beggars can't be choosers, eh?" he said. "Let's go see what's up with this young lady."

After confirming that no one had taken over the case yet, Sam and Peter headed over to Interrogation Room 1. Sam peeked through the one-way glass to observe the woman waiting for them. She was pretty, but not in a remarkable way that would cause heads to turn if she was walking down the street. Straight sandy blond hair and a naturally skinny, almost bony physique, the woman's leg bounced, and she picked at her fingernails. The sound of Sam opening the door caused her to jump.

"I'm Detective Samuel Marlowe, and this is Officer Peter Marsden," he said. "And who might you be?"

"Lydia Frederickson," the woman said.

"And what can I do for you, Lydia?"

"I need to report ... a murder," Lydia said, her voice trembling.

Sam was surprised by this but kept his expression calm.

"You've come to the right place," he said. "Tell us whatever you can."

"It happened fifteen years ago, in mid-July. I was attending a summer camp up at Lake Odette; I'd gone there for quite a few years with my best friend, Arlena Graves."

Sam, who had been jotting down Lydia's account, looked up at the woman across from him after the words "best friend" left her carnation pink lips. The term did not seem to be one of endearment but said, rather, in spite.

"Former best friend, I take it?" Sam asked.

"She's the murderer!" Lydia slammed a hand on the table.

Sam motioned for her to continue.

"Arlena and I were the popular girls at camp; everyone always wanted to hang out with us. The last year I went to camp, there was this new girl from upstate. She was a total geek, but kind of sweet. Kind of like an annoying little sister that idolizes you. Her name was Misty Taylor ... I'll never forget that name ..." Lydia paused. "She desperately wanted to hang out with us. Arlena thought it would be fun to play pranks on Misty, you know, if she wanted to be cool like us, she would have to 'work' for it."

"Charming," Sam lowered his head so Lydia couldn't see him roll his eyes. "And what were these 'pranks?'"

"It was harmless fun! At least, that's what Arlena told me," Lydia said. "We made some of the other girls do it too, and nothing ever happened to them, so we thought it would be fine for Misty to do it. We'd make them do stuff like eat dirt or streak through the cabins."

Good to know the mean girls from school didn't take a vacation once the semester ended; they found new victims, Sam thought.

"Mean as hell and emotionally scarring, but, yes, typically harmless," Sam said. "What went wrong with Misty?"

"Misty wasn't deterred by Arlena's usual tactics, so she decided to come up with something new. Arlena convinced Misty she could hang out with us if she completed one last test. Arlena stole some supplies from the supply cabin, and we also lifted a couple bottles of beer from the general store when the counselors took us there to pick out some snacks for our bonfire. That night, we invited Misty into our cabin after the counselors did a roll call and all that stuff. We made Misty drink a bunch of beers as fast as she could and then try to cut her hair. After that, we made her strip down to her t-shirt and shorts and do laps around the campsite. If she did all that without throwing up, we figured that would be pretty impressive and a good enough reason to let her spend time with us."

"Let me get this straight; you left a young girl in only a flimsy t-shirt and shorts outside in the cold after forcing her to drink a shitload of booze and after making her essentially run a freakin' marathon for your amusement?" Sam summarized in a tone like a scolding parent.

Lydia shrunk down in her chair. Her eyes shimmered as she teared up.

"It was an accident, I swear!" Lydia said. "It was all Arlena's idea. I didn't want to make Misty do all of that stuff. If we didn't, she might still be alive today ..."

"What makes you think she's dead?"

"Arlena and I went back into the cabins and left Misty running around the campsite. The next morning, during roll call, Misty wasn't there. The counselors called us all into the mess hall and gave some stupid lecture about pranks and that kind of stuff. They talked about how all of that stuff could, depending on the circumstances, kill someone. We figured Misty must have died for the counselors to make that big of a scene."

"What you two did to Misty was terrible," Sam said. "But what makes you believe that she died?"

"The camp was closed down after Misty's family sued–I think they settled but I don't know for sure since I was only about fifteen at the time," Lydia said. "I know there were plenty of other 'hazings,' if you want to call it that, at other schools and camps and they weren't closed down. It had to be something serious for the entire camp to close down like that."

Lydia grabbed the small silver shoulder bag she had slung over the back of her chair and proceeded to pull out a few pieces of paper. She laid them down on the table in front of her for Sam and Peter to see.

"There's also these," Lydia said.

"Remember Misty," "Murderer," and other sentiments were typed in bold black block letters along with pictures of a teenage girl whom Sam surmised was Misty Taylor.

"I've been getting these notes for weeks now," Lydia said. "Arlena and I made a pact to never tell anyone what happened to Misty and I kept my end of the bargain. I think Arlena is doing this for revenge because, last month, she 'claimed' she had been dating my boyfriend for the past year, which I didn't believe for an instant! I think she's trying to get me out of the picture so she can get with Colin!"

"When man candy is concerned, friendship and loyalty go out the window," Sam said.

A knock on the interrogation room door interrupted Sam's conversation with Lydia. He glanced over his shoulder at Peter, who stepped outside into the hall after answering the door.

"Detective Marlowe," he whispered to Sam when he returned. "Apparently, Arlena Graves has arrived at the station and wants to meet with the top detective."

"Hmm ... She does, does she?" Sam reflected on Peter's news. "What are the odds?"

He popped up from the table, handing Peter his notepad and pen.

"Okay, Marsden, you stay here and finish up with Lydia. I'm going to go check in with our new guest."

"Sure thing, Detective," Peter said, as he exchanged places with Sam.

Sam, meanwhile, made his way across the hall to Interrogation Room 2, where Arlena Graves was waiting. As he did before with Lydia, he observed the woman in question through the one-way glass. If Lydia was pretty, then Arlena was gorgeous. Sleek auburn hair and mesmerizing hickory eyes, Arlena was shorter than her former best friend but had the upper hand in physique. She probably spent hours at the gym and watched what she ate, based on the muscle definition that Sam could see as she leaned against the window in her scarlet red t-shirt and navy blue skinny jeans. Her cherry red lips pursed together, she checked the time on her elegant gold watch on her wrist time and again before folding her arms right beneath her chest and letting out a huff.

"Ms. Graves," Sam began as he headed into the room. "I was informed by Officer Marsden that you wanted to speak to me; what can I do for you?"

"I need to report a murder," Arlena said, her tone matter-of-fact.

"Let me take a guess," Sam took a seat at the table in the center of the room. "This murder is a cold case that happened about, oh, let's say, fifteen years ago."

Arlena blinked.

"Yes, actually," she said. "How did you know?"

"Hey, I'm not the lead detective in this department for nothing."

"A well-deserved title, I see."

"Let's hear your story," Sam said, motioning for Arlena to commence her tale.

Arlena strolled over from the window and took a seat at the table across from Sam and began her story. He was admittedly curious as to what the good-looking gal had to say but, at the same time, was trying to hold back his feelings of disgust for her. If half of what Lydia said about Arlena was true, then she was an absolute bitch.

Sam discovered that Arlena's version of events was quite similar to Lydia's, save for one crucial detail: she claimed torturing Misty was Lydia's idea.

"She was always jealous of me, and so she took it out on poor Misty," Arlena sniffed, though Sam saw no tears smudging her flawlessly applied makeup. "Lydia always envied me and my possessions, including my boyfriend. She saw Colin desirable not because he is a successful agent at CS Financial. No, she wanted him because he was with me. Lydia resorted to framing me for what she did to Misty to try and get with my man!"

Arlena produced several notes and photos similar to what Lydia showed him. Sam looked them over before excusing himself from the room. He knocked on the window of Interrogation Room 1 to get Peter's attention. The rookie cop stepped out of the room moments later.

"Arlena is pointing the finger right back at Lydia," Sam said. "In fact, she showed me those same 'Remember Misty,' and 'Murderer' notes that Lydia did."

"Do you think they sent them to each other?" Peter asked.

"It's possible. It's also possible that one of the girls, whoever was guilty, sent a duplicate copy to herself to appear innocent and throw suspicion off of her," Sam paused. "Or there could be a whole separate third party that's punishing both Lydia and Arlena for what happened."

"Both women have accused the other of murder; should we book them?"

Sam shook his head.

"Not yet. We'll hold both, but there's not enough evidence to make the charges stick since right now all we have is a case of 'she said–she said.' We need to investigate the claims before Lydia or Arlena, or both, would be brought up on charges," Sam said. "Did you get any more details on the two-timing boyfriend?"

"His name is Colin Dennings," Peter read from his notes. "He is a financial advisor at CS Financial in downtown Odette. Apparently, Mr. Dennings is successful, according to Ms. Frederickson. Anyway, Ms. Frederickson stated that she began a relationship with Mr. Dennings approximately one year ago after he approached her at a party they both attended."

"Hmm," Sam frowned. "That's quite the enigma since that's essentially the same story Arlena told me about meeting her Prince Charming."

"It sounds like he was playing both of them," Peter said. "But it can't be a coincidence that he's cheating on these two women and they both show up to the police department to report the same crime."

"My thoughts exactly," Sam said. "All right, Marsden, let's stick these two ladies into holding cells—on opposite sides of the room, of course—and then pay a visit to Mr. Dennings to find out what his story is."

★★★

Colin Dennings lived in one of the newly built and modern condos near downtown Odette.

"Hello, officers," a handsome, fair-haired man in a gray t-shirt and blue sweatpants answered the door. "Can I help you?"

Sam and Peter presented their badges.

"I am Detective Marlowe and this," he thumbed behind him at Peter. "is Officer Marsden. Are you Colin Dennings?"

"I am. What can I do for you, officers?"

"We have some questions for you about two acquaintances of yours," Sam said. "A 'Lydia Frederickson' and 'Arlena Graves.'"

An amused smile crossed Colin's lips.

"Yes, I am personally acquainted with both ladies," he said. "But I take it you're not here to simply ask about my dating history."

"And you would be correct."

Colin stepped aside to allow Sam and Peter to enter.

"Please, come in. Pardon the mess; I'm working from home today, so I have papers and reports all over the place."

The interior of the condo was as tasteful as the exterior, having a modern art deco theme. As Colin said, there were various papers and folders laid out on the coffee table in front of the ivy green couch.

"Who's at the door, Col?" a woman called from another room.

Sam raised an eyebrow at Colin, who looked back at him with a pleasant expression.

"We have two of Odette's finest officers visiting us," Colin called back in response.

A woman a few years older than Sam, probably no more than thirty, with onyx black hair tied off to the side in a braid strolled into the living room. She, like Colin, was dressed casually, wearing black yoga pants and a simple bubblegum pink tank top.

"Officers, this is Zoey Phoenix," Colin said.

"And who are you, Miss Phoenix?" Sam asked.

"A friend," Zoey said.

Sam looked at her expectantly, waiting to see if she'd expand on the details of her relationship with Colin. Zoey folded her arms across her chest, giving the detective a good look at the tattoo on the underside of her forearm, written in a foreign script.

"What's your tattoo say?" Sam asked.

"It's a quote from the sacred Sikhism scripture," Zoey said. "'As she has planted, so does she harvest; such is the field of karma.'"

"Karma?" Sam repeated. "Not sure how much credence I put into that stuff. Karma has been having more fun kicking me in the ass than helping me out for my good deeds."

"Maybe the universe is waiting for the right moment," Zoey said. "Or, perhaps, you need to go out there and take karma into your own hands."

"Okay, I came here to ask some questions about a possible crime, not to receive a lecture on philosophy, so do you mind if we get back on topic?"

"Of course, make yourselves comfortable," Colin said.

He took a seat on the couch while Sam, and Peter sat down across from him in the two armchairs.

"I made a fresh pot of coffee," Zoey told Sam and Peter. "Would either of you care for a cup?"

Peter passed while Sam accepted the offer. His stomach clenched in pain as a wave of nausea washed over him. His hand holding the coffee had a slight tremor; Sam put the mug down on the end table between the two armchairs.

"Marsden, why don't you start off the questioning while I run to the little boy's room," he said, before turning his attention to Colin. "Where's your restroom?"

"Down that hallway. First door on your right," Colin pointed toward the west hallway.

"Thanks."

Sam hurried out of the living room and into the bathroom. The door barely closed behind him, he frantically shoved a hand into his pants pocket, and quivering, pulled out some pills and popped them in his mouth. His back against the door, Sam slid down until he was sitting on the cold tile floor. *What the fuck am I doing?* He wondered as he rode out the nausea and stomach pains. *At least Marsden's keeping the investigation going while I'm sitting here on my ass.*

After a few minutes, Sam felt steady enough to leave the bathroom and return to the living room. Peter was asking Colin about his relationship with Lydia and Arlena.

"It's true," he said. "I dated both of them."

"At the same time," Peter said.

"How did you pull that one off?" Sam asked as he returned to his seat. "Also, why? Those two seem like a handful on their own; if they ever found out about each other, which they did, you were going to be looking death straight in the face."

He eyed Zoey to see her reaction to what Colin had to say. Her face remained placid, and she listened to the conversation from her spot on the couch opposite Colin.

"Yeah, they can both be exhausting at times," Colin said. "But, well, I had to admit that my curiosity got the best of me and I sought them both out. You see, there was this girl that I grew up with back in Golden who knew both Lydia and Arlena. I was attending a party last year and found out that Lydia was there, so I went to find her. I did the same with Arlena a few days later at another event. Much to my surprise, both women were beautiful and successful, and well, I kind of got carried away and had some fun …"

"This girl you grew up with upstate in Golden," Sam said. "Did she happen to attend a summer camp with Arlena and Lydia?"

"Yes, actually," Colin said.

"Was her name Misty Taylor?"

Colin exchanged a surprised glance with Zoey.

"That seems like a yes," Peter said to Sam.

"Yes, Misty was my neighbor growing up. She was like my little sister," Colin said.

"You heard about Arlena and Lydia from Misty," Sam said. "But did you ever hear about Misty from Arlena and Lydia?"

"Not directly," Colin shook his head. "I mean, I did ask about their pasts, but who doesn't do that when getting into a new relationship? I tried to ask about that summer camp, but Arlena and Lydia would usually clam up or change the topic before I could get too much information out of them."

"How about any notes or messages concerning Misty?" Peter asked. "Did either ever mention or show you anything like that?"

"Sort of. Lydia mentioned something about receiving a note that scared her," Colin said. "So, I told her to contact the police if it kept up."

"And Arlena?"

"Not scared so much as pissed off. She was angry someone was digging up her past but didn't say why, though, in hindsight, I assume it's probably similar to what Lydia received. Not much rattled Arlena, so I decided to let it go."

"Did Lydia or Arlena give you any indication of who they believed was responsible for the messages?"

"They assumed the other was behind it. The notes were received shortly after they found out the three of us were in a kind of love triangle. I guess that both believed the other was trying to sabotage the relationship."

He glanced between Sam and Peter.

"Has something happened to them?"

"It's an ongoing investigation," Sam said with a slight shrug. "Can't really talk about it."

"I understand," Colin said.

Sam looked over at Peter before getting up from his chair, the rookie officer doing the same.

"Well, thank you for your time, Colin. We'll reach out to you if we need any more information," he said.

"Officers?" Zoey spoke up. "Please do whatever you can to get justice for Misty; don't let Arlena and Lydia continue to get away with the horrid things they did."

Sam stopped at the door. He turned to face Zoey.

"How do you know Misty?" he asked.

"She was like family," Zoey said, picking at some of the black polish on her nails. "Arlena and Lydia need to get their just desserts."

"Just desserts," Sam repeated.

Edwin, he thought. *Edwin used to say that* ... Sam shook his head.

"We'll do whatever we can, Miss Phoenix," he said. "Because, as you said, some people need to get their just desserts."

★★★

Leaving Colin's condo, Sam and Peter drove out to the district courthouse to do some research. He left Peter in the court records room while he stepped outside to grab something to eat for the two of them from the hot dog vendor down the street at the corner of Main and Transit. Sam returned a few minutes later.

"Mind if I sit?" he asked, pulling up a chair and sitting down. "Physical therapy has helped me get the strength back in my leg, but I'm not Superman yet."

Peter motioned toward the chair.

"Please do," he said. "May I ask if the injury you're referring to is the gunshot wound you sustained from the Odette High School shootings that happened a few months ago?"

"You can ask, and you'd be right, but I don't want to talk about it."

"Of course, Detective. I don't want to pry. The only reason I was asking is because I want to make sure I have the chance to say something before this case gets too hectic and I miss the opportunity to do so."

Sam cracked open the can of soda pop he bought with the hot dogs.

"What's that, Marsden?"

Peter, who was standing at one of the filing cabinets, turned to face Sam.

"My sister is a teacher at Odette High School. You saved her life the day of the school shooting. I'm sure you've heard it a million times since that day but thank you. You, Detective, are a hero. So, thank you. It's an honor to work with and learn from you."

Sam's body went rigid at the mention of the school shooting; the wound was still fresh, even though the incident happened months ago. The hand gripping the can of soda pop tightened around the blue can, causing some of the fizzy brown liquid to bubble up and out, collecting in a puddle on the desk where he sat.

"Don't ... don't mention it," Sam managed to say through clenched teeth, grabbing some of the napkins the vendor gave him to clean up the spilled soda pop. "I'm not kidding. Don't mention that day again. Ever."

"Of course," Peter replied. "I didn't mean to—"

"It's fine," Sam waved him off. "I'm glad your sister made it out alive and well, truly I am. Now, let's get back to business, okay?"

The records room was quiet while Peter searched through the files. When he located the file Sam wanted, he joined the detective at the desk.

"I found the Taylor case," Peter placed the open file on the desk.

"Great," Sam said. "Give me the details."

"Charges were filed against the summer camp Misty, Arlena and Lydia attended after the incident occurred. The family alleged negligence, child endangerment and other charges against the camp for failing to stop some of the campers from hazing Misty."

"Were Arlena and Lydia named as the guilty parties?"

"No," Peter continued reading, searching for the information. "Actually, it says here that, because Misty refused to say who the people responsible were, her parents were willing to settle out of court instead of going to trial since the lack of evidence would have hurt their case."

"Wait a second," Sam said. "'Because Misty refused to say …' You know what that means? Misty *didn't* die from the incident."

"Right, but that doesn't explain what happened to Misty afterward. She may still have died."

"True. Let's contact the authorities in Golden and see if we can find any trace of Misty."

★★★

Arriving at the police department the following morning, Sam found Peter waiting at his desk.

"You're here early, Marsden," he said.

Peter briefly glanced at his watch.

"It's ten o'clock; is that early?" he asked.

"It is for me," Sam said. "Anyhoo, what's up? Did we get any news from Golden?"

"Yes, Sir."

"Why don't you sound happy about that?"

"Well, it's not the most helpful information," Peter said.

He handed Sam his notes.

"There is no death certificate on file for anyone named 'Misty Taylor' in Golden. I also checked the death records in Odette, to be safe, and there's no one by that name here either."

"That means she's alive," Sam said. "Why isn't that a good thing?"

"Actually, no death certificate doesn't mean Misty's alive," Peter said.

"How so?"

"Because there are no records for Misty after that summer camp. No school records, medical records, driver's license records, nothing."

Sam read over Peter's thorough notes.

"Huh, that's a real head-scratcher, isn't it?" he drummed his fingers against the file folder. "It's like Misty completely disappeared."

"What's the next step, Detective?" Peter asked.

"It is possible to get a conviction for Arlena and Lydia without Misty's body to prove murder," Sam said. "But I still don't think there's enough circumstantial evidence to prove murder beyond a reasonable doubt. If we were charging them as horrible human beings, yeah, I'd say we're good but, otherwise, not so much. We still need more evidence."

Sam thought for a moment.

"Say, Marsden, what did you think of Colin's lady friend, Zoey?"

"It seems like she knows more than she's saying," Peter said.

"That it does," Sam handed Peter's notes back to him. "Call CS Financial and see if Colin is in the office today; if he is, I'd like to pay Zoey another visit and see what other information she can give us without Colin around, just in case she's hiding something from him."

"Yes, Sir."

Sam excused himself while Peter reached out to CS Financial. In the bathroom, Sam locked himself in a stall and popped some of the painkillers he had in his pocket into his mouth. Stepping out from the stall, he headed over to the sink and splashed cool water on his face. Dabbing his face dry with a paper towel, Sam heard the door to the bathroom open, followed by some footsteps.

"Good morning, Marlowe," Captain Buchanan said.

"Hey, Cap," Sam said, tossing the paper towel into the trashcan.

"How are things going with the case?"

"About as good as they can be. The case is a real doozy, but Marsden and I have a lead we're about to follow up on."

"Marsden is doing well?"

"Yep. He's a good kid. Cooke is lucky to have him."

"And how are *you* doing?" the Captain asked.

"Much better than sitting on my ass filling out paperwork," Sam said.

"Good, good," the Captain said. "Well, I won't keep you from your work."

"I'll take your word for it," Sam said before heading out of the bathroom.

★★★

"Oh, hello, officers," Zoey said when she opened the door to the condo. "Colin's at the office today."

"That's fine," Sam said. "Because we actually came to see you."

"Me? I'm not sure what I can do to help you with whatever it is you're investigating."

"We have a couple of questions for you regarding Misty."

Zoey motioned for Peter and Sam to head inside the condo.

"Can I get you guys anything?" she asked as she closed the door behind her.

"Nah, I'm good," Sam said. "Marsden?"

"No, thank you," Peter said.

"Okay, what about Misty?" Zoey perched herself on the couch on the edge of the cushion.

She leaned forward with her elbows on her knees, and her hands clasped together. Zoey rested her chin on her fists and dedicated all of her focus to Sam, who shifted slightly in his seat. *What is with this girl?* He wondered. *I feel like she's challenging me ...*

"You said you knew Misty like Colin did," Sam said. "How did you know her?"

"I grew up with her," Zoey said.

"Did you attend the same summer camp as Misty, Arlena, and Lydia, by any chance?" Peter asked.

Zoey looked down at her hands.

"I did," she said.

Sam motioned for Zoey to elaborate. She sighed.

"I saw what Arlena and Lydia did to Misty and those other girls. None of them deserved what those two bitches did to them, especially not Misty. She was only trying to make friends, to fit in, and Arlena and Lydia took advantage of that."

"Did you or any of the other girls ever say anything to the camp counselors?"

Zoey shook her head.

"No, we never did. But even if we had, I doubt the counselors would have believed us. Arlena and Lydia were brown-nosers to the extreme; they had the counselors wrapped around their little fingers. When they wanted to be charming and sweet, they could be. That's the side of them that the counselors saw," she paused. "Plus, I think that either Arlena or Lydia, or both, were wealthy, and well, money talks."

"What happened to Misty after the incident at camp?" Sam asked.

"Misty's parents wanted to sue the camp for what happened, but, from what I know, Misty refused to identify who it was that hazed her like that, so they settled out of court. Plus, all of our parents had to sign some release form that waved all liability and whatnot on the camp's part, so I'm not sure how far the lawsuit could have gone. Regardless, the camp closed down after that."

"Why didn't anyone else come forward to point the finger at Arlena and Lydia?"

"I guess we were all too scared," Zoey said. "I mean, if they did all that to Misty, what would they do to us if they found out we squealed?"

"Zoey, this question is crucial, so we need you to answer to the best of your knowledge," Sam started to say. "Is Misty alive or dead?"

Zoey scooted back in her seat and folded her arms across her chest.

"Misty is dead," she said.

"Dead?" Sam repeated. "Can you give us more details about her death?"

"She's gone, plain and simple."

"But there is no evidence to prove that Misty is, in fact, dead," Peter said. "How do you know that she is?"

"I told you," Zoey said. "I lived in Golden. I knew Misty. Like Colin did, I saw what happened after Arlena and Lydia tortured Misty. That's how I know."

She stood up from the couch.

"I'm sorry, officers, but I have somewhere to be. Would you mind showing yourselves out?"

"Sure thing," Sam said with a frown.

Peter followed him out of the condo.

"She clammed up rather quickly, didn't she?" Sam said to Peter as they walked back to their squad car.

"She did," Peter said. "That makes me question whether or not she truly knows if Misty is, in fact, dead."

"Yeah, the reasonable doubt keeps increasing, doesn't it?"

Getting into the driver's seat, Sam tapped the steering wheel thoughtfully. Peter quietly watched him from the passenger's side.

"The camp is closed down, but I wonder if it's possible to get information from its records," Sam said.

"We could try contacting the former counselors," Peter said. "It's been fifteen years, so I'm not sure how much they'll be able to remember. Were you looking for something specific?"

"Let's call it a hunch."

★★★

Returning to the police department, Sam tasked Peter with looking into and then contacting the former counselors at the camp that Misty, Arlena and Lydia attended. He headed down to the holding cells.

"Detective Marlowe!" Lydia was a mess when Sam poked his head into her cell. "When can I go home? I want to go home!"

"Hopefully this will be wrapped up soon," Sam said, ignoring her pitiful pleas. "Actually, I have a question for you."

Lydia sniffled. She sat dejected on the holding cell bench. "What?"

"Does the name 'Zoey Phoenix' mean anything to you?"

"No, why?"

"It doesn't ring a bell?" Sam asked, Lydia, shaking her head. "Nothing from childhood, maybe? Summer camp?"

"No."

"Okay, thanks."

Sam departed from Lydia's cell and headed down the hallway to Arlena's. The other woman was in a far better condition than Lydia, though she looked pretty pissed off about her current situation.

"Zoey Phoenix?" Arlena repeated the name. "No. I've never heard that name in my life."

"Interesting," Sam said. "Thanks, Ms. Graves."

Peter met him in the hallway leading back to the bullpen.

"There you are, Detective," he said. "I finished speaking with Mr. Hague, one of the camp counselors."

"Oh, good. What did he have to say?" Sam asked.

"He remembered the incident with Misty," Peter said. "In fact, he was able to identify the two girls he thought responsible for the incident: Arlena and Lydia. Of course, he had no evidence to prove that they were responsible at the time, but he was sure that they were the ones who did it."

"And how about Misty? Did he have any information about her post-hazing?"

"Yes. Following the incident, Mr. Hague and the other counselors went to the hospital to visit Misty. He swears that she was alive."

"Colin, Zoey, Arlena and Lydia all believe that Misty is dead, but one of the camp counselors, not to mention all of the evidence and records, claim that Misty is alive," Sam scratched the back of his neck. "I guess the question is: is Misty actually alive or dead?"

"How do we find out?" Peter asked.

"I have an idea," Sam said. "But we're going to need some help to do it."

★★★

Sam and Peter each visited the holding cells to bring Lydia and Arlena, separately, of course, on what Sam liked to call 'a little field trip.' Taking separate patrol cars, they drove the women up to the campgrounds at Lake Odette.

"Why do we have to come all the way up here?" Lydia shuddered as she followed Peter up the trail to the campgrounds. "I hate coming here."

"Unfortunately, it's necessary for you to be here," Peter said. "But this hopefully shouldn't take too long."

The gravel on the path changed to well-trodden dirt as the cabins came into sight. Peter led Lydia toward the cabins.

"What is *she* doing here?" Arlena's eyes narrowed when Lydia and Peter approached.

Standing on the front porch of the cabin, illuminated by only a lantern, Sam gave the woman next to him a shrug.

"Because," he said. "You're both involved in this mess, so you both have to be here."

"Officer Marsden, Lydia," Arlena's tone was ice cold on her former best friend's name.

"Detective Marlowe, Arlena," Lydia replied with equal animosity.

"Now that we've gotten our heartwarming reunion out of the way," Sam took a step forward to stand in the middle of the group. "Let's get down to the important stuff, like what happened to Misty."

"Yes," Arlena folded her arms across her chest. "What evidence do you have of Lydia's guilt?"

"My guilt?" Lydia placed a hand over her heart. "Are you kidding me? You're the guilty one!"

"Actually, you're both guilty."

Both Arlena and Lydia whirled around in time to see Colin emerging from the dark woods surrounding the cabin. Zoey followed behind him.

"Colin, honey, what are you doing here?" Arlena asked.

She started to step forward, but Sam put his arm out to stop her.

"Screw you, Arlena!" Lydia said with a huff. "Colin's mine!"

"I don't belong to either of you," Colin said with a dismissive wave.

"What?" Arlena and Lydia cried in unison.

"He was playing both you girls," Sam said. "And I bet you'll never guess why."

Arlena and Lydia looked from Colin to Sam and back again.

"I looked for both of you to get the truth," Colin said. "I needed to know who hurt Misty."

"You what?" Arlena fingered the bracelet on her wrist as she stared at Colin.

Must have been a gift from Colin, Sam figured. *It's probably going to end up in the trash once this is all over.*

The news rattled her; Arlena's jaw was agape, and her eyes were wide as she stared dumbfounded at Colin.

"You heard me," Colin said. "The only reason I wanted to start a relationship with either of you was to find out what you did to Misty fifteen years ago. You know, keep your friends close but your enemies closer? Do you honestly think it was a coincidence that I was 'dating' both of you at the same time and would be careless enough to have you find out about each other? I'm a financial advisor; strategy and planning are part of my job. No; the only reason I did it was to turn you two against each other so you'd reveal the truth. The truth of how you destroyed Misty was the one leverage you had on each other, and I thought it would come out when it came down to it."

"And it obviously worked, seeing you're both here, pointing the finger at each other," Zoey said.

"And who the hell are you?" Arlena asked.

"Let's say that I'm someone who was very close to Misty, who wants to see you two monsters finally have karma catch up to you and kick you both in the ass," Zoey said. "Those pictures you received, 'Remember Misty' and 'Murderer,' I sent them to you. I couldn't let either of you forget what you did on that night fifteen years ago."

Arlena's usually cool and aloof demeanor had slowly broken down, and she now looked worried and fearful. She turned to Sam, her eyes pleading with him to do something.

"Can't you arrest her or something?"

"Don't worry, Ms. Graves," Sam said. "Zoey will be getting in trouble for sending those notes, but that's not the most important thing right now."

Peter and Sam pulled their handcuffs off their belts, moving to handcuff Lydia and Arlena respectively.

"Arlena Graves and Lydia Frederickson, you are both under arrest for the attempted murder of Misty Taylor," Sam said.

"Attempted murder? What are you talking about?" Lydia cried. "I thought Misty was dead!"

"Shut up, you dumb bitch!" Arlena snapped. "You're making things worse!"

"Very true, Arlena. Anything you say *can* and *will* be used against you in a court of law," Sam said. "But the charge is 'attempted murder' and not 'murder' simply for one reason."

"And what's that?" Arlena asked.

"Misty isn't dead."

★★★

Sitting in the bullpen at his desk, Sam frowned. He'd run out of excuses over the past couple of days to put off finishing the paperwork from the Misty Taylor case, so he knew he'd have to start it eventually. Pushing aside some stray papers on his desk, Sam snagged a pen and let out a breath as he grabbed the case file.

"Hey, Marlowe!" an officer called to him. "You've got visitors!"

Sam immediately threw down his pen and headed over to the officer who had addressed him.

"Interrogation Room 1," the officer said.

"Got it," Sam said before making his way over to the room in question.

Taking a quick look through the one-way glass, he found Colin and Zoey waiting for him. Sam fetched Peter from the break room to join him in the interrogation room.

"Detective Marlowe, Officer Marsden," Colin said with a smile and a handshake when Sam and Peter entered the room.

"Nice to see you two," Sam said. "What can I do for you?"

"We came to say thank you again for helping to hold Arlena and Lydia accountable for their actions fifteen years ago," Zoey said. "Playing games or pranks is one thing, but the way they tortured Misty? That crossed the line."

"It's a relief to know they'll finally be prosecuted for their wrongdoings," Colin said, his fingers brushing against Zoey's.

"I think the DA is working on a plea bargain for a possible reduced sentence and to avoid a trial in exchange for a confession," Sam said. "But, since Arlena and Lydia pretty much already confessed to Officer Marsden and me, I don't think the DA will have a problem."

"That's all Misty wanted," Zoey said with a tearful smile. "To have Arlena and Lydia admit to what they did is more than enough. Thank you."

She stepped forward to embrace Sam. As she did, Sam whispered a response to her:

"You're welcome, Misty."

Zoey pulled away and regarded Sam with surprise, curiosity, and awe.

"You ... knew?" she asked.

"Not at first," Sam replied. "I started to put the pieces together when Marsden and I kept getting the run around when we were trying to figure out if Misty was alive or dead. It was quite the coincidence that Zoey Phoenix appeared shortly after Misty Taylor disappeared. What sealed the deal, Ms. Phoenix, however, was your name and that tattoo of yours; Phoenix, the bird of legend who rises from the ashes and the quote about karma. How could you not be Misty?"

"I thought it was fitting," Zoey said with a laugh as she brushed away a tear. "The only way to make Arlena and Lydia sorry for what they did was to pretend Misty died. After what happened, I was so stupid because I kept believing that, by keeping my mouth shut about what happened, I would be doing what Arlena and Lydia wanted and we could all be friends. What an idiot, right? Of course, when that didn't happen, I realized what bitches they were and how badly they treated me. I couldn't be Misty anymore. I couldn't be the doormat that everyone walked over. I had to become someone new; someone who wouldn't stand for that sort of thing."

"How about you?" Sam looked at Colin. "How did you get roped into this whole charade?"

"Zoey and I have been friends since childhood, back when she was Misty," Colin said. "It took some convincing and persuading, but I eventually got her to tell me what happened that night at camp. I was so horrified at how they could treat someone like Misty like that, so I promised her that I'd do whatever I could to help her fix what happened fifteen years ago."

"Including dating two criminals? Now *that* is dedication."

"Whatever it took," Colin said. "Zoey changed her hair color and style, wore color contacts to alter her eye color and also changed her legal name to complete the transition. If she could do all that, I could pretend to date Lydia and Arlena for a bit."

"Now that's all settled," Sam said. "I think it's about time you two finally got together, isn't it?"

Colin coughed, and Zoey blushed. Peter chuckled.

"I think we need to be going," Colin said.

"Sure thing," Sam replied.

He watched with a knowing grin as Colin and Zoey walked hand in hand out of the police department.

★★★

Captain Buchanan read over the case report from the Misty Taylor case. Sam seemed to work well with a straight shooter like Peter, he mused. They managed to solve a cold case together from fifteen years ago after only meeting each other only a few days prior. That was impressive. But perhaps what was more impressive, the Captain considered, was that he saw glimpses of the old Sam. Maybe returning to full duty was the best thing for him instead of sitting at his desk on limited duty.

Sam seemed to relish in teaching the new recruit what it took to be a top-notch detective. Edwin had taught and mentored him as a new recruit, and it paid off, as the man was one of the lead detectives of the department and he was not yet thirty years old. Perhaps what Sam needed was a partner. Being forced to always be on his best behavior to serve as a role model to a bright and fresh rookie out of the police academy might rub off on him too. Peter was already assigned to work with Cooke, and a transfer might tip Sam off on what he was trying to do by giving him a partner. The man was not stupid.

The Captain tapped his chin thoughtfully. Maybe, just maybe, a partner was what Sam needed. It was at least worth a shot.

SOMETHING FROM NOTHING

Detective Samuel Marlowe frowned as he looked at the man seated across from him, the Captain of the police department. He wasn't happy and made no attempt to hide his displeasure from the Captain.

"This is bullshit, Cap," Sam said. "And uncalled for."

The Captain, unfazed by his lead detective's usual forwardness, folded his hands together and placed them on his desk.

"Listen, Sam," he replied. "You're good at what you do. That's why we want you for this."

"Yeah, but I work alone. Solo. By myself. Me, myself and I."

"I know what alone means," Captain Buchanan said. "But you weren't alone during the Misty Taylor case. In fact, you worked quite well with Officer Marsden."

"Don't get me wrong, Cap," Sam said. "Marsden's a good guy, but I only agreed to work with him so I could get back on active duty. I don't need or want a partner."

A gentle knock on the closed office door interrupted the conversation. The Captain rose from his seat behind the desk and headed toward the door.

"Humor me, Sam," he said, hand on the doorknob. "I'm sure you will get along extremely well with her—"

"Her?" Sam asked, turning around in his seat to look at the Captain.

"Perfect timing, Detective Bennett. Please, come in. I'd like to introduce you to your new partner."

The Captain smiled and stepped aside to allow the visitor to enter the office. The young woman, this "Detective Bennett," marched into the Captain's office.

"Sam," the Captain smacked Sam on the shoulder to make him stand up. "This is your new partner, Dahlia Bennett."

Sam stood up, adjusting his lilac dress shirt and coffee-colored hair.

"Detective Bennett," the Captain turned his attention to Dahlia. "This is Detective-"

"Samuel Marlowe," Dahlia finished before the Captain could get the words out. "It is an honor to work with such a distinguished detective."

She offered her hand to Sam.

"Yes, it is," Sam replied, shaking Dahlia's hand.

He was both surprised and impressed by her firm handshake, but did his best to keep his expression calm and collected. The Captain rattled on, speaking to Dahlia about something that Sam immediately tuned out. Instead, he took the opportunity to observe his new "partner." She was petite in stature, but stood tall and confidently. Her naturally curly obsidian colored hair had been pulled back neatly into a bun that rested at the nape of her neck. Dahlia kept direct eye contact with the Captain throughout his monologue, suggesting to Sam that she either had some military or law enforcement in her background. Or she was an arrogant ass kisser. Either way, according to the Captain, he was stuck with her.

"Now that we're all acquainted," the Captain said, snagging two file folders off his desk. "We have a case."

He handed one folder to Sam and the other to Dahlia.

"The director of CS Financial, the wealthiest institution in Odette, received an anonymous note this morning threatening the welfare of her daughter unless a large sum of money was paid."

"Is it legit?" Sam asked, an eyebrow raised.

"That's where you two come in," the Captain said. "I want the two of you to speak to Ms. Shea, determine if this threat is credible and pursue it accordingly."

"Yes, Sir," Dahlia replied.

Rolling his eyes at his partner's exuberance, Sam closed the file folder before looking up.

"Yeah, on it," he said.

Sam turned and abruptly stomped away from the Captain's office. Dahlia caught up with him moments later, much to his chagrin. No words were exchanged between the two as they made their way through the police department and out to the parking lot to Sam's police cruiser. Getting into the driver's seat, he purposefully left the passenger's side door locked. Undeterred, Dahlia knocked on the window. She stared him down, making a small motion with her hand toward the locked door. Grumbling, Sam flicked the lock open, and Dahlia slipped into the passenger's seat.

CS Financial was in the heart of Odette. The glass building in the business complex was palatial and aesthetically designed. Sam pulled the cruiser up to the building, parking in a spot marked "reserved."

"Detective Marlowe, this spot says 'reserved,'" Dahlia said, pointing at the signpost in front of them.

"Yes, you're very observant," Sam replied.

"You can't park here."

Sam gripped the steering wheel, annoyed.

"Then why don't you find a vacant spot, which is like a freakin' county away, and then patrol the parking lot or something while I work on the important things?"

"The Captain said we are to work together."

"The Captain said," Sam repeated in a whiny, high pitched voice. "Now, if you'll excuse me, I have work to do."

Sam exited the vehicle without another word. Dahlia let out an irritated huff but followed him toward the building. Once inside the spacious lobby, Sam introduced himself to the receptionist, who immediately escorted the two detectives up to the second floor to the director's office.

"Ma'am, I have the detectives from the Odette PD to see you," the receptionist said upon entering the office.

The director rose from her seat behind her desk.

"Thank you, Shawn. Please fetch my daughter and personal assistant," the director said.

She turned her attention to Sam and Dahlia after the receptionist hurried from the office.

"Thank you for arriving so quickly, detectives. Please, have a seat," she said, motioning to the chairs in front of her desk.

Cynthia Shea was in her late fifties, with salt and pepper hair and steel blue eyes. A consummate professional, she inherited the business from her father, the founder, and ran the company with a mix of integrity and shrewdness, as evidenced by the various photographs, news articles and accolades decorating the walls of the office.

"Here is the note," Cynthia said as Sam and Dahlia sat down. "It arrived this morning."

She handed a copy of the note to both detectives.

"Who delivered it?" Sam asked.

"My assistant brought it to my attention this morning when he brought in all of the mail and paperwork I needed to look over when I arrived at the office."

Cynthia appeared ready to elaborate on her response but fell silent upon the cacophony of chatter approaching her office doors. The double doors burst open, and a young man and woman strolled in, acting as if they owned the place. They were followed by a red-faced receptionist, embarrassed by the pair's intrusion without warning.

"Mother!" the girl said dramatically. "Al and I were about to go to the boutique and then go for drinks at the new club downtown!"

"Detectives, this is my daughter, Hannahly," Cynthia said. "My apologies for her behavior; I don't believe she's grasped the true gravity of the situation yet."

She had a pleasant look on her face, but Sam figured it was to mask the true feelings of horror and shame she felt at her daughter's disregard to her current situation.

Hannahly was what Barbie would look like if she had become a real person instead of a doll. Golden blond hair, stunning blue eyes, a slim figure and flashy-and presumably expensive-designer clothes and accessories, she seemed like she would be more at home in Malibu or New York City instead of a small town in Colorado. Sam did his best not to roll his eyes at her air-headedness.

"It's my fault, Ms. Shea," Hannahly's male companion said with a small bow. "I have been trying to keep Hannahly's mind off of things."

Sam's eyebrows furrowed in confusion when, out of the corner of his eye, he spied Dahlia tense up momentarily at the sound of the man's voice before relaxing and then looking down at the pristine turquoise tiled floor beneath her feet.

"I appreciate your efforts, Alistair, but, unfortunately, we are going to need to discuss this matter," Cynthia said. "Detectives Samuel Marlowe and Dahlia Bennett are here to assist with the case."

Sam and Dahlia both rose from their chairs and turned to face Hannahly and Alistair. Alistair's eyes instantly settled on Dahlia, who seemed to shrink under his gaze.

"Hello, Dahlia," he said, a smirk revealing his pearly white teeth as he took her hand and planted a kiss on the back of it.

Sam cleared his throat loudly. The slick dressed man turned to him.

"Alistair Kinney, Ms. Shea's personal assistant," he held a hand out to Sam.

Sam, however, did not move. Alistair held his hand out for another couple of seconds before letting it fall to his side.

"Ms. Shea, have you shown the detectives the letter?" Alistair changed the subject to avoid the awkward tension between himself and the detectives.

"I had started to when the two of you boisterously entered the discussion," Cynthia said. "I would very much like to continue so we can determine if my daughter's life is at stake!"

"Of course, forgive the intrusion Ms. Shea, and please, continue."

Cynthia let out a breath as she sat down in her desk chair.

"I apologize for being short with both of you, but I am absolutely on edge with this threat," she sighed. "Detectives, do you believe this is credible?"

Sam opened up the folder again to study the note once more. It was a plain white piece of paper with letters cut out from various newspaper types and fonts. It read:

```
Cynthia Shea,
    If you value the life of your daughter, you will
leave $250,000 in a duffel bag in the trashcan near the
fountain in the center of Odette Town Park by tomorrow
at noon. If you don't, say goodbye to your darling
Hannahly. DO NOT contact the police. Or Else.
```

"Well," Sam said as he closed the folder. "This sounds like a load of bullshit to me."

Alistair raised a manicured eyebrow at him.

"And how do you come to that conclusion, Detective?" he asked.

"This note sounds like a sad attempt to extort money from Ms. Shea," Sam said. "Okay, so what happens if the money isn't delivered at noon tomorrow? Is some magical ninja going to appear out of a puff of smoke and snatch up Hannahly at 12:01? I highly doubt it."

Cynthia seemed relieved, but Alistair didn't appear convinced. He turned to Cynthia.

"Ms. Shea, I must insist that we don't take this threat lightly," Alistair said. "I still think that this threat could very well be credible."

"I'm sorry, Alistair, but what police academy did you graduate from?" Cynthia said.

Alistair's lips came together in a thin, firm line. He turned from Cynthia, his attention on Dahlia.

"How about you, Dahlia?" Alistair asked.

Dahlia's head jerked up. Sam frowned. What the hell was going on with her?

"I … I—"

"You what?" Sam asked.

Dahlia cleared her throat.

"I agree with Detective Marlowe."

Alistair said nothing and stomped over to the sofa where Hannahly sat. She didn't notice as he plopped down next to her, slinging his arm up and over the back of the couch, as she had her face buried in her phone while she chomped away on her bubblegum.

"That being said," Sam turned back to Cynthia. "That doesn't mean we won't look into the threat. It's still a crime, so, credible or not, the people behind this will still be getting into trouble."

"It is much appreciated, Detective," Cynthia said.

"Ms. Shea, is there anyone you can think of that would want to hurt you or Hannahly? An ex-boyfriend, a disgruntled employee, or a pissed off client, that sort of thing?"

Hands resting on her desk, one on top of the other, Cynthia tapped the back of her bottom hand with her index finger.

"That's a tough question," she said. "I am the heiress to the wealthiest financial institution in Odette, so, naturally, I have my enemies. However, no one immediately comes to mind … except for one person, though I can't imagine him doing something like this—"

"You'd be amazed at what people are capable of, Ms. Shea," Sam said. "Who is this person?"

"My ex-husband, Joseph Falconer," Cynthia said.

"Daddy?" Hannahly looked up from her phone. "Mother, you can't seriously think that Daddy has something to do with this!"

Cynthia ignored her daughter.

"I hate to think ill of Joseph, but we didn't end our relationship on the best of terms," she said. "When my father passed away, he left all of the CS Financial holdings and assets to me. He told me to protect the company and its integrity. When Joseph and I got married years ago, my attorney advised me to have him sign a prenuptial agreement to protect the company. When we did divorce, Joseph was quite angry with the fact that he didn't receive a dime from CS Financial or me."

"I'd say that's a pretty good motive," Sam said. "If you don't mind me asking, what led to the divorce?"

"I'd rather not say."

Cynthia flushed. Sam made a mental note to ask Joseph about the cause of the divorce.

"Is there anyone else you can think of?" he asked.

"Not at the moment, unfortunately. I will think things over and submit a list to you as soon as I can," Cynthia said.

Sam turned in his seat to face Hannahly.

"How about you?" he asked her. "Any angry ex-boyfriends or anything like that?"

Hannahly tapped a few more buttons on her phone. The bubble she was blowing with her gum popped.

"Sorry, but no," Hannahly said. "All of my ex's love me. I mean, who wouldn't?"

"Whoever doesn't would surely be an idiot," Alistair said.

He grinned and leaned into Hannahly, who giggled.

"Those two are going to make me barf," Sam said under his breath.

Out of the corner of his eye, he caught Dahlia's lips turning upward with a small smile.

★★★

Sam and Dahlia departed from CS Financial to meet up with Cynthia's ex-husband and Hannahly's father, Joseph Falconer. Initially driving in silence, Sam's curiosity got the best of him.

"What's the deal with you and that ball-less wonder back there?"

Out of the corner of his eye, Sam could see Dahlia's head snap around to face him before turning again and locking her gaze on the passing scenery outside her window.

"Nothing, Detective Marlowe," she said.

"Okay, two things," Sam said. "One, enough with the 'Detective Marlowe' crap. It's a friggin mouthful. It's 'Sam,' unless you piss me off. And two, if there is any potential for this whole partner thing to work–and I stress 'if'–then don't bullshit me. If I want a heaping pile of bullshit, I'll go visit a farm."

Dahlia suppressed a smile as she continued to stare out the window.

"You're right, Detec–I mean, Sam," she said. "It is important for partners to have open and honest communication, but I'd rather not talk about what happened."

Sam's mind was full of ideas and theories as to what could have transpired between Dahlia and Alistair.

"Were you two an item?" he asked.

"An item? There is no way in hell that I would ever touch that rapist pig."

"That's what the deal is, then."

Dahlia cursed under her breath.

Sam laughed.

"Rapist pig? You've told me quite a lot with those two little words, Miss Bennett. I guess the score is now Sam, 1, Dahlia, 0."

"Well played, Sam," Dahlia sighed.

"Hey, I'm one of the top cops in Odette for a reason."

"Yes, thanks for the reminder."

"Care to expand on the whole 'rapist pig' comment?"

"Not really."

Sam dropped the conversation. He'd get Dahlia to tell him what he wanted; it was only a matter of time.

★★★

When Joseph Falconer answered the door, he was opposite of what Sam had pictured Cynthia Shea's ex-husband to be. His raven black hair had been spiked to a sharp point, and his tight gray t-shirt and fitted blue jeans displayed a formidable physique.

"So, it's true," Joseph said after Sam and Dahlia presented their police credentials. "Hannahly is in danger."

"That's what we're trying to determine," Sam said. "What do you know about the situation?"

"I got an anonymous letter this morning, stating my daughter was in trouble."

"What did it say?"

Joseph grabbed the letter from the next room and handed it to Sam and Dahlia to look over.

```
Joseph Falconer,
    If you value the life of your daughter, you will
leave $250,000 in a duffel bag in the trashcan near the
fountain in the center of Odette Town Park by tomorrow
at noon. If you don't, say goodbye to your darling
Hannahly. DO NOT contact the police. Or Else.
```

"It sounds like the other letter," Dahlia whispered to Sam.

"Mr. Falconer, we heard that when you and Cynthia had divorced a few years ago," Sam said. "She got to keep everything. Do you have the money they are asking for?"

Joseph stared at Sam, cracking each individual knuckle with a loud pop.

"Not ... exactly," he said. "But, I'll find a way. I'll rob a bank to keep my daughter safe if I have to."

"I'd rather we not go to those extremes," Sam said.

"If Cynthia hadn't screwed me over like that, I wouldn't have to be worrying about how to come up with the money to protect my sweet little princess," Joseph said.

"Screwed you over?" Dahlia asked.

"Hold the brakes, there, pal," Sam said. "You signed a prenup agreement when you and Cynthia tied the knot years ago, didn't you? You knew that, if anything happened, she'd get to keep her company's assets and property; how did she screw you over?"

"Because," Joseph said. "I wasn't the one to cause the divorce; Cynthia did. She cheated on me."

"Really? Do you know the guy?" Sam asked. "Or gal? Hey, I don't judge."

"No, I don't know him," Joseph said. "Believe me, if I did, that son of a bitch would be eating through a straw after I got through with him!"

"You found out about the affair, then what?"

"I told Cynthia that there was no way we could fix our relationship after she broke our vows like that. She said it was an accident and that it would never happen again, but the trust was completely gone. I told her I wanted a divorce, and well, the rest is history."

"Did this guy ever try to hook up with Cynthia again?" Sam asked. "Or did he ever try to maybe blackmail or extort money from her to keep it a secret?"

"Not that I'm aware of. The finances were Cynthia's thing, which is understandable since she was being groomed to become the next head of CS Financial."

"Is the company doing well?" Dahlia asked. "Has anyone been laid off or fired due to downsizing or anything like that?"

"No. In fact, CS Financial is as prosperous as ever. But, you know, if you're looking for funny stuff, there's this one agent at the company that shot through the ranks faster than I can ever remember anyone besides Cynthia moving up. Do you think that might be something?" Joseph asked.

"It's possible," Sam said. "Maybe this person's price for his silence was a few promotions; got a name?"

"It's Jayden something. I don't remember his last name, but I'm sure his first name was Jayden."

Sam scribbled down the information.

"Well, thanks, Mr. Falconer," he said. "We'll check this out."

"What about the note?" Joseph asked. "The note said to have the money put together and delivered by tomorrow at noon; if I have to get that money, I need to know immediately so I can start planning-"

"Hold your horses, bud. We have no proof that this threat is even credible," Sam said. "We saw your daughter this morning, and she was doing fine. Unless the kidnappers magically get a hold of her, you have nothing to worry about."

"I guess I'll have to take your word for it," Joseph said, his eyebrows drawing together and rubbing the back of his neck.

★★★

Cynthia went from reclining in her desk chair to sitting straight up with her hands folded across her desk. She stared at Sam with intensity.

"I assume you spoke to Joseph?" Cynthia asked. "He's the only other person who knows about the affair, besides myself and the, let's call him, 'third party.'"

"Maybe we spoke to your lover and not Joseph," Sam said. "It doesn't matter where we got the information from; what does matter is what information you're willing to share with us to help in our investigation."

Cynthia let out a breath.

"You believe it's important, Detective?" she asked.

"I'd rather find out it had nothing to do with the possible threat against your daughter by investigating it than not looking into this possible lead and something does happen to Hannahly."

"Fair enough," Cynthia's posture softened. "It's true; I did have a bit of an indiscretion while married to Joseph. It was a onetime thing, and I assure you, Detectives, it was not intentional."

"Intentional or not, it doesn't make a difference. We need the name of the man you had the affair with."

"I can't give that to you."

Sam frowned.

"Why not?"

"This person and I agreed to keep what happened between us a secret," Cynthia said. "I can't reveal his name or else I have breached my side of the deal. If that happens, then he can reveal all of the details and CS Financial does not need negative press, especially when it comes to the director of an institution people trust with their finances."

"I get that, but keeping that under wraps won't help Hannahly, especially if the guy in question is the one trying to extort money from you."

"It's not him," Cynthia sounded adamant.

"How can you know for sure?" Dahlia asked. "Have you heard of the phrase 'street angel, house devil?' We sometimes trust people without knowing their true intentions or what they're truly like when no one's around."

Sam eyed Dahlia, who kept her focus firmly planted on Cynthia.

"I understand that, Detective Bennett," the financial director said. "But, I have been keeping an eye on this individual, just in case."

"Then he's a part of the company," Sam said.

"Interpret that as you will."

Sam tapped the arm his chair.

"Let's make a deal, Ms. Shea," he said. "You give a list of CS Financial employees to Bennett and me to investigate. If we figure out who the 'third party' is, you'll have complete deniability that you revealed his name. You can keep up your end of the bargain. Bennett and I can continue our investigation; deal?"

Cynthia mulled over the terms for a few moments.

"All right, deal," she said.

Cynthia buzzed her assistant over her intercom.

"Yes, Ms. Shea?" Alistair asked. "What can I do for you?"

"Alistair, please provide the detectives with a list of the company employees," Cynthia said.

"Of course, Ms. Shea," Alistair said. "I'll have it for you momentarily."

True to his word, Alistair arrived in the office moments later. He handed one copy of the list to Sam and the other to Dahlia.

"Do you think the person threatening to harm Hannahly might be an employee?" Alistair asked.

"We are simply covering all bases," Sam said.

"Okay," Alistair said as he exited the office.

The two detectives stepped out of Cynthia's office and reviewed the list of names.

"What was the name Joseph gave us—Jayden?" Sam asked as he scanned the list.

"Yes," Dahlia said.

"There's a 'Jayden Delano' on here, and he seems to be the only Jayden employed here, so odds are he's the guy Joseph was talking about. Let's go pay him a visit."

The two detectives waited in the lobby while the financial advisor finished his meeting. A few minutes later, a man in an impeccably tailored gray suit escorted two individuals in expensive designer clothes and matching gold Rolex watches to the door.

"Thank you, Mr. and Mrs. Morgan. It was great to see you again. Don't hesitate to contact me with any questions," he said to the couple before they left.

"Jayden Delano?" Sam asked.

"That's me," Jayden said. "Are you the two detectives my secretary mentioned?"

"That's us, Marlowe and Bennett," Sam said. "Say, where's your accent from? You sound like you're more from the East Coast than from around here."

"Good call, Detective," Jayden said. "I'm originally from Boston."

The financier motioned for Sam and Dahlia to follow him to his office.

"What made you come out west?" Sam asked as they walked.

"A story as old as time," Jayden said. "Love. My spouse has family out here, and after we got married, we moved out west to be closer to them."

Reaching the office, Jayden took a seat at his desk, indicating for Sam and Dahlia to make themselves comfortable in the visitor's chairs.

"What can I do for you two?" he asked.

"We're looking into a matter that may be connected with the employees of CS Financial," Sam said.

"What kind of matter?"

"It's an ongoing investigation, so we're not at liberty to say."

"Oh, of course," Jayden said. "I'll try to help however I can. What do you need to know?"

"How is your relationship with Ms. Shea?" Dahlia asked.

"Ms. Shea is a great boss," Jayden said. "She is very knowledgeable about the company and is shrewd, but fair. I like my coworkers too. Everyone here is open-minded and accepting, which is great in today's day and age."

"How have things been since Ms. Shea and her ex-husband got divorced?" Sam asked.

"No different. Ms. Shea is the consummate professional; she can compartmentalize work and personal life better than anyone I've ever known."

"Has anyone been paying, let's say, extra special attention to Ms. Shea? Is there any awkwardness between Ms. Shea and any of your coworkers?"

Jayden shook his head.

"No, not at all," he said.

"How long have you been working here at CS Financial?" Sam asked.

"It's been a little over three years now."

"Three years and you're already a senior financial advisor? That's impressive."

"Yes, I made senior advisor pretty quickly, but that's because I managed to land some big accounts," Jayden said, as he reached for the mug of coffee on his desk. He took a sip.

"So, it has nothing to do with the possibility of you having an affair with the director?" Sam asked.

Sam and Dahlia moved out of the way in time to avoid the spray of coffee that came from Jayden at Sam's suggestion. The financial advisor coughed and grabbed some tissues to clean up the spilled beverage.

"I'm sorry, what?" Jayden asked, still wheezing a little. "You think I'm having an affair with Ms. Shea?"

"A source mentioned the possibility," Dahlia said. "Can you confirm or deny this allegation?"

Jayden smiled, and he let out a small chuckle. He ran his fingers over the golden band on his ring finger.

"I'm not sure who you were speaking to, but they apparently don't know me very well," he said.

Jayden picked up a picture frame from next to his computer screen and turned it around for Sam and Dahlia to see.

"This is my husband, Carter," he said. "Ms. Shea's a great lady but, she's not exactly my preferred gender."

"What a world we live in, eh?" Sam said. "Someone gets ahead by doing hard work, and there's always someone else to assume that he got that far through sinister means."

He stood up.

"If that's the case, then you're probably not the guy we're looking for," he said. "Thanks for your time, Jayden. We'll see ourselves out."

★★★

In the lobby, a few moments later, Dahlia asked, "What now?"

"This investigation is going nowhere," Sam said. "I'm pretty sure this threat is a hoax."

"Is that what we're going to tell Ms. Shea?"

"Pretty much, yeah."

Dahlia sighed.

"All right, if you say so."

She followed Sam as he marched back toward Cynthia's office.

"Ms. Shea," he said as he strolled into the office. "Based on our investigation so far, it's becoming more and more likely that this threat is merely a hoax."

Cynthia looked up from her computer screen.

"You're sure?" she asked.

"Yes, Ma'am," Sam said. "I'm sure."

"That is quite the relief. Detectives, would you mind telling Hannahly that directly, so she doesn't worry?"

"Of course," Sam said.

Cynthia summoned her daughter, who made her way up to her mother's office a few minutes later, Alistair tagging behind her. Sam relayed the news.

"Ms. Shea," Alistair turned to Cynthia. "While I respect the decision of these two fine detectives, I would be very relieved if one of them could keep an eye on Hannahly until noon tomorrow, to be safe. Perhaps Detective Bennett? Wouldn't you agree that it would be in her best interest?"

"I would rather be safe than sorry," Cynthia said. "Detectives, thoughts?"

Sam looked over at Hannahly. She seemed as disinterested as before, with her focus entirely on whatever she was doing on her phone.

"We can do that for you," Sam said. "Detective Bennett would be happy to stay with Hannahly as her personal bodyguard."

Dahlia glared at Sam, who simply smiled as he mouthed the word 'seniority' to her.

"Thank you, Detective Bennett," Cynthia said, placing a hand over her heart. "I can rest easier knowing that someone will be watching over my darling daughter tonight."

Her posture stiff, Dahlia replied through pinched lips and clenched teeth.

"Happy to be of service, ma'am."

★★★

It couldn't have been more awkward and uncomfortable if she had shown up to the police department with nothing but her bra and panties on. Dahlia sat curled up on the couch in the living room of Hannahly's pricey condo, 'babysitting" Hannahly while keeping as much distance as possible from Alistair, which was made rather tricky based on the fact that the latter wouldn't leave Hannahly's side. Resting her chin on her hand, she sighed. This was not how she expected to be spending her first day on the force.

The lights were off in the living room, and there was a movie playing on the impressive and expensive flat screen smart TV. Hannahly and Alistair were seated next to Dahlia, with only a half-empty bowl of popcorn to separate them. The phone she had tucked between her knees vibrated, so Dahlia checked the message. It was from Sam.

Having fun?

Dahlia envisioned the smirk on his face. Sam was certainly ... something. What that something was, she wasn't quite sure, but he was definitely something.

Everything is fine.

When Captain Buchanan informed her that she was going to be partnered with Sam Marlowe, the lead detective in the department, Dahlia was sure she looked like a high school girl whose crush asked her to the homecoming dance. She had heard from her father about an 'up and coming policeman' who'd been involved in some cases at the college he worked at, and after doing some research, she discovered it was Sam. "I want to work alongside someone like him," she solemnly swore to herself. If she was going to become a celebrated heroine one day, she needed to learn from the best.

Disillusion? Dahlia considered, her lips pursed. She wasn't entirely sure how to describe her first day working with Sam. Either way, Dahlia pushed her thoughts aside when the movie ended, and Hannahly stood up and stretched like a cat who had been sunbathing in a window.

"That was fun. I'm going to take a bubble bath and then go to bed," she sashayed toward the archway leading out of the room. "Alistair can show you to the guest bedroom, detective. Later!"

Dahlia grimaced at the feel of the bile rising in her throat as Hannahly strutted from the room and left her alone with Alistair. She gulped it down as if it were a glass of water. It didn't make her feel any better.

Dahlia was relieved when Alistair walked out of the living room, but before she could let out a sigh of relief, he returned a few minutes later. He had a bottle of wine and two wine glasses in his hands. Alistair joined her on the couch. Dahlia tried to discreetly scoot away, but she was already in contact with the arm of the couch, which prevented her from moving any further.

"My dear Dahlia," Alistair said, placing the glasses down on the coffee table in front of the couch. "It's been quite some time since I was last able to bask in your radiance, and I am ashamed to say, I remember us parting on bad terms. I owe you a tremendous apology. What happened two years ago was ... tragic, and my heart still mourns the loss every day."

Dahlia looked away from Alistair so he couldn't see her roll her eyes at him. What a load of shit.

"Will you give me another chance, Dahlia?" Alistair asked, taking one of her hands in his.

Dahlia shuddered. Her skin felt as though spiders and centipedes were crawling up and down her arms. She remained silent. She had no words, but, even if she did, she wasn't sure he was worthy of them. Alistair slid closer and brushed a strand of her hair back. Dahlia could feel his breath on her neck.

"I know it's sudden, Dahlia," Alistair said. "I mean, we just reunited today. Please, take your time, but don't take too long; we've already been apart for longer than we should have been."

He uncorked the bottle of wine and poured some of the burgundy liquid in each glass before handing one to Dahlia and taking the other for himself.

"Cheers to new beginnings?" Alistair asked, raising his glass.

Dahlia said nothing. Alistair brought the glass up to his lips, watching Dahlia through the glass. *He's waiting for me to take a drink,* Dahlia considered. *Maybe he'll leave me the hell alone if I do.*

Dahlia lifted the wine glass and took a drink. Alistair watched her with a smile.

★★★

Sam's eyes were locked on his phone. It had been a little too long since the last time Dahlia responded to one of his messages. What the hell was going on there? He was confident that the threat had been a hoax, but sent Dahlia to watch Hannahly as a precaution. As an added bonus, it got her out of his hair for the night.

Sitting in his chair in his mother's room at the long-term care facility, Sam leaned back, crossing one leg over the other. Dahlia was occupied babysitting Hannahly and wasn't bothering him by continually texting him every few minutes; he thought that would be a good thing, yet it didn't *feel* like a good thing.

"I'm getting a little worried, Mom," he said to his comatose mother. "She's not answering. She's been quick to respond the entire time and now, nothing."

Wait, why do I care? Sam asked himself. *I don't even want a partner. I work alone. Plus, a partner might get in the way of the things I might need to do …*

A small ping sounded throughout the otherwise quiet room. Sam immediately checked his phone.

All is fine, Detective Marlowe. He stared at the message and then let out a little laugh.

"False alarm, Mom," Sam said. "She wrote back that all is fine over there. See? I knew the whole thing was a hoax …"

He paused, mentally running through the message again. **All is fine, Detective Marlowe.** Pursing his lips, Sam skimmed through his previous correspondence with his new partner. They'd exchanged several text messages over the past few hours and not once had she referred to him as Detective Marlowe; Dahlia had been calling him "Sam," like he had directed her to earlier in the day. *Why the sudden change?*

Sam slipped his phone into the breast pocket of his dress shirt and got up from his chair.

"You know, it wouldn't hurt to swing by and check up on things," he said, kissing his mother's forehead. "I'll be back later."

It was to check up on the investigation, Sam reminded himself as he hustled down the hallway toward the exit of the facility. Nothing more.

★★★

Her head hurt, and her mouth tasted like vomit. Dahlia tried to lift her head but dropped it back down as she was hit with a wave of dizziness. She buried her face in the pillow and … wait, *pillow?* Dahlia's eyes jolted open, and she forced herself to roll over and sit up, pushing through the pangs of nausea that struck her.

She was in bed. Not her bed, but a bed. *How did that happen?* Dahlia let out a shaky breath as she ran a hand through her hair. The last thing she remembered was sitting downstairs in the living room with Alistair and having a drink of wine. Dahlia looked around the room. Based on the luxurious furniture and décor, this must be the spare bedroom at Hannahly's condo. Hannahly said that Alistair was supposed to show her to the spare bedroom, but where the hell was Alistair?

Dahlia threw back the covers and put her feet on the cold wooden floor. She went to stand up but froze in place when she made a gruesome discovery. Scattered on the floor around her feet was her clothing, along with a few articles of men's clothing.

"No, no, no, no, no," Dahlia repeated, feeling her heart pounding against her ribcage with tremendous force.

There is no way in hell that I actually slept with Alistair, is there? She wanted to cry, or vomit. Or both. *How the fuck could I have let this happen? I'm a cop, for Christ's sake!* Elbows resting on her knees, Dahlia put her head in her hands.

"I'm sorry, Iris," she whispered to herself. "I made a mess out of this …"

Her head snapped up at the sound of her cell phone vibrating on the end table next to the bed. *Shit! Sam!* He was probably going to give her hell for not answering for however long she'd been out.

Snagging her phone off the end table, Dahlia checked her messages. Much to her surprise, there was only one new message waiting for her. I'm outside, Bennett. Open up.

He's here? Outside? Right now? Dammit! Be right down, Dahlia typed before tossing her phone aside and throwing her clothes on faster than the one day she was running late to school back in junior high. She flew down the stairs, her feet barely touching the plush pink carpeting as she raced to the door.

"There you are, Bennett," Sam said when Dahlia opened the door. "Sleeping on the job?"

"What?" Dahlia cleared her throat after her voice cracked.

"Lighten up, Bennett," Sam said with a frown. "Don't you know a joke when you hear one or do you not have a sense of humor?"

He made his way past Dahlia into Hannahly's condo. Sam looked around.

"Where are Hannahly and Alistair?" he asked.

"Well," Dahlia played with a stray piece of her hair that fell from her messy bun. "After the movie ended, Hannahly went upstairs to take a bubble bath and then go to bed. Um, Alistair and I had a drink and …"

Sam turned around to face her.

"I thought he was, and I quote, a 'rapist pig,' and now you're sharing a drink with him?" he asked.

Dahlia opened her mouth to respond, but words failed her. Sam walked over to her, standing a few inches away from her face. She felt self-conscious under his scrutiny as his eyes roved her body, clasping her hands behind her back and blindly picking at her fingers.

"Did you drink too much?" Sam asked.

Dahlia shook her head.

"I only had one glass," she said.

"Pale skin, dilated pupils, bloodshot eyes," Sam said. "Either you're completely shitfaced, or there's something else causing you to act like you've come home from a bender."

"You mean, like being drugged?"

"I have no idea, but something's up," he said. "Remember what I told you earlier today about addressing me as 'Detective Marlowe?'"

"Yes, you said not to call you that unless I piss you off; why?"

"Then, you didn't send this message to me?"

Sam pulled out his cell phone and showed Dahlia the message in question.

"If I did, I don't remember," Dahlia said.

She heard him curse under his breath.

"We need to find Hannahly and Alistair," Sam said, turning and heading toward the stairs.

Dahlia hurried behind him. Upstairs, they checked the various rooms, finding them empty and undisturbed, until reaching Hannahly's bedroom at the end of the hallway. Alistair was face down on the floor, his hand clutching a piece of paper. Dahlia turned white at the sight of him.

"Alistair, wake up!" Sam shook the man's body.

With a groan, Alistair began to stir after a few moments.

"What happened? Where's Hannahly?" Sam asked.

Alistair pushed the paper forward toward Sam, who read it over. Dahlia could tell by the death grip he had on the piece of paper and his unblinking stare at the words on the paper in front of him that whatever happened wasn't good.

"Sam?" she bit the inside of her cheek. "Where's Hannahly?"

"She ..." Sam cleared his throat. "She's gone ..."

★★★

The next morning at the police department, Sam was on the phone at his desk when someone placed a piece of paper in front of him. Catching a glimpse of the header, Sam abruptly hung up the phone and addressed the letter's deliverer.

"Get back here, Bennett. That's an order!"

Dahlia stopped mid-stride and returned to Sam's desk in the bullpen.

"What the hell is this shit, Bennett?" Sam asked, holding up the letter.

"It's my resignation," Dahlia replied.

She stood tall and looked straightforward, though her gaze was somewhere above Sam's head, avoiding eye contact with him.

"Yeah, I can read," Sam said. "Care to explain this?"

"I failed in the assignment you gave me on my first day. I believe it is best if I do not continue, thus not jeopardizing any future cases or anyone else's safety."

Sam stood up from his chair to stand directly in Dahlia's line of sight. Before she could break her gaze, Sam looked her straight in the eye and tore the letter in half. He tossed the shreds into the garbage next to his desk.

"You are not quitting, Bennett," Sam said, tapping the edge of his desk with his fingers with each word he spoke. "You screwed up, big deal. I've fucked up and disobeyed the rules so many times, it's a wonder I'm still employed. You know why? Because I'm a good cop and I know I am. I may not know all the details about what happened between you and Alistair, but I know enough to see that you truly hate that piece of shit. There was someone in my life that I hated that much too and I refused to let him get away with what he did. Don't let him win, Bennett."

Dahlia averted her gaze while Sam spoke, her shoulders slumped, and her chin tucked into her chest. About a minute after he finished speaking, her posture straightened and she looked directly at him.

"I've been working on the case while you were getting checked out at the hospital," Sam changed the subject before things could get too sentimental. "I am pretty sure that the person responsible for kidnapping Hannahly is an employee at CS Financial."

"What makes you say that?" Dahlia asked.

"Read the ransom note again," Sam handed her a copy of the note they found in Alistair's hand.

We know you think this was a hoax. We have taken Hannahly to prove it wasn't.

If you want to see her alive again, you MUST follow our instructions to the letter!

Don't speak to anyone about this, including family.

Don't contact ANY authorities or private parties, like a private investigator.

Prepare a duffel bag and place $500,000 in small, unmarked bills inside.

Place the bag containing the money into the trashcan by the fountain in Odette Town Park.

This must be completed by noon tomorrow.

No excuses! No exceptions!

Remember, we're watching everything, and if you or those two arrogant detectives think you can outsmart us, it will cost Hannahly her life.

"Notice," Sam began to speak once he figured Dahlia had had enough time to go through the letter, "the note says that we think the first letter was a hoax; I distinctly remember saying that while we were at CS Financial. Plus, the note also mentions 'two arrogant detectives,' which is very specific. The kidnappers didn't say cops or anything generic; they specifically said, two detectives. Again, we were the only two detectives at CS Financial. It has to be someone from there."

"But who? Only a select few people knew why we were really at CS Financial."

"True, unless Cynthia's office was bugged," Sam said. "I'm sending a tech team down to the building to scan the office for any listening devices. But, in the case that Cynthia's office was not bugged, who were the people that knew the true reason we were at CS Financial and that we believed the original note to be a hoax?"

"Well, there's Cynthia Shea, of course," Dahlia said. "We also talked to her ex, Joseph, but he wasn't at CS Financial; we stopped by his house. Hannahly knew, Alistair knew, and … that's it, actually. We talked to that one guy, Jayden, but we never said that it was about the kidnapping."

"Bennett! Marlowe!" Captain Buchanan stepped out into the bullpen and did not look pleased. "My office. Now."

"We're working on the case, Cap," Sam motioned to the paper in Dahlia's hand.

"Great, we can discuss it in my office."

With an annoyed huff, Sam followed the Captain to his office, Dahlia behind him. Captain Buchanan closed the office door with more force than usual and stomped over to his desk. Lips pressed together in a firm, thin line, he stared hard at the two detectives.

"Listen, Cap," Sam said. "I know it looks bad."

"The daughter of the director of one of the wealthiest institutions in town has been kidnapped after my so-called 'lead detective' dismissed the first threat against her?" the Captain said. "Gee, and I thought everything was fine and dandy."

"Actually, the first note was bogus. The kidnappers resorted to extreme measures because we didn't take the bait from the first note. I mean, they had to be desperate enough to drug Bennett to knock her out to get to Hannahly, right?"

Captain Buchanan looked from Sam to Dahlia and back again.

"Drugged?" he repeated.

Dahlia gave Sam an incredulous stare, one that mirrored the Captain's.

"Work with me, Bennett," Sam nudged her foot with his.

"Um, yes," Dahlia said. "We're waiting for the tests to return from the hospital, but it's very likely that I was drugged last night."

"I see," Captain Buchanan said. "I'm glad you're all right, Detective Bennett. Well, if the kidnappers are getting desperate, it goes without saying that you two need to find Hannahly before things get worse. The first twenty-four hours in a missing person's case are crucial, so get going."

"On it," Sam gave the Captain a small salute before heading out of the office.

"Sam, wait up!" Dahlia jogged to catch up with him.

"What is it, Bennett?"

"Do you honestly think that I was drugged or were you buying time before the Captain disciplines us for screwing up this case?"

"I think you were drugged, actually," Sam said. "Even though we only met yesterday, I've gotten an idea of what you're like. Quite frankly, you're a goody-two-shoes little girl scout. I can't imagine you getting drunk while on duty, especially not on your first day. Now, if you were old and jaded like me, maybe. The only explanation I can think of is that you were drugged."

"But who would have drugged me?" Dahlia asked. "The only people at the house were Hannahly, Alistair and me."

"Gee, that's quite the pickle now, isn't it?" Sam replied.

"Are you implying that it was one of them?"

"Seeing as that Hannahly is gone, that only leaves one person, unless you drugged yourself, in which case I say you're more fucked up than I am."

"Alistair did this," Dahlia said.

"You tell me; is this something he's capable of?"

"Y-yes."

"How do you know? What's your evidence?"

Sam stared her down, hoping it was enough for her to reveal her background with Alistair. It was beyond his own insatiable curiosity now; there might be some details that could assist with the case, at least, that's what he told himself. Dahlia shifted, folding her arms across her chest.

"Fine," she let her arms fall to her sides. "Is there someplace more private we can go to discuss this?"

"Interrogation Room 2 is open, I believe," Sam said before he turned to head toward the room in question.

Dahlia followed behind him. As Sam said, Interrogation Room 2 was vacant, so the two detectives headed inside. Sam took a seat at the table.

"All right, Bennett," he said. "I'm all ears."

Dahlia turned her back to him, resting her hands on the sill of the one-way window.

"Growing up, I had a best friend named Iris. My dad and her mother served in the same unit on the military base we lived on. We became instant friends. I mean, we both had flowers for names; once we discovered that, there was no turning back. Iris was very shy and sweet. She literally couldn't hurt a fly; she would release it outside, even in the middle of winter. I guess Alistair thought she would be an easy target because of her personality."

"Easy target?" Sam repeated.

Dahlia turned from the window.

"Have you heard of Major William Bennett?" she asked.

"You mean the dean of Hammett College?"

"Yes, that Major Bennett, the same Major Bennett who is dean of a prestigious school is also my father," Dahlia said. "Because of our connection, my brothers and I could get into the school no problem. Iris was also able to get into the school with us, which was great."

"Where does Alistair come in?" Sam asked.

"Iris and I were meeting up with friends to study at a coffee shop close to the campus. Alistair was there and took an immediate interest in her. I thought it was great; Iris was far from outgoing, so she would never make the first move on a guy, even if she were desperately in love with him. It was nice to see someone good looking paying attention to such a great girl."

"How did the shit hit the fan?"

"Well, a few weeks into their relationship, Iris told me that Alistair was getting pushy, wanting to sleep with her. Again, my best friend was not that kind of girl; she didn't want to jump into bed with just anyone. I guess growing up in the military made her morals and values strong. It was admirable for Iris to stick to her guns like that, though Alistair didn't appreciate it.

"Shortly before mid-terms, Iris sent me a message asking me to stop by her apartment, which I did. I found her a complete mess. She was sitting on the floor in her bathroom with a towel on, sobbing. I asked what happened and she told me that Alistair had shown up at her apartment and raped her. I told her that she needed to call the cops, but Iris didn't want to do that. She said she didn't want to deal with him or what he did to her. I didn't agree, but I couldn't force her to press charges, so I spent the night with her, trying to help my best friend through the worst night of her life."

"Christ, Bennett," Sam ran a hand over his face.

That wasn't the story he was expecting.

"But that's not the end of it," Dahlia said, folding her arms across her chest and turning her eyes toward the ceiling, resting her head back against the wall. "I did my best to help Iris recover from what happened, and things seemed to be getting better. But, right before the holidays, I headed over to Iris' apartment and found she had slit her wrists and bled out. She was rushed to the emergency room, but there was nothing they could do to save her; she'd already lost too much blood."

She paused to let out a breath.

"I swore that I would do whatever I could to make the bastard who killed my best friend pay. Alistair must have figured out that I was gunning for him because he started causing problems for me."

"Like what?" Sam asked.

"Alistair managed to convince my father and brothers that I wasn't cut out for law enforcement. Somehow, he got my father to agree and my father, the dean, tried to switch my major to a different program. Something 'safe' that a girl could do. My father went so far as to threaten to expel me if I didn't switch my major from criminal justice to something else. I refused and transferred out of Hammett," Sam noticed a flicker of pain in Dahlia's face as she spoke. "Alistair made them doubt me, made them think I wasn't good enough. The one person that would have told me otherwise, Iris, was dead because of Alistair, the same man who brainwashed my family into thinking those very things. And being forced out of state to a college where my father's influence likely wouldn't reach, I lost valuable time and evidence to get justice for Iris ... Alistair ... got away with what he did."

Alistair is her Seth. The thought burst into Sam's mind as if it had been shot out of a cannon. Alistair Kinney caused the death of someone close to Dahlia, like his stepfather, Seth Tucker, practically killed his mother, Charlotte, leaving her in a vegetative state after brutally beating her in a drunken rage nearly twelve years ago.

She understands, she's been there. She knows what it's like to lose someone you love. She knows what it's like to have people think you're not worthy of anything. Sam could hear his heart beating loudly in his chest. *She's just like me ... just like I was when Edwin ... saved me.*

"I understand," he started to say.

Dahlia turned her attention from the ceiling to his face.

Sam caught himself before he could finish his statement, quickly closing his mouth. *I know what it's like to be doubted and how it feels to have the one person who always believed in you ripped out of your life.* He cleared his throat instead.

"Listen, Bennett," Sam said. "We're going to get this guy. We may not be able to get him for what he did to Iris, but we're going to make sure he goes to prison for a long, long time."

Dahlia brushed away a tear from her eye.

"How?" she asked.

"It's not going to be easy, but I think I know how to do it."

★★★

Pulling the edges of her body-hugging silver dress down to keep her modesty, Dahlia silently cursed as she made her way up the cobblestone driveway of the fancy townhouse. The small garden lanterns illuminated the pathway up to the front door, on which Dahlia promptly-though reluctantly-knocked.

"Dahlia, what a pleasant surprise," Alistair said when he opened the door.

His eyes roved over Dahlia's body, and as evidenced by the sly grin that crept onto his face, he appreciated her choice of outfit. Sam was right about the dress' effect on Alistair, even though Dahlia didn't want to admit it.

"Are you going to invite me in or stand there ogling me?" Dahlia asked, raising her hand to rest it on the doorframe and batting her eyelashes.

"Of course," Alistair said, stepping aside.

Dahlia entered the luxury residence. She, admittedly, was surprised by the apparent good fortune that befell Alistair. Swallowing her pride, Dahlia forced a sultry smile before turning to face Alistair.

"How are you feeling?" she asked, brushing a finger against his cheek.

"I'm all right," Alistair said. "My head still aches from where the kidnappers brutally attacked me."

Liar, Dahlia thought. *The doctors at the ER said you didn't even have a scratch.*

"But," he caught her hand and kissed her fingertips. "I'm mostly worried about Hannahly. The poor girl ... she must be terrified and alone ..."

Dahlia wrapped her arms around his neck, and he, her waist. She momentarily contemplated strangling him, but he potentially had valuable information, so she couldn't. *Darn.*

"Alistair," Dahlia purred. "I need your help with something."

"I'm at your service, darling," Alistair replied.

Dahlia looked away, biting her lip in pretend-though it probably held a bit of truth-embarrassment.

"When Hannahly disappeared yesterday, my partner was furious with me," she sniffed as if she were about to cry. "He fired me."

"He can do that?"

Shit. He's on to me ... I have to come up with something.

"I didn't think he could either," Dahlia said. "But Sam has a lot of pull at the department. I'm going to file an appeal but ... I don't know what I'm going to do! I have no job, no money! My life is over!"

She looked up at Alistair, her eyes pleading with him.

"I ... I didn't know who else to turn to—"

"You came to the right place," Alistair said. "Let's sit down, open some wine and talk, okay?"

"Thank you, Alistair," she said, sniffling again for effect. "Do you mind if I use your restroom first? My mascara feels like it's starting to run from these stupid tears."

Alistair showed Dahlia to the restroom.

"Take your time, honey," he said, opening the door for her. "I'll go down to my wine cellar and pick out something special for us."

Closing the door, Dahlia pressed her ear against it, listening for Alistair's footsteps to fade. Once he was gone, she slipped off her high heels and quietly left the restroom. Poking around the house for a few moments, Dahlia found the basement entrance and promptly locked it by jamming the doorknob with a dining chair. With Alistair temporarily locked away, Dahlia began searching the house.

The downstairs portion of the townhouse held nothing of interest; its primary purpose seemed to only be to flaunt Alistair's apparent wealth and prestige through expensive furniture and décor. Dahlia made her way upstairs to the second floor.

She peeked into the first room on the right, making sure the coast was clear before stepping inside. The room was quite palatial, with a king-sized bed, flat screen TV, walk-in closet and a desk with a computer, but also somewhat unkempt. Clothes were scattered across the blue carpeted floors which, Dahlia noted, upon further inspection, included women's clothing. A quick check of the nearest feminine clothing article showed it was a size small. Frowning, Dahlia headed over to the desk and rummaged through it. Several notes and letters caught her attention. She snapped some pictures of the papers on her cell phone before replacing them into the desk.

Turning away from the desk, a noise in the hallway caused Dahlia to freeze. Tiptoeing to the bedroom door, she opened the door a crack and peered into the hallway. There was no one outside ... perhaps in one of the other rooms? Dahlia headed down the hallway and carefully checked the other rooms. The first two rooms yielded nothing.

"And behind door number three," Dahlia whispered her hand on the doorknob.

Pushing the door open, Dahlia gasped at the sight before her. "Hannahly!"

★★★

Cynthia blinked, stunned, after hearing what Sam and Dahlia had to say the following day.

"So, it was all a setup?"

"Sort of," Sam said with a shrug. "The ransom demand was real, but the threat to your daughter wasn't. I mean, she was in on the whole thing."

Closing her eyes, Cynthia put her hand up to her chin and exhaled slowly. Joseph, standing with his arms folded next to his ex-wife in her office at CS Financial, eyed Sam and Dahlia.

"Run this by me again," he said gruffly.

"Alistair is an asshole," Sam started off with. "He was only interested in whatever he could do to benefit himself, including stealing and attempted kidnapping."

Sam glanced behind him at Dahlia, who took a step forward and produced some copies of photos she had in the file folder she was carrying, which she placed on Cynthia's desk.

"I found these photos at Alistair's place last night," Dahlia said. "He had taken pictures, Ms. Shea, of you after your one-night stand. It appears that he was holding on to them in case he ever needed to hold that over your head."

"Wait," Joseph held his hands up. "Alistair? You had an affair with that fucking little jerk?"

"I told you, Joseph, it was all an accident!" Cynthia said. "We'd had that huge argument, and I went to get some fresh air. I ended up at a bar downtown, hoping to get a few drinks to calm my nerves and clear my head. Alistair came up to me, and he was so nice, sweet and caring. He played me. Before I realized it, we were at a motel. I'm sure you can figure out what happened after that."

"Seriously? Alistair?"

"It was a mistake. End of story."

"Anyhoo," Sam said, trying to rein the conversation in before it got too far off track. "Alistair, now having something to hold over your head, Cynthia, wormed his way into your company and why not? CS Financial is only one of the wealthiest institutions in the whole city."

"Yes, I admit that I did hire Alistair to keep him quiet," Cynthia said. "I thought that if I made him my assistant, I could keep an eye on him to ensure that word of what happened between us never got out."

"And then he met your daughter, Hannahly," Sam said. "Both are young and beautiful, so there was an immediate connection between them. Alistair must have seen how devastated Hannahly was over your divorce and used that to his advantage."

"Alistair concocted the ransom plot," Joseph started to say but stopped upon seeing Sam shake his head.

"Actually, Hannahly was the mastermind," he said, surprising both Cynthia and Joseph, the two parents exchanging a look. "She came up with the ransom story because she knew how important CS Financial and its wealth were to you, Cynthia, and to you as well, Joseph, since you do get some alimony from your ex."

"The first note was, as Detective Marlowe figured, a hoax," Dahlia said. "When Alistair and Hannahly realized that we weren't going to fall for the note, they changed their plans and came up with the fake kidnapping. If you recall, Alistair was the one who suggested that I watch over Hannahly for the night. While at the condo, he gave me some wine that he drugged to knock me out."

"He drugged you?" Cynthia asked.

"Yes. The lab reports came back, and traces of Rohypnol were found in my system," Dahlia said. "He drugged me and then set me up to make it look like ... well, that part doesn't matter. What does matter is that Alistair and Hannahly waited until I was unconscious to set up the scene. Hannahly took Alistair's car back to his apartment to hide while Alistair pretended to have been knocked out while struggling against the kidnappers. Of course, the doctors were able to confirm that Alistair had no defensive wounds or any wounds for that matter, so there was no altercation between him and the kidnappers. Instead, he simply lay on the floor with their new ransom note and waited until either Detective Marlowe or I found him. Hannahly would have been gone by this point, so it would have looked like she had been taken and Alistair was knocked out trying to stop her from being kidnapped."

"Alistair wanted Detective Bennett, here, to be the one at the condo for two reasons," Sam said. "The first, being a lot smaller and skinnier than I am, it would take a lesser amount of drugs to knock her out. The second was a little more personal, and it's something up to Detective Bennett on whether or not to share."

Cynthia and Joseph turned their attention to Dahlia. She let out a breath before speaking.

"Alistair … hurt … someone I was very close to. I promised one day that I would try to bring him to justice for what he did, so he knew that I had it out for him. Not that it would ever stop him from trying to sweet talk me; charm and charisma were weapons to him. Hell, he even tried to set it up to look like I slept with him, which, thankfully, didn't actually happen," Dahlia said. "Alistair figured that if Hannahly was kidnapped on my watch, it might ruin my career as a cop and hopefully lessen his chances of being caught for what he did to my friend."

"Instead, it sealed his fate," Sam said. "The tech team from the police department did not find any listening or recording devices anywhere in your office, Cynthia, so that eliminated numerous people as suspects. The only people who knew Bennett and I believed the first note to be a hoax were you, Joseph, Alistair, and Hannahly. Seeing that we weren't going to fall for the trap and give them the money they wanted, Hannahly and Alistair ended up coming up with the staged kidnapping."

"But what were they planning to do with the money?" Cynthia asked.

"I found plane tickets and rental information for a charming little villa in Mexico," Dahlia said. "I also found correspondence between Alistair and a girl in Mexico he planned to shack up with once he and Hannahly got down there. It looks to me that he was planning on taking the money and running, leaving Hannahly to fend for herself, alone in a foreign country."

Cynthia glanced over at Joseph, who said nothing. With a stoic expression, she turned back to Sam and Dahlia.

"Thank you both for your assistance," Cynthia said with a heavy sigh. "I requested the best detectives, and that's what I received. The result of this case may have been undesirable, but the truth was revealed, and for that I am grateful."

Sam and Dahlia shook hands with both Joseph and Cynthia before leaving CS Financial. The drive back to the police department was quiet. Sam parked in his usual spot and turned the car off. Neither he nor Dahlia made any effort to get out of the vehicle immediately.

"Sam?" Dahlia said after a moment.

Sam turned his head to look at her but said nothing.

"Thanks for not letting me quit," her voice was light and sincere. "I know you didn't want a partner, but I appreciate you helping me finally see that Alistair was put behind bars, where he belongs. I know it's not because of what he did to Iris, but he's in prison, which is all that matters."

Dahlia waited a few moments to see if Sam had a response, but he stayed silent. She gave him a small smile before starting to exit the cruiser.

"I know what it's like."

Halfway out of the car, Dahlia paused. She sat back down in the passenger's seat.

"You know what that's like?" she asked.

Sam's grip on the steering wheel tightened.

"I know what it's like to be doubted," he managed to get out. "And to lose the one person who always believed in you."

Dahlia said nothing, not wanting to push Sam and cause him to clam up on her for good. Instead, she sat there silently, her hands folded in her lap.

"No one expects a kid from the projects to get anywhere in life," Sam's hands fell from the wheel.

He turned his head to look out the window.

"My mom always said that I could be anything I set my mind to, but sometimes I questioned if she even believed that herself. Kids like me don't grow up and suddenly get a fairy tale ending. Instead, everyone expects that when you come from nothing, you stay nothing, and are always destined to be nothing. My stepfather sure as hell didn't believe that I'd be worth anything and neither did my biological father, at least, I assume so since he didn't stick around."

"But you proved them all wrong," Dahlia tried to reassure him.

Sam shrugged.

"Yeah, I thought so," he said. "But, you know, life has this funny habit of knocking you on your ass the moment you feel like you're getting somewhere. My stepfather beat my mom within an inch of her life, leaving her in a vegetative state and my foster father, the one other person who actually gave a shit about me and helped me turn my life around after what happened with my mom, well, he's gone too … and I couldn't do anything to stop it. Do you know why? It's because of the system."

"The system?" Dahlia repeated.

"Yeah, the system. Think of what happened to Iris. Alistair got away with what he did to her because of the system."

"No, it's because Iris chose not to report him. No report of a crime essentially means that the crime didn't happen in the eyes of the law."

"You can view it that way if you want," Sam said. "But I know the truth."

And it's my job to do something about it.

"Sam, I …" Dahlia paused. "I'm not sure if this means anything, but I'm proud of you. I said it is an honor to work with such a distinguished detective because it truly is. You knew how to get the truth from Hannahly and Alistair while helping me to get justice in a roundabout way for Iris. I'm glad I got to be your partner, even if it was for one case."

Dahlia extended her hand out to Sam, who turned his head to look at her. After a moment, he shook his head.

"You sound like you're going somewhere," Sam said to her.

Dahlia cocked her head to the side, confused.

"But I thought …" she started to say.

"Listen, Bennett, if you want to be a good, no, great cop, you need to learn from the best, and let's face it, I am undeniably the best."

Dahlia smiled, bringing a hand up to her chest and placing it over her heart. Like she had done only minutes before, Sam extended his hand for a handshake, which Dahlia happily accepted.

Maybe having a partner wasn't so bad after all.

SHOOTING STARS

Dahlia pulled her damp curly hair back into a ponytail as she emerged from the woman's locker room at the Odette Police Department. She usually arrived early to get in a workout in the department's fitness center before starting her scheduled shift. Freshly showered and dressed in a lemon colored blouse and beige dress pants, Dahlia made her way up to the bullpen. She dropped her gym bag over by her desk before joining her partner over by the window.

"Morning, Sam," she said.

"Bennett," Detective Samuel Marlowe said, still focused on something outside.

Dahlia followed Sam's gaze out the window and found the ground below buzzing with activity. There seemed to be an endless line of people holding brightly colored posters or photos, along with several individuals from local media outlets, as evidenced by the cameras and microphones. Something big happened, and word had spread like wildfire through the small town of Odette, Colorado.

"They're all here for her?" Dahlia asked though she was well aware of the answer.

"Nah, Bennett, they're here for me," Sam said with a smirk and a wink. "Didn't you know the show, *The Pretty and the Powerful*, was about yours truly?"

Dahlia chuckled, and out of the corner of her eye, she could see Sam smirking.

"Sure, Sam, if you say so," she replied.

"I suppose we should get down there," Sam said, stepping away from the window. "She should be here any moment, and we'll need to usher her inside before the media sharks get to her."

Dahlia followed him away from the window and out of the bullpen. Sam instructed Dahlia to wait at the back entrance while he kept the gawkers, fans and the media at the front door of the department occupied by answering their questions. The diversion would hopefully allow Tamsen Wilde to slip into the police department unnoticed.

The crowd ate up the ham Sam gave them, with most people still interested in hearing about the 'hero cop,' the title, Dahlia discovered, that came from his heroics during the shooting at Odette Senior High School nearly two years ago. Dahlia could hear every few words from her partner as he addressed the spectators via the podium microphones, causing her to roll her viridian green eyes and shake her head.

"Is it true that Tamsen Wilde is being brought in on suspicion of murder?" one reporter asked.

"Where are you getting your news from? The tabloids?" was Sam's retort.

Dahlia laughed softly.

"Are you sure you didn't see a scene from the movie they're filming here?" Sam asked.

He sounded like he was on a roll. While Sam played the entertainer, Dahlia watched as an unmarked police car quietly pulled up to the back of the building where she was waiting.

"Thanks for creating the diversion, Detective," Officer Denomy said as he stepped out of the driver's seat. "People have been mobbing us since we left the hotel. Seriously, we had to throw a blond wig on one of the forensics techs and pretend she was Tamsen and stuff her in the back of a patrol car to give the press a red herring while I snuck the real Miss Wilde out the service entrance."

Dahlia waved him off.

"No problem; my partner's having fun out there anyway," she replied. "Are you ready to bring her in?"

"Yes, ma'am," Denomy said. "We're ready."

He came around the front of the car to the rear passenger's side door. Denomy opened the door and helped a stunning bleach blond twenty-something out of the back seat. Tamsen Wilde, an up and coming Hollywood starlet, had been brought in on suspicion of murder. She looked frightened, Dahlia observed, with her ordinarily bright caramel eyes appearing watery and swollen, an indicator that she'd been crying recently. Tamsen seemed genuinely distraught, but she still was an actress, and based on the promos Dahlia had seen advertising a television show Tamsen was in, she could convincingly turn on the waterworks when the cameras were rolling.

However, the cameras, journalists, and adoring fans were all out front; there was no one for Tamsen to perform for. Perhaps the starlet was not pretending after all.

Denomy escorted Tamsen inside to an interrogation room while Dahlia fetched Sam. They then joined the actress in Interrogation Room 3.

"Well, Ms. Wilde," Sam began to say as he and Dahlia entered the room. "It's great to meet you, though I wish it were under better circumstances."

Tamsen dabbed her eyes with a tissue, the expensive silver bracelets around her wrists tinkling slightly from the movement.

"Thank you for not making me come in through the front," she said, her voice hoarse and tired. "The press would have a field day with that one. And the last thing I need right now is more bad press after my whole rehab stint a few months ago."

As her name implied, Tamsen Wilde enjoyed the glitz and glamour of the celebrity lifestyle, earning her a reputation of a party-girl and the nickname "Wilde Child." She and some co-stars were filming a scene for a movie up at Lake Odette over the past few days, staying at a local hotel until the end of the shoot. Tamsen, along with fellow actors Xander Mathis and Kora Sheerwood, had been seen partying at some local establishments, drinking and with rumored drug use.

"What happened last night?" Sam asked. "Can you help us figure out how Xander Mathis wound up dead in your hotel room?"

"I ... I don't remember ..." Tamsen's voice trailed off.

Sam and Dahlia exchanged a knowing look. Feigning a lack of recollection was the oldest trick in the book. Tamsen glanced between the two detectives with a frown.

"I know what you're thinking," she said. "And I'm not lying. I wouldn't hurt Xander. I loved him."

"Loved?" Sam repeated. "Last I saw in the tabloids, you and Xander had broken up because of infidelity."

Dahlia raised an eyebrow at Sam.

"You read celebrity gossip magazines?" she asked, a smirk on her lips.

"No," Sam said, waving her off. "My foster mother does and my foster sister, Clarice, has some copies in the waiting room of her law office."

"Yeah, that's what the story was," Tamsen said. "But it was only that, a story. Our managers fabricated the story for free publicity. We're playing the leads in this rom-com, and Xander's supposed affair has generated a lot of hype for the movie."

"Sure."

"Seriously! You can ask Ross all about it!"

"Oh, we will," Sam jotted down the name Tamsen had given him. "But, for now, let's try and figure out what happened last night. Several witnesses put you, Xander and Kora at a club downtown; what time did you leave?"

"The club closed at two in the morning, so we headed back to the hotel right around then," Tamsen said. "Kora said she had more booze in her room, so we went there to keep partying."

"If Kora had the alcohol in her room like you said," Dahlia said. "How did you and Xander end up in your room?"

"Kora had a morning radio interview, so her manager cut her off early," Tamsen replied. "Kora gave Xander and me some of the beer and champagne she had, and we went to my room."

"What did the two of you do when you returned to your room?" Sam asked.

"That's where it gets ... fuzzy ..." Tamsen said, looking down.

She brought her hands up to fiddle with a strand of her hair as she nibbled on her bottom lip.

"Please tell us what you do remember," Dahlia said.

Tamsen let out a breath.

"After we got the booze from Kora, we headed across the hall to my room," she said, her brows furrowing. "Xander and I talked. He started telling me how he planned to 'rekindle' things with me for the press to see to add some additional hype during the premiere party. After a while, we laid on the bed, watching television and smoking pot. The next thing I remember after that is Ross coming into my room this morning and telling me Xander was dead ..."

Sam scribbled a word down on his notes for Dahlia to read. She nodded in agreement to his suggestion of 'poison.' Before any further questions could be asked, the interrogation room door flew open.

"All right, detectives, that's enough; there will be no more speaking to Ms. Wilde until the studio attorney arrives."

Sam and Dahlia looked at the girl with glasses wearing the striped shirt.

"And you are who, exactly?" Sam asked.

"I'm Mr. Serrado's assistant, Nichole," the girl adjusted her glasses. "Mr. Serrado said that I am to stay here with Ms. Wilde until the attorney arrives to make sure that no one speaks to her until she has legal representation present."

Sam rolled his eyes and Dahlia sighed.

"Fine. Whatever," he grumbled. "Let's go, Bennett."

Nichole stood with her chest puffed out as Sam and Dahlia passed by her on their way out of the interrogation room.

★★★

Without being able to speak to Tamsen again until she had an attorney present, Sam and Dahlia drove out to the hotel where Tamsen was staying to investigate instead. The parking lot was packed with newshounds and fans all trying to get a glimpse of something, anything. Sam and Dahlia fought their way through the crowd and headed inside the five-story neoclassical style building.

The fifth floor housed the suites, which was where Tamsen, Xander, Kora and their managers were staying. Police officers were stationed at both stairwells on the top floor, the elevator banks, and outside room 508 to ensure no unauthorized personnel gained entry into the crime scene.

"Is everything all photographed and documented?" Sam asked one of the crime scene technicians as he put on a fresh pair of latex gloves.

"Yes, Sir, Detective," the tech replied. "Scene's all yours."

With the go-ahead given, Sam and Dahlia proceeded inside room 508. The room was an exquisite suite, decked out with several luxury accommodations, two queen-sized beds, a large flat screen television, full kitchen, and Jacuzzi. The picturesque image of the deluxe room was ruined by the body of Xander Mathis on the queen-sized bed furthest from the door to the room.

The body of one of Hollywood's "Top 50 Hunks" was lying face down near the edge of the mattress. He was still dressed in the outfit he was seen wearing when out with Tamsen and Kora the previous night, a designer white polo, custom-made dress shoes, a stunning gold watch and several gold chains, which hung off the bed from around his neck. Xander's auburn colored hair was still styled neatly, a faint odor of hairspray and cologne still lingering. On the deep jade-green carpet was several empty beer and champagne bottles. An ashtray with a couple of roaches sat on the nightstand next to the head of the bed.

"If Xander's still wearing his clothes from last night, at least based on the millions of pictures that were shown on the news last night about the three of them," Dahlia began to say as Sam examined the body. "It's likely that Tamsen's telling the truth about leaving the club and coming back to her room after having some drinks with Kora in her room."

"It seems that way so far," Sam said.

Carefully moving Xander's right arm, Sam's silver eyes narrowed.

"Bennett," he called over to Dahlia. "Look around for any used needles; Xander's got fresh pockmarks."

Sam continued looking over the body while Dahlia searched every nook and cranny of the room for any needles, ultimately coming up empty-handed.

"There are cameras in every hallway, right?" Dahlia said to Sam. "Can we pull the recordings to see if anyone entered or exited Tamsen's room? Maybe a staff member changed the garbage or something."

"Good idea, Bennett," Sam replied. "Go make friends with security and get those tapes. If not, call Judge Mars; he should be able to get you a court order for the tapes ASAP."

"On it," Dahlia said as she headed toward the door.

Sam looked around to ensure he was entirely by himself before stepping over to the nightstand. There were a few prescription bottles on the mahogany wood surface, the contents of which were a variety of pills. Sam slipped some of the tablets into his pocket and replaced the bottle back to the place he found it. His stock of painkillers was starting to run low. Besides, it wasn't like the dead guy had any further use of them.

A knock on the hotel room door made Sam jump, causing him to drop the bottle of pills on the floor.

"Fuck," he said through gritted teeth.

"Sam, what happened?" Dahlia asked when she poked her head in the room.

Shit. Why are you here, Bennett? Why aren't you making friends with the people in security?

"I, uh, was checking out the prescription bottles and dropped one when you scared the shit out of me when you knocked on the door," Sam said.

"Oh. Do you think they're important?"

"Maybe."

"We can take a closer look when we get back to the station," Dahlia said. "I ran into the Medical Examiner on my way down to the security office and thought I'd bring her up here. Are you ready for her?"

"Yeah, send her in," Sam said.

Well, shit.

★★★

Dahlia frowned to herself as she made her way toward the elevator. Sam seemed unusually jumpy when she went to inform him that the medical examiner had arrived. He looked like the kid who was caught with his hand in the cookie jar. But why?

Dahlia pressed the button to take her down to the ground floor. She folded her arms across her chest as the elevator began its descent with a soft hum. *Maybe it's because this is a high-profile case, with tons of media coverage. But, then again, didn't Sam thrive on that sort of attention? He seemed to, at least.*

Reaching the ground floor, Dahlia stepped out of the elevator. She stopped by the front desk to get directions to the security office so she could collect the security footage. The head of security was a serious young man in his early thirties.

"Yes, Detective," Al Linklater said. "It shouldn't be a problem to secure those tapes for you-"

The phone rang, interrupting Al. He excused himself for a moment to take the call. Dahlia observed the wall of security monitors while the head of security answered his call.

"O-oh, I see ..." Al seemed surprised with whatever the caller was saying. "Um ... yes ... that should be fine ... I-I-I'll ... yes, I'll be looking forward to it. Yes ... it's a great help. Thank you."

Listening to the conversation caused Dahlia's eyebrows to furrow. That didn't sound like a regular business phone call. It sounded personal.

"Is everything okay?" Dahlia asked Al when he joined her at the wall of monitors.

Al began straightening his uniform and removing invisible specks of lint and dust.

"Oh, yes, everything's fine, Detective Bennett," he said.

Dahlia waited a few seconds before speaking again.

"How about those security tapes?" she asked.

"Oh! Right!" Al said. "I-I-I'm sorry, Detective Bennett, but you will need to get a subpoena if you would like the tapes."

"A subpoena?" Dahlia repeated. "I'm a bit confused. You were about to get them for me before the phone call came in; did something happen?"

"No, everything's fine," Al said, ushering her toward the door. "If you'll please excuse me, there is nothing further I can do until you have a subpoena."

Before she could say anything further, Dahlia was out in the hallway, and the security office door was closing behind her. It was time to call Judge Mars.

★★★

Concluding their investigation of the crime scene, Sam and Dahlia returned to the police department. Upon arrival, the Captain informed them that Kora, Xander and Tamsen's co-star, and Ross Serrado, Tamsen's manager, were present to give their statements, accompanied by their attorneys who both arrived on red eyes to get into town as quickly as possible. Sam met with Kora while Dahlia spoke with Ross.

Kora was young, talented and beautiful, like Xander and Tamsen, Sam considered as he observed her through the interrogation room window. She had wavy chocolate brown hair that cascaded down the ivory skin of her back, which was revealed by the low cut of her silky red blouse. Her makeup was meticulously applied, as if she were going to be walking the red carpet that day instead of making a statement down at the police department. Having seen enough, Sam headed into the interrogation room.

"Miss Sheerwood, thank you for coming down to the department."

Despite being indoors, the starlet had on a pair of dark aviator style sunglasses. Kora lowered her glasses minutely with a perfectly polished hand and her dark smokey-eyes, which appeared almost black under the interrogation room's lighting, roved over Sam's face before becoming shielded once again by her sunglasses.

"You're pretty cute for a police officer," she told Sam.

"Well, thank you," Sam grinned. "I thought so too."

Kora let out a melodious laugh. The door to the interrogation room burst open, and a tall man in a garish silver suit strolled inside. He headed to the table and took a seat next to Kora, placing his briefcase on the table, folding his hands on top of it, and then looking at Sam with turquoise blue eyes that seemed bright and eager.

"Bryson Lobos, Kora's attorney," he said. "You are not to speak to my client unless I am present, Detective."

Sam held his hands up in mock surrender.

"No worries, bud," he said. "I was only introducing myself to our up and coming starlet."

Kora put her hand on Bryson's arm.

"Bry, do the special introduction," she said. "Please?"

Bryson flashed her his million-watt grin. *No wonder she wears sunglasses all the time with this walking disco ball,* Sam mused.

"Anything for you, Kora," Bryson said. "My name is Bryson Lobos. Lobos, Spanish for wolves. I am a wolf, ready to stalk my prey before landing the deadly strike!"

The attorney finished his spiel with a dramatic growl while bending his fingers to resemble claws. Kora smiled and clapped. Sam closed his eyes and took a breath. *These two ... I have no words.*

"Good work, Lobos," he said instead. "But do you mind if we get down to business? There's a dead guy who isn't going to solve his own murder."

"That would make *such* a good show, wouldn't it, Bry?" Kora said to Bryson.

"It would, Kora. You are a genius," Bryson replied.

Shoot me now.

"Anyway," Sam tapped his pen on his notepad. "Back on Xander Mathis; what can you tell me about last night's incident?"

"Tamsen killed Xander," Kora said with a sniff, lifting her head and giving off an air of smugness.

"That's what we're trying to determine."

"No, I mean I know she did it."

"How so?"

Kora turned to Bryson.

"Go ahead," he said.

"Because of the cheating scandal. Tamsen was distraught over Xander's cheating."

"Tamsen said it was a setup," Sam said to the starlet.

"Oh no, it was definitely real."

"Where's your proof?"

Kora turned to Bryson again.

"Detective, this information cannot leave this room," the attorney said. "Kora is under contract with the studio to keep this information secret from the press for the time being."

"Listen, the only thing I care about is figuring out what happened to Xander," Sam said. "I don't give a shit what your client may or may not have done concerning the cheating scandal."

Wait, so did Kora cause Tamsen and Xander to break up? What a bitch.

"It's okay, Kora," Bryson placed his hand on top of Kora's. "You can tell the detective what happened."

"You want proof?" Kora asked Sam.

She pointed to her smirking blood red lips.

"I was the woman Xander was kissing in the photo."

"Did Tamsen know that?" Sam asked.

"She didn't have a clue," Kora replied, sounding triumphant. "I had on a wig and six-inch heels so I wouldn't be immediately recognizable."

"Aren't you and Tamsen supposed to be friends? Why would you do something like that?"

Kora flipped her hair over her shoulder with her hand. She leaned back in her chair and folded her arms across her chest.

"The media assumes we're friends because we've been to some parties and clubs at the same time," Kora said, a hint of annoyance in her voice. "In reality, I can't stand her."

Sam eyed Kora for a moment. He remembered something about Tamsen winning a role over Kora being mentioned in a magazine a while back. Perhaps the latter's resentment stemmed from that.

"Say, Kora, what did you think of Tamsen's role in that office drama? You know, the one she was nominated for an award for?" Sam asked with a smile, seeing if poking the lioness would yield any answers.

"Kora, don't say anything," Bryson's smile was quickly replaced by a serious expression.

I must be on to something, Sam noted.

"No, Bryson! I can't pretend anymore!" Kora slammed her palms down on the table. "That was my role … that was my Emmy, not Tamsen's … that bitch—"

"Call me crazy if you want," Sam started to say. "But it almost sounds like you're throwing Tamsen under the bus simply because you don't like her."

Kora smirked.

"You're correct, Detective. I do believe you're crazy."

"Am I? The only evidence you've given me regarding Tamsen's guilt is the supposed anger she felt over Xander's infidelity."

Bryson leaned over to Kora and whispered something to her. She got up from the table, getting up to grab her purse from off the window sill before returning to her seat. She withdrew a clear Ziploc bag. Inside, there was a needle with a bright orange cap. She placed it on the table and slid it forward to Sam. Kora's face lit up victoriously at Sam's dumbfounded expression.

"I can tell by your face that you are well aware of what this is," she said. "It's proof positive of Tamsen's guilt. I thought you were competent enough to arrest Tamsen without it, but it appears not."

Sam instantly seized the bag.

"And how, pray tell, did this little gem end up in your possession, since you claim you're not the killer and all," he asked.

"It came in a box with a bouquet of flowers I received this morning," Kora said. "The note attached to the vase-which is still in my room, by the way-said that the needle was an insurance policy in case Tamsen was not arrested for Xander's murder. In this case, it's insurance to guarantee that I am not suspected of Xander's murder."

Stepping out of the room, Sam immediately arranged for the needle to be taken down to the lab to be analyzed.

That story sounds like a bunch of bullshit to me, Sam thought with a frown. *Complete and utter bullshit.*

★★★

The attorney waited until the detective left the room to speak to his client.

"Good work," Bryson said to Kora.

Kora smiled smugly at her attorney.

"My finest performance yet, don't cha think?"

"You never cease to amaze me, my dear."

★★★

Dahlia headed into Interrogation Room 2, where Ross Serrado was pacing back and forth impatiently.

"Sorry for the wait, Mr. Serrado," she said when she entered the room. "My partner and I just returned from the crime scene."

Ross met Dahlia at the doorway and offered his hand. After a handshake, he kissed her hand. Dahlia did her best to keep the pleasant expression glued on her face. *As soon as this is done, I'm pouring a gallon of hand sanitizer on my hand.*

"All is forgiven, my dear," Ross said, his grin as brilliant and shiny as his bald head. "I hate to be rude, honey, but we need to make this quick; my phone's been blowing up non-stop ever since the news of Tamsen's involvement in Xander's death was leaked. Her publicist and I have a ton of damage control to attend to."

"Of course," Dahlia said. "I'll do whatever I can to get you out of here as soon as possible, okay?"

She looked over at the professionally dressed blonde sitting at the table with a briefcase on her lap.

"Are you Mr. Serrado's attorney?"

"Yes, I'm Emilia Cochrane," the woman said. "I'm also assisting with Ms. Wilde's case, so I guess you could say that I'm doing double duty right now."

"Nice to meet you," Dahlia shook hands with Emilia before turning her attention back to Ross. "I'm ready whenever you are, Mr. Serrado."

"Well, I won't beat around the bush and waste your time, Detective," Ross said. "Tamsen is guilty."

Dahlia pursed her lips. *Well, that was straightforward. But why does he think that?*

"And what makes you say that, Mr. Serrado?" she asked.

"Ross, honey, please," the manager said with a wink.

Dahlia bit her tongue.

"And what makes you say that, Mr. ... Ross?"

"There was no one else around to kill Xander. Kora was in her room, and I was in my room. That eliminates two people. Out of four, that only leaves you with two more people, Xander and Tamsen. If one of them ends up dead, then it's the one who's left who's guilty, am I right? Plus, Tamsen had a motive, something clearly all over the news right now with Xander's recent actions and all that."

"Have you read Agatha Christie's, *And Then There Were None*?" Dahlia asked. "The one person who's still standing at the end doesn't necessarily mean he or she is the guilty party."

"Touché," Ross said. "But, regardless, my statement still stands. Tamsen is guilty."

★★★

Sam and Dahlia met back at their desks in the bullpen afterward.

"What words of wisdom did the manager have to share with you, Bennett?" Sam asked as Dahlia took a seat at her desk.

"He thinks she's guilty," Dahlia replied, arms folded across her chest as she leaned back in her desk chair.

"Motive?"

"He didn't say explicitly, but Ross implied it was over Xander's alleged affair."

"Wait a second," Sam frowned. "Didn't Tamsen say that it was all a setup and that her manager was in on it?"

"She did."

"Okay, one of them is lying, but which one and why?"

"I don't think we have enough evidence to determine that yet," Dahlia said. "What about the medications you were looking at in the hotel room? Maybe this wasn't even murder, but a suicide or an accidental OD."

Shit. I was hoping she forgot about that.

"I'd ... rather wait for that lead," Sam said.

"Why? It might be something."

"Exactly, it *might* be something, but we don't know for sure that it is. I'd rather wait to find out the toxicology results from the ME before we head down that route."

Their conversation was halted when Sam received a phone call.

"Marlowe," Sam answered his desk phone.

Dahlia watched her partner's confused yet intrigued expression as he listened to the caller.

"What was that about?" she asked as he returned the phone to its cradle.

"Apparently, there is some dude who is being irritatingly insistent that he needs to see Tamsen," Sam got up from his chair. "You stay here and watch the security video that came in, and I'll go see what's going on downstairs."

Sam left Dahlia in the bullpen and made his way downstairs to the booking area.

"You rang?" he said to the desk sergeant on duty.

"Yeah," the desk sergeant said. "Kenney's keeping an eye on this guy. He didn't say anything except that he needed to see Tamsen. He *needed* to see Tamsen. When we said he couldn't see her, he, well, to put it frankly, threw a hissy-fit. We threw him in a holding cell to cool off."

"I see," Sam replied with a chuckle at the sergeant's impression of the man. "Thanks, Shannon."

Sam found Officer Kenney waiting with a plain looking middle-aged man.

"You the one asking for Tamsen?" he asked as he leaned against the door frame of the holding cell.

The frumpy man practically flew over to Sam.

"Yes. I need to see her," he said. "I need to see my darling angel."

"Angel?" Sam repeated, an eyebrow raised.

"Yes, yes, yes," the man bobbed his head, his coke-bottle glasses sliding down his nose from the movement. "Tamsen is my girlfriend."

A bemused smile crossed Sam's lips. Tamsen was dating this guy? Sure, and he was the king of Sweden.

"All right, Romeo," Sam said. "Tamsen gave me a couple of questions to ask you before she sees you; think you can handle that, big guy?"

"Of course," the man couldn't contain his smile. "Anything for my angel."

Sam dismissed Kenney, taking the officer's seat after his departure. He motioned for the man to join him on the bench and he shuffled over to where Sam sat, staring at the bench for a moment with a frown.

"Don't worry, the bench won't bite," Sam said.

The man looked up at him, then to the bench and back again before he decided to take a seat next to Sam.

"I'm Sam. I'm working with Tamsen. Who might you be?"

"My name is Devon Sinclair."

"You from around here, Devon?"

"No. Tamsen and I live in Hollywood."

"How did you manage to score a babe like Tamsen Wilde?"

"It was after I saw Tamsen on television for the first time. She was playing such a mature, complex role at only fifteen years old that most women three times her age couldn't pull off," Devon said, a dreamy look in his coffee brown eyes. "I knew we were meant to be together. I wrote to Tamsen, professing my love for her."

"And she wrote you back?" Sam asked.

"No; instead, she'd send me messages through her roles on television," Devon said. "She told me she loved me too and asked me to move to California with her."

"Can't turn down an offer like that."

"Right. Can I please see my angel now? I've been worried sick ever since that man got into her hotel room. I tried to get to her last night, but I couldn't."

"What man?" Sam asked.

He fully expected Devon to describe Xander, so he was surprised at the response he received.

"This man was older," Devon said to Sam. "Last night, he went into Tamsen's room. She was with her friend, well, the guy she used to be friends with until the media tried to say they were together, which was untrue, of course. Tamsen and I talked it over and-"

"Focus, buddy."

"Tamsen and her friend were watching television on the bed together. Whatever they were watching must have been boring because they both fell asleep. The guy went into the room and did something to the friend—"

"What did he do?" Sam asked.

"I don't know, but I got it on tape."

Sam let out a slow breath.

"Okay, Devon, I have two questions for you," he said, doing his best to keep his voice even, as he was unsure of whether he wanted to punch the man or hug him. "One, do you have the recording? Two, where the hell were you recording from?"

Devon fished around in his coat pocket before pulling out a USB.

"I made a copy for Tamsen to prove she was innocent of hurting her friend," he replied. "That's why I need to see my darling angel."

"In that case, Devon," Sam said. "You and I are both trying to help Tamsen. I'll take the video—"

"No!" Devon clutched the USB to his chest. "You take this and then you won't let me see her ... I won't give this to you until I see my angel ..."

Sam ran a hand through his golden-brown hair.

"Devon, I'll make you a deal," he said. "I'll let you see Tamsen, but you can't talk to her. Department rules or some shit like that. In return, you give me the USB so I can do my job and help your woman."

Devon thought over Sam's proposition for a moment. His rigid posture relaxed.

"All right then, let's go see her," Sam said.

He got up from the bench and headed out of the holding cell, motioning for Devon to follow him. They passed a few occupied cells, pausing in front of cell 8, Devon nearly bumping into Sam when he stopped.

"There you are, lover boy," Sam said. "Miss Tamsen Wilde, safe and sound."

Devon eagerly peered through the window of the holding cell. Sam could see the immediate reassuring and calming effect it had on Devon. He waited a few moments and then cleared his throat.

"All right, Devon, it's time to hold up your end of the bargain," Sam said, holding his hand out.

Without looking away from the cell, Devon placed the USB in Sam's hand.

"You never answered my second question," Sam pointed out as he put the USB in the breast pocket of his lilac dress shirt. "Where, pray tell, did you put your recording devices?"

"I went up to the roof and installed a hidden camera in the window," Devon replied. "She likes me to keep an eye on her when we're apart; helps her feel safe."

Sam momentarily imagined Devon scaling the roof, a la Spiderman, to install the camera outside the window, before shaking his head.

★★★

Examining the contents of the USB was put on the back burner when Sam returned to the bullpen. He found Dahlia's desk vacant and a note on his computer.

Sam,
Got the name of the doctor that prescribed all of the medicines.
Going to check him out.
Meet me at Dr. Stanley Sharpe's office on Blayden Avenue
—Dahlia

"Goddamn it, Bennett!" Sam threw the note down on his desk and grabbed his keys before heading out the door to join Dahlia at the doctor's office.

She's really hell-bent on this medication-angle, he considered. *I need to find a way to get her off this lead.*

The drive to Blayden Avenue took approximately twenty minutes. When Sam rushed into the office, he found Dahlia sitting in the lobby, waiting for him.

"Oh, good, you got my message," she said, rising from the chair she had been sitting in.

"Yeah, I did," Sam said with a frown. "What the hell are you doing?"

"What do you mean?" Dahlia asked. "The various medications that were at the scene were all prescribed to Xander. Since he's not from Odette, the doctor he saw is obviously not his primary care physician. Before prescribing anything, Dr. Sharpe should have requested Xander's medical records to check what prescriptions he was on, in case one of the meds conflicted with another one. That negligence could have led to Xander's death."

"Good point," Sam admitted through gritted teeth.

Damn, this is getting out of hand.

"Bennett, why don't you take the lead on this one?" Sam said. "If you're so dead set on seeing this lead through to the end, then you should be the one asking the questions."

Dahlia's eyes widened in surprise for a split second.

"You want *me* to lead the questioning?" she asked.

"That's what I said, isn't it?"

"Well, yeah, but it's kind of a surprise."

"I'm full of surprises, Bennett, get used to it," Sam said. "Now, go get 'em, tiger."

Dahlia turned and headed toward the door leading into the office. Making a left turn, she arrived at Dr. Sharpe's personal office, Sam right behind her.

"Dr. Sharpe," Dahlia said to the tiny old man sitting at his desk after knocking on the open door-frame.

Stanley Sharpe looked up from his paperwork, his brown eyes moving from Dahlia to Sam and back again from beneath his thick brown glasses.

"Hello, deary," he said. "What can I do for you?"

"I'm Detective Bennett, and this is Detective Marlowe," Dahlia said. "We have a couple questions for you about a patient of yours, Xander Mathis."

"Who?" Dr. Sharpe asked.

He scratched his head with a wrinkly, crooked finger.

"Oh, you mean the boy from the movies? Yes, he stopped in here a few days ago."

"What can you tell us about him?"

"He's a nice boy, but kind of all over the place," Stanley said. "He came to me to get a refill on some of his prescriptions since he was going to be in town for a while."

"Yes, he had several painkillers and some sleep aids prescribed to him," Dahlia said. "Why did you prescribe all of those medications to Xander?"

"Why?" Stanley repeated, adjusting his glasses. "He had a script for them. I passed them along to the pharmacy like he asked me to."

"Did you check the side effects of the drugs? If they conflict with any of the other medications?"

"I was going to do that, honey, but the boy was in a hurry to get to the movie set; he wouldn't let me get out my books and check the medications."

"Get out your books?" Sam repeated. "You cross check everything by hand?"

"Yes. I never got the hang of that computer gizmo," Stanley said. "Besides, it's worked for me for fifty years. My father always said 'if it ain't broke, don't fix it.'"

After a few additional questions, Dahlia and Sam excused themselves from Stanley's office.

"What's your verdict, Bennett?" Sam asked.

"I believe what Dr. Sharpe said about Xander not wanting to spend too much time hanging around the office," Dahlia said. "If you're a drug addict abusing pills, you probably don't want to be spending a lot of time around people that can call you out on it, right?"

Sam let out a little laugh, which sounded more like an indignant snort.

"That's pretty much junkie 101," he said.

"Right. Plus, if Xander wanted his medications that bad and Dr. Sharpe wouldn't fill them for him, Xander could have gone to the hospital in an attempt to get a script there."

"Exactly. Xander probably chose Dr. Sharpe because he is practically the definition of 'old-fashioned.' Less of a chance of digging into his little drug problem, right?" Sam said. "But does that equate to negligence on the doctor's part, Bennett? I don't think it does."

"Probably not."

"Also, we have to wait for Tamsen's drug test to come back, but I'm guessing that her results are going to show similar drugs to what Xander took and she's still alive."

"Okay, you've made your point," Dahlia said. "Do you think that Kora will submit to a drug test? See if she took any of the drugs too?"

"My guess is no, but it never hurts to ask," Sam said. "You can ask because she had no interest in hearing what I had to say."

"Fine. I'll ask her," Dahlia said before heading toward the waiting room door.

"Good plan."

Shoving his hands in his pockets, Sam let out a quiet sigh of relief as he followed Dahlia out of the office.

★★★

Sitting on the patio of a five-star restaurant, Kora sipped daintily at her glass of wine. She would occasionally flick her hair or tip her dark sunglasses down to appease the fans that had gathered on the sidewalk some feet away to catch a glimpse of her.

"It's my job to throw them a bone now and then," she told Bryson before sending him off to shoo the onlookers away. "But enough's enough."

Bryson, the ever-obedient wolf, did what Kora requested and left the table to deal with the crowd.

"Excuse me, Miss Sheerwood?"

Kora turned her attention away from Bryson dealing with the crowd and looked at the woman who had approached her table. She lowered her sunglasses.

"What do you want?"

"I'm Detective Bennett. I'm working with Detective Marlowe on Xander's case," Dahlia said.

"Oh, right," Kora replaced her sunglasses. "What do you want?"

"We'd like you to submit to a drug test."

"A drug test? For what?"

"There were narcotics found at the scene," Dahlia said. "We'd like to determine who may have taken them. Standard procedure."

Kora folded her arms across her chest.

"Sorry, sweetie, but no can do. The last thing I need is for my drug results to mysteriously find their way into the tabloids."

"It would remain confidential, only for the investigation—"

"I said no. End of story. If you want a drug screen, get a warrant or whatever it is you legal people call it," Kora said. "Now, if you'll excuse me, I have to make a phone call."

★★★

Once Dahlia had left her alone, Kora whipped her cell phone from her purse and placed a call.

"It's me. We have a problem."

"What kind of problem?"

"A huge problem."

"That didn't answer my question, Kora."

"Just get your ass down here."

"Fine. I'll be there in ten."

★★★

Sam made his way to the bullpen the following morning, file folders in hand.

"Here's the preliminary autopsy report, fresh from the ME's office," he held up the files.

Dahlia looked up from her computer screen.

"Great," she said. "What's it say?"

"The Doc found some interesting things in Xander's stomach."

"Like what?"

"Undigested pills," Sam said. "And only a few of them."

"Wait, so you mean that Xander likely didn't overdose on pills?"

"It doesn't seem that way. We still have to wait for the tox screen to come back to confirm, but it doesn't seem that the pills were what killed him."

"Then it still might be murder after all," Dahlia said.

"It's possible," Sam said.

He pointed to Dahlia's computer.

"What are you working on?"

"I'm reviewing the video footage from the hotel," Dahlia said.

"I don't understand how people can be so wishy-washy. 'Oh, we want to help you in any way we can to find out what happened,' but when we ask for video footage from the hallway, it's like you're asking for the crown jewels," Sam said. "Thank god for Judge Mars granting us the subpoena, right?"

"Yeah, that did seem a little strange. The security manager seemed completely on board with sharing the footage, and then five minutes later, it was like I was speaking to an entirely different person. Thankfully, Judge Mars issued the subpoena to get the tapes, and I'm taking a look at them now to see if there's anything on there. He's going to get a warrant for a drug test too, for Kora, since she won't voluntarily take one."

"Speaking of which, anything suspicious on the tapes?"

"Well, Tamsen's manager was surprisingly on the prowl the night before the murder, and spending some 'quality time' with Kora, but other than that, not really. Tamsen's timeline seems accurate, which is good for us, but bad for her. No one except for her manager, who was in there for no more than five minutes, went into Tamsen's room that night."

"Hmm ..." Sam said as he took a seat at his desk and inserted the USB into his computer.

"What's that?" Dahlia asked.

"A video the Fruit Loops guy from yesterday shot by installing a camera in Tamsen's hotel window."

"Say what?"

"I'm not repeating myself, Bennett," Sam said as he pulled up the video in question. "I never got a chance to check it out yesterday since you decided to go spend your time interrogating little old men instead."

Dahlia rolled her eyes at him. The video gave Sam and Dahlia a fly-on-the-wall view inside Tamsen's room. It showed Tamsen and Xander lying on the bed, drinking, and smoking. A short time later, they both seemingly passed out. As if he had been lying in wait for that very moment, the man Devon was referring to appeared in Tamsen's room minutes after the two stars fell into unconsciousness. Sam paused the video.

"What time did you see him go into the room on the hotel cam?" he asked.

Dahlia consulted her notes.

"Time stamp said 3:15 a.m."

Sam examined the time stamp on Devon's video; it was a match. He let the video continue. The two detectives watched with anxious anticipation as the man produced a needle and headed directly over to Xander's body. The man inserted the needle into Xander's arm, forced the contents into his body and then removed the needle. He carefully wrapped the unconscious Tamsen's hand around the syringe before putting it into a fresh Ziploc bag. The man checked Xander's pulse and breathing. Seemingly satisfied, the man hurried from the hotel room. Sam paused the video.

"What time did you see him leave?" Sam asked.

"About three twenty-one," Dahlia replied.

Sam spun around in his desk chair to face Dahlia.

"Well, we now have another nail in the coffin of our killer," he said. "But the question still remains of whether the killer was the mastermind behind the crime or if someone else was the brains and he was merely the executioner. We need to make absolutely sure that we have all our ducks in a row before we arrest our killer or else another guilty person might go free; we can't let that happen, especially with all of the press covering this case. How bad would it make the Odette PD look if that happened?"

"Doesn't it seem odd to you that someone so involved with film and the movies would be so easily caught on security camera like that?"

"You would think so," Sam paused. "Wait a second; Bennett, you said that the security guard was all on board with helping us until he received a phone call and then he changed his mind, right?"

"Yes."

"What if our killer bribed him to not give us the tapes because he knew what was going to be on there?"

Dahlia's eyebrows shot up.

"I think you might be right, Sam," she said. "I'll get a warrant for the phone records and the security guard's bank account."

"Might be right?" Sam repeated. "Bennett, I'm always right."

★★★

Tamsen sat in the interrogation room, her hands around a hot cup of tea. She stared silently into it as if it held all of the answers she was longing for.

"I'm sorry to have to break this news to you, Tamsen," Sam said, folding his hands together and placing them on the table.

Tamsen shook her head.

"I have to know," she said. "Play the video. Let me see what happened."

Sam pressed play on the laptop sitting on the table. Tamsen watched as her manager, Ross, slipped out of his room and made his way across the hall to Kora's. The latter greeted him with a long, dramatic kiss before pulling him into her room. Ross did not return to his room until shortly before eight the next morning.

"They've been having an affair," Tamsen said.

The tears welled up in her eyes as she watched the video.

"You didn't know about their relationship?" Dahlia asked.

"No, I swear. If anything, I would have thought she was sleeping with the lawyer guy, Bryson," Tamsen looked between Sam and Dahlia. "Why? Why would they do this?"

"We're still working on that one," Sam said. "Wait, you think Kora might have been having an affair with that attorney guy?"

"Yeah," Tamsen shrugged. "I've seen him come out of her trailer a few times when we were on set in California. His clothes were all rumpled, and he looked like he ran a marathon, you know, all sweaty and stuff. I figured they were sleeping together, but I don't think Bryson's married, so it didn't matter to me 'cause they weren't technically cheating on anyone."

"What about conflict of interest?" Dahlia asked.

"I don't know about that. Ross or Emilia usually take care of that kind of stuff for me."

"How about Xander? Did Kora ever put the moves on him?"

"Sure, but Xander wasn't having any of it. We may do drugs, get drunk and party, but Xander and I were always faithful to each other. Anything said in the papers or magazines was for show, like the publicity stunt of Xander and me breaking up."

Dahlia motioned for Sam to join her out in the hallway.

"What do you think about Tamsen's claim that Bryson was sleeping with Kora?" she asked.

"Based on how they interacted when Kora came to make her statement, I'm inclined to believe it," Sam said. "But I'm not sure how much information we can get out of him because he's an attorney and it might fall under attorney–client privilege."

"True, but I wonder if maybe Bryson the person would be more willing to share information when compared to Bryson the attorney," Dahlia said. "If he has feelings for her, maybe he might reveal some information, especially if he finds out about Kora's affair with Ross."

"Let's hope affairs of the heart win out over affairs of the court so we can figure out if anyone else was involved in Xander's death," Sam said.

★★★

Bryson was reclining in the Jacuzzi in his hotel room when there was a knock on the door. He called for the person knocking to enter.

"Working hard, I see," Sam said.

Bryson smiled at him.

"You know it, Detective," he said. "Now, to what do I owe this honor?"

Dahlia produced a photograph from the file folder she'd been carrying. She showed it to Bryson.

"Did you know that Kora and Ross were having an affair?" Dahlia asked. "This is a photograph from the security footage from the night before Xander Mathis was killed, so their relationship is still current."

Bryson scooted across the Jacuzzi to get a closer look at the photograph. He blinked, and his mouth opened, but no sound came out.

"You're kidding," Bryson said. "This can't be real. This is a forgery or a setup."

"Nope, it's the real deal," Sam said. "We got a subpoena for the footage, so it's all wrapped up in a nice, pretty legal bow. This, my friend, is the truth."

Bryson did not immediately react. He looked away from the photo and down at the bubbling water. He then smacked the water with his hand, the spray hitting Sam and Dahlia.

"Oh, good, I got my shower for today," Sam shook the water off his hands, causing Dahlia to smirk.

"I can't believe her!" Bryson placed the photo on the floor near the Jacuzzi. "She tricked me! She told me she loved me! I left my wife for her! That bitch!"

Bryson got out of the Jacuzzi, grabbing a towel from off of the end table next to it. He turned to Sam and Dahlia.

"Detectives," he said. "As I'm sure you know, there are certain exceptions to the attorney–client confidentiality rule, which can vary. One exception is the duty of a lawyer to not conceal incriminating evidence, be an accessory to a crime, or intentionally destroy evidence of a crime."

"Yeah, thanks for the Law 101 reminder," Sam said.

"The reason I'm telling you this is because of a request that Kora made to me," Bryson said. "We were at lunch earlier at a restaurant downtown. She asked me to do her a favor."

"What kind of favor?"

"She asked me to help her fake her drug test that you were going to require her to submit to by providing her with a clean urine sample. Kora said that it was because the studio was going to terminate her contract if they found drugs in her system and she didn't want that to happen because it would ruin her career, but, having read over her contract before, I know that it's not true. I didn't think much of it until now. She wanted me to help her get a clean drug test so she would not be incriminated in Xander's murder. There were drugs found at the scene, right? Well, Kora didn't want to have drugs in her system otherwise it would appear that she was right in the room with Xander and Tamsen instead of being in her room, as she claimed. If she were the only one in the room that didn't get knocked unconscious, it would be awfully suspicious, wouldn't it?" Bryson said. "I realize now, that if I helped her to pass her drug test like she wanted me to, I would essentially be helping her conceal a crime. I refuse to become an accessory and lose my job over … her."

"You think Kora murdered Xander?" Sam asked.

"I don't know if she's the one who actually did it, but it wouldn't surprise me if she were involved. You know she hated Tamsen, right? I mean, deeply hated Tamsen. It wouldn't surprise me if Kora orchestrated this whole thing to finally get her enemy out of the way and out of the way permanently."

"Right, because other tries to get her out of the picture, like sending her to rehab, didn't work," Dahlia said.

"Exactly," Bryson said. "They have a Tonya Harding, Nancy Kerrigan thing going on, except far deadlier."

He walked over to the desk behind Sam and Dahlia and grabbed his cell phone from it.

"I'm sorry, but if you'll excuse me, detectives, I have to call my ex and apologize for being a complete asshole and ruining a perfectly happy marriage … or, at least, what I thought was one …"

Sam gave Bryson a salute and mouthed the words "good luck" before he and Dahlia headed out of the hotel room.

★★★

"It helps to have friends in high places," Sam said as he hung up the phone at his desk in the bullpen at the police department.

Dahlia looked at him.

"Why, what's up?" she asked.

"Normally, toxicology reports can take weeks, even months, to get the results," Sam said. "But, I asked my friends in the ME's office to put a rush on Xander's results, and ta-dah! They emailed me the initial findings, one week to the date."

"Impressive," Dahlia said.

She got up from her desk and stood behind Sam to read over his shoulder.

"Okay, let's see …" he skimmed the results. "Yikes, that's quite a cocktail of drugs he's got going on there."

"Yes, it's a lot of drugs," Dahlia said. "But if you look at the amount of each drug, they're all relatively low dosages. Maybe being mixed together, the drugs created a problem, but I don't think that's what caused his death."

"Neither do I. We know that Xander was injected with something by Ross. Unless we find out what the deadly substance was, the defense might be able to successfully argue that it was a drug overdose and what was injected wasn't anything harmful."

Dahlia moved in closer to Sam's computer screen.

"Wait, that's Propofol," she pointed at the screen. "That's not a standard prescription drug. It's typically used to sedate someone, usually in a hospital setting where it can be properly monitored because it slows the brain and nervous system activity. Why would Xander have that in his system?"

"Okay, since it's not a regular old prescription drug that anyone can get, can we find any record of any of them, Tamsen, Kora, Ross or Xander, being admitted to the hospital where one of them could have access to the Propofol?" Sam wondered aloud.

"When Tamsen was first brought in under suspicion of Xander's death, she mentioned that she had been to rehab a few months ago," Dahlia said. "Was she brought to the hospital before that? Maybe she OD'd and was sent to the hospital to have her stomach pumped or something prior to being sent to rehab? If she were, that would have provided Ross with access to the Propofol."

"It's possible," Sam said. "Give her a call, Bennett and see what she has to say about it."

Dahlia returned to her desk and phoned Tamsen while Sam continued skimming the results of Xander's toxicology report. He grabbed his phone and placed a call of his own.

"Hey, Carruthers, it's Marlowe," Sam said. "I got another request for you lovely crime lab folks."

"Sure, what's up?"

"The syringe that I sent down last week, I need you guys to test it for a specific drug."

"What are we looking for?"

"See if you can find any traces of Propofol."

"Like the anesthetic used in hospitals?" Carruthers asked.

"That's the one."

"Can do. I'll get that queued up and see what I can do for you. By the way, Detective, we got the results on the alcohol bottles from the evidence you sent us."

The bottles of alcohol Kora gave Xander and Tamsen before the two returned to Tamsen's room. My gut says they were drugged; let's see if I'm right.

"What have you got for me?" Sam asked.

"I'll have the report down to you tonight, but I can confirm there were traces of a sedative found in them."

Bingo. Tamsen and Xander ingested a sedative, which caused them to pass out, making them easy prey for our killer.

"Thanks."

Sam hung up the phone and Dahlia did the same shortly afterward.

"Tamsen confirmed that she had been at the hospital before being sent to rehab," she said.

"Well, hot damn," Sam said.

"Wait, it gets better. Tamsen said that she had to have her stomach pumped because she had taken too many pills. The hospital staff put her under anesthetic during the procedure."

"Let me guess, the anesthetic used was Propofol."

"She doesn't know for sure, but she's going to have someone get the copy of the medical records and drop them off to us for our investigation."

"Bennett, did Tamsen say who put her in rehab? If she's still doing drugs and partying, I highly doubt she checked herself in because an addict usually won't change unless he or she wants to."

Ain't that the truth.

"Yes, she did. Tamsen said that Ross sent her to rehab. He was the one who brought her to the hospital to have her stomach pumped and made all of the arrangements for rehab while she was recuperating in the hospital for a few days."

"If he was at the hospital, then Ross had access to the Propofol, which he could use to kill Xander by injecting him with it with the syringe we saw in the video from the camera Fruit Loops Guy put in Tamsen's room," Sam said.

"That makes sense," Dahlia said. "But what still bugs me is why Kora and Ross went after Xander. If they were so hell-bent on destroying Tamsen, why target Xander?"

"That," Sam cleared his throat. "I'm still working on."

"I thought you were supposed to have all the answers, Mr. Lead Detective."

"I do, but not right this second."

Dahlia rolled her eyes and shook her head.

★★★

As promised, Tamsen had Nichole stop by the department shortly after one that afternoon. She gave a copy of her hospital records to Sam and Dahlia.

Sam skimmed through the paperwork and then handed the folder to Dahlia to review. He grabbed the phone and called Tamsen at the holding center.

"Tamsen, we're close to wrapping this case up," he said. "But we need your help on one more thing."

"Sure," Tamsen said. "What's up?"

"How was Xander's relationship with others, like Ross and Kora?"

"It was all right. He got along with Ross pretty well. Kora was kind of a flirt with him. It kind of got on his nerves sometimes," she paused. "You know, Xander did tell me one time that I should look for a different manager and stay away from Kora and her drama."

Sam perked up at this information.

"Stay away from them?" he repeated. "Did Xander say why?"

"No, nothing in particular. The only thing he said is that he was afraid they'd hurt me. I thought he meant that I'd get hurt with the fake feud with Kora and Ross wouldn't do anything to stop it because it was good press."

There was a pause on the other end of the line.

"Why? Do you think he suspected them of something?"

"He might not have known the extent of what Ross and Kora were capable of," Sam said. "But we have a pretty good idea, and even though he was uncertain, I think Xander was right on warning you off of them."

There was a bang, followed by some shuffling and mumbling. *Tamsen must have dropped the phone,* Sam figured.

"Sorry," Tamsen said, her voice quivering. "It's been a tough few days, between losing Xander and then dealing with the withdrawal symptoms."

"Don't worry about it," Sam said.

"It's hard not to when it's likely that two people I thought I trusted ended up screwing me over and destroying my life and killing the man I loved," Tamsen sniffed. "Please get justice for Xander."

"Your wish is my command."

★★★

"Good evening everyone, this is the six o'clock news. Our top story tonight is the arrest by the Odette Police Department in the murder of Xander Mathis. Our cameras were there as actress Kora Sheerwood and Ross Serrado, the manager of actress Tamsen Wilde, were arrested and taken into custody by the police. A representative of the department stated that both will be facing charges in the murder of actor Xander Mathis that occurred two weeks ago. Our reporters reached out to Tamsen Wilde, but she was unavailable for comment ..."

Sam muted the television in the bullpen and turned around to face Tamsen and Dahlia.

"Well, it's finally over, Tamsen," Dahlia said.

Tamsen sighed.

"Yeah. I'm glad it's over," she said. "But now, I have no idea what to do. I mean, I lost Xander. My manager and my friend double crossed me and tried to get me arrested for murder because they couldn't get rid of me any other way. How am I supposed to move on after that?"

"Maybe you could go into public speaking," Dahlia said. "Speak about your ordeal to other survivors and victims working through their own struggles; it might be helpful for them and for you. Your fans love you, so why not give back to them?"

Tamsen seemed to consider Dahlia's suggestion.

"That's not a bad idea," she said, fiddling with the charm on her necklace.

"You know," Sam said. "Speaking of people who love you, there is a guy who helped us catch Ross and Kora. I think he would greatly like to meet you as a reward for helping to exonerate you."

"He helped clear my name?" Tamsen repeated. "I'd like to thank him."

Keeping a close eye on the exchange, Sam and Dahlia watched as Tamsen thanked Devon in person for his help. The man appeared as though he died and had gone to heaven the moment Tamsen smiled at him.

"So, you do have a sentimental side," Dahlia nudged Sam in the side with her elbow.

"I guess I'm a sap for happy endings," he replied.

"Then I suppose you'll be happy to know then that your case has made every news outlet and newspaper in the area," Dahlia said. "You're a celebrity."

Sam shrugged, a brilliant grin on his face. "What can I say, Bennett? People love me."

Dahlia rolled her eyes and shook her head, but smiled at her partner nonetheless.

THE GRAY AREA

Not guilty.

Those two little words caused a great deal of relief to settle over young Roderick Morgan. The groans and gasps of anger and disbelief of the spectators packed shoulder to shoulder in the gallery of the courtroom turned the relief that Roderick felt into jubilation and a smile crossed his lips, revealing his pearly white teeth. While his stunning smile would have normally caused nearly every woman in the court to go weak at the knees, on this particular afternoon, Roderick's grin only served to further infuriate the numerous people seated behind him.

"Murderer!"

"Spoiled rotten rich kid! Nothing's ever good enough for people like you!"

"This is a court of law, not a damned sporting event!" the judge banged his gavel repeatedly to silence the outbursts of the crowd. "And, as much as you all may disagree with the verdict, a jury of his peers has spoken. Mr. Morgan, you are free to go."

Roderick was immediately pulled into a giant bear hug by his attorney, the linebacker of a man named Brian Davies.

"Congrats, Roddy boy!" Brian said with a hearty slap on the back.

Roderick coughed, the wind knocked out of him.

"Thanks," he wheezed in response. "C'mon, Davies, let's get out of here. I need to celebrate."

The bailiff unlocked Roderick's handcuffs before Brian escorted his client out of the courtroom. The attorney quickly filled out the necessary paperwork to get his newly acquitted client officially released. Once that was all squared away with the court, they hurried through the courthouse in an attempt to avoid a confrontation with the mob of people from the courtroom that were angered by the verdict. Roderick attempted to open the thick solid oak doors of justice that, once he stepped through them would render him a free man, but Brian put a hand on his shoulder to stop him.

"There's a ton of press out there," he said to Roderick. "Let me go first."

Brian stepped forward, opening the massive doors with ease, and walked straight into the sea of microphones, camera flashes, and video recorders. Roderick followed a few steps behind his loyal attorney and stood at his side as he waited for the onslaught of the inevitable media coverage that was a result of the trial's conclusion.

"People, please," Brian started to speak, holding his hands up to halt the millions of questions that were being voiced to him all at once.

Once the media crowd quieted down, Brian addressed them:

"I am pleased to announce that my client, Mr. Roderick Morgan, was found not guilty for the deaths of his parents, Walter and Cassidy Morgan. Mr. and Mrs. Morgan adopted Roderick and raised him as if he was their own flesh and blood. There was no way that he would repay their love and kindness by brutally murdering them as they lay sleeping in their beds."

Roderick nudged Brian, who turned to look at him.

"May I?" he asked.

"Of course," Brian said.

Roderick stepped in front of Brian to better face the endless crowd of media before him.

"I would like to extend my gratitude to everyone who supported me throughout this dreadful ordeal," he said, speaking in the sweet and innocent tone that had helped him to win over the jury a short time ago.

Roderick's gentle eyes and sincere expression then suddenly transformed to that of smugness accompanied by a sneer. "But that proves that you are all stupid as hell," he said with a wink. "Because I got away with murder. Adios!"

Roderick pulled his designer sunglasses out of his designer suit coat pocket and put them on as his personal driver pulled up in front of the courthouse with his golden Maserati. The media watched in stunned silence as Roderick descended the concrete steps to his car, not a care in the world. Brian followed solemnly behind him, his head lowered in shame at the admission of guilt by his client.

"Stupid spoiled rotten son of a bitch," he grumbled to himself, not caring if Roderick heard him or not.

★★★

Detective Samuel Marlowe cracked his neck as he leaned against the wall outside of the parole board meeting room at the Odette Penitentiary. He was growing restless the longer he had to wait for the meeting to begin. He'd gone to several parole board hearings over the years, sometimes a job necessity, other times because he knew that it was where he needed to be to help see justice served. Now was an instance of the latter.

His cell phone vibrating in his pocket drew Sam from his thoughts. Checking the message, Sam was surprised to find an alert from a local news app.

Verdict reached in the Roderick Morgan case.

That didn't take long, Sam considered. He clicked on the alert, and it brought him to the full article.

Roderick Morgan found not guilty on all counts.

Sam shook his head slowly.

"The jury fucked up that one big time," he mumbled to himself as he stuffed his phone back into his pocket. "The kid was absolutely guilty. Hopefully, he gets what's coming to him."

Once the parole board was ready to commence with the meeting, Sam and the few others in attendance filed into the meeting room. The detective took a seat at the back and watched silently as the other people took care of their business with the parole board. Despite having done this a few times before, Sam couldn't deny the feelings of anxiety and anger that bubbled through his veins as the presiding Board Commissioner addressed the other members concerning the next case on the docket.

"Okay, next we have a parole consideration hearing for Seth Tucker, regarding his charge of attempted murder, case number J-07042017. Bailiff, please bring in inmate 0195218."

A few minutes later, the bailiff brought in the inmate as requested. Clutching the paper with his statement on it, the white-hot rage against the atrocities the man had committed against his mother burst through the dams and came flooding back through Sam's system. Charlotte, his mother, was still in a vegetative state, being kept alive by machines and now Seth had a chance to walk free after thirteen years? That was nowhere near enough time. He was going to make sure the bastard served every day, every hour, every minute and every second of his twenty-year sentence. Sam had succeeded before and knew he could do it again.

★★★

A beer in one hand and the television remote in the other, Roderick flipped through the channels on the large television screen as he reclined in his plush armchair in the sitting room of the Morgan family mansion; at least, what was left of the Morgan family. He couldn't help but smile at the fact that he had graced the airwaves and was featured on each news station: **Roderick Morgan found not guilty but confesses to murders.**

"You seem pretty pleased with yourself," a voice said from behind Roderick.

Roderick glanced over his shoulder and discovered his head housekeeper standing in the doorway, carrying a silver tea tray in her hands.

"Ah, Evie, perfect timing, as usual," Roderick said.

He beckoned her over, and Evelyn Norris made her way toward Roderick after what seemed like a moment or two of hesitation. She gently nudged some of the empty liquor bottles out of the way so she could set down the tea tray on the table next to Roderick. Evelyn picked up the porcelain teapot and poured a cup of tea when Roderick raised a hand to stop her.

"Instead of tea, why don't you join me and party with my friend here, Jack Daniels?" Roderick offered, raising his bottle in a mock salute.

"I'm not much of a drinker," Evelyn said.

Roderick remembered that Evelyn, indeed, was not one to indulge much in alcoholic beverages.

"Why don't you take a seat and take a load off and join me for some tea?" he said.

After appearing to be mulling it over for a split second, Evelyn obliged the young man and sat down on the couch. Roderick observed his beloved head housekeeper curiously as he watched her over the end of the clear glass bottle that he had brought up to his lips.

"What's up, Evie?" he asked after he swallowed his swig of alcohol. "You seem tense."

Evelyn glanced up from the frayed piece of string she had been picking at on her gray uniform.

"Is it true?" she blurted out before she could stop herself.

Roderick let out a small chuckle as Evelyn's hands flew up to cover her mouth.

"You mean that?" he asked, nodding his head toward the television.

This particular station was showing video footage of Roderick speaking to the media after his acquittal, with the headline: "Acquitted, but Admits He Did It." Roderick's expression sobered, at least as much as it could after six beers, and he looked Evelyn straight in the eye.

"Evie, you know how I feel about you; you've been like a mother to me all these years," he began to tell her. "I'm going to be honest with you. Yes, I did it. I killed my parents."

Roderick saw Evelyn shudder. He decided to speak up to quell his beloved housekeeper's nerves.

"I'm sure you have a million things you want to ask me, Evie, so I'll try to answer whatever I can," he said, motioning with the bottle in his hands. "I'm going to guess that why I did it is probably your biggest question. Well, my parents were going to disinherit me. They said that my partying and drinking was destructive and putting a strain on the family name. They were going to take away the money that rightfully belonged to me because I enjoyed having fun now then. I had to do something about it."

"And you decided you'd shoot them," Evelyn said with a frown.

Roderick smirked.

"Yep. I took one of my dad's gun and shot them while they slept," he said, pointing his fingers like a gun. "Bang, bang, dead."

"Why would you admit to it?" Evelyn asked. "You were acquitted; no one would have known."

"Where's the fun in that? Besides, there's double jeopardy, so I'm untouchable. Plus, I am all over the media. Think of the book deals, film rights and the money from Hollywood! I'll be set for life, and believe me, Evelyn, I will take good care of you."

"I could never profit from your parents' deaths," Evelyn looked away. "Besides, are you sure you'll get the money? Aren't there trustees and attorneys that watch over the family estate? Will they let you get away with what you did?"

Roderick waved her off. He undid the clasp on his designer watch and removed it from his left wrist, revealing a birthmark there. Roderick placed his drink on the table, got up from the couch and walked over to Evelyn. He got down on his knees in front of her and took her hands in his. Evelyn tried to pull away, but Roderick's grip only tightened further.

"We'll worry about all of that stuff later. You are going to stay with me, right Evie?" he asked. "I would pay you handsomely, Evie, if you stayed on as my head housekeeper, so you wouldn't be profiting from my parents' deaths."

Evelyn stayed quiet, not entirely sure how to respond.

"Can I have a night to think it over?" she asked.

"Of course," Roderick gave her hand a light squeeze. "But, please, I truly would appreciate it if you'd stay."

Evelyn gave Roderick a weak smile.

★★★

Sam frowned as he stood at the end of the long cobblestone driveway looking up at the mansion sitting at the end of the road.

"Honestly, do we need to be here?" he wondered aloud. "Whoever did this should be hailed as a hero and not as a criminal."

"This is still a crime scene," his partner, Dahlia, said, hands on her hips. "It doesn't matter what our personal feelings are about the individuals involved in this case; it is our responsibility as the police to investigate this case thoroughly and figure out who is responsible for what happened and seek justice accordingly."

Sam flashed her one of his trademark smug grins.

"Funny, Bennett," he said. "If only I cared, I'd probably take that little speech into consideration but, news flash, I don't. This dick got what was coming to him."

Dahlia rolled her eyes.

"What's with you today, Sam?" she asked. "You seem grumpier than usual."

Sam fixed his hair and adjusted his suit coat before turning from the police car to walk up the cobblestone driveway to the Morgan mansion, Dahlia right behind him.

"Nothing," he said. "I … I had a bad morning." *I guess the fact that I didn't sleep at all last night since I was a little preoccupied with my stepfather being granted parole is making me a tad bit grumpy, Bennett.*

It took some clever maneuvering and threats of arrest for obstruction of justice to get through the media that had swarmed the mansion grounds. Once Sam and Dahlia arrived at the front doors, they showed their badges to the officer stationed there and were immediately greeted with an overly enthusiastic salute.

"Hello, Detective Marlowe! Sir!" the rookie officer shouted, the saluting hand quivering in his excitement. "And Detective Bennett! Ma'am! It is an honor to be here with two amazing detectives!"

Sam smiled to himself at the reverence given to him by the young cadet. A recent case they'd worked on involving some celebrities had, in turn, made Sam and Dahlia into instant stars in the department. Well, according to Sam, it made Dahlia a bit of a celebrity, as he already viewed himself as one.

"We're here to investigate the crime scene," Dahlia said.

"Yes, ma'am! The chief informed us of your arrival!" the officer said.

With another salute, he stepped out of the mansion doorway to allow Dahlia and Sam to enter inside. They walked together through the grand front foyer toward the back of the house, specifically, the sitting room.

The sitting room was something out of a magazine for the lifestyles of the rich and famous. Sam let out an appreciative whistle as he looked around at the lavish furniture and elegant décor.

"Looks like a murder–suicide," Rusty said when they entered the room.

Sam shook the Senior Detective's hand.

"Thanks for securing the scene, Caldwell. So, what have we got here?"

Both Sam and Dahlia's eyes were immediately drawn to the ground about two feet away from where Rusty was standing. Lying on top of the Persian rug that spanned the gap between the couch and the armchair was the body of Roderick Morgan.

"Looks like the rotten bastard got his just desserts," Sam said to himself as he observed the body before him.

"Really, Sam?" Dahlia asked, apparently having heard him.

She glared at Rusty, who was nodding in agreement with Sam's sentiment, and he quickly stopped before averting his gaze by turning his attention to Roderick's body as well.

"What do you want me to say, Bennett?" Sam said. "Oh, boo, the poor double murderer is dead! There are so many people lining up to be one of the pallbearers at his funeral that they're going to need to fight each other off."

"We have a job to do, Sam," Dahlia reminded her partner. "Regardless of the victim's criminal history-a truly despicable man, I agree-our job is to find whoever did this and bring them to justice."

"You're so cute, Bennett, with your little morals and ideals," Sam said. "You need to drop those immediately."

"Let's just investigate, okay?" Dahlia said with a huff.

She turned to Rusty.

"You said that you believe this is a murder-suicide?"

"Yes, and amazingly enough, the other victim lived," he said. "She was in pretty bad shape, though. Medics said she barely had a pulse and was hardly breathing."

"She?" Sam repeated.

"The other vic was found right next to Roderick, Evelyn Norris," Rusty said. "She was the head housekeeper for the Morgans for the past twenty-five years. My guess would be poisoning, but, like I said, it's only a guess from an old cop who's been around the bend a time or two."

"Interesting," Sam mused aloud. "Bennett, go speak to the other staff and see what you can find out about the relationship between Roderick and Evelyn."

Dahlia was about to open her mouth to protest, but Sam quickly reminded her that she was the junior detective and thus needed to obey his orders. She relented, but that did not stop her from giving her senior partner an annoyed huff before stomping away from the sitting room.

★★★

Not a common occurrence, Dahlia was surprised to find Sam at his desk in the bullpen when she arrived at the department the next morning. He appeared to be hard at work, diligently filling out some documents.

"Good morning, Sam," Dahlia said as she headed over to her desk.

Sam's head whipped up, and he immediately flipped the papers he'd been working on over so they were face down on his desk. Dahlia frowned as she sat down and placed her messenger bag on the floor next to her.

"Is everything okay?" she asked.

"Peachy keen," Sam said.

"Sure. And I'm the Queen of England."

Sam grabbed a manila envelope from off his desk and handed it to Dahlia.

"Well, here's the preliminary autopsy report then, Your Majesty," he said.

Dahlia rolled her eyes as she opened the envelope and began to read the report.

"Huh, that's interesting," she said more to herself than Sam.

"I'm assuming you're talking about the large amounts of calcium oxalate crystals in the vic's urine and in some of his tissues?" Sam said.

"Yes, actually. That's not a normal thing, to have that much in your system."

"No, it's not. I called Dr. Rochester and asked about the results, and she explained it to me. Granted, it was in all that sciencey-mumbo-jumbo, but I think I got the gist of it," Sam said. "I'll save you the science lesson and give you the abridged version. The Doc is certain that the high levels are a result of ethylene glycol poisoning."

"Ethylene glycol? You mean, like, anti-freeze?" Dahlia asked.

"Exactly," Sam said.

"It seems that Rusty was right about poisoning."

"Yep. I've contacted the hospital to get Evelyn's test results to see if her tox screen came up with the same thing, as well as the folks down at the crime lab to check the evidence for any traces of the chemical. I'm getting a subpoena for the hospital records, and as soon as that's signed by Judge Mars, I'm off to the hospital to get those results. That being said, I wouldn't be surprised one bit if Evelyn's results were the same as Roderick's."

"Okay, so it's likely murder," Dahlia said. "But that leaves us with a ton of suspects since Roderick was, well ..."

"An asshole who, essentially, was a waste of life?" Sam said.

"To put it nicely."

"I guess a good place to start would be Roderick's attorney. He was the one who got the slimeball out of a murder sentence, so he might either have information on someone who wanted to give his client a taste of his own medicine or give us clues that he, himself, is guilty of ridding the world of a truly despicable being."

"I caught part of the news broadcast yesterday," Dahlia turned to her computer and tapped some keys and clicked the mouse a few times. "And I remember hearing his attorney's name … here it is, Brian Davies. Looks like he's a partner at the law firm, Davies, Hemings, and Simpson."

"All right then, let's pay Mr. Davies a visit," Sam said.

"You go on ahead," Dahlia said. "I'll meet you at the car."

Sam eyed her for a moment, Dahlia doing her best to sit firmly beneath his scrutinizing gaze. After a few minutes, he spun on his heel and made his way out of the bullpen. Once he was out of sight, Dahlia got up and checked the hallway to make sure that Sam was, in fact, gone. With the coast clear, she hurried back to Sam's desk and searched for the paperwork he had been filling out when she arrived.

"He's filing an appeal to a parole decision?" Dahlia whispered to herself.

She snatched a post-it note from her desk and jotted down some of the pertinent information from the form and then shoved that sticky note into her desk to look at later. Dahlia then returned the papers to where Sam had stashed them before hustling out of the bullpen to catch up with her partner.

★★★

Pulling into the parking lot of the law offices of Davies, Hemings, and Simpson, Sam was annoyed, but not surprised, to find several reporters and news vans camped out front.

"How mad would you be if I ran over a couple of reporters?" he asked Dahlia as he drove into an open parking spot.

"Very," Dahlia said. "So, don't even think about it."

"You're no fun," Sam said with a sigh.

They fought their way through the news reporters, who swarmed them with questions about the death of Roderick Morgan.

"Detectives! Do you have any suspects?"

"Detectives! Do you think it had anything to do with Roderick's confession?"

"Can we get a comment?"

Sam turned around to face the reporters.

"To answer your questions: no comment, no comment, and if you insist," he paused. "Comment."

Dahlia put her head down to hide the smile that appeared on her face before following Sam inside the building. Brian Davies worked on the third floor of the building. He was standing near the windows, frowning as he looked out the window, a cup of coffee in his hand.

"I feel like a hostage," Brian said to Sam and Dahlia after introductions were made. "They've been here since I got back from the trial yesterday. Good thing I have a change of clothes and a couch, huh? Came in handy last night."

"Speaking of that whole debacle," Sam said. "We'd like to ask you a couple of questions about it."

Brian left his spot by the window, taking a seat at his desk.

"What do you want to know?" he asked.

"So, Roderick admitted he did it after you got him off the hook; thoughts?"

"Well, that was straight to the point," Brian frowned.

"Excuse my partner," Dahlia said. "He has no brain to mouth filter."

"No worries. Actually, I had to bite my tongue to prevent myself from saying something in front of all those cameras and recorders when Roderick said what he said. I was going to say some things that weren't very professional sounding."

"Though probably completely justified," Sam said.

"No kidding," Brian sighed. "I don't get it. I've been the Morgans' attorney for a few years now, and my father was their attorney before that; I, essentially, grew up around them. Walter and Cassidy were wonderful to Roderick. They gave him anything and everything that he wanted. The Morgans couldn't have children of their own, so they adopted Roderick. I suppose that they spoiled him rotten out of love, but it backfired and turned him into a little demon."

"Did Roderick have any other offenses on his rap sheet?"

"He was charged a time or two with little things like drunk and disorderly and underage drinking. My father and I managed to get him off the hook for those and the DUI he had a year ago," Brian paused, rubbing his stubbly chin. "Actually, I think it was the DUI charge that led Walter and Cassidy to threaten to disinherit Roderick."

"Threaten?" Dahlia repeated.

"Yes, threaten. The Morgans didn't actually have the heart to do it. Like I said, they loved Roderick with every fiber of their beings."

"But Roderick had no idea that the threat of disinheritance was an empty one," Dahlia said.

"He must not have otherwise Walter and Cassidy would likely still be alive," Brian said.

"You've known Roderick his entire life, right?" Sam asked.

"Yes, though, after yesterday, it's not something I want to admit to."

"Would you say Roderick was a smart cookie?"

"He was. I mean, he was never interested in school, so his grades didn't reflect it, but he was actually a very bright kid."

"Okay, then why didn't he know that admitting to murdering his parents could potentially disinherit him?" Sam asked. "A simple internet search would have told him all about the 'slayer' rule, which prevents killers from inheriting from their crimes. There are both criminal and civil provisions in Colorado, so, even if Roderick beat the criminal charges, the money still may not have been his if someone brought a wrongful death suit or something like that against him."

"That's actually something that I've been trying to wrap my head around, too. Like I said, Roderick was not a stupid kid. He was a narcissistic bastard, though; that's probably the best answer I can offer. You know, it wouldn't surprise me if he did it as a backup plan."

"Backup plan?" Sam repeated. "What's that supposed to mean?"

"Say that Roderick hadn't died and he had to go to civil court for a wrongful death suit against his parents. If he lost that, he'd lose all the money he wanted so desperately, right? Well, if he has offers upon offers from news outlets, Hollywood agents, and writers for his story about murdering his parents and pretty much getting away with it, he'd be rolling in the dough regardless. The worst part is that there have already been calls of interest into Roderick for his story; I know because a couple of them have contacted my office already."

"I see."

"Mr. Davies, is there anyone that had problems with Roderick?" Dahlia asked. "Anyone that might want to harm him?"

"Beside me after the way he screwed me over on national television?" Brian said with a laugh. "I'm kidding; I've been here all night, so I didn't kill him. Roderick pretty much had Walter and Cassidy make all his problems disappear by throwing money at them. They were very wealthy, so I'm sure there were a lot of people that were envious of their financial status, but there's no one that I'm aware of personally. Roderick did have some ex-girlfriends that he didn't part with on good terms, but I highly doubt they'd do anything like this."

"We'll still need their names," Sam said.

"Of course; I'll put a list together. Oh, and to be clear, I'm giving this to you as a friend of Roderick's and *not* as his attorney,"

"If anyone asks, it was from a friend," Sam said. "No names."

"Good."

Brian turned to his computer and began compiling a list of Roderick's ex-girlfriends for Sam and Dahlia. His typing was steady until it slowed and came to an abrupt stop.

"You know, detectives," Brian said. "I thought of something. Walter and Cassidy were talking about possibly adding a second beneficiary to their wills; someone to either share in the inheritance or to receive the money should anything happen to Roderick before they died."

"Now you're talking," Sam said. "Any idea who this new beneficiary might be?"

"Unfortunately, no. The Morgans never got much further than thinking about it, at least, from a legal perspective. You may want to check with their financial advisor at CS Financial. He may have some more information about the possible beneficiary."

Brian finished typing up the list of ex-girlfriends, printed it and gave a copy to both Sam and Dahlia. The two detectives then left the law offices, en route to CS Financial.

★★★

Sam and Dahlia arrived at CS Financial and headed up to the second floor to meet with the financial advisor in charge of the Morgan account.

"Nice to see you again, detectives," Jayden said. "Though, I wish it was under better circumstances."

The agent in charge of the Morgan account was Jayden Delano, a young Boston-born man with sandy brown hair who was a rising star at the financial institution.

"You and me both, buddy," Sam said as he and Dahlia followed Jayden into his office. "It'd be nice to walk in here one day and *not* have to discuss a crime."

Jayden took a seat at his desk while Sam and Dahlia sat down in the visitor's chairs in front of it.

"The Morgan account," the advisor began to say. "Is quite extensive. After their original advisor retired a few years ago, they were looking for a new financial manager. I liked a challenge, so I volunteered to try and win the Morgans over to the CS Financial side. Thankfully, my job was made a little easier because their retiring advisor actually recommended us."

Jayden's frown deepened, and he sighed.

"It's still unbelievable what happened to them. Walter and Cassidy were truly nice people," he said. "I can't understand why Roderick would want to do something like that to them."

"Well, he got his comeuppance, so we don't have to worry about him anymore," Sam said. "However, the justice system has this idiotic notion that I should have to care about finding out who killed Roderick instead of giving his killer a medal of honor. That's where you come in, Jayden."

Dahlia glared at Sam, presumably over his comments to Jayden. He gave her a small shrug in response.

"Jayden, we just spoke to the Morgan family attorney," Dahlia said. "He told us that the Morgans were considering adding another beneficiary to inherit their fortune should Roderick die; do you have any idea who this person is?"

"I do, actually, which is what makes this whole incident so strange," Jayden said. "The Morgans were considering leaving a significant amount of their fortune to a member of the staff. I can't exactly say who for legal reasons, but you're more than welcome to list off names, and I can tell you who was *not* up for consideration."

"I like the way you think, Jayden," Sam said with a smile. "I can see why you've made it this far so quickly. Loopholes can be a cop's best friend sometimes."

Dahlia pulled her notebook out of her pocket and began listing off the names of the Morgan family staff members. Jayden denied name after name until only one remained.

"The only one left is Evelyn Norris," Dahlia said, reviewing the list.

"The housekeeper?" Sam asked. "Do you know who that is, Jayden?"

"Yes," Jayden said. "Evelyn's been a member of the staff for at least twenty years. The Morgans told me that Evelyn played a huge role in Roderick's life; she was his favorite staff member, by far, they said. Based solely on that information and *not* because I know anything further, Evelyn would be a candidate for the Morgans to consider leaving their fortune to if anything happened to Roderick."

"If the Morgans wanted to leave Evelyn with a shitload of cash," Sam said. "Then it's reasonable to assume that they trusted her and pretty much considered her a member of the family?"

"I'd say so, yes," Jayden said. "I can't imagine there being any ill-will between Evelyn and her employers and vice versa."

"Did Evelyn know about this arrangement?"

"No. Actually, I'm pretty sure that *if* they were going to tell her, it would have been as a surprise to celebrate her twenty-five years of employment with them."

"When was that supposed to take place?" Dahlia asked.

"Oh, that wouldn't be for another year," Jayden said. "We were only in the planning stages. Nothing was concrete yet. If it were, Mr. Davies would have been in the loop as the family attorney. He'd have to draw up all the legal documents and what have you before the actual finances were altered."

"Shit," Sam turned to Dahlia. "Just when I thought we had something."

★★★

Returning from CS Financial, Sam and Dahlia made their way back to the bullpen at the police department. Sam set Dahlia with the task of looking up information on the list of ex-girlfriends that Brian had provided them with.

"Here you are, Sam," Dahlia said as she handed him a piece of paper. "The names, addresses, phone numbers and everything else you requested for Roderick's long list of ex's."

Sam took a quick look at the list before turning his attention back to his computer screen.

"Good work, Bennett," he said. "Now, get going. Those names aren't going to check out themselves."

"I'm looking into all of the ex-girlfriends?" Dahlia asked. "You're not coming with me?"

"I know you'll miss me, Bennett, but you're a big girl and can do that yourself. I have a bunch of things I need to look in to and take care of here at the department."

Dahlia walked back over to her desk and began gathering her essentials to go out investigating.

"Does your to-do list happen to have something to do with a parole hearing?" she asked, her head down, but her eyes still focused on her partner.

Sam's head whipped up.

"What did you say?" he asked.

"You heard me," Dahlia said, keeping eye contact with him. "I saw the parole decision appeals form on your desk."

"More like you were snooping and looking at things you had no right to lay eyes on," Sam said in a scolding tone.

"Hey, I learned from the best."

Sam let out a breath.

"Listen, Bennett, the parole decision appeal is a personal thing, and I'd rather not discuss it, thank you very much," he said.

"Can I help in any way?" Dahlia asked.

"No."

"Are you sure?"

"Yes."

Dahlia sighed.

"Okay, Sam," she said.

Dahlia gathered her materials and stuffed them in her messenger bag, which she then slung over her shoulder.

"My offer still stands if you need any help," she said before turning and making her way toward the exit.

Sam watched her leave. There wasn't anything that could be done, he knew. Seth was eventually going to be released from prison; it was only a matter of when. Unfortunately, that 'when' came a little sooner than expected, but that wasn't going to stop Sam from doing everything in his power to keep that man behind bars.

★★★

Maria Charron was a teacher at Odette Junior High School. In her early thirties, she was a few years older than Roderick, and from what Dahlia gathered, held no ill-will against her former boyfriend.

"Roderick was a real sweet talker," Maria said as she wiped down the dry erase board after classes had been dismissed for the day. "He loved to shower me with gifts of all sorts. I felt kind of awkward and bad about taking lavish gifts, like jewelry and even a car, but Roderick insisted."

"How did the relationship come to an end?" Dahlia asked.

"Well, I'm sure you've guessed that Roderick enjoyed a party lifestyle. He was into going out on the town to dance, go to clubs, see concerts and all sorts of other things. I'm not that kind of girl. I mean, I like to go out, like anyone, but only once in a while, not every night like Roderick did. It was obvious that we weren't compatible, so I ended the relationship. I didn't want to keep him captive."

Maria paused. She put the eraser down and turned around to face Dahlia.

"Though, I suspect that if I did, he probably would have found another woman to occupy himself with."

"Serial cheater?"

"I guess you could say that," a small smile tugged at the corners of Maria's lips. "I found out that I was the 'other woman' a few months into our relationship. I wanted to end it with Roderick right then and there, but he convinced me to stay and broke up with the other girl right on the spot. It's not hard to believe that if he cheated on someone to get with me, he would cheat on me as well."

"Past actions can predict future behavior," Dahlia said in agreement. "In your relationship with Roderick, did you interact at all with his parents?"

"I did. Walter and Cassidy were wonderful people." Maria closed her eyes and bit her lip. "I still can't believe what happened to them. They adored Roderick. When we first started dating, I remember thinking about how lucky I would be if Roderick and I got married and Walter and Cassidy became my in-laws. They were … amazing. That's all I can think to say. Amazing."

"What did Roderick think about his parents?"

"I'm certain he hadn't appreciated them the way he should have, but, then again, he was only in his early twenties when we were together, so I can't expect him to act too mature, right?"

"I have three brothers, so I understand completely," Dahlia said. "Growing older is mandatory, but maturity is optional."

Maria laughed.

"Yes, that's a good way to put it," she said. "I see now that it wasn't because Roderick was young, but it was because he was … I- I'm sorry, I can't … even bring myself to say the word—"

"I get it," Dahlia said. "Was there anyone else that Roderick was particularly close to? A friend? A member of the staff, maybe?"

"Um, yes, actually," Maria said. "You know, there was the one housekeeper, Evelyn, I believe her name was, that Roderick was close with. Thinking back, he was extremely close to her, closer than he was with me. I mean, that's understandable since he's known her for far longer than he's known me. At the same time, there was a butler at the estate that was with the family for even longer than Evelyn and their relationship was like that of an acquaintance, not a friend or even family member."

"What's your definition of close? Like friend-friend close? Parent-child close? Lovers close?"

Maria pursed her lips and ran a hand through her jet-black hair.

"You know? That's a good question," she said. "I guess I'd have to say lovers close. They got each other naturally. It was odd at times but also impressive."

"Interesting," Dahlia said.

She scribbled down Maria's information on her notepad. Sam was going to love this.

★★★

Sam coughed and sputtered, choking on the coffee he'd been drinking while he listened to Dahlia's summary of her meeting with Maria Charron.

"Need some paper towels?" Dahlia said.

"No, I'm good," Sam said. "I guess I wasn't expecting you to say that one of Roderick's ex's thought he might be fucking a housekeeper who's old enough to be his mother."

"Hey, love can come in all shapes, sizes, colors, genders, and ages. Remember Jayden from CS Financial and his *husband,* Carter?"

"In this fucked up world, if you can find your special someone, regardless of shape, size, color, gender or age," Sam said. "I say more power to you. My problem is that Roderick sleeping with Evelyn doesn't seem to fit with what we know of him so far. I mean, he's a spoiled-rotten rich brat that likes flashy cars, partying, gorgeous young women and flaunting his wealth. You saw that golden Maserati on the news reports, right? From what I've been able to dig up about Evelyn, she seems like the complete opposite of those things."

"What have you learned about Evelyn?"

"It's quite the pickle. Evelyn Norris didn't appear in any records past twenty-five years ago. Anything I could find on her comes from the last two and a half decades."

"Twenty-five years?" Dahlia repeated. "That's nearly the same amount of time that Evelyn's been employed with the Morgans, right?"

"According to Jayden," Sam checked his notes. "The Morgans were planning on surprising Evelyn with her inclusion in the will during her twenty-fifth anniversary next year."

"Evelyn's probably close to her sixties, so that doesn't make sense that she would only have a record dating up to twenty-five years back."

"Exactly. A riddle wrapped in a mystery inside of an enigma, to quote Winston Churchill. What did the other household staff members say about Roderick?"

"Nothing of importance," Dahlia said. "They practically all said that they got out of the house as soon as they could after hearing that Roderick admitted to the murders of Walter and Cassidy. I cross checked the security system and the video surveillance with their alibis and found that all of the staff members that claimed they left did, in fact, leave. The IT department confirmed that the video was not altered in any way, so their alibis seem credible."

"I'm going to check in with the crime lab tomorrow morning and see if they have any details for us. There might be some evidence in there to make the other Morgan estate staff members talk if they saw or heard some suspicious," Sam said. "How about their views of Evelyn? Did they have anything to say about her?"

"They all liked Evelyn. Actually, the staff seemed more heartbroken about what happened to her over what happened to Roderick. Given the circumstances, I guess that's understandable."

"Okay, so the other staff members left the estate, but what about Roderick and Evelyn?"

"Evelyn lives in the Morgan house in the spare bedroom on the ground floor, so she did not leave from the mansion," Dahlia said. "According to the staff, Evelyn was in shock that Roderick had committed the crime, like the rest of them. She volunteered to go and speak to him about it on behalf of the others. They all wanted to know if what he said about killing Walter and Cassidy was true or if it was some stupidity on Roderick's part or a publicity stunt or something like that. Apparently, Evelyn said that she would hold a staff meeting the following morning and let everyone know what Roderick told her."

"Hmm ..." Sam tapped his fingers on his desk. "That makes it sounds like this wasn't premeditated, at least, on Evelyn's part. If Evelyn was planning on holding a staff meeting the next day, it sounds like she didn't plan on being poisoned."

"No, I guess not," Dahlia said. "But what if Roderick was the one that poisoned Evelyn? If they were as close as Maria said, it would make sense. Think about it this way: Roderick is acquitted and admits to the murders, thinking he is going to inherit the family fortune. Of course, he finds out after all is said and done that he's not going to see a dime because of the slayer statute. He knows he's screwed and is desperate for a way out of the hole he created. If he loved Evelyn, maybe he wanted to take her with him."

"Your theory is pretty good, Bennett, but it doesn't seem to fit Roderick. Does he seem like the poisoning type to you? If he wanted to get away with his parents' murders, there were hundreds of other ways that he could have done it. Instead, he decides to shoot them while they sleep. I don't think it's a big stretch to imagine that Roderick would make some sort of grand exit if he were going to off himself," Sam paused. "On the other hand, Evelyn, a woman, might be more likely to have chosen poisoning as a method of murder."

"'An autopsy or tox screen may reveal death's why, But I hope the case will just slip by. My crime is quiet and well thought through, for you're used to violence. Can I fool you?'" Dahlia recited.

"Nice," Sam said. "That was the poem the prosecutors used as part of their closing statement in the Julia Lynn Turner case."

"The same woman who murdered who two husbands by poisoning them with anti-freeze."

"Gee, what a coincidence."

★★★

Sam and Dahlia met up with the physicians attending to Evelyn Norris the following morning.

"What's her prognosis, Doc?" Sam asked, folding his arms across his chest.

"She's lucky to be alive, quite frankly," Dr. Hailey Rogers said as she pushed her glasses back up the bridge of her nose.

"Do you think she'll make it?"

Dr. Rogers let out a breath, causing her platinum blond bangs to flutter momentarily before coming to rest on her forehead once again.

"Evelyn was essentially dead until we revived her and pumped her stomach to help get rid of some of the poison," she said. "We're doing everything we can to keep her alive. We've given her charcoal, sodium bicarbonate in her IV and dialysis to help her body remove the toxins faster."

"I'd like to see her," Sam said to Hailey, who looked at him curiously.

"You can see her if you'd like, but I'm not sure what good that'll do," Hailey said. "Evelyn has been unconscious since she was rushed here a few days ago and we're keeping her sedated to reduce any unnecessary stress on her body while she recuperates. She's also on a ventilator."

"Well, my charms have been known to work miracles," Sam grinned at Hailey.

Hailey smiled and batted her eyes at Sam while Dahlia rolled her eyes.

"Let's go, Romeo," she said, grabbing Sam's sleeve and pulling him toward Evelyn's hospital room.

Evelyn's room in the ICU was easy to spot, based on the presence of the two uniformed police officers stationed at the doorway. Sam and Dahlia flashed their badges to the officers, who saluted them in response.

"Why don't you head down to the cafeteria and grab some coffee, guys?" Sam said. "I highly doubt that Evelyn Norris is going to get up and walk out of the hospital."

The two officers chuckled before heading off to the cafeteria for a much-needed break. Sam and Dahlia then headed inside the hospital room. The room was quiet compared to the hustle and bustle of the rest of the hospital. The lifeless body of Evelyn was resting in the large bed in the middle of the room amidst a mess of wires and machinery. Sam took a closer look at the beeping and blinking machines while Dahlia sat down in the armchair next to Evelyn's bedside.

"Gee, no wonder she's not waking up, they're pumping with enough drugs to fill a pharmacy," Sam said, looking over the IV bags.

"Well, ethylene glycol poisoning is serious," Dahlia said.

"Thank you for that, Dr. Bennett."

"We'll be very fortunate if she pulls through."

"Yeah," Sam sighed. "It does seem like it's all up to her now."

He turned and started for the door.

"Let's go back to the department, Bennett. Maybe the crime lab will have some gifts for us when we get back."

★★★

With the report from the crime lab, Sam and Dahlia laid out all of their notes, statements, and photographs to begin piecing together what had transpired at the Morgan estate.

"They were both poisoned," Sam reviewed the papers spread out on the table in front of him. "The ethylene glycol was enough to kill Roderick Morgan but didn't strike down Evelyn Norris. Instead, she's on a ventilator while her body is trying to remove all of the toxins from the poisoning."

"Did the lab discover how Roderick and Evelyn were poisoned yet?" Dahlia asked as she taped another crime scene photo to the bulletin board in the conference room.

"Traces of ethylene glycol were discovered in the teapot and two of the teacups," Sam read aloud. "The two teacups were tested for DNA, and the saliva on the cups was positively identified as belonging to Roderick Morgan and Evelyn Norris."

Dahlia jotted the information down on the dry erase board.

"There was poison in the tea, eh?" Sam put the report back down on the table. "What did you discover about the movements of the two victims, Bennett? Did any of the staff members see them make or drink the tea?"

"Uhh ..." Dahlia scanned the documents on the table. "Yes, here it is. Mrs. Morgan's personal maid, Joyce Foster, said she was speaking with Evelyn while the head housekeeper was preparing the tea in the pot that forensics confirmed had ethylene glycol in it."

"Did the maid see Evelyn spike the tea?" Sam asked.

Dahlia shook her head.

"No," she replied. "The maid said that Evelyn had been preparing the tea like she had done a million times before, so she didn't think anything of it."

"But was that maid present in the kitchen watching Evelyn make the tea the entire time?"

"The maid claimed that she left the mansion shortly before Evelyn put the tea on the serving tray to take with her when she went to speak to Roderick," Dahlia paused. "Which means that Evelyn did have the opportunity to murder Roderick."

"Bingo," Sam said. "Now we need a motive."

"If only Evelyn would come out of her coma," Dahlia said with a sigh.

Sam said nothing. His attention was entirely focused on one of the sheets of paper in front of him on the table.

"Hey, Bennett," Sam started to say. "Evelyn Norris only came into existence twenty-five years ago; if that's the case, then there must be another woman out there that disappeared around the same time."

Standing at the dry erase board, looking over some photos, Dahlia turned to face her partner.

"That's a good point," she tapped the end of the dry erase marker against her palm. "Evelyn would have been about twenty-five to thirty years old back then, and a fully grown adult woman can't materialize out of thin air, so there must be a record of another woman somewhere that can explain where she came from."

"Good, I'm glad you agree," Sam said. "Happy hunting."

"Wait, what?" Dahlia asked. "How the hell am I supposed to find that information?"

"Don't know, don't care. Just find it."

Dahlia let out a huff.

"Fine," she said before she sulked her way out of the room.

Sam waited a few minutes before leaving the room and heading out of the department entirely. Hopping in his car, he drove out to the post office.

"I need this sent priority, certified and any other fancy things to ensure that this makes it to its destination as soon as possible and as safely as possible," Sam said to the clerk at the counter.

"Sure, Sir," the unenthused clerk said, popping his gum.

"This letter is crucial," Sam tapped the letter with his index finger. "It's going to the National Appeals Board to appeal a parole decision; you don't want a vicious criminal walking around on the streets, do you?"

The clerk looked up from placing a label on the envelope, and seeing Sam's serious expression, shook his head vehemently.

"Good, that's what I thought."

With the letter all set to be sent off to its destination, Sam paid for his delivery and returned to his car. Hands gripping the steering wheel, he let out a breath. *That bastard can't get out of prison yet, he can't ... he just can't.*

Stopping at a fast food restaurant down the street from the post office, Sam texted Dahlia to ask if she wanted him to bring her anything to eat before he returned to the department. Much to his surprise, her response was some information instead of a food order.

I think I got something.

Like what? Sam texted back.

There was a woman named Eve Norman that seemed to drop off the face of the Earth right around the time Evelyn Norris came in it.

Nice! Keep digging. I'll be back in a bit.

Instead of driving back to the department, Sam made a trip back up to Odette General Hospital.

"Hey, doc," Sam asked one of the attending physicians. "Any chance that Evelyn Norris could be taken off the ventilator? She's a crucial witness in a murder case."

The doctor pulled up the chart on the computer behind the desk at the nurses' station.

"Let me see here," he read over the report.

Sam watched him intensely, hoping for good news.

"It's been a few days, and her stats are improving," the doctor said. "What I can do is a spontaneous breathing trial to see if Evelyn might be able to start breathing independently, but while still attached to the ventilator, in case she's not quite at that point yet. If she does well, we can start weaning her off of it."

"All right, I guess. As long as she stays alive, I can't argue, can I?" Sam said. "Oh, by the way, doc, there's been an update in the contact information at the police department. If Evelyn Norris wakes up, only contact me. I'll give you my card with my information on it, so you have it. I am the one to be contacted, not Detective Bennett like originally written in the reports."

"Sure. I'll update the records with that information."

"Thanks, doc."

Sam fished a business card out of his wallet and handed it to the doctor to update Evelyn's records.

★★★

Sam nearly ran directly into Dahlia, who was returning from the break room, while he was hurrying out of the bullpen the following afternoon.

"Is everything okay, Sam?" she asked.

"Yeah," Sam said. "I have somewhere to be."

"Does it have to do with Evelyn? Did she wake up?"

Do I tell her? Do I tell her that Evelyn actually is awake? My goody-two-shoes partner might interfere with the information I need to get out of Evelyn to get to the bottom of what really caused Roderick's death. Sam exhaled slowly.

"Yeah, she's awake," he said. "Let's go to the hospital."

"That's great news! I'll grab my files and meet you at the car," Dahlia said before scurrying off.

Sam brought a hand up to his face and cursed to himself.

Now, why the fuck did I do that?

★★★

Sam and Dahlia sat quietly by Evelyn's bedside, watching closely as the sleeping woman's eyes fluttered open.

"What ... happened?" Evelyn asked in a tone barely above a whisper. "Where ... am I?"

"You're in the hospital, Evelyn," Dahlia said, gently rubbing the older woman's arm.

Evelyn looked up at Dahlia, confused.

"I'm Detective Dahlia Bennett, and that is Detective Samuel Marlowe," Dahlia introduced herself and Sam.

"I did it," Evelyn said, her voice a little stronger.

There was a brief moment of silence, primarily because Dahlia and Sam were both somewhat stunned.

"Does that mean what I think it means?" Dahlia asked and looked over at Sam.

"You're talking about Roderick, right?" Sam asked Evelyn, coming over to her bedside.

"Yes, I did it. I killed him."

"That was easy," Dahlia pulled her phone out of her pocket to record the conversation. "Can you tell us why you did it?"

"He killed Mr. and Mrs. Morgan because he was going to lose his inheritance because of how he had been acting, rude, lazy, and entitled and so many other terrible things ..." Evelyn closed her eyes and sighed.

"That's a good story," Sam said. "Now how about the truth?"

"What do you mean?"

"You already admitted to killing Roderick, so why don't you tell us the real reason you killed him, *Eve Norman?*"

Dahlia's eyes traveled from Sam's face to Evelyn's and back again.

"Eve Norman?" Evelyn repeated.

"You heard me; Eve Norman," Sam said. "You see, when we began searching the database for information on Evelyn Norris, we discovered that Evelyn didn't come into existence until about twenty-five years ago. No offense, honey, but you are not twenty-five. We did some further digging for similar ladies who vanished right around the same time that Evelyn appeared, and we came up with a near perfect fit: Eve Norman. How am I doing so far?"

Evelyn closed her eyes and sighed.

"What were you running from that you had to change your identity?" Sam asked. "Did it have anything to do with Roderick?"

Sam knew that he hit a nerve when he saw the tears beginning to well up in Evelyn's eyes.

"What's your connection to Roderick?" he asked.

"It wasn't that I was running from anything," Evelyn started to explain, pausing as she tried to swallow her tears. "I changed my identity because I wanted to keep an eye on my son."

"Say what?" Dahlia nearly dropped her phone after hearing that bombshell. "Roderick was your son?"

"Yes," Evelyn said. "Roderick was my son."

"But you gave him up for adoption," Sam said. "Why did you do that?"

"I couldn't care for him, even though I wanted to," Evelyn said, tears welling up in her tired eyes again. "I had been in a relationship with Roderick's father, and I truly loved that man. I thought he loved me, but I learned otherwise when I discovered that he had a wife and children. If I had known that, I never would have started a relationship with him, but I can't do anything about that now. I found out a short time later that I was pregnant and I told Roderick's father. He told me that he wanted to end the affair and he wanted nothing to do with this child."

"I'm so sorry, Evelyn," Dahlia said when Evelyn paused.

Evelyn patted the young woman's hand before continuing her tale.

"I didn't know what to do. I wanted to have Roderick, but there was no way that I could take care of him. I did the best thing for him that I could at the time: I gave him up for adoption," she said. "After a year or so, I desperately wanted to know what happened to my little boy. I never stopped thinking about him since the moment I gave him up, and I needed to know if my son was all right. I saw that the Morgan family had adopted a child and immediately knew that it was Roderick. He had a distinct birthmark around his left wrist, so I knew for sure that my son was with them."

"So, you became an employee of the Morgan family," Sam said.

"Yes, I thought that I could get a good job while watching my son grow up at the same time. It was the perfect opportunity to help raise my son," Evelyn said.

"But why did you change your name?" Dahlia asked.

"My name was on Roderick's birth certificate. If the Morgans discovered that I was Roderick's mother and that I wanted a job from them, they might have thought that I was either reconsidering the adoption, wanted money or something else. I figured it would be easier if I left that life behind and became someone else."

"You secured a job with the Morgans, then what?" Sam asked.

"I watched my son grow up. It was so wonderful. He and I actually grew very close, as if he knew deep down that I was his biological mother," Evelyn closed her eyes and let out a breath. "But then I noticed him starting to develop some of his father's tendencies. Roderick started drinking, womanizing and partying. I was so crushed because the Morgans were so good to him. I tried to instill good values in him, but I guess his father's genetics won out."

"And then you find out that Roderick murdered his adoptive parents," Dahlia said.

Evelyn began to tear up again, and Sam quickly pulled out a handkerchief and handed it to her.

"My heart broke when Roderick told me straight out that he did kill Mr. and Mrs. Morgan," she said in between sobs. "I couldn't live knowing that I brought this monster into the world. I couldn't bear to keep going and see Roderick benefitting from murdering Mr. and Mrs. Morgan. The worst part was that he probably wouldn't get the money because he admitted to killing them. That meant that Mr. and Mrs. Morgan died for no reason."

"You put ethylene glycol in the tea that night," Sam said.

"Yes. I sneaked into the garage and took a bottle of anti-freeze. I've heard it tastes sweet, so I didn't think that Roderick would notice if I put it in the tea. I chose a sweet tea flavor that evening to help mask it," Evelyn shook her head. "I thought that he and I could drink the tea and then drift off to sleep together and be out of this world. Instead, here I am."

She weakly lifted her arms.

"I'm ready to pay my dues," Evelyn said to Sam and Dahlia.

Sam looked at Dahlia out of the corner of his eye and saw her hand hovering over her handcuffs.

"Bennett, can I see you outside in the hallway for a second?" he asked.

Dahlia followed him out into the hallway.

"What's wrong?"

"Listen, let's not rush to arrest Evelyn," Sam said. "I mean, she just woke up from this horrific ordeal. Arresting her now would be cruel. Let's wait until she's released from the hospital to bring her into the station, okay?"

"But Sam, she confessed," Dahlia said. "She killed someone; we can't let her go."

"Yes, she did, you're very observant. I'll tell you what, Bennett," Sam said. "Let's go back to the station. You can type up her confession and make it all pretty. Once that's done, we'll bring it here for Evelyn to sign and then you can arrest her after she's cleared to leave the hospital, okay?"

Dahlia frowned and folded her arms across her chest.

"Fine, if you say so."

★★★

Dahlia arrived at the hospital the next day with Evelyn's typed up confession. She headed into Evelyn's hospital room and was immediately stunned by what she saw.

"Sam?" Dahlia asked.

Her partner was seated on Evelyn's bed. Evelyn was gone, and the bed looked like it had been recently changed and prepped for a new patient.

"Where's Evelyn?" Dahlia asked him.

"Evelyn Norris is dead," Sam said.

"Say what? Dead?"

"Yes. Dead. Gone."

Dahlia's heart sank.

"But … she seemed to be doing so well yesterday. How could she just die like that?"

Sam patted the space on the bed next to him. Dahlia joined him, flopping down next to her partner.

"Don't forget, Bennett, Evelyn was poisoned. It looks like she gave a valiant effort to remove all the poison from her life but couldn't keep going on after all the damage it had done."

Dahlia let out a breath and thought about what Sam told her. After mulling it over for a few minutes, she looked up at him.

"Wait, how did you know before me?" she asked. "I thought the doctors were supposed to contact both of us if anything happened with Evelyn. Something doesn't feel right about this."

"What doesn't feel right?" Sam asked. "Is it because you didn't get to put the cuffs on Evelyn and bring her into the station to be charged with murder? Is it because the killer didn't get brought to justice in court?"

Dahlia opened her mouth to respond but stopped before any words came out.

"I don't know," she said eventually. "Something doesn't feel … right."

"Listen, Bennett, you did good. Sometimes, justice isn't always black and white. Eve, in this case, was a gray area. I know you like the rulebook, Bennett, but, damn, you need to lighten up!"

"Sam, if I acted like you, I'd be doing time in the penitentiary," Dahlia said, folding her arms across her chest, a small pout appearing on her lips.

Sam wrapped his arm around Dahlia's shoulders.

"As long as you're in the cell next to me, Bennett, then I'd say that justice has been served," he said with a grin.

Sam stood up from the bed. He pulled his wallet out of his pocket and gave some money to Dahlia.

"Here, why don't you go buy some lunch and head back to the station?" Sam said. "We'll wrap up the paperwork and give a sound bite to the media to wrap up this case."

"What are you going to tell them?" Dahlia asked as she took the money from him.

"Roderick killed Evelyn after he found out that he wasn't going to inherit his parents' money in a murder-suicide pact."

Dahlia sighed.

"Well, it won't make Roderick seem any worse," she said.

"He's a good scapegoat."

Dahlia eyed him warily.

"You know, you're a little too nonchalant for losing a crucial witness in such an important case," she said. "Are you sure you didn't sneak her out of the hospital or something so she could go back to being Eve Norman and not have to pay for her crimes against Roderick?"

"That's funny, Bennett," Sam said. "I couldn't do that because we'd know her secret identity and you, my dear girl scout, could easily go and find her, and as you put it, bring her to justice."

He watched as Dahlia left the hospital room, shoving his hands into his pants pockets.

'Are you sure you didn't sneak her out of the hospital or something so she could go back to being Eve Norman and not have

to pay for her crimes against Roderick? Sam chuckled as he recalled Dahlia's words.

That's kinda funny, Bennett. And do you know why?

Because that's precisely what happened.

Eve has a new identity and is now finally free.

AFTERSHOCKS

Sam sat on the couch in the living room of his foster sister's apartment. Elbow resting on the arm of the couch, he held his chin in his hand.

"What the hell am I supposed to do, Nin?" Sam asked.

Nina Hill softly sat down next to him and put a hand on his shoulder.

"You knew this was going to happen eventually, Sam," she said.

Sam let out a breath.

"I know," he said. "But I wasn't ready for it yet. He still was supposed to have another seven years in prison. I was supposed to have another seven years to prepare before Seth was released from prison for what he did to my mom."

"I wish I had answers for you," Nina said, resting her head on Sam's shoulder.

After a few moments, she lifted her head and looked at Sam.

"I may not have answers, but I might have a little something to help take the edge off."

"Take the edge off?" Sam repeated as Nina got up from the couch and crossed the living room, disappearing into her bedroom for a few seconds.

He eyed her with a mixture of suspicion and surprise when she returned with two joints.

"Marijuana?" Sam asked. "Since when are you a drug user?"

"Well," Nina said with a shrug. "After Dad … died … I was in bad shape."

"I remember."

The death of Nina's father, Edwin Hill, hadn't been easy for anyone. Sam's best friend, mentor, former partner on the police force and foster father had been killed during a school shooting at Odette Senior High nearly four years ago. The tragic death, combined with the gravity of the incident, had sent shockwaves out across Odette, with several individuals, like Sam and Nina, still feeling the aftershocks.

"One of my friends gave me a little something to help me relax," Nina sat back down on the couch. "I was able to forget about … things … for a little while, which was an amazing feeling."

Oh, I'm well aware of what drugs can do, Nin. I'm in the same boat you are.

"There was no way that I was going to pass that up," she said. "It's one of the things I can use to make things feel a little better for a while. Maybe it can help you, too."

Without saying anything, Sam accepted the joint from Nina, who grabbed a lighter from the nearby end table. They sat in silence, Sam's arm around Nina, his head back against the top of the couch, his eyes closed. It was nice, he considered, not having to feel for a while. It was something he longed for; searching for it with the various painkillers he'd been taking over the past four years.

When his cell phone rang, Sam wanted to throw the contraption out the window.

"You don't have to answer that, do you?" Nina murmured into his shoulder.

"Yeah, I do," Sam groaned. "I set the ringtone to be a specific song when my pain-in-the-ass partner calls or texts, so I know it's her."

Nina shifted to allow Sam to pull his phone out of his pocket. Reading the text message, he let out a long sigh.

"Sorry, Nin," he said. "I gotta go. Bennett, apparently, has someone down at the station reporting something that I need to hear."

Nina grabbed Sam's hand and gave it a light squeeze. He repeated the gesture before letting her hand go and making his way toward the apartment door.

★★★

Sam eyed the girl across from him in the interrogation room of the Odette Police Department with aloofness, though he did his best to project an air of professionalism.

"Okay, so you were snooping around the house you were babysitting in," he checked his notes. "What did you find?"

Honestly, he wasn't expecting much from this report. Gabby McGowan was a fifteen-year-old girl who, after putting the kids she was babysitting to bed, decided to poke around her employer's fancy house. Maybe the guy was into some kinky shit, and it scared her. Either way, things didn't seem promising. Dahlia was going to hear it for calling him in for this.

With a shaky hand, Gabby pulled her cell phone out of the pocket of her ripped stonewashed jeans. Tapping a few buttons, she accessed the phone's photo gallery.

"I … I took photos, 'cause I was afraid that if I took anything, he'd notice," Gabby pushed her phone across the table to Sam.

"And what did you find?"

"I found drugs. In a hollowed-out book in the upstairs study."

Sam raised a tawny eyebrow in surprise. Nope. Definitely not expecting that.

"How do you know they weren't legal prescription drugs?" Sam asked. "The guy is a doctor, after all."

"I go to high school. The kid with the locker next to mine, I've seen him give pills like that to some of his friends. I know they're not legal 'cause he got busted by Principal Porter and is now in rehab or something," Gabby said. "I also found a small leather-bound book. It had a bunch of people's names in it."

Sam flipped through the photos of the names in the black book. He was unfamiliar with most, though he did recognize a couple. *Benedict Stoner. Shit. Hope he knows to keep his mouth shut*, Sam thought.

There was one other name, however, that snared his attention. Sam's charcoal gray eyes stared at the photo, unable to move.

"Um, Detective?" Gabby said after Sam's prolonged silence.

Sam blinked a few times in an attempt to bring his attention back to the present.

"I'm going to need you to make an official statement," he cleared his throat but was still unable to look away from *that* name. "We'll look into the matter. Thank you for bringing this to our attention."

Gabby seemed visibly relieved, slowing the nervous bouncing of her leg.

"I'll have my partner come in to take your formal statement while we get these photos from your phone uploaded onto our system."

Sam fetched his partner, Junior Detective Dahlia Bennett, to have her take Gabby's official statement while he had the photos uploaded onto the Odette Police Department's system. Barely finished uploading the photos, Sam practically pushed the IT rep out of his desk chair. He needed to see if that name had actually been there or if he merely imagined it. Sam desperately hoped that the name was like an optical illusion and wasn't truly in those pages.

Button-mashing his mouse, Sam flew through the photos. The blood in his veins felt as though it had been struck with a bone-chilling coldness that caused every cell in his body to freeze. The only movement he felt was the beating of his heart, which pounded deafeningly in his ears as if he was standing next to the speakers at a rock concert.

Nina Hill.

★★★

Having finished taking the young girl's statement, Dahlia dismissed her from the interrogation room before heading to the bullpen to find Sam. She saw him at his desk, staring at his computer screen with a dumbfounded expression on his face.

"Are you trying to crack the Zodiac Killer code?" Dahlia said to Sam. "Because that is some serious concentration."

He whipped his head up to look at Dahlia.

"What did you say, Bennett?" Sam asked, apparently not having heard what she said.

Dahlia frowned. She'd been expecting a snarky comeback from her partner, not for him to sit and stare at his computer screen like a character in a movie that had been paused. They'd been working together long enough for Dahlia to be able to recognize something was deeply troubling Sam.

"You okay there, Sam?" she asked, her viridian eyes regarding him with concern.

"Dandy," Sam grumbled in response.

"Sure, if you say so."

"I do say so."

He clicked out of the photo he'd been looking over and turned around to face Dahlia. She was somewhat taken aback by the look of him. Sam's pupils were dilated, and his eyes were bloodshot. The bags under his eyes were puffy and swollen and made him look exhausted as if he hadn't slept for a few nights.

"Really? 'Cause you kind of look like you spent the weekend at a cannabis festival," Dahlia said.

"A weekend at a cannabis festival is better than your permanent residency at ass kissers anonymous."

Dahlia let out a huff.

"You can be a real ass sometimes, you know that?"

"It's why you love me, Bennett, don't deny it," Sam said. "Now let's go see what Dr. Trenton has to say about little Miss Nosey's discoveries."

He stood up from his chair and started heading toward the door of the bullpen, Dahlia following behind him.

★★★

Aaron Trenton was a well-respected physician with a flourishing practice in Odette, Colorado. Given the nickname "Dr. Stud Muffin," Trenton was not only popular for his medical abilities, but also for his good looks and charm. Gorgeous and feathered golden hair, bright cyan blue eyes, chiseled jawline and naturally muscular physique, Trenton enjoyed his appeal to the masses and entered into the realm of fame, becoming a regular guest contributor on the local television program, AM Odette. Doing so increased the business at his practice considerably, especially with the female portion of the population.

According to the receptionist at Trenton's practice, the celebrity doctor was at the television studio in downtown Odette, preparing to film a segment for an upcoming broadcast. Sam and Dahlia drove out to the news studio, and after being reluctantly allowed back to the set by the office manager, the two detectives found the good doctor sitting on the set's couch having his make-up done.

"Gee, and here I thought you were a natural beauty," Sam said as he and Dahlia walked onto the set. "Ah, well, I guess we all can't be as pretty as me."

Dahlia opened her mouth to say something but opted to shake her head instead. Trenton shooed aside the make-up artist to allow himself to get a clear view of the two individuals who had approached him.

"Sorry, kids, autographs will have to wait until after the taping," he said.

"Yeah, we're not here for autographs," Sam replied as both he and Dahlia showed their police badges to Trenton. "We're here to discuss a rather intoxicating secret of yours."

Trenton's expression remained pleasant.

"Intoxicating secret?" he repeated. "I'm not quite sure what you're referring to, detectives, but I'm always willing to assist my fellow public servants."

Trenton suggested speaking in a dressing room for more privacy. He left the couch and began leading Sam and Dahlia off the set and down the hall where the dressing and storage rooms were located. While doing so, they passed by the show's host, who looked at Trenton questioningly. With a wink, the doctor reassured her that he'd be back momentarily. Her confusion alleviated, she smiled and continued sipping on her frappe as she headed toward the set.

"So," Trenton began once the three of them entered the guest dressing room. "What is this 'secret' you wish to discuss?"

"Care to enlighten us on how a whole shitload of hardcore drugs ended up in your possession?" Sam asked.

"I'm sorry, what?" Trenton asked in response.

"It has come to our attention that several illegal drugs were found in your residence," Dahlia said. "Along with a book of names, presumably your customers."

"We don't know they're customers," Sam said to Dahlia with a scowl.

Dahlia glanced up at him quizzically. He seemed annoyed at her implication, which was reasonable to assume, that the names in the book Gabby found were Trenton's clients. She decided to brush it off for now.

"I assure you, detectives," Trenton said. "I haven't the faintest idea what you're referring to."

Sam pulled his cell phone from out of his black dress pants pocket. He was sure to have the IT rep back at the department download Gabby's photos onto his phone as well as the system.

"Recognize this room?" Sam asked, showing Trenton one of the photos.

The doctor took a look at the photo.

"It appears to be my home office."

Sam flipped forward to the next photo.

"And is this the bookshelf in your study?"

"Well, yes," Trenton's smile slowly began to disappear. "My grandfather made that bookshelf; you can see where he carved his initials into the wood on the inside of the top shelf. There's no denying it's mine."

"Based on that information, then this fake book filled with drugs and a list of names must be yours," Sam said.

Trenton did not respond immediately.

"Where did you get those photos of my house?" he asked. "If you entered my residence without my permission, then those photos were illegally obtained, and therefore, inadmissible—"

With a tsk, tsk, Sam shook his head slowly.

"Gee, all pleasantries seem to always go out the window when the perp's faced with irrefutable evidence," he said to Dahlia.

"I know, right?" Dahlia said in agreement. "If only all his fangirls saw him now; they'd think this man was an imposter and drop him like a hot potato."

Trenton glared at Sam and Dahlia, his clear blue eyes darkened, like the calm, crystal clear ocean waters suddenly succumbing to a nasty squall.

"I refuse to say anything further until I have spoken to my attorney," Trenton growled.

"What do you need your attorney for?" Sam asked, looking at Dahlia with a smile. "You're not under arrest; we're having a friendly chat, right, Bennett?"

"Right, Sam," Dahlia agreed on cue.

"Unless, of course," Sam said, a sly grin creeping onto his face. "You'd like us to arrest you, and by doing so, we could speak to the DA on your behalf and try to recommend a good deal for you in exchange for your cooperation."

Trenton gave Sam a grin that nearly matched his own. *That smile doesn't seem right,* Sam thought. *What's he up to?*

"You know what? I think you're right, Detective," the doctor said, looking squarely at Sam. "I think you and I might be able to work something out."

The tone of the doctor's voice caused Sam's grin to fade. His police instincts were telling him that Trenton knew about his own dark drug secrets. But how?

"I'm sure we could come to a *mutually* beneficial agreement," Trenton said to him.

"Sam," Dahlia whispered and nudged him. "What are you doing? Why are you letting this scumbag drug dealer get to you?"

Because I have no choice, Bennett. He's got me by the balls, and he knows it.

"You tell me I'm an ass earlier and now you're giving me hell for trying to be a calm and professional guy?" Sam said. "You're sending me mixed signals, Bennett."

Dahlia rolled her eyes and shook her head.

Hopefully, that will keep her off my back for a bit.

The show host, who happened to have blown a bubble with her gum at the moment the detectives and the doctor emerged from the dressing room, stopped inflating the bubble, causing it to splatter on her face.

"Wait, what the hell is going on?" she whined. "Where are you taking Aaron? And why is he in handcuffs?"

"Because," Sam said. "Dr. Trenton has been a bad boy and needs a time out."

The host blinked as the three continued forward toward the exit.

"But what about my show!?"

★★★

Sitting in the interrogation room at the Odette Police Department, as he had done earlier in the day, with Trenton and his flashy and costly attorney, Adrian Ellwood, Sam leaned back in his chair, a deep frown set on his face. How the hell could this have been happening in his city right under his nose? Trenton had a sweet operation running right out of his medical practice. His 'clients' would come to see him at his practice. They would be given a script for some medicine, which was actually the illegal narcotics and prescriptions, which would then be filled at the pharmacy.

"Okay," Sam motioned to Trenton and his lawyer. "Let's hear all the details."

"My wife, Lauren, owns a pharmacy; she took over her grandparents' convenience store when they retired and added the pharmacy. Lauren would fill my patients' prescriptions, both the legal and not so legal ones."

"And she agreed to do this why?"

"Medical school is not cheap," Trenton said. "Besides, it's a lucrative business, as I'm sure you know, Detective."

Sam muttered to himself, causing Trenton to smirk.

"Continue," Sam said, doing his best to keep his voice calm and even.

"Lauren and I composed our own code to write on the prescriptions to designate the patient's drug of choice."

"Do you have a legend of all your codes?"

Trenton's lawyer opened up his briefcase, fiddled around with some papers, and then produced a piece of paper.

"We will provide a copy of the code and legend contingent upon a deal with the DA," the lawyer said.

"That's not my decision," Sam said. "I can recommend stuff to the DA, but she has the final say."

"Oh, don't worry, Detective, I've already contacted the DA to open up the discussion for a deal."

Adrian returned the paper to his briefcase and gestured for Trenton to continue his story.

"The patients would come into my clinic to get their prescription, which Lauren would then fill down at the pharmacy. They would look like any other person coming to have their scripts filled."

"This leather book that you had in your study," Sam said. "Are those your clients' names inside?"

Please don't let that be your book of clients.

"Yes, that is a list of my clients," Trenton said. "Should anything happen, where one of them would try to turn me over to the police, let's say that I would have no qualms about providing evidence of their illegal drug use to the police in return or the public in the case of some of my well-known clients."

"But those can't all be your clients," Sam said. "In looking through the extensive list, I believe I recognized the name of a dealer or two."

Trenton's knowing smirk returned.

"Yes. Some of the people in the book are other dealers. I provide the product, and they sell it. We split the profits; it's as simple as that."

The doctor turned to his lawyer.

"Adrian, you're dismissed," he said.

"Aaron, I can't—"

"I said, you're dismissed," Trenton was far more adamant. "The good detective, here, and I have a personal matter to discuss. Now, leave."

Adrian stood up, fixed his suit coat and glared at Trenton as he stormed toward the door.

"If the DA doesn't agree to a deal, Trenton, know that it is your fault," he grumbled before leaving, slamming the door behind him.

Sam's stomach churned and his throat burned from the bile bubbling up in it even thinking about some of the names in the book that could link him to Trenton's operation and expose his drug habit.

"Well, you've got me all to yourself, doc," Sam said. "What did you want to talk about?"

"As you pointed out, not all of the names in the book are my patients; some are dealers," Trenton said. "Including Benedict Stoner."

Fuck. He knows.

The pen Sam held in his hand snapped from his death grip on the plastic.

"What about him?" the detective feigned ignorance.

How much does Trenton actually know?

"Please, Detective," Trenton let out a small laugh. "Don't play coy with me. You're a client of Stoner's. He's told me so."

"Sure, because drug dealers are such reliable people."

"I mean, I have proof."

Shit.

"Do you now?" Sam asked, his tone challenging the doctor. "Pray tell, what is this alleged proof?"

"Oh, you know, only your fingerprints on some bottles and bags," Trenton said.

That stupid son of a bitch! He played me! Fuck you, Stoner! Sam let out a slow breath.

"Fine. What do you want?" he asked.

"Make these charges disappear, Detective, and I'll forget I ever heard Stoner say you were one of his clients," Trenton said.

The doctor leaned back in his seat and folded his arms across his chest. It took every ounce of self-restraint Sam had to not leap over the table and begin pummeling Trenton's pretty-boy face in.

How the hell was he supposed to pull this off? Dahlia knew about Trenton's drug empire, so there was no way that he could make the case just disappear.

On the other hand, could he risk sending Trenton to trial and letting the possibility of his drug habit come up? That would completely ruin him as a police officer. Sam's frown deepened. There had to be another way, one that put Trenton away, but one that didn't have the risk of his secret getting out.

I thought that bastard Stoner was going to keep his mouth shut in exchange for me keeping his ass out of prison ... I think we need to have a little chat. Sam stood up from the table and headed toward the door.

"I'll see what I can do to make this little problem disappear," he said, hand on the doorknob. "Don't go anywhere."

"I'll be anxiously awaiting your return," Trenton said with a little wave.

Fuckin' dirtbag.

★★★

"Christ, Bennett," Sam said when he laid eyes upon the numerous boxes of evidence Dahlia and some additional officers had collected from Trenton's residence while he questioned the doctor. "How the hell did we miss this one?"

Dahlia put her hands on her waist as she surveyed the extensive collection of evidence.

"Probably because the drug dealers were two well-respected citizens with squeaky clean records and the manner in which they conducted their business was so ordinary that there was no way eyebrows would ever be raised."

Sam rubbed the nape of his neck.

"Yeah, but I'm a cop, Bennett," he started to say.

"And what am I? A girl-scout?"

Sam let out a slow breath.

"You and I are cops, happy now?" he grumbled. "We're detectives. The root word is detect; we discover and investigate things, yet we couldn't detect a mondo drug dealing operation taking place in a town whose number of residents is only a fraction of the capacity of the Pepsi Center in Denver!"

"We're only human, Sam," Dahlia tried to reassure him. "We're not superheroes like Superman or Wonder Woman; we're not infallible."

"Says the perfectionist."

Dahlia gave her partner a small smile.

"While it would be great to be able to stop crime before it happened," she said. "It isn't possible. That's why the Odette Police Department exists. What matters is that we put a stop to the Trenton drug dealing enterprise before it could claim any more victims."

"Yeah, but only because a fifteen-year-old girl with an unhealthy curiosity happened to stumble across some evidence," Sam said with a huff.

"Don't you remember what the new recruits are taught at the academy regarding witnesses?" Dahlia asked. "Witnesses are never perfect."

"You are an incurable optimist, you know that, Bennett? It's disgusting."

"But you're stuck with me," Dahlia said with a grin.

"Gee, thanks for the reminder. Say, Bennett, I might as well drown my sorrows and take a peek into some of this evidence; grab me a pop from the cafeteria, will you?"

Before she had a chance to question if his feet were broken, Sam played both the seniority and the "that's an order, Bennett" cards. Dahlia gave her partner a mock salute before heading down to the police department cafeteria. Once she was a safe distance away, Sam locked the door to the evidence room. Putting on a fresh pair of latex gloves, he rushed over to the box that contained the book of Trenton's clients' names. Carefully skimming through the pages, he searched through the book until he found the page that held Nina's name. Sam meticulously tore out that page, taking care not to leave any trace of tampering behind. He then repeated the action with the page containing Benedict Stoner's name.

"Well, Mr. Emmons, Mr. Young and Mr. Donato," he said to himself, referring to the three other names on the page besides Nina's. "Looks like the three of you get a free pass. For now. Don't fuck it up. And as for you, Mr. Stoner, we need to talk."

Folding up the pieces of paper, Sam slipped them into his pocket. He then replaced the book into its evidence box, discarded his latex gloves and unlocked the evidence room door shortly before Dahlia returned.

"Here's your pop, your majesty," she said as she handed him the can.

"Took you long enough," Sam replied with a grin.

Dahlia rolled her eyes and shook her head.

"You're such an ass," she said.

"What was it you said to me earlier?" Sam asked. "'But you're stuck with me'?"

Dahlia couldn't help but smile at her partner's comment.

"Did you start sorting through the evidence yet?" she asked.

"Yeah, I was going to, but that's when I remembered that's what rookie partners are for," Sam patted Dahlia on the shoulder. "Have fun, Bennett."

Opening up his soda and taking a swig, Sam strolled out of the evidence room, leaving Dahlia behind. He headed up to his desk in the bullpen. Firing up his computer, Sam logged into the system under the test credentials that all the members of the IT department used to check or test the department's computer system. He pulled up the file of the photos Gabby had taken, located the page with Nina's name and promptly deleted it, followed by the picture of the page with Stoner's name.

Sure, it was probably not the way Edwin would have wanted him to protect Nina, but he didn't have much choice. As Dahlia said, it wasn't possible to prevent all crime, and even if it was, Nina's addiction came entirely out of left field, or, at least, not as bad as he convinced himself it was. Sam was sure few, if any, people knew, including Nina's mother and sister. Knowing Nina the way he did (including the fact that he and Nina had sneaked out a few times together as teenagers), he was aware that she inherited her father's stealthy skills and habits. But, now that he did have proof of her problem, Sam was ready to deliver the wakeup call his foster sister so clearly needed.

★★★

By making Dahlia sort through the evidence, Sam hoped to buy himself a few hours. Benedict Stoner owned a garage a few blocks over from the Englewood Apartments, the rundown complex where Sam used to live before his stepfather beat his mother into a vegetative state. Parking on the street outside the garage, Sam stuffed his hands into his pockets and made his way up the chipped and cracked blacktop driveway.

Wearing a pair of navy overalls, a dirty towel hanging out of his rear pocket, his hands covered in grease, Benedict Stoner was fiddling around underneath the hood of a car when Sam approached.

"Stoner, we need to talk."

Stoner looked up from the engine.

"Marlowe, hey, wasn't expecting to see you again so soon," the grizzled gray-haired man said.

He pulled the towel from his back pocket and began wiping his hands.

"What do you need, Marlowe?"

Sam glanced around the garage. There were no other workers in the immediate vicinity, but some pedestrians were walking by on the sidewalk a few feet away.

"Can we talk somewhere private?" Sam asked.

"Sure. Let's go to my office," Stoner motioned for the detective to follow him.

Inside the mechanic's cramped and cluttered office, Sam shut the door, discreetly locking it as Stoner headed over to his desk.

"You out of stock already?" Stoner asked. "Hard week at the department?"

"I guess you could say that," Sam turned to face him. "In fact, I'm working on a real doozy. Apparently, there's been a drug ring that's been operating right under our noses. It's run by a doctor named Aaron Trenton; ever hear of him?"

"The TV doc?" Stoner said. "Yeah, I heard of him. He was supposed to be on AM Odette this morning, but seems like he was booked up or something and couldn't make it."

"Know why he couldn't make it to the filming? It's because he's been arrested. Trenton's down at the police department as we speak."

"Shit. That sucks."

Sam stepped forward, placing his hands on Stoner's desk and leaning forward to close the distance between the mechanic and himself.

"Yeah. You know what else sucks?" he asked. "Trenton's book of names."

"His what?" Stoner asked, scratching his cheek, the action leaving a trail of dirt and grime.

"A book of names. Of his clients. And partners. Take a guess, Stoner, on whose name I found in there."

"Damn Trenton," Stoner threw the towel over his shoulder. "I figured he'd kept records and shit, but I didn't think he kept that much detail."

"He's a doctor, Stoner; he's supposed to be detail oriented!" Sam said, smacking his hands down on the desk.

"Can you make it go away?"

"What do you think I'm trying to do? Serve myself up on a silver platter? Of course, I'm trying to make it go away! The problem is that I don't know how."

"What's that supposed to mean?" Stoner asked.

"You see, Trenton's put me in a bit of a pickle. He wants this whole mess to go away like you do. If I don't make it go away, he plans on ratting me out to the cops. Do you know what happens if I fail my drug test or am implicated as a conspirator in the purchasing of illegal narcotics?"

Stoner leaned back in his chair, trying to back away from Sam as the detective continued to decrease the distance between them.

"I know you're one of Trenton's purchasers," Sam said. "You get stock from Trenton and then split the profits with him. Were you bragging to him about me keeping your ass out of prison? Were you?"

"Yes!" Stoner blurted out. "But it wasn't bragging! I got picked up, and then you made my charges disappear. When I came back to my garage the next day, Trenton called and asked me if I said anything about our arrangement. I told him that I had help in getting the charges dropped. He asked me how and I said I had a cop as a client."

"And so, you gave him my name, you fucking idiot?"

"Trenton asked for your name! He said it would be good to have a cop on our side to help with the business! I thought it was a good idea!"

"Christ, Stoner! I think you've been indulging a little too much in your own product because your brain is completely fried."

Sam closed his eyes and pinched the bridge of his nose. He felt a headache coming on.

"Trenton said you had evidence against me," Sam said. "What is it and where is it?"

"Evidence?" Stoner's question sounded genuine. "What are you talking about?"

"He said you had my fingerprints on some evidence that could be used to link me to you and your drug dealing activities; where is that evidence? I need it."

"I ain't got evidence against you! You know me, Marlowe; I'd never do that to you!"

"And I'm supposed to believe you?" Sam asked the man cowering in his chair behind the desk.

"Of course! If any one of my clients gets in trouble, I don't know them, and they don't know me. That's how it works, Marlowe! You gotta believe me!"

Sam did not immediately respond. He stood rooted to his spot, silently mulling over the situation. Stoner watched him with wide eyes. Sam cracked his knuckles.

"Sorry, Stoner, but I can't take that chance."

★★★

Leaving Stoner's garage, Sam drove out to Nina's apartment. He sat in the driver's seat of his car, eyes blankly staring forward and hands clenching the steering wheel. A few raindrops plopped down on his windshield, and Sam blinked. The sky had been cloudy majority of the day, but it now appeared the gray clouds turned dark and sinister in preparation for the impending storm. Sam got out of his car and headed up to Nina's apartment, aiming to get inside the building before the inevitable downpour commenced.

Arriving at apartment 2B, Sam rapped on the cheery creamy pastel yellow door. When she'd been apartment hunting, Sam remembered remarking to Nina that the color of the door reminded him of her, warm, sunny and cheerful. Of course, that was years ago, when things were happy. Now, he had an inkling that the two of them now resembled the black, stormy skies outside. Stuffing his hands into his pockets, Sam turned away from the door as he waited for his foster sister to come to the door.

"Sam?"

He whirled around to find Nina standing in the doorway.

"Uh, hi, Nin," Sam stammered.

He looked her over quickly, now seeing the truth of her addiction in her appearance; he could no longer deny it or try to ignore it. She, on the surface, appeared to be the same. Deep chocolate brown pin straight hair that fell a few inches past her shoulders and bangs that came to rest above wise and entrancing moss green eyes. She was naturally petite in both height and weight but made up for her lack of stature with a big and bright personality.

However, the woman standing before him was different. Her skin was flushed, eyes tired looking with bags beneath them. The gray t-shirt she wore was baggy and unflattering, her jeans, tattered and ripped. Sam's heart plummeted at the sight of his dear, sweet Nina. *I must have caught her right after she shot-up. Christ, Nin …*

"May I come in?" Sam asked.

Nina stepped aside to allow him to enter. Once Sam was inside, Nina closed the apartment door and then turned around to face her foster brother. Neither spoke, instead standing before each other for a few seconds before embracing. They clung tightly to each other as if the other was their lifeline.

They eventually separated, moving from the doorway to take a seat on the couch.

"Sammie! What happened to your hands?" Nina asked, holding his hands in hers.

Sam looked down at his knuckles and fingers. They were bruised and bloodied, with scratches and cuts coming in. *I guess Stoner's face was harder than it felt when I was beating the shit out of him at the garage.*

"I've got some bandages and disinfectant," Nina said. "Let me clean you up."

Sam watched quietly as Nina left the couch for a few minutes, returning from her bathroom across the room with a bundle of medical supplies in her arms. She cleaned the cuts and applied antibacterial ointment before bandaging Sam's most injured fingers. Once she was finished, Nina curled up to Sam's side, and he wrapped an arm around her small frame, keeping her close to him.

"Nina," Sam said, pausing as he thought of what he wanted to say. "I need to ask you something, and I need you to be completely honest with me."

Nina adjusted her position so that she could look him straight in the eye. Gazing upon her lovely face, Sam found it hard to speak. He slowly exhaled before addressing his reason for visiting.

"Nin, today we broke up a large drug-dealing ring."

"That's great, Sam," Nina said with a smile and giving Sam's hand a squeeze.

"Yeah, it would be except for one problem. Your name was in the book of clients."

Nina pulled away from Sam, getting up from the couch and walking over to a nearby table. Sam's eyes widened in shock as he watched her withdraw a cigarette from the mahogany carton and attempt to light it with a blue lighter. He stormed over to her and yanked it from between her lips.

"Hey!" Nina protested.

"Nina, look at me," Sam tossed the unlit cigarette aside and put his hands on her shoulders. "What the hell is wrong with you, Nin? I'm trying to talk to you about your problem, and you're going to light up right now? What the hell? Why are you doing this to yourself?"

Nina's eyes began tearing up. "Why are *you* doing this to *yourself?*" she tried to knock away his hands.

"What are you talking about?"

"I know about your little problem, Sam. I saw you slip some pills a couple of times, even at Clarice and Raymond's engagement party when you thought no one was looking," Nina replied. "You come in here and chastise me for what I've done, and yet you're a freakin' hypocrite!"

"Yeah, I am," Sam replied. "I might be a hypocrite, but that's because, even though I have a problem, I don't care because I stopped giving a damn about myself years ago. But you, on the other hand, you can't do this to yourself, Nin. I care too deeply to let you do this to yourself."

"Care too deeply?" the tears were streaming down Nina's face by this point. "That's bullshit, Sam! How can you say you care when this is probably the most time we've spent together since my Dad was killed! Did you ever once stop to think that Mom and Clarice needed you after he died? That I needed you? Why do you think I turned to drugs and alcohol, Sam? It was something to take the pain away because *you weren't there* to help make things better! You weren't there when we needed you, when I needed you. What happened yesterday, when you came to see me to tell me about what happened with Seth, I thought you finally understood, but I guess I was wrong."

Sam was speechless. He let his hands slide off Nina's shoulders and fall to his sides. He had distanced himself from his foster family after Edwin's death. Like Nina, he turned to self-medication to numb the pain from experiencing such a monumental loss. In an attempt to save his family from his self-destructive grieving, Sam deliberately alienated himself from the people whom he loved most and who desperately needed him at that same time. Instead of protecting them, the only thing he accomplished was to inflict more pain on Gloria, Clarice, and Nina.

"I ... I'm sorry," was all Sam could get out.

"Please, just leave," Nina said.

Without a further word, Sam respected her wishes and left the apartment.

★★★

Stretched out on the couch in his apartment, Sam continued drowning his sorrows in Southern Comfort and OxyContin. Nina's words stung. *I fucked up big time.* How the hell was he supposed to remedy this colossal mess?

Sam's cell phone buzzed and with an annoyed sigh, he grabbed it off of the end table next to the couch where he was seated. It was Dahlia. Of course it was.

"What, Bennett?" he asked.

"Sam, we have a problem," Dahlia said.

Sam pulled the phone away from his ear, Dahlia's voice coming in a little too loud for the liking of his drugged up sensitive hearing.

"What kind of problem?" he asked.

"I've been going through the evidence, specifically the book of names that Gabby found."

"And?"

"Pages are missing."

Great. She noticed.

"Maybe," Sam said, finding that thinking was a bit difficult in his current state. "Maybe Trenton had some high-profile clients that he didn't want us to find and tore out the pages to protect them."

"But that doesn't make sense," Dahlia said. "We went to talk to Trenton at the studio this morning and brought him into the police station shortly after that. He's been at the department since we brought him in; when would he have had time to destroy evidence? Are you drunk?"

"Hell, I don't know, Bennett," Sam said. "Listen ... this case ... it's going to go to vice so you can leave it alone."

"It's what?" Dahlia sounded shocked. "Wait, why are we giving this case up? We got the lead from Gabby; we did the investigating; we did the-"

"I know what we did. I was there, in case you forgot. But this case is under the jurisdiction of Vice and Narcotics. Like we would be called in for homicide, Vice and Narcotics would be called in for this kind of thing. There's nothing we can do about it, Bennett. Them's the rules."

If Vice and Narcotics arrest Trenton, then he can't use my problem against me. Plus, I know Stoner's not going to talk after I left him a bloody mess in the garage. Even if he did, no one's going to believe him over me anyway. I think ... I think I fixed my problem ... for now, at least.

In a haze from the mixture of pills and alcohol and being lost in his thoughts, Sam did not even flinch at the sound of knocking on his apartment door, breaking the silence around him.

"Gotta go, Bennett," Sam said and abruptly hung up on his partner.

Slowly making his way to the door, he was surprised, even in his inebriated state, to see who his visitor was.

"Hi Sammie," Nina said in almost a whisper.

"Hi Nina," Sam replied.

He motioned for her to come inside, which she did.

"Sam, I ..." Nina began to say, but Sam held up a hand to stop her.

"No, I'm sorry, Nina. I forgot that it wasn't only me dealing with the pain of what happened with Edwin. I mean, I knew you guys were also suffering, but ..." Sam let out a breath.

He hated sentimental crap.

"But I was afraid of losing anyone else that I loved by going down that path I chose for myself."

"I love you too, Sam. You know that. I always have and I always will," Nina replied. "And I want to say that I'm sorry, too. I also could have done more after Dad died. I should have been there to comfort you, too, instead of doing stupid shit to ease the pain."

"Guess we both screwed up royally."

"Well, they do say misery loves company."

Both smiled slightly at that thought.

"Hey, if I have to be miserable with someone," Sam said. "I'm glad it's you, Nina."

Nina laughed.

"And I'm glad it's you, Sam," she said.

BIG FISH

Junior Detective Dahlia Bennett entered into the bullpen of the Odette Police Department and a curious smirk and accompanying expression instantly jumped onto her face. She spied the golden-brown hair of her partner, Detective Samuel Marlowe, in the mirror's reflection as he primped his appearance to perfection. Sam was never this early. Ever. That, combined with the fact that he was thoroughly grooming himself, indicated to Dahlia that a major case was probably on the horizon.

"Ah, there you are, Bennett," Sam said, his mercury colored eyes focusing on Dahlia via the mirror.

He adjusted the cuffs of his crimson red dress shirt as Dahlia approached him.

"Hi Sam," she replied. "Do we have a case?"

"Not yet, but I have an inkling one is on its way," Sam replied. "The Captain—"

He leaned over to Dahlia and lowered his voice to a whisper.

"The Cap said two feds are in town, requesting the assistance of the local authorities."

Dahlia's green eyes were sparkling like fresh dew on grass. Colorado Bureau of Investigation? FBI? CIA? Regardless of the acronym, working alongside some federal law enforcement agents, Dahlia was sure, was to be a highlight of her career. Who knows? Maybe, if the case went well enough, it could include a job offer for her. Agent Bennett? A shiver of excitement shot through her petite body at the thought.

"Well, what are we waiting for?" Dahlia bounced, her curly obsidian hair swinging from side to side.

"We're waiting for the Captain to call us," Sam said, turning from the mirror to face his partner.

Dahlia turned around after Sam indicated that Captain Buchanan had stepped out into the bullpen from his office.

"Sam, Dahlia," the Captain said. "I need the two of you in my office."

"Sure thing, Cap," Sam called in response.

After a discreet fist bump, Sam and Dahlia followed the Captain into his office. Inside, they found two individuals whom neither detective recognized. They wore matching navy jackets which gave no indication of what agency they might have come from. Dahlia's eyes moved from the two guests to the file folders on the Captain's desk, which prominently displayed the FBI emblem, much to Dahlia's delight.

"Detectives, this is Agent Shawn Martell and Agent Florence Calvert from the FBI," the Captain introduced the man and woman seated in the visitor's chairs in front of his desk respectively. "And, agents, this is Samuel Marlowe and Dahlia Bennett, my finest detectives, as you requested."

Sam and Dahlia exchanged handshakes with Shawn and Florence. Shawn Martell was a similar height to Sam, falling a tad under the six-foot mark. Auburn colored hair, caramel brown eyes, and an overall aesthetically pleasing appearance, Shawn looked as though he could easily portray the 'hunky agent' role on an FBI television drama, Dahlia considered. *Christ, I'm even starting to think like Sam.*

Florence could hold her own against her partner, with a long and slender frame, sleek black hair that hung down to the middle of her back and celeste blue eyes. She was taller than the average woman, nearly measuring up to Shawn, save for an inch or two. If her partner fit the hunk role, Florence appeared to be apt for the "woman in charge" role in the drama.

"We're obviously not here to sightsee," Shawn began to say.

"We're investigating a human trafficking ring," Florence said. "And would like the assistance of the local authorities."

"You know, Flor and I," Shawn thumbed toward his partner. "Would stand out like a sore thumb in a small town like this."

"Seeing some FBI agents could cause the potential perps to run like hell," Sam said, understanding what the agents were getting at. "But two local cops poking around would be far more discreet."

"Exactly," Shawn said. "Could we get your assistance?"

"Absolutely," Sam and Dahlia replied in unison.

★★★

Sam and Dahlia followed Shawn and Florence to the Dellaria Inn, the no-questions-asked motel on the outskirts of Odette, where they and the remainder of their team were staying over the course of the investigation. After introductions were exchanged with the rest of the team, Shawn and Florence brought the detectives up to speed.

"Okay, here's the deal," Shawn said as Florence handed Sam and Dahlia a copy of their reports. "Our Nevada office notified us recently about an influx of girls between the ages of twelve and eighteen being used for prostitution in Reno. Obviously, these girls are not willing participants, as several girls from previous rescues assured us; they were kidnapped and pimped out. Some, however, were runaways who were conned or coerced into the lifestyle, so they are as much victims as the other girls that were kidnapped."

"The victims have come from various states across the US," Florence said. "Montana, Idaho, Arizona, you name it. We believe they're taken from other states so that when they're delivered to Nevada, their chances of escape are diminished from a lack of resources and unfamiliarity with the area."

"How does Odette fit in?" Sam asked.

"We triangulated the different routes taken during the previous deliveries of the girls to the prostitution rings in Nevada and most, if not all, passed through Colorado," Florence replied. "Our searches of major cities like Boulder, Denver and Colorado Springs yielded nothing."

"While big cities are good to disappear into, there are also a lot more people to possibly rat someone out," Shawn said. "In smaller towns like Odette, it's easier to blend in and disappear. You know, live quietly and don't make waves; nobody will suspect a thing, not to mention you'd fall off the police's radar in most cases."

"How can we help?" Dahlia asked, gluing her arms to her sides to prevent herself from breaking out into a happy dance.

"Witnesses from previous deliveries informed us that the drop-offs were completed via a tractor trailer," Florence said to the detectives. "We need the two of you to investigate any and all trucking companies in Odette."

"That shouldn't be too difficult," Sam said. "There's only one trucking company in Odette, Ramsey Trucking, Co."

"The owner is Wilson Ramsey," Dahlia said. "I think he began the company about forty years ago. There was a business profile done on the company on the news a few weeks ago, and I remember some bits and pieces of what they said. Business is steady; supplies trucks to businesses and private parties across town in addition to interstate commerce."

Shawn grinned at Florence.

"These guys are great," he said to her.

★★★

A well-respected company, Ramsey Trucking, Co. employed multiple tractor trailers for long or major hauls, as well as smaller trucks for additional business opportunities when a semi was too cumbersome.

"Mornin', detectives," Ramsey said, taking his feet encased in heavily stitched cowboy boots off the desk. "What can I do for you?"

"A nasty accident occurred on the highway near Nevada's border with Utah. According to the investigators of that incident, a truck driver from Colorado is believed to be a relevant witness," Sam said, improvising a cover story without batting an eyelash. "We're trying to identify the driver and would appreciate your assistance, Mr. Ramsey. We're going to need to see a list of all your employees, as well as the records of your trucks' pickups and deliveries over the past month."

"Sure," Ramsey said, picking up the phone on his desk to forward Sam's request to his secretary.

She appeared a short time later to take Sam and Dahlia to the records room.

"Mr. Ramsey said that all of his records are at your disposal and not to hesitate if you require any additional assistance or information," the secretary said.

The records room was small but efficient. There was a place for everything, and everything had its place. The rows of gray metal filing cabinets kept extensive records of the transactions throughout the business' forty-plus years of operation.

"These files are older than I am," Sam said as he skimmed through the files in the first cabinet.

"At least it's all neatly organized," Dahlia replied as she started searching through the files on the opposite end. "We don't have to fight our way through a paper jungle."

Eyeing the dates on the first couple of files, Dahlia found they were recent. She beckoned Sam over to her. They photographed the records and then forwarded those pictures to Florence and Shawn to review.

"Wait a sec," Sam paused as one of the names on the list caught his eye. "I know this guy."

Dahlia glanced up from the record she was currently reviewing.

"Who is it?" she asked.

Sam pointed to the name for his partner to see.

"Jeremy Nagel is a creep," he said. "He's done time for a few things like drug possession and robbery. Apparently, he's out on parole."

"Would he stoop to human trafficking?" Dahlia asked. "It's quite a different crime from robbery or drugs."

"Yeah, but if Nagel got a cut of the profits, it wouldn't matter what the crime is."

"What does his driving record say? Any trips to Nevada?"

Sam studied the records.

"Looks like Nagel took a trip out west a few weeks ago," he replied. "Bennett, contact the feds and let them know about Nagel. I'll go see if I can find him."

Sam headed toward the loading bays.

"Excuse me," he addressed a smart, motherly looking woman with glasses and a clipboard standing at the helm of the loading bays. "You look like you're in charge."

"Indeed, I am," the woman said with a pleasant smile, her nose wrinkling from the gesture. "How can I help you, honey?"

"I'm Detective Marlowe from the Odette Police Department," Sam showed the woman his badge. "I'm looking to speak with Jeremy Nagel; seen him around recently?"

"I'm Michelle Farina, and I'm the manager on shift," the woman replied. "I believe Jeremy went on break. He usually takes a smoke break around this time."

Michelle's pleasant expression vanished as she knitted her eyebrows together and bit her bottom lip.

"Jeremy's not in trouble, is he?" she asked. "I know he's made mistakes in the past, but he's not a bad guy–"

"Don't worry, Ms. Farina," Sam held a hand up. "I only have a few questions for Jeremy that I'm hoping he can shed some light on. He's not in trouble."

"That's good, I suppose," Michelle replied.

Sam exited the loading bays through one of the open garage doors. Glancing around, he found a dark-haired man lighting up a cigarette near a public ashtray at the corner of the building. Strolling over to the man, Sam pulled a cigarette out of his own pocket, a recent bad habit he picked up from his dear foster sister, Nina, though he would never for a moment blame her for it.

"Got a light?" Sam asked as he leaned against the side of the building.

Jeremy Nagel glanced up.

"I didn't do nothing, I didn't hear nothing, and I didn't see nothing," he said, letting out a puff of smoke.

Sam ignored Jeremy as he lit his own cigarette.

"Well, all three of those statements are double negatives, so that means that you saw, heard or did something. Or, all three," he said.

"What, are you the grammar police now?"

Sam grinned. "Only when necessary," he replied. "Actually, I'm here on a different matter. A few weeks ago, you made a delivery out to Nevada; tell me about it."

"Typical job," Jeremy shrugged. "Got my job details from Mrs. Farina. Loaded up the truck and set off."

"How long was that trip?"

"We can only drive for about eight hours, unless we've had a break in there somewhere or are coming from off-duty, so, factoring in pit stops for food, sleep and to take a piss, it took about two and a half days," Jeremy replied. "Give or take a couple of hours."

"What were you hauling?"

"Beef. There's a lot of hotels, casinos, and restaurants down in Reno, so it's a good market for beef. Gotta make all those fancy burger and steak dinners somehow, right?"

Jeremy tossed the butt of his cigarette into the ashtray.

"Why are you asking me all of this?"

"There's been a report of the transportation of illegal items over state lines," Sam said.

"Illegal items?" Jeremy repeated with a frown. "Like what?"

"You tell me."

"Dude, I got no freakin' idea. And if I did, why would I tell you? I mean, that'd be like putting the handcuffs on myself, you know?"

"And I'm supposed to believe you know nothing about this, why?" Sam replied, motioning with his cigarette.

"First, I don't pick my routes; I'm assigned them, so there is no guarantee when I'll make another trip to Nevada. Two, you can check the report and with the warehouse in Reno; I went directly from Odette to Reno and back," Jeremy said. "I mean, yeah, I stopped for a few minutes here and there to eat or sleep, but so does every other trucker out on the road. But, most importantly, you gotta believe me because I haven't done anything stupid since I got paroled. Do you know how hard it is to get a job with a felony on your record? I'm lucky I got this job, and I'm not gonna screw it up. My girlfriend ... she's pregnant. I'm not gonna mess this up and go back to prison when I got a kid on the way. I'm not that stupid."

Sam did not reply immediately. Instead, he finished his cigarette and crushed it in the ashtray.

"If you say so," Sam quoted one of his partner's usual responses. "But, a word of advice: don't leave town."

★★★

Sam and Dahlia drove out to the apartment where Jeremy and his girlfriend lived. The two detectives noted that Gwen McCormick was undeniably in her third trimester when she answered the door.

"This has been a huge change for both of us, especially since this wasn't a planned pregnancy or anything," she said as she led Sam and Dahlia into the living room. "I've quit smoking and drinking, and Jeremy's gone straight, so, like my grandma used to say, it's been a blessing in disguise."

Sam helped Gwen take a seat on the couch and then joined Dahlia on the loveseat across from it. Dahlia gave him a small smile, a reaction, Sam figured, to him letting her see his compassionate side.

"Don't say anything," he whispered to her. "You'll ruin my image."

Dahlia chuckled quietly.

"Is everything all right with Jeremy?" Gwen asked. "Last time Jeremy checked in with his parole officer, he said that Jeremy was doing well. He didn't do something stupid, did he?"

"Actually, that's what we're here to find out," Sam said. "Gwen, can you tell us about Jeremy's job at Ramsey Trucking?"

"Sure. He's been there for about a year and a half now after he passed his commercial driving test. It sucks that he has to be on the road for days at a time sometimes but it pays the bills and Jeremy seems happy with what he's doing. I mean, there's not that many job opportunities out there for people with a long rap sheet, but Mr. Ramsey's company has been good to Jeremy and me. You see that stroller over there? Some of the other drivers and workers all chipped in and bought that for us."

"That's sweet of them," Dahlia said. "I take it the other employees like Jeremy?"

"Yeah," Gwen said. "Jeremy's a good guy, really, he is. He hasn't always made the best decisions, you know? We've gone out a couple times with some of the other drivers and had a few beers together. One of the girls he works with is also a tattoo artist; she's going to do a new tattoo for me after the baby's born. I'm going to get his name and birth date on the inside of my wrist here."

"How about the manager, Michelle Farina?" Sam asked. "Have you met her?"

"No, I haven't met her, but Jeremy's mentioned her a few times. She sounds like a nice lady. She's been cool about Jeremy taking fewer out of state routes so he wouldn't be too far away now that I'm in my third trimester."

"Jeremy hasn't been taking many trips out to other states recently, then?"

Gwen shook her head.

"Nope, he hasn't, which has been kind of a relief and a big help. I think the last trip he did was to Nevada or something a few weeks ago," she paused. "Oh! It was Nevada; I remember Jeremy saying that it was a repeat customer that orders a bunch of frozen meat or something every six months. He won't have to do that route again for another, like, four months; the baby will be born by then, so it shouldn't be a problem."

"That's the only trip out of state?" Dahlia asked.

"Yeah, that's the last one," Gwen pointed toward a messy desk off near the kitchen. "There's some papers and stuff Jeremy's got from work in there detailing all his trips. You can take a look at it if you'd like."

Dahlia went over to the desk to look through the papers.

"Sam," she called him over.

He joined her at the desk.

"What's up?" Sam asked.

"Based on all this, it seems like Jeremy and Gwen are telling the truth," Dahlia said. "It doesn't look like he was out to Nevada except for the one trip a few weeks ago."

"Hmm ... well, I guess that's both good and bad news."

"Detectives?" Gwen called to Sam and Dahlia.

The two detectives both turned around to look at her.

"Please tell me that Jeremy's not in trouble."

Dahlia looked at Sam, who let out a breath.

"As of right now," he said. "It seems like Jeremy's been on the straight and narrow."

Gwen let out an audible sigh of relief.

★★★

Back at the motel, Sam and Dahlia reported their findings to Shawn and Florence.

"I like Jeremy Nagel as a suspect," Shawn said, fists against his hips. "He's got priors, the resources, and opportunity. It's like a hat trick of crime."

"Plus, the trip from Odette to Reno that Jeremy took has a couple hours unaccounted for," Florence reviewed her notes. "Despite his claims of making pit stops for personal reasons, Jeremy could actually have been making a delivery in the human trafficking ring."

Dahlia eyed Sam as Shawn and Florence continued discussing the good fit Jeremy was for their criminal. Arms folded across his chest, Sam was leaning back in his chair, so much so that it was only resting on the rear legs.

"What are you thinking?" Dahlia asked, leaning over to him so they could speak somewhat privately.

"Nagel does fit the suspect mold pretty well," Sam began to say.

"But?"

"Butts are for ashtrays."

Sam grinned as Dahlia let out a breath and rubbed her temples.

"Focus, Sam," she said.

"It seems too easy for it to be him," Sam said. "Nagel said it wasn't his decision what routes he took; he was assigned them. I mean, that could be a load of bullshit, but it didn't seem like that. Plus, when Nagel was talking about his girlfriend, he seemed sincere. I think he's telling the truth this time."

Sam abruptly let his chair fall forward so that it was on all four legs and he was sitting up straight. He looked at Dahlia with a frown.

"Plus, you heard what his girlfriend said about him not taking as many interstate routes," Sam said. "The only time he'd take them was if he was assigned them. If that's the case, there'd be no guarantee that he'd be going to Nevada, right?"

"Detective Marlowe, are you still with us?" Florence's voice drew Sam and Dahlia back into the conversation.

Sam gave her a little salute.

"Yes, ma'am, we're still with you," he said. "Now, what did you say?"

Shawn smirked while Florence folded her arms across her chest.

"I said that Shawn and I were going to go and verify Jeremy's alleged pit stops. There should be surveillance cameras at the truck stops and the convenience stores he stopped at, so we should be able to confirm if he did, indeed, stop where he said he did."

"Great, you guys do that," Sam said. "Bennett and I will stay here and review the records again."

Dahlia moved a chair next to Sam's at the computer after Shawn and Florence left.

"What are we looking for?" she asked.

"Not a clue," Sam replied as he clicked through the photos.

"In other words, you're looking for a needle in a haystack?"

"Essentially," Sam looked at his partner. "Actually, I want to see who else was assigned a Nevada route and by whom."

"You think the trafficker might be someone higher up?" Dahlia asked, an eyebrow raised.

"Maybe. I guess I can't see someone like Jeremy Nagel orchestrating, let alone executing, an elaborate scheme like this. There's got to be someone else involved."

Reviewing the Nevada trips, the detectives uncovered no distinct pattern of assignment.

"The only odd thing, if you could call it that, is that a 'T. Farina' would always be assigned a Nevada trip by 'M. Farina'," Dahlia pointed to a line on the screen. "One's a driver, and one's a manager."

"I met Michelle Farina while looking for Nagel," Sam said. "She seems nice."

"I'd like to know how she assigns the jobs," Dahlia said. "Do you think she'd be willing to talk to us and explain how she does that?"

"Can't hurt to ask."

★★★

Returning to Ramsey Trucking, Co., Sam and Dahlia asked the secretary to speak with Michelle. She arrived a few minutes later and suggested going to her office.

"Nice to see you again, detective," she said to Sam. "And it's great to meet you, Detective Bennett."

"We have a couple of questions for you, Michelle," Sam said. "How do you assign routes?"

"It depends," Michelle replied. "A driver might request a certain route, and if it's available, I'll assign it. Otherwise, it's whoever is available for the next assignment."

"How about Jeremy Nagel? Did he request any Nevada routes?"

Michelle did not respond immediately.

"Michelle?" Dahlia asked to get her attention.

"Oh, I'm sorry," Michelle said. "I … I was thinking … about Jeremy. He … he goes to Nevada all the time … he always wants those routes …"

Sam and Dahlia exchanged a look.

"That's not what it says in the records we reviewed," Sam said. "In fact, most of the work that Jeremy has been doing has been intrastate, not interstate. Bennett, do you have a copy of those records?"

Dahlia pulled out her cell phone and produced the photo of the record in question.

"The records indicate that Jeremy stopped taking any out of state trips, for the most part, starting about five months ago," Sam said. "I also chatted with him and his girlfriend earlier, and they both said the same thing."

"But there is someone who has made quite a few Nevada trips," Dahlia said. "Someone by the name of 'T. Farina.'"

"That's my husband, Tommy. He works as a driver. He'll take on extra shifts or routes when needed."

"Does he have an affinity for the Reno area?" Sam asked.

Michelle, who was sitting at her desk, began tapping her fingers. She dropped them into her lap and cleared her throat.

"I, uh ..."

"Michelle, something bad happened, didn't it?" Sam said. "Is that why you're trying to push suspicion on to Jeremy?"

"I can't say ..." Michelle squeezed her eyes shut and shook her head.

"We can help you, but you need to tell us what happened."

Michelle turned to her computer and pulled up a word processor, where she began typing away furiously. When she finished, she rotated the monitor to show Sam and Dahlia.

AFRAID OFFICE BUGGED.
CAN'T TALK OUT LOUD.
NEED HELP.

"Okay," Sam said. "Why don't we step out for some coffee and chat—"

Michelle was typing away again. Her first message was erased and was replaced by:

WATCHING US.
CAN'T RISK IT.
JOANNA'S LIFE AT STAKE.

Dahlia whipped out her cell phone and wrote on the device's notepad while Sam and Michelle continued to talk, in case the office was, in fact, bugged.

WHO'S JOANNA?

Michelle responded: MY DAUGHTER.

SHE WAS TAKEN.
NEED TO COOPERATE TO KEEP HER SAFE.
ALSO, CAN'T TELL ANYONE.

PLEASE HELP.

Dahlia assured the distraught woman across from her, **WE CAN HELP.**

★★★

The information was relayed to Shawn and Florence, and a plan was put into place to get Michelle and Tommy to a safe location where they could discuss the details of Joanna's kidnapping with Sam, Dahlia and the two federal agents. Meeting Shawn and Florence at a cemetery, the Farinas explained their situation and the two agents then shared that information with Sam and Dahlia. Every month, Michelle and Tommy would be delivered orders on where to pick up and then drop off several girls for the human trafficking ring, where they would then be distributed to a brothel in Reno. Michelle would assign Tommy the route through Nevada as per the instructions, and he would follow them. Their reward was that the life of their seventeen-year-old daughter, Joanna, was spared for another month.

It was a little over a week later that the instructions were delivered to the Farinas. Sam, Dahlia, Shawn, and Florence reviewed the instructions and put a plan in place. Dahlia and another FBI agent, Kelly, would switch places with the girls Tommy would be picking up in this shipment. Tommy loaded his truck and made the pickup, as dictated by the instructions. Shortly after midnight on a remote stretch of desert road, he pulled off to the side of the highway to where Sam, Dahlia and the FBI agents were waiting to make the swap. The three terrified teenaged girls were ushered out of the truck and into waiting cars. Dahlia and Kelly finished up their last-minute preparations for the sting before getting into Tommy's truck.

"Good thing you're short," Sam joked to Dahlia. "You can definitely pass off as a teenager."

Dahlia stuck her tongue out at her partner before she and Kelly were loaded into the trailer of Tommy's truck.

The drive was long and arduous, even with mattresses and a supply of food and water for them. They stopped a few times during the trip at truck stops, and under cover of darkness, Dahlia and Kelly stretched their legs before returning to the trailer to continue the journey. After nearly two days on the road, Tommy informed them they were almost at their destination.

"We're here," Tommy warned Dahlia and Kelly as he parked the truck. "Be ready."

Dahlia and Kelly assumed their positions of lying on the floor of the trailer near each other, scattering empty beer bottles and cans and syringes around them to give the appearance of being drugged and drunk. Opening her eyes slightly, Dahlia watched as the trailer doors opened and a man wearing a holster stepped inside.

"Two?" Holster man growled. "Why's there only two bitches here? There's supposed to be three! What are you doing, Tommy?"

Dahlia cursed internally. There was no mention of how many girls were supposed to be picked up by Tommy in the instructions, probably a safeguard against law enforcement stings like this. She could see the worry on Tommy's face, his eyes wide and his mouth slightly agape; she knew she needed to come up with something and fast.

"T-Tommy?" Dahlia asked, slurring her words. "Is Heather … uh, um … out for a swim?"

Kelly caught on to her plan and backed her up.

"Yeah … uh, what's your name again? Donny?"

Dahlia gave a giggle and moved to playfully push Kelly, deliberately missing and falling to the ground. Kelly laughed and collapsed next to her.

"It's Tommy!" Dahlia said. "It's Tommy, right?"

"Oh! Tommy! Now I remember!" Kelly tapped her temple. "You said that Heather wasn't feelin' good, so she was gonna go for a swim. Is she back yet?"

Holster looked at Tommy, his arms folded across his beefy chest.

"Oh, right," Tommy said. "Listen, the other girl … Heather … she … couldn't handle her booze and heroin. She … overdosed … I-I-I figured you guys wouldn't want a dead body on your hands, so I dumped her in the Colorado River … Figured it'd be easier on all of us … I told the girls that she was going for a swim …"

The man appeared to think over the story they presented for a few moments before letting his arms fall to his side.

"It'll probably look like she got drunk and went swimming and drowned," he said. "Good thinking, but don't ever do shit like that again. You got a problem, you let us handle it. We don't need your stupid ass putting our entire operation at risk, ya feel me?"

Tommy held his hands up in surrender.

"Of course. My mistake. I promise it will never happen again," he said.

"Good," the man walked over to Kelly and Dahlia and yanked them both up from the floor. "Let's go."

The man put zip ties around both of their wrists and used one to lock the two girls' wrists together. Once they were secured, he produced a gun from his holster and stood behind Dahlia and Kelly.

"Move," he ordered.

Still acting as if they were under the influence, Dahlia and Kelly eventually made their way out of the trailer, landing with a wobble on the soft grass. The property was expansive and well maintained. By all appearances, it was a high-class spa. The two-story building rivaled any hotel in Las Vegas. The terracotta tile leading up to the building diverged into two separate paths, one leading around to the front of the spa and the other leading up to the back. The latter was where the man directed Dahlia and Kelly to go.

Inside, the women were greeted by the sound of running water from a waterfall cascading down into an indoor pond and soft music playing in the background. The monochrome art deco room was empty. Holster pushed them down a hallway to their right and shoved them through a doorway.

"Welcome girls," a man seated behind a massive mahogany desk greeted them in a tone that made Dahlia's skin crawl.

The gunman bolted the door behind them. The bile bubbled up in Dahlia's throat as she saw red stiletto heels briefly appear beneath the desk before disappearing as their owner changed positions. Lovely.

"Damn, you girls are sure pretty," the man licked his lips. "I don't think we'll have any problems putting you two to work. In fact, I got some clients that are into … virgins."

Gee, what a charming place.

★★★

Through a camera and microphone implanted in a pair of fake glasses Kelly wore, Sam, Shawn, and Florence were able to see and hear everything the two officers did from inside their van.

"Christ, what a pig," Sam's nostrils flared as he watched the man at the desk chat up Dahlia and Kelly while one of his workers serviced him from beneath the desk.

"Rarely are the people that commit crimes like sex trafficking upstanding citizens," Shawn said with a frown.

"No shit."

"Boys, quiet," Florence said. "I want to hear what he's saying."

"I don't think we'll have any problems putting you to work. In fact, I got some clients who are into ... virgins."

"I am going to fucking rip his head off—" Sam's hands balled into fists.

"Shhh!" Florence brought a finger up to her lips.

"Calm down, Marlowe," Shawn put a hand on Sam's shoulder. "We're going to get these guys. Give it time. We need to collect a little more evidence before we storm the castle, okay? Your partner's going to be fine. Don't worry."

★★★

Dahlia wondered how Sam was dealing with listening to the spa "manager," as he called himself. The poor guy was probably giving Shawn and Florence hell. Oh, well; it was probably better to be stuck with an irritated Sam in the truck than dealing with this bastard.

"Girls, I know we got off to a rough start, but I'd like us to be friends," the manager said.

Reaching under the desk, he shoved the girl that was beneath it.

"Get outta here," he said. "I got business to take care of."

The girl got out from under the desk and scurried out of the room. Once she was gone, the manager continued speaking.

"I'd like you girls to call me Rich," he said. "And what are your names?"

"I'm Connie," Kelly said.

"I'm ... Iris," Dahlia swallowed hard.

Closing his robe, Rich got up from behind the desk and walked over to the two girls. With a small knife, he cut the zip tie connecting Dahlia and Kelly, and he then placed a hand on each girl's shoulder.

"Here's the deal. When you're booked by a client, you do what they want. As long as you do that, we shouldn't have any problems, capiche?"

"What ... what if we don't want to?" Kelly asked.

"You don't do what the clients want, then you don't get your dope," Rich said. "Also, you don't do what the clients want, you don't eat, you don't drink, and well, we're out in the middle of nowhere, you'll die before you make it halfway to the city."

Strategic location, Dahlia considered. *The girls practically have no option. They have to participate in the prostitution ring to survive.*

"Like I said, let's be friends; that way, everyone's happy, and I don't have to beat the shit out of you girls, okay?" Rich said.

Neither Dahlia nor Kelly responded, which Rich took as acquiescence.

"Good. Now, let's get you girls broken in," he said. "On your knees. Now."

They didn't move. Rich backhanded Kelly across the face, sending her glasses flying across the room. Dahlia darted over to the agent, who had stumbled backward and fallen from the strike. Before she could get to Kelly, Rich grabbed hold of Dahlia's curls and yanked her back. She squealed from the sudden pain shooting through her scalp.

"On your fucking knees! Now!" he spat, shoving Dahlia forward, causing her to crash into Kelly. "You heard me! Knees! Now!"

Dahlia and Kelly both did as he commanded.

★★★

Without another word, Sam burst out of the van and was tearing toward the building.

"Sam, what the hell?" Shawn called as he chased after the cop.

"My partner is in there. I'm not letting some fat prick hurt her," Sam replied, still marching forward. "If anything happens to Dahlia, I won't let you two live to regret it, you hear me? If you want to stop me, you'll have to fucking shoot me."

Shawn backed off, his hands up in surrender.

Upon reaching the front door of the establishment, Sam paused. He adjusted the fake mustache and the gaudy shirt he wore, which he had picked up at a local store during one the pit stops, just in case he needed a disguise for the sting operation. He strolled inside like he owned the place.

"You need something?" a guard immediately asked Sam, putting a hand out to stop him in his tracks.

"Yeah, I need a lady," Sam said, slinging his arm over the guard's shoulder. "I won big at the casino in Vegas and want to celebrate. I heard this is the best place to do it."

The guard didn't seem convinced. He opened up his jacket enough to allow Sam to get a glimpse of the gun in his holster.

"Hey, man, no need to get testy," Sam held his hands up in mock surrender. "Your buddy, Rich, I think his name was, he told me that I could come here and get one of his new hires. I'm into all that shit and rumor has it that a new shipment has arrived."

"Wait here," the guard said.

When he returned, he motioned to Sam to follow him. The guard led Sam through the spa and toward the back of the building to a door locked with a keypad. Punching in the code, the guard unlocked the door, and he and Sam continued forward. At the back of the spa, they headed down a hallway, stopping in front of another door. The guard knocked and received a yell from the inside to enter.

"Who are you?" Rich immediately asked Sam when the guard shoved him into the room.

Dahlia had to bite her tongue to keep herself from laughing at her partner's ridiculous disguise.

"I'm a guy who knows people," Sam said. "I know that you have some special services here that I want to take advantage of. I heard that you got some fresh fillies in from the pasture and I want to check them out."

Rich eyed Sam for a moment. Sam pulled a wallet out of his pants pocket and produced several fresh, crisp hundred–dollar bills.

"It will be worth your time, I'm sure," he grinned, waving the cash like a fan.

"In that case, you've come to the right place," Rich said, a sleazy smirk on his lips. "The two ladies behind you are new. Take your pick."

Sam grinned. "Don't mind if I do!" he clapped his hands together.

"Pay up first," Rich said.

Sam handed over a wad of cash, which Rich greedily snatched from his hand. Sam walked over to Dahlia and Kelly and winked at them.

"This one seems spunky," he said, playing with a piece of Dahlia's curly black hair. "I'll take her."

"Good choice," Rich joined Sam and Dahlia. "Now, remember, sweetheart, quid pro quo."

Dahlia averted her gaze. Rich pressed the intercom on his desk.

"Otto, show this nice man with the deep pockets and his lady friend to a room."

A big man with a ton of tattoos and a visible weapon escorted Sam and Dahlia from the office to the second floor. They entered room 203, as directed by Otto. He closed the door once the three of them were inside, standing with his back against the door as he watched Sam and Dahlia.

"Uh, hey bud, the hallway's on the other side of the door," Sam said.

Otto didn't respond. He stood in place unmoving like a guard at Buckingham Palace.

"I suppose you're here to make sure our rookie girl, here, does what she's supposed to, eh?" Sam scratched his chin.

He looked at Dahlia.

"I feel like you might be here a while," Sam said. "It looks like my lady friend is about to spill her guts in the bathroom."

On cue, Dahlia hurried into the bathroom and began making vomiting noises. Sam took a seat on the bed.

"Hey, you got any mints?" he asked Otto. "Call me crazy, but I'm not into vomit tasting kisses."

Sam rolled his eyes when Otto did not respond.

"Tough crowd," he sighed.

Sam gave it a few minutes before he got off the bed and headed toward the bathroom door.

"You okay, there, babe?" he tapped the door with his knuckle.

He got no response, so he turned around to face Otto.

"Time's a-wastin', bud," Sam thumbed toward the bathroom door. "Think you can get her out of there?"

Otto moved from his place by the door and tried the bathroom door handle, finding it locked. While the guard worked on opening the door, Sam grabbed a lamp from the nightstand next to the bed, and after carefully creeping up behind Otto, smashed it down on the guard's head. Otto collapsed to the floor, a cut on his head bleeding from the impact.

"You okay, Bennett?" Sam asked when he opened the bathroom door.

He helped Dahlia get up and over Otto's unconscious body.

"A little sore from the ride and Rich smacking me around, but, yeah," Dahlia replied. "Nice disguise, Sam. You lose a bet?"

"This shit is hot, right?"

Dahlia ignored his comment.

"What's the plan?" she asked.

"First, we need to tie up Otto and stuff him in the bathroom, so he's out of the way. Then, we need to find Joanna, but quickly and quietly. If anyone suspects that Tommy and Michelle spilled the beans about being coerced into participating, Joanna's good as dead," Sam said. "Once we find her, we give the word to Shawn and Florence, and they'll call in the cavalry."

Sam opened the door to the room a crack to check the hallway. No one appeared to have heard anything, so he shut the door again. Grabbing a razor from the bathroom, Sam removed Dahlia's remaining zip ties. They hurriedly searched the room for anything they could use to tie up Otto. In the armoire, Sam came across chains, handcuffs and zip ties.

"This should be interesting," he motioned to Dahlia to help him with the items. "I've never tied up a man like this before."

"Stop there, I don't want to know," Dahlia said.

Sam chuckled as he and Dahlia tied up Otto and then rolled him into the bathroom. Sam took the guard's gun and stuffed it into his waistband. The two of them pushed the armoire in front of the door to block it. With Otto out of the way, Sam headed toward the room door and motioned for his partner to follow him. Dahlia slipped down one end of the hallway while Sam went the opposite way.

"Hey, I'm looking for Joanna," Dahlia said to a girl who exited a room.

"Sorry, haven't seen her."

"But she's here."

"Sorry, gotta go. If I don't get ready for my next appointment, I'll be in big trouble. You should probably get moving too; Rich doesn't like it when we're late."

And with that, she scurried off.

On the opposite end of the hall, Sam came across a blonde girl who was about to head into the stairwell.

"Hey, honey," he called out to her. "I, uh, 'booked a session' with Joanna; have you seen her?"

"Joanna?" the blonde asked. "Are you sure?"

"Yeah. I talked to Rich about it."

The woman seemed confused.

"I think you should talk with Madison," she said.

"Who's Madison?" Sam asked.

"A friend of Joanna's," the blonde said. "You might have to wait a bit, though. She's with a customer."

"Do you know what room?" Sam asked.

"Her usual room, 227."

Sam whirled around and raced back down the hallway toward room 227. The door was closed with a sign that said 'Occupied' hanging on the door handle. Carefully opening the door, Sam poked his head inside. A sad looking teen girl with sandy brown hair and the standard skimpy attire was seated on the bed while a sloppy, middle-aged man was removing his shirt a few feet away from her, his back to Sam.

The girl spotted Sam as he surreptitiously slipped into the room. He put a finger up to his lips. Her eyes widened, and she froze. Creeping forward, Sam came up behind the man and tapped him on the shoulder.

"Excuse me," he said.

The man turned around. Face to face with the john, Sam punched him hard and square in the jaw. The man fell backward, crashing into and breaking the little wooden desk in the corner of the room.

"Who are you?" the girl asked, her tone shaky and frightened as she scooted back on the bed.

"Are you Joanna?" Sam asked.

"Joanna? No. I'm not Joanna. I'm Madison. Jo ... was my friend."

"*Was* your friend?"

He didn't like where this conversation was heading.

"Jo ... she's dead ..." Madison's lower lip trembled.

Sam closed his eyes and ran a hand over his face.

"What happened, Madison?" he asked, doing his best to keep his voice calm. "I'm a cop; it's okay, you can tell me."

"Rich kidnapped us from a party we were at downtown in Odette," Madison fixed the pleats on her skirt. "I think he knew that Jo's mom and dad worked at a trucking company, so he could use her to make them help him get more girls like us."

"How did he get to you?"

"Jo and I liked to do party and do, um, drugs, with our friends sometimes. One time, I think we must have passed out because, when we woke up, we weren't at the party anymore. We were in a truck. He brought us here and made us do things with people. Rich shot the guy that drove us here, right in front of us, once Mr. Farina agreed to be the new driver. Jo freaked out. Like, she started puking and crying right in front of Rich. He said he didn't want to deal with her, so he shot her up with a bunch of stuff. Jo … never woke up."

"You're telling me that Joanna's been dead this whole time?" Sam blinked rapidly, trying to keep himself from crying or screaming or punching something.

"Yeah," she said, looking down at her fishnet stockings. "I miss her so much …"

Sam said nothing as he reached a hand out to the young girl on the bed. She looked at him with curious, fearful eyes.

"Come with me," Sam said. "I'm going to get you out of here."

Stepping out into the hallway, Sam held Madison close to him. He waved down Dahlia, who was down at the opposite end of the hall.

"Sam, is this—" she started to ask.

Sam shook his head.

"This is a friend of Joanna's, Madison," he said. "I need you to take care of her and also call Shawn and Florence and tell them to get in here."

Letting go of Madison, Sam turned and began making his way down the hallway.

"Where are you going?" Dahlia called loud enough for him to hear.

"I need to talk to Rich about Joanna."

Before Dahlia could say anything further, Sam hurried down the stairs and toward Rich's office. When he arrived, the manager was sitting with his feet up at his desk, counting the money Sam had given him a few minutes earlier.

"Back so soon?" Rich asked when he saw Sam enter the office. "I hope she didn't disappoint."

Sam didn't say anything. Instead, he pulled out the gun he took from Otto and pointed it at Rich. The man immediately dropped the money and put his hands up.

"Joanna Farina," Sam said. "Where is she?"

"Who?" Rich asked.

"Joanna! The girl whose parents you conned into trafficking your sex slaves in exchange for their daughter's life!"

"Oh, that Joanna ..."

It was silent for a moment.

"Well?!" Sam growled.

"She's dead."

"You killed her!"

"No, I didn't kill her. The stupid bitch shot up too much, and OD'd. Not my fault."

Sam took a few more steps forward toward Rich, rotating the man in his chair and pushing the barrel of the gun directly against his forehead.

"*You* are the one who pumped her full of drugs because *you* didn't feel like dealing with her after *you* killed the truck driver right in front of her! You fucking killed a man in front of a little girl and then you drugged her to death because you didn't want to deal with her!" Sam cocked back the hammer. "You killed her. Joanna is dead because of you."

From outside the door, Sam could hear movement; he knew it was Shawn, Florence and the other agents storming the spa.

"Please don't kill me!" Rich pleaded. "Please!"

Sam figured he had no more than a few minutes before the FBI agents found him in the room with the manager. His eyes moved from Rich's face to the door and back again. Time was ticking down for him to decide what to do with Rich.

"Please ..."

"This ..." Sam said. "Is for Joanna."

★★★

Sitting outside on the edge of the FBI's van, Sam stared down at the tile beneath his feet.

"Sam?"

He didn't bother to look up when he heard Dahlia speak to him, nor when she sat down next to him.

"Madison told me what happened," Dahlia said.

Sam did not respond. Dahlia put her hand on his shoulder.

"Are you okay?" she asked.

"Peachy," Sam mumbled.

"Hey kids," Shawn walked over to where the two detectives were sitting. "How are you guys doing?"

"It's … a lot to take in," Dahlia said.

"Detective Bennett?" Florence joined them. "I need you for a moment."

Dahlia gave Sam a small nudge before heading off to speak with Florence. Shawn took Dahlia's spot next to him.

"Was that your first time shooting someone?" he asked.

Sam lifted his head to look at Shawn.

"I thought you feds would have read over my file before we started working together," he said with a humorless laugh.

Shawn gave Sam a grin.

"You're right, we did," he admitted. "But I needed to say something to get you talking."

"Touché."

"Regardless of if it's the first time you pull the trigger or the hundredth time, it's never easy," Shawn said. "Say, Sam, you did well in there. Did you ever think of applying to the FBI? We could use a great investigator like you."

Sam was genuinely surprised and touched. He wasn't sure how to respond. It must have shown on his face because Shawn chuckled.

"I know, it's a big decision," he said. "I'll give you my card. Think it over and let me know."

Shawn pulled a business card out of his wallet and handed it to Sam, who stared down at the letters and numbers as if they were foreign to him.

"Detective Bennett," Florence said to Dahlia when she approached. "Good work in there. How are you doing?"

"I'm all right," Dahlia said. "It's been a long case, so I'm glad it's over."

"How is Detective Marlowe doing?"

"He's … doing. That's all I can say. He's a little shaken up, given the circumstances."

Florence let out a breath, causing Dahlia to feel a bit uneasy.

"Listen, Detec-Dahlia," the agent began to say. "It's obvious that Detective Marlowe is a brilliant detective with an unwavering commitment to justice."

"Right."

"But ... there's something that leads me to believe something is amiss. I can't put my finger on it, but something's not right. Please, watch your back, Detective Bennett. Keep an eye on your partner. If you have any concerns or suspicions, feel free to reach out to Shawn and me. We'll do whatever we can to help you."

"Thanks, I guess ..."

With a frown, Dahlia headed back over to Sam as Shawn was leaving.

"What's that?" she asked.

"Shawn's contact info," Sam replied. "He invited me to join the FBI."

Dahlia blinked. She felt a mixture of surprise, excitement and something she couldn't quite describe ... disappointment? Sure, it would be a fabulous opportunity for Sam, and he was a great cop, so he'd fit in very well and be a tremendous asset to the team. Even though she hated to admit it, if he left, Dahlia knew she'd miss him. After a rough start to their partnership, they ended up developing a close relationship; it'd be like losing a brother.

"Congrats, Sam," she said instead. "That's a great honor and well deserved."

"Thanks," Sam said, staring off into the distance.

Florence doesn't know what she's talking about. Dealing with Sam might be like hugging a cactus sometimes, but I know he's been through a lot. Florence is reading too much into it, that's all.

★★★

Dahlia sat at her desk in the bullpen of the Odette Police Department, staring blankly at the report in front of her. She tried to focus but she couldn't, no matter how hard she tried. Sam was meeting with Shawn and Florence that morning before they left Colorado. She figured he probably went to accept the job at the FBI.

Letting out a sigh, Dahlia knew it was probably for the best. In Odette, Sam was a big fish in a small pond; he needed to move on to bigger and better things, even if that meant going off to do so on his own. It was going to be quite different without her partner around.

Shaking her head, Dahlia attempted to return to her paperwork. She nearly jumped out of her skin when someone whispered, "Boo!"

"Boo!"

"Sam!" Dahlia brought a hand up to cover her heart.

"Did you see the papers this morning?" Sam asked, sitting down and then putting his feet up on his desk. "I made the front page for breaking up the human trafficking ring. I'm sure they mentioned you and the feds in there somewhere, but I didn't check for that."

"Speaking of the feds," Dahlia said. "How'd your meeting go?"

"Went great," Sam replied.

He eyed Dahlia for a moment.

"Oh, do you mean the job offer? How did that conversation go?"

He was playing coy, which made Dahlia want to punch him.

"Since you brought it up ..." she said.

"Bennett, to be honest," he paused, and Dahlia held her breath. "I turned them down."

"You did?" Dahlia was stunned.

"As great as being an FBI agent would be, Odette needs me," Sam smirked. "And I know you need me, Bennett. You'd be completely lost without me."

Dahlia laughed.

He was an arrogant ass at times, but he was her arrogant ass, and she was happy that it was going to stay that way.

PASSIONS IGNITED

Sam and Dahlia found the bullpen of the Odette Police Department in its usual state of activity, with police officers coming and going, answering phones or finishing paperwork and various other duties, when they returned from lunch. Sam was lounging at his desk with his feet up and his arms behind his head while Dahlia was organizing her already pristine desk.

"Sam?" a blonde woman asked Sam as she approached his desk.

Dahlia watched with amazement and intrigue as her partner practically flew out of his seat and over to the woman. Adding to her initial surprise was when Dahlia saw Sam embrace the female visitor. There was undeniably some history between them, as Sam was typically not the hugging type.

"Hey Bennett," Sam called over to her.

Shit. He saw her watching him.

"I have someone I'd like you to meet."

A relieved smile popping onto her face, Dahlia left her desk and came over to her partner and the woman in the powder blue blouse and gray pinstripe pencil skirt.

"Clarice, this is Dahlia Bennett, my partner," Sam said to the woman. "And Dahlia, this is Clarice Hill, soon-to-be Navarro, my foster sister."

"It's wonderful to finally meet you," Clarice said. "I know Sammie thinks highly of you."

Dahlia threw an intrigued glance at her partner as she and Clarice shook hands. She could tell she wasn't supposed to know that little tidbit of information that he talked about and praised her in front of his family when Sam averted his eyes to the floor and rubbed the nape of his neck.

"And I couldn't ask for a better mentor," Dahlia said earnestly, genuinely meaning what she said.

Clarice turned back to Sam.

"Sam, I need your help," she said.

"Whatever you need," Sam replied.

He led Clarice to his desk and offered her his chair.

"What's going on, Clarice?" Sam asked.

"One of Raymond's coworkers and a good friend of ours has been dealing with some trouble recently," Clarice said.

"What kind of trouble?"

"He received a note threatening his family."

"Yeah, I'd say that's trouble," Sam leaned back against his desk. "But I assume Ray's friend hasn't reported it?"

"Exactly," Clarice said. "Ray noticed that Greg was not himself and asked him about it. After some pestering, Greg finally revealed the letter, which said not to involve the police. However, being a lawyer, I love loopholes. I figured, instead of asking the police for help, I'd ask my brother—who also happens to be a cop—to look into things."

"See, this is why Clarice is a successful lawyer," Sam said to Dahlia, who smiled. "Bennett and I would be happy to help, Clarice."

"Thanks, Sammie," she said. "Ray's at the fire station with Greg now."

Sam and Dahlia walked Clarice to her car, Sam walking uncomfortably between the two ladies as they chatted about him.

"My mom has a bunch of newspaper articles about Sammie's cases framed and hanging on the wall at the house," Clarice said. "She especially loved the picture of the two of you with Tamsen Wilde, the actress from that case a couple years ago. I can only imagine how excited Sammie must have been when he got to work with her."

Dahlia grinned at Sam, who rolled his eyes.

"I was surprised at how much Sam knew about Tamsen, Xander, and Kora," she said. "Does he read those celebrity tabloids like I think he does?"

"Oh, of course. That and he watches terrible reality TV shows," Clarice said. "He used to say that Nina picked the show when he lived at home with us and he was watching it with her to be a good guy, but I know it was because he got emotionally invested in the shows. He had to know if the bachelorette was going to choose the fan favorite, the hunky pool boy or the rebel."

"I knew it!" Dahlia said with a chuckle.

"TMI, Clarice," Sam grumbled. "TMI."

Clarice embraced them both before getting into her car and driving off. The two detectives headed toward Sam's car to drive out to meet with Raymond and Greg.

"Your foster sister is great," Dahlia said as she slipped into the passenger's seat.

"Yep. She is," Sam replied in a tone that implied the statement was an indisputable fact rather than an opinion.

"Sam?"

"Bennett?"

"I know what happened to your mom," Dahlia started to say. "But why don't you talk about your foster family? If Clarice is any indication, they obviously love and trust you."

"Guess the subject never came up."

Dahlia looked out the window with a frown.

"Really? As far as I remember, we've approached the topic many times, but you've refused to participate," she said.

"I'll make you a deal, Bennett," Sam began to say.

He put the key in the ignition and started the car.

"I'll tell you about my family when you tell me more about yours," he said.

"Good talk, Sam," Dahlia sighed.

Sam grinned, and Dahlia rolled her eyes at him. She knew he loved getting the upper hand over her when they bantered.

★★★

Sam pulled into the parking lot of the Odette Fire Department, finding a spot in the back. Exiting the car, the two detectives headed through one of the open garage doors of the station house. Inside, a female firefighter, with her shirt sleeves rolled up past her elbows, was kneeling next to a toolbox, which had most of its contents on the concrete floor next to her as she tinkered with the fire truck.

"Can I help you?" the woman asked, a wrench in her hand.

"We're here to meet with Ray Navarro," Sam replied.

The woman picked up a rag from on top of the toolbox next to her and wiped her hands.

"Does Lieutenant Navarro know you're coming?"

"Sort of. He's set to become my future brother-in-law and my sister asked if I could swing by and ask him something."

The woman smiled.

"Oh, right!" she said. "You're Sam. I remember seeing you at Ray and Clarice's engagement party a few months ago. I don't think we were ever properly introduced; I'm Lacey Savage."

"Nice to meet you," Sam replied.

"C'mon, I'll take you to him."

Sam and Dahlia followed the blonde woman with the messy bun into the station to Ray's office. Lacey knocked on the door before entering.

"Hey Lieutenant," she said. "I have some visitors here to see you."

Ray, who was working at his desk, lifted his dark head of mocha colored hair. His smile reached his light brown eyes.

"Hey Sam," he stood and shook Sam's hand. "Great to see you, man."

"You too, Ray."

Sam turned to Dahlia.

"Bennett, this is Ray Navarro," Sam said. "And, Ray, this is Dahlia Bennett, my partner."

"Great to finally meet you, Ms. Bennett," Ray shook Dahlia's hand.

When Clarice began dating Ray in their late teens, she tried to describe him to Edwin, her protective cop father. She said his personality reminded her of a German Shepherd, brave, loyal and protective. In his years of knowing Ray, Sam wholeheartedly agreed. A good man, Sam had no qualms about giving Clarice away to Raymond at their wedding, something she asked him to do, as the late Edwin would not be able to.

"Thanks, Lacey," Ray said, dismissing the other firefighter.

"No problem, Lieutenant," she blew a kiss and winked before leaving Ray's office.

Ray closed the office door.

"That's one way to make an exit," Sam said.

"Lacey is a good firefighter, but she's kind of a flirt. She's harmless, and some of the single guys are flattered by it, so we ignore it."

Ray motioned for Sam and Dahlia to take a seat.

"Did Clarice talk to you about Greg?"

"She did," Sam said.

"Greg's really affected by this. He's been a good buddy of mine for quite a few years now, so I want to help him out. Besides, as firefighters, we all have to have each other's backs. I'm sure as cops, you understand."

"Of course."

"I'll contact Greg and have him explain the details."

Ray texted Greg, asking him to come to his office. He arrived a few minutes later. Ray introduced the detectives.

Greg was the same age as Ray and Clarice, also in his early thirties. Sam met him briefly at the engagement party and when Ray met with his groomsmen to go over some of the details for the wedding. A few inches shorter than his friend, he had a stocky build, but not to the point where he was overweight. His brown hair was of a very dark hue, making it look nearly black.

"I found the note under the wiper blade on the windshield of my car last week," Greg said to Sam and Dahlia. "I had parked on the street in front of my house that night, so I thought maybe someone hit my car, dented it and left a note or something like that. Obviously, that wasn't the case."

"What did the note say?" Sam asked.

Greg's blue eyes moved between Sam and Dahlia, Sam noting the deep bags under his eyes and the stubble on his chin and cheeks. Poor guy probably hasn't slept in days.

"It said: 'You know what you did. Your charmed life will be destroyed, and you will burn in hell unless you pay for your sins. Get the cops involved and you'll suffer even more. If you don't fix the problem YOU created by the wedding, your life will be over.'"

"Charming," Sam said with a frown. "I have to ask, Greg, what did you do?"

Greg shrugged, a distraught expression firmly planted on his face.

"That's what gets me; I don't know. I don't have any idea what the note's referring to. If I did, I'd clear it up ASAP, especially since Ray and Clarice's wedding isn't that far off. I was planning on proposing to my girlfriend then."

"Instead of tossing the bouquet at the reception, Clarice is going to give it to Eleni and then Greg is going to pop the question," Ray said. "We were planning on keeping it a secret, but, since Eleni might be in danger too, I think you guys should know."

"I take it Eleni doesn't know about the note," Sam said.

"No. At first, I wasn't sure what to make of it. I thought it might be a hoax, but then, this past Wednesday, I found my tires slit. I figured the guy behind this was pretty serious," Greg replied.

"That's when I found out," Ray said. "We left the station at the same time that night, and I saw the tires. Greg told me what happened."

"Wait, your tires were slashed here at the station?" Dahlia asked turning to Sam. "The suspect knows where Greg lives and works."

"Hmm, good point," Sam drummed his fingers on the arm of the chair. "I know firefighters are supposed to be heroes and all, but, let's face it, people are weird as fuck. Did anyone ever get pissed at you for being a good guy and saving their asses from an impending fiery doom or some other form of danger?"

Ray and Greg exchanged a look.

"You know, now that you mention it," Greg said to Ray. "Do you remember that string of fires that we responded to at the end of last year?"

"Yes, I do," Ray said. "You two may have heard about this case at the police department; last year, there were a bunch of small but suspicious fires in this one neighborhood. Working with arson investigators, we determined it was the work of some bored teenagers. Greg testified against them in juvenile court."

"They obviously weren't pleased with me testifying against them," Greg said. "But you don't think they'd come after me for that, do you?"

"Witness Protection is a thing for a reason," Sam said. "We'll look into it and see if those kids had anything to do with this."

★★★

Back at the police department, Dahlia went to look up the arson case while Sam poked around on Greg's social media profiles. Dahlia's heels clacked against the wooden floor of the bullpen as she approached. She dropped a file folder on his keyboard.

"Fifteen-year-old Donny Bishop and fourteen-year-old Christian Diangelo were arrested last year for criminal mischief and destruction of property," Dahlia said to Sam. "They were first time offenders, so they were sentenced to six months in juvie plus community service."

"Great, both little delinquents are back out, terrorizing the community," Sam breezed through the file. "Good work, Bennett. Why don't you track them down and see what they have to say about Greg?"

"What are you going to do?" Dahlia asked, heading over to her desk to grab some necessities before heading off.

"The guy or gal who sent the note said that Greg committed some horrible sin; the problem is Greg doesn't know what that sin is. Now, it's either something he didn't consider a bad thing, forgot about or something harmless that someone else perceived as a sin," Sam told his partner. "People tend to post a lot of stupid shit on the internet; I'm going to keep looking online, see if that gives us any indication of what this 'sin' is. When you get back, we can take a trip to visit Greg's girlfriend."

"Sounds like a plan," Dahlia said before heading out of the bullpen. "Well, have fun."

★★★

Donny and Christian were scheduled for community service that afternoon. Along with some other parolees, they were cleaning up graffiti on some buildings in downtown Odette. Upon arrival, Dahlia sought out the activity supervisor, Amy Olsen.

"Detective Bennett, Odette PD," Dahlia showed the woman her badge. "I'm looking for Donny Bishop and Christian Diangelo."

"Oh, yes, I spoke to you on the phone earlier," Amy said. "What can I help you with?"

"My partner and I are following up on some leads for a case, and we came across Donny and Christian's names. What can you tell me about them?"

"Donny and Christian have been very active and helpful," Amy said. "They've shown up and actually worked. That's more than I can say for some people that are assigned to my group. Granted, it could all be an act, but I believe they're genuine."

"I hope you're right because threatening a firefighter and his family is serious business," Dahlia replied.

Amy called the two boys over.

"Boys, this is Detective Bennett from the Odette Police Department," Amy said to the teenagers. "She has a couple of questions for you. Please help her out to the best of your ability and be courteous."

"Boys, do you recall a man by the name of Greg Romero?" Dahlia asked.

"Yeah, we know 'im," Donny said, pushing the red bandana back up over his dark brows. "He's the firefighter who testified against us in court."

"Tough break," Dahlia said. "I mean, firefighters are supposed to help people, right? Instead, it's a firefighter that ends up putting you two away and forcing you to spend your free time cleaning up graffiti."

Donny and Christian both shrugged.

"Yeah, it sucks, but it's either this or we go back to juvie," Donny replied. "And I ain't going back to juvie."

"I take it you two are still pissed at Mr. Romero for what he did?"

"Not really," Christian said.

"Christian and I were bored and lookin' to do something fun," Donny said. "We thought it'd be cool to try and do some of the stuff we found on the internet in these bad ass videos we were watching."

"We didn't know we'd get in trouble!"

"You blew up people's mailboxes and set their lawn and garden decorations on fire," Dahlia said. "How did you not know arson was illegal?"

"We know that ... now," Donny said as he dug the toe of his dirty sneaker into the sidewalk. "But we didn't think about it at the time."

"And we won't ever do it again, right, Donny?" Christian looked up at his buddy.

"No way," Donny said. "Mr. Greg showed us pictures of people that got burned with fireworks and stuff like that. They were nasty as hell. No way I want to have skin from my ass grafted onto my face!"

"What do you think about Mr. Romero?" Dahlia asked the boys.

"Guy was doin' his job."

"Then you two aren't angry with him for getting you in trouble?"

"Not really. We were when we first got sent to juvie, but not now."

"Our counselor said we have to take ownership of our actions and not blame it on others," Christian said, removing his white baseball cap for a moment to scratch his blond hair.

"Why are you askin' us all these questions about Mr. Greg?" Donny asked. "Is he okay?"

"To be honest," Dahlia began to say. "Mr. Romero is in a bit of trouble right now. Someone is giving him problems, and my partner and I are trying to help him out."

"Can we help?" Christian asked. "We'd like to help, right, Donny?"

"Sure," Donny said.

A small smile crossed Dahlia's lips.

"That's nice of you boys," she said. "I'm not sure if there's anything you can do, but, if there is, I'll let you know."

"Yeah," Donny said. "We'd kinda like to make up for callin' Mr. Greg an asshole and a bastard and all that. He's not a bad guy, and well, we kinda feel bad about it."

"Well, at the very least, I'll pass on the message," Dahlia said. "I know he'd appreciate hearing that from you two."

Dahlia glanced between the two boys. Letting out a slow breath, she knew her gut reaction was right, and these boys probably weren't responsible for the threats to Greg and his girlfriend. Hopefully, Sam found something because, otherwise, their one good lead was erased like the graffiti on the walls of the building the parolees were cleaning up.

★★★

Speaking with Ray on the phone, Sam spied Dahlia entering the bullpen.

"Thanks, Ray," he said before hanging up the phone. "Any luck with the chain gang, Bennett?"

"Not really," Dahlia replied, taking a seat at her desk. "They were two bored kids who did something stupid. I think the whole experience scared them straight."

"Let's hope so," Sam said.

"How'd your afternoon go?"

"I may have found something. There is someone who is practically leeching on to Greg through social media. She-I'm assuming it's a she-comments on practically every post, likes every picture and is essentially being a creeper."

"Who is it?"

"That's the thing," Sam turned to the computer and clicked the mouse button a few times. "When I pull up the stalker's profile, there's practically no information on it, except for a name."

Dahlia leaned forward to get a look at the name on the profile Sam pulled up on his computer screen.

"Eleni Dimitriou?" she asked. "Isn't Eleni the name of Greg's girlfriend?"

"It is, and it's not a common name either, so what are the odds that he's got two girlfriends named Eleni?"

"Probably very minimal."

"Right," Sam said. "It's likely that this Eleni is probably a fake identity for whoever the bad guy, err, gal, is."

"We should visit Eleni then," Dahlia said. "Maybe she'll have some insight into Greg's relationships, both past, and present."

"It's worth a shot."

★★★

Greg yawned as he sat down on the bench in the locker room of the fire station. He felt a little better now that Ray's future brother-in-law was looking into the threats, but he still couldn't help but worry. Maybe after a nice dinner at home with Eleni, he could actually get some sleep. Greg sighed as he ran a hand over his face. It was probably a long shot, but he still hoped that he could at least log a few hours' rest.

"Hi, Greg!"

The fireman looked up and saw Lacey entering the locker room.

"Hey, Lacey," he said with a small wave.

Lacey gave him a brilliant smile as she took a seat next to him on the bench.

"You look exhausted," she said.

"Yeah ... I've had a lot on my mind, I guess," Greg said.

"Well, let me see if I can help take your mind off things."

Lacey pulled her cell phone out of her pocket and played with it for a few moments before showing it to Greg.

"This is my dress for the wedding," she said. "What do you think?"

The dress was a royal blue colored halter dress that fell below the knees of the model in the picture.

"It's very pretty, Lacey," Greg said. "That's a good color for you; matches your eyes."

"Aren't you a sweetie?" Lacey said with a giggle. "By the way, I heard about your special surprise at the wedding."

"My special surprise?"

"You're proposing, duh!"

Greg's eyes darted up from the picture on the phone to Lacey's smiling face.

"Wait, you know about the proposal?" he asked. "How?"

"Well," Lacey played with the charm on her crucifix necklace. "I may have accidentally overheard you talking about it with Lieutenant Navarro when you two were leaving the station one night."

"Lacey, please don't say anything to anyone, it's supposed to be a special surprise," Greg said.

Lacey put her fingers on Greg's lips.

"Don't worry," she said. "I know it's supposed to be secret. I won't say anything, cross my heart. And I'll act surprised, like everyone else."

Greg gave her a relieved smile.

"Thanks, Lace," he said. "I want it to go perfectly because it's a huge deal to me. Plus, Ray and Clarice were nice enough to let me steal the spotlight from their wedding day for a bit to do this, so I don't want to mess anything up."

"I know you do and that is why any girl would be lucky to say yes to you," Lacey said. "I am so excited about seeing you get down on one knee and ask that wonderful question!"

"Yeah, me too," Greg said. "I do have to admit that I'm kind of nervous, though."

"Don't be. I have no doubt your answer will be a yes."

"Thanks, Lacey."

Lacey gave Greg a quick peck on the cheek before standing up from the bench and giving him a wink. Greg found himself smiling as Lacey left the room after a quick stop at her locker. Suddenly, he was feeling much better.

★★★

Eleni Dimitriou was a pilot. Having recently returned from a trip out to the east coast, she had the day off. Sam and Dahlia met up with her at the house she shared with Greg.

"What can I do for you, detectives?" she asked, taking a seat on the couch in her living room.

"We have some questions for you about your boyfriend, Greg," Dahlia said.

She and Sam took a seat in two armchairs across from Eleni.

"Greg? Is he okay?" Eleni asked, alarmed.

"He's fine, don't worry," Sam replied. "How long have you two been together?"

"Thank goodness," Eleni paused. "We've been together for three years now but have known each other for about five, so I obviously know him very well, but what are you asking questions about him for? Greg's a great guy. He doesn't even have a speeding ticket on his record."

"We're looking into a case of stolen identity," Sam said. "Eleni, do you have any social media accounts?"

"Yeah, I have a couple. It's a nice way to connect with passengers and other pilots."

Dahlia showed Eleni her cellphone.

"Does this profile look familiar to you?" she asked.

Eleni looked over the page on Dahlia's phone.

"No, it doesn't," she paused. "Wait, why is my name on there?"

"We were actually hoping that you could tell us," Sam said.

"I haven't the faintest idea," Eleni grabbed her tablet from where it was charging on the end table next to the couch. "Here's my profile page."

Sam and Dahlia examined the page on Eleni's tablet. Unlike the one on Dahlia's phone, this profile was fully used and updated often. There were pictures from some of the destinations Eleni had flown to, candid shots of Greg and her, and photos of Eleni with her family and friends. Skimming through her list of friends and contacts, Sam and Dahlia discovered several firefighters from Greg's station.

"You're friends with the other firemen and women at Greg's company?" Sam asked.

"Some more than others," Eleni said. "Greg is close with Lieutenant Navarro and his fiancée."

"His fiancée is my sister," Sam said.

Eleni smiled brightly.

"She is?" she snapped her fingers. "That's where I recognized your name from! Greg and I have gone out with Ray and Clarice a few times, and she mentioned that she had a brother named Sam who worked at the police department. It's nice to finally meet you in person."

"You too."

"How about the other firefighters?" Dahlia asked.

"Most of them are great people," Eleni said.

"Most of them?"

"Well, I hate to talk about her this way, I mean, she is a firefighter and puts her life on the line on a daily basis ..."

"It's okay, Eleni," Sam said. "We're not here to judge."

"The one girl, Lacey," Eleni began to say. "She's a huge flirt. I mean, she'll hit on anything that moves, I swear."

"Including Greg?"

"Including Greg. Some of the guys are single, and they enjoy the attention. I don't know; I think they view it as harmless fun."

"And what do you view it as?" Sam asked.

"Annoying and rude, but harmless," Eleni said.

"Eleni, I'm sorry to have to ask this," Dahlia said. "But how is your relationship with Greg?"

"Are you asking if he's ever cheated on me or been abusive? The answer to both is no, never," Eleni replied. "Well, not that I know of, cheating-wise. Greg is a big homebody; he and I spend a lot of time at work, so, when we both have off, Greg and I usually spend it at home, watching a movie with some takeout or something like that. I mean, as a pilot, I'm gone quite a bit, so he'd have ample opportunity to do so, but that's not in Greg's character."

She paused.

"Is this where the social media account comes in? Is someone stealing my name to get to Greg?"

"We don't know," Sam said.

"But what would they want from him?"

"Again, we are investigating that right now."

"Do you happen to have Greg's passwords to his social media accounts?" Dahlia asked.

"Yes, I do. Greg and I are pretty open with each other when it comes to that stuff."

"Good," Sam said. "We need you to monitor Greg's account and let us know if your doppelganger has any activity on your boyfriend's account. Think you can do that?"

"Definitely."

★★★

Leaving Eleni and Greg's house, Sam and Dahlia stopped at a nearby restaurant to grab some dinner.

"Lacey gets on some people's nerves with her flirty behavior." Dahlia poked at her salad with her fork. "Do you think Eleni may have misinterpreted this as Greg cheating on her?"

Sam sipped his coffee.

"I don't think so. I mean, it makes sense as a theory, but I'm not getting that from Eleni," he said. "She doesn't seem like the type to threaten the lives of others. Eleni is a pilot, so she has the responsibility of the lives of her passengers and crew in her hands every time she goes up in the air."

"Right. Plus, Eleni said that Greg is a good guy and didn't have anything like a speeding ticket on his record. We can check that out when we get back to the station, but I'm pretty sure she's telling the truth," Dahlia said. "If that's the case, then Eleni doesn't seem to think that Greg has any 'sins' to pay for."

"Well, legal sins, at least," Sam motioned with his fork. "What if the sin we're talking about isn't one that can be punished by the legal system or at least usually isn't?"

"Like what? Adultery?"

"Bingo. Adultery is still illegal in some states, but usually not enforced."

"Do you think this is a case of vigilante justice?" Dahlia asked. "You know, the system 'failed' Eleni because she can't do anything to stop Greg from cheating on her when she's not around, so someone is seeking justice for her?"

About to take a bite of his pasta, Sam stopped moving, the fork full of fettuccini alfredo hovering a few inches away from his mouth. Dahlia shrank back in her chair at the expression on his face.

"No, I don't," Sam said, staring at his partner with intensity. "Vigilante justice is a bunch of bullshit; don't ever mention it again."

"Lighten up, Sam," Dahlia said, stabbing some lettuce with her fork. "It was only a suggestion."

Sam put his fork down and ran a hand over his face.

"Okay, back on topic," he said. "We need to find out who is behind this fake Eleni profile. Whoever it is is obviously keeping tabs on Greg. If we could find out who it is, we might be able to piece together what his or her motive is. This person might be the one threatening Greg, and if not, at the very least, might have some additional information for us since this person is watching practically every single thing the man does."

"You know, I might have some people that can help me with tracing the origin of the account activity," Dahlia said.

"Great. You do that," Sam said. "I'll go and talk to Lacey about her behavior toward other women's boyfriends and husbands."

He tossed his napkin on the table and stood up from his chair.

"Get a box for me, will you, Bennett?"

"Wait, Sam!" Dahlia called as Sam began to walk away. "What about the check?"

His response was a wave.

"Jerk."

★★★

Sam caught up with Lacey as she was heading into the parking lot to leave the fire department.

"Oh, hello, Detective," Lacey smiled at him as he jogged over to her. "Nice to see you again."

"Hi Lacey," Sam said. "I have a couple of questions for you."

"For me? Okay. Not sure how I can help you, but shoot."

"I've heard from several others that you are, let's say, pretty flirty to the guys at the station."

Lacey giggled.

"I don't mean to sound stuck up, but I'm rather pretty. I mean, I was offered a modeling job when I was a teenager; why not use what I've got to my advantage? Besides, it's all in fun. The guys like it, too."

"How about the other ladies you work with and the spouses or significant others of your male coworkers? Do they find it fun?"

"They should," Lacey sounded dismissive as she put her duffel bag in the back seat of her car. "I mean, I'm not going to take any of their men, you know? Besides, if the guys can joke around with each other, why can't I?"

"How are they supposed to know that you're not making the moves on someone else's man?" Sam asked, folding his arms as he leaned back against the firewoman's car.

"Because," Lacey shut the car door. "I'm engaged, or, well, soon to be engaged."

"Are you now?"

"Yes. I know for a fact that my true love is planning to propose to me. It was supposed to be a secret, but I overheard him talking about his plans with Lieutenant Navarro."

"Since you brought it up," Sam said. "Spill the details, sister."

"It's supposed to be a surprise, Detective; didn't you get that I'm not supposed to talk about it when I said it was a secret?" Lacey said.

"If you know about it already, that doesn't make it much of a secret anymore, does it?"

The firewoman crossed her arms and gave Sam a small pout.

"Your charms aren't going to work on me, sweetie pie," he said.

Lacey let out a huff.

"Fine. If you want to know," she said. "My love is going to propose to me at Lieutenant Navarro's wedding."

"During the bouquet toss?" Sam asked.

"Yes."

"Gee, that's awfully funny."

"Why? What's so funny about that?"

Sam opened his mouth to respond but decided against it.

"Nice talking to you, Lacey," he said instead. "I've got to head back to the police department."

Sam ran back toward his car without another word to the firewoman.

★★★

"Okay, boys, walk me through this," Dahlia said.

Sitting at her computer at the police department, Donny and Christian next to her, the boys instructed her on how to trace the IP address of the source of the posts from the duplicate Eleni profile. *I'm not too shabby with computers and technology,* Dahlia considered. *But the boys might be more fluent in social media and catch something that I might miss. Besides, they seem to be happy to help Greg out.*

"What's going on here?" Sam asked as he strolled into the bullpen.

"Sam, this is Donny, and this is Christian," Dahlia said, motioning to each boy respectively. "They're assisting me in tracking the IP address of the computer that was used to post and reply on the fake Eleni account."

"I see," he said.

"Boys, this is Detective Marlowe. He's my partner," Dahlia said.

"Hi," Donny and Christian said in unison to Sam.

"So," Dahlia said. "How'd it go with Lacey?"

"I think I may have gotten something," Sam said as he took a seat at his desk. "But I want to see what you three come up with first."

"Okay, then let's see what we can find."

Donny and Christian assisted Dahlia in tracing the IP address while Sam finished up his dinner from the restaurant. It took a few minutes, but the trio was eventually able to get a result.

"See? Look at that, boys," Dahlia said. "You should be doing work on computers, not posting videos of you committing crimes."

"Yeah, I guess you're right," Donny looked down at his plump fingers. "Thanks for letting us help."

"No, thank *you*," Dahlia said with a smile.

"C'mon, Donny, we gotta go," Christian said. "We gotta go home before curfew."

"Oh, right."

Donny and Christian waved to Sam and Dahlia before hurrying out of the bullpen.

"Why, Bennett, I didn't realize you were a cradle robber with the way those boys were crushing on you," Sam grinned.

Dahlia rolled her eyes. She crumpled up a piece of paper and threw it at him.

"Shut it, Sam," Dahlia said. "I thought it might be nice ask them for help, so they feel like they've done something to help Greg. Who knows? They might find something to do with their lives instead of committing crimes and giving us more work to do. Maybe they'll become computer technicians or something."

"If those blushes on their cheeks were any indication, then I'd say you made your point, Bennett," Sam paused. "And good thinking."

"Thanks."

"What did you find?"

"This is both good and bad," Dahlia said. "We traced the IP address back to the Odette Fire Department."

"You did, huh?" Sam grabbed a napkin from the takeout bag to wipe his mouth.

"Yeah. Now, what did you find out from Lacey?"

"Let me ask you this," Sam said. "What are the odds that Ray and Clarice are not only letting Greg propose to Eleni during the bouquet toss but Lacey's boyfriend as well on the same day and at the same time?"

"Say what?" Dahlia said. "You're kidding."

"Nope. She told me. Ray never mentioned anything about a second surprise proposal at the wedding."

"Is it wishful thinking? Or jealousy?"

"Or a delusion?"

Dahlia thought over Sam's suggestion for a minute.

"That makes sense. What if, somehow, some way, Lacey believes that *she* is the one that Greg is proposing to? Could there be something in their history that led Lacey to believe that there was something between them?"

"It's possible," Sam said. "Bennett, check that fake Eleni profile, see when it was opened."

"It looks like … three years ago," she said.

"Three years ago; that's right around the time that Eleni and Greg got together," Sam said.

"Is Lacey pretending to be Eleni so she could act out her fantasy of being with Greg? You know, comment on all his pictures and posts like she was his real girlfriend?" Dahlia asked.

"That's also possible," Sam said. "And if the IP address can be traced back to the fire department, it also points the finger at Lacey."

"But why wouldn't she use a different computer that couldn't be so easily traced back to her? There's the library she could have used or a computer at the coffee shop; those wouldn't immediately point to a firefighter as the culprit."

"True, but, like my foster father used to say, we don't catch the smart ones."

Dahlia chuckled.

"What do we want to do about this? Is there a way we can catch Lacey in the act?" she asked.

"Well," Sam tapped his desk. "Let's see … what if Greg does some additional posts to see if Lacey takes the bait and comments on them through the fake Eleni profile? If she does, I'll see if Ray can maybe snap a picture or something of her on the computer for confirmation. We can get her for identity theft, at the very least."

"All right, it's a start."

"Baby steps, Bennett," Sam said as he reached for his desk phone. "First, let's see if the person that's pretending to be Eleni even is Lacey, though I'm pretty certain it is. If we can confirm that, we can put a plan into place and put Miss Looney Tunes in prison so Greg and Eleni can live happily ever after."

"Gee, Sam, just when I thought you didn't believe in fairy tales," Dahlia said.

Sam ignored her as he dialed Ray at the fire station.

★★★

Sam and Dahlia headed out to a local bar, where Ray had invited several firefighters to get together after work. They slipped into a nearby booth that allowed them some distance but still provided a good vantage point to observe the firefighters, who were seated at the bar counter. Seeing as they had no plans of going anywhere anytime soon, Sam suggested they order drinks, and an appetizer and Dahlia agreed. They ate and drank in silence, which was quite the contrast from the lively chatter carrying on around them.

"I have three older brothers," Dahlia said, moving some nachos onto her plate.

Sam raised an eyebrow as he peered down the end of his glass at Dahlia.

"You said that if we ever wanted to discuss our families, it was a two-way street," Dahlia said, reminding him.

"I remember," Sam said, putting his drink down.

"Donovan is the oldest. Cody and Ashton are next; they're twins."

"Good to know."

"Okay, I know Clarice," Dahlia said. "And I know there's a picture of you with your foster family on your desk; the brunette is Nina, right? How old is she?"

"My age, but a few months older," Sam said.

A little grin appeared on Dahlia's lips.

"Then, you're the baby of the family?"

"I guess so," the edges of Sam's lips curled upward ever so slightly.

"Sam—"

"Hold that thought, Bennett," Sam held a hand up.

Ray came up to their table and handed the detectives an envelope.

"I had one of the other firefighters sit with Greg in the common room while he went through some posts and pictures. I hung around the computer room, pretending to do some last-minute wedding research and stuff like that," he said. "Lacey came in. She used a private browser so she wouldn't leave any web history, but I managed to get a couple of pictures of her computer showing her logged in to the account you told me about."

Sam grabbed the envelope and skimmed through the pictures.

"Great. We know that Eleni was in the air at the time of the posts on the second account, so we know for sure that Lacey is at least impersonating Greg's girlfriend," he said. "Now, let's see if we can push her a little bit further. Is Greg ready?"

"About as ready as he'll ever be; he's got his phone on the bar, and it's set to record, so we should be ready to get the truth," Ray said, hands fidgeting with the ends of his shirt. "I'll let him know."

Ray left the table and headed over to where Greg and the other firefighters were seated at the bar. He bid Greg a good night before leaving the bar.

"Sticking around, Romero?" another firefighter patted Greg on the shoulder.

"Yeah," Greg replied. "No rush to get home."

"Enjoy it, bud! Once you get married and have kids, your days of partying are poof, gone!"

"Thanks for the reminder," Greg let out a dramatic sigh.

Lacey slid onto the bar stool next to him. "You okay, Greg?" she asked.

Greg wrapped his hands around his beer bottle.

"Eleni's off on a cross-country flight again," he said. "There's no reason for me to go home right now. I mean, the only thing I'll be going home to is an empty house."

Lacey gently placed a hand on Greg's arm.

"That's terrible, Greg," she cooed. "You should be greeted with open arms by someone who loves you and has dedicated her life to you."

"Yeah, that'd be nice, but I know that Eleni loves her job like I love mine. Can I," Greg paused. "Can I tell you something?"

"Of course. You can tell me anything."

"I've always considered you to be one of my closest friends at the station. I'd like to show you something extremely special."

Lacey had maneuvered herself to be closer to Greg.

She's going to be on his lap if she gets any closer, Sam thought.

Greg slipped his hand into his pocket and pulled out a small black box. Lacey's eyes lit up at the sight of it.

"Is that ... what I think it is?" she asked.

"It's the ring I'm going to propose with," he said as he opened up the box.

"Greg, it's beautiful!" Lacey said. "I ... I'm so happy!"

"Me too. I mean, I can't wait to see the look on Eleni's face—"

"Eleni?" Lacey's smile vanished instantly. "Eleni? You're *still* planning on being with that bitch?"

"Actually, I'm planning to propose to her," Greg said, snapping the box shut. "Shouldn't you be happy for me instead of bad mouthing the love of my life?"

"*I* should be the one you're in love with!" Lacey said.

"What makes you say that?"

Lacey scooted her barstool closer to Greg's, the distance between them now no more than a few inches.

"I've known that we've been destined to be together since the night we made love for the first time," she brushed some strands of Greg's hair.

Greg pulled away.

"Whoa, whoa, whoa," he held his hands up. "That was a onetime thing, and it was a complete accident, a spur of the moment kind of thing. It was after the shooting at the high school when we all went out to let loose. I mean, my best friend's girlfriend lost her father because he gave his life to save the kids and teachers from the shooter. So, yeah, I got drunk, so I could forget. And yeah, we kissed and ended up back at my place—"

"We ended up there because you knew that my love was the only thing that could heal you," Lacey said. "I knew we were meant to be together from the first moment our lips touched."

"Did you miss that entire conversation we had at the fire station the next day?" Greg asked. "I told you what happened was a mistake and that I was extremely sorry for leading you on like that. Besides, I had already started developing feelings for Eleni, so there was no way this was going to work out between us."

"I knew you were hurting, Greg, so I didn't push you that night," Lacey said, tenderly touching Greg's cheek. "I've waited patiently for you to come to your senses. I'm going to give you one last chance."

"Or what?"

"Well," Lacey giggled. "Let's say you won't have to worry about Eleni anymore. I've dealt with your decision to stay with that bitch after the shooting, so I'm giving you one last chance to repent for your sins against me and our love."

"'Repent for my sins ...'" Greg repeated. "Those are the same words from the notes; Lacey, you wrote them."

"Of course. You needed a wakeup call, sweetie, to realize that I'm the one who's supposed to be the love of your life. I'm the one you're supposed to be proposing to at the Lieutenant's wedding. I'm the one you're supposed to come home to every night. Me! Not Eleni! Me!"

"Get it through your head, Lacey, *I don't want you.*"

Lacey clenched her jaw. Silently, she reached down into her pocket and whipped out a switchblade. She held it up to Greg's throat.

"I gave you a chance. You should be with me and if I can't have you, no one will—"

Sam and Dahlia hurried over and grabbed hold of Lacey.

"Wait! Let me go!" Lacey whined and struggled as Sam wrenched the switchblade out of her hands. "Greg! Honey! Do something!"

"You threatened my life and Eleni's!" Greg said, eyes wide and aa hand covering his throat. "You expect me to save you now? You *are* insane!"

"Lacey Savage, you are under arrest," Sam said.

Despite her protests and pleas, Sam handcuffed Lacey and escorted her from the bar, much to the interest of the other patrons.

"Show's over folks!" Dahlia shouted to the gawkers. "Back to your nachos and beer! All of you!"

Once the bar returned to its normal state, Dahlia turned to Greg. He was slumped back against the bar, his mouth still agape as he stared at the floor.

"Come on, let's step outside and get some air," she said.

Greg slid off the stool and wobbled a bit. Dahlia caught his arm and led him outside.

"Sorry," he said with a laugh. "I guess I was a little more rattled than I thought."

"You did well," she reassured him.

"I … I can't believe that happened," Greg let out a shaky breath. "I thought things had been okay between us after that one-night stand. I told Lacey straight out that night was a mistake and that I didn't want to lead her on by thinking there was a chance for us to be together … I—"

"Honestly, I don't think it would have mattered what you said to Lacey. In fact, I think this would have happened to anyone who may have been in your predicament. You just happened to be the one to draw the short straw, Greg."

Ray, who had been waiting outside to keep an eye on his friend, hurried over to them.

"Greg, are you all right?" he immediately asked.

"A little rattled, but, otherwise, yeah," Greg replied.

"Are you okay to drive home? I can take you home, or you can take the guest room at my house-"

Greg shook his head.

"I'm going to go home. I need to go home and write down all the things I want to say to Eleni. I need to explain to her what happened between Lacey and me before we got together. And … I might propose to her when she gets home in a few days … I could have lost her, and it made me realize I need to tell her how much she means to me."

Dahlia and Ray watched Greg leave before speaking again.

"Miss Bennett?"

"Please, call me Dahlia."

"Right, Dahlia," Ray said. "Keep an eye on Sam. I can't even imagine how he must be feeling right now after hearing what Greg had to say."

"You mean about the shooting?" Dahlia asked.

"Yeah. I was there at the school shooting, responding to the incident; do you know the details?"

"Most of them. I was out of state in college when it happened, but I've read over the case file and saw the news reports."

"Then I'm sure you know that the school security guard, Edwin Hill, was Clarice and Nina's father and Sam's foster father."

"I did," Dahlia said.

"I was in the ambulance with Sam when he was being rushed to the hospital for the bullet wound in his leg," Ray said. "I think it was the pain meds that we were administering that made him so talkative, but he said some things to me that I think you should know as his partner. Sam said that he blamed himself for Edwin's death."

"How? I thought that he was shot by the assailant when the kid was trying to get into the school."

"That's correct. Edwin told Sam to leave him and take care of business; Sam didn't want to, but he didn't have a choice. I don't think he's ever forgiven himself for it, based on how he's changed over the years. You can ask Gloria, Clarice, and Nina all about it. He's not the same guy from before Edwin's death," Ray paused. "The kid that committed the crime, Dillon, this I don't think anyone knew besides a few people, but Sam tried to mentor him."

"He did?" Dahlia took a few steps back and fell down onto the wooden bench when the back of her knees hit the wood.

Her heart dropped.

"The mentoring program at the police department was started by Sam. He wanted to give back to the community as his way of thanking Edwin and the Hills for saving him. I remember when he first mentioned it; the pride in his voice and the smile on his face, Edwin was as happy and proud as Sam."

"And Dillon was someone that Sam was trying to take under his wing like Edwin did with him."

"I don't know all the details but, from what I heard from Sam before the shooting was that Dillon's mom was a terrible human being and that she refused to let her son be helped by anyone, including Edwin and him."

"Why the hell would she do that?" Dahlia asked. "Was she so miserable that she wanted to inflict suffering on those around her to make them miserable too?"

"Probably," Ray stuffed his hands into his pockets. "It's not for lack of trying, though. I've worked with Sam a couple times at crime scenes, and I know he did his best to reach out to Dillon and turn the boy's life around but the mother stood in the way."

Sam. No wonder you don't want to let down those emotional walls, Dahlia thought. *You've been burned so badly, even though you were only trying to make a difference in someone's life.*

"What I'm getting at is that Sam will probably find a way to blame himself for Lacey's actions, too," Ray said, jarring Dahlia from her thoughts. "You know, something along the lines of 'if I had saved Edwin's life, we could have stopped the shooter and avoided the tragedy, which would mean that nothing happened between Greg and Lacey and this whole incident wouldn't have occurred.'"

"Yeah, that sounds like his abstract thinking," Dahlia said with a sigh, resting her chin in her hand. "I'll keep an eye on him, Ray. You don't have to worry. He's my partner, and I'll make sure he's okay, even if I have to beat the information out of him."

Ray let out a soft chuckle.

"I don't think Sam could have been assigned a better partner."

"He is a huge pain in the ass," Dahlia said. "But he's my huge pain in the ass."

★★★

The next day, Clarice and Raymond stopped by the department to personally thank Sam and Dahlia for their assistance with Greg.

"We checked in on Greg this morning, and it's like he's transformed back into himself," Ray said. "Thank you both so much."

"Glad we could help," Sam replied.

"He said he told Eleni the whole story once she landed and she was very understanding about the whole incident. Greg's going to catch the next flight out to where Eleni is, and they're going to spend a couple days together, and I think Greg's going to propose."

"That's wonderful," Dahlia said with a smile. "I'm glad Greg's life is finally going to get back to normal."

Clarice reached into her purse and pulled out a thick white envelope, which she handed to Dahlia.

"What's this?" Dahlia asked as she accepted the envelope.

"A wedding invitation," Clarice replied. "We'd love to have you there."

Dahlia smiled down at the envelope in her hands.

"Thank you," she said. "I'd be honored to attend."

Hugs were exchanged before Clarice and Raymond left. Sitting down at her desk, Dahlia opened and read over the invitation, which announced the wedding and reception, the latter of which would have a special moment of remembrance on behalf of the bride and groom to honor the late Edwin Hill.

"I take it you figured it out?"

Dahlia looked up and saw Sam watching her.

"Figured what out?" she asked.

"Why I don't talk about my family."

Dahlia set aside the invitation and turned her attention toward Sam.

"Yes, I know about Edwin. Ray told me the rest of the story," she said. "And I am so, so sorry for your loss. I cannot even imagine how terrible—"

"Which is why I don't think about it," Sam held a hand up to stop her. "And neither should you, Bennett."

"I am proud of you, though, for the way you've kept it together all these years," Dahlia ignored him. "You know that none of what happened to Greg is your fault, right? There's nothing you could have done differently that would have stopped what was going to happen. It could have been a terrible car accident that caused Greg to go out to the bar and get drunk and end up in bed with Lacey. The incident that sparked Lacey's delusions happened to be the shooting. You have no reason to blame yourself for anything that happened."

"Don't you have paperwork or something you should be doing?"

"Oh, right, of course," Dahlia turned back to her desk, pretending to busy herself with some paperwork. "I admit that I never got the honor to meet Edwin personally, but, from the things I've read about him in the case files and in the old newspaper clippings hanging around the department, Edwin was a hell of a guy."

Sam crumpled up a piece of paper and tossed it into the nearby wastebasket like a basketball.

"Bennett?" he said.

"Yeah, Sam?"

Sam let out a breath.

"What you said just now … means a lot," he said. "Thanks."

Dahlia smiled at him.

"Anytime, Sam," she said. "Anytime."

ESTRANGED

Junior Detective Dahlia Bennett shook her head in response to her partner's statement but smiled nonetheless.

"Sure, Sam," she replied. "If you say so."

Senior Detective Samuel Marlowe grinned back at his partner. They'd stopped by a hot dog vendor in downtown Odette, Colorado to grab a quick meal while discussing a recent case.

"Don't believe me, Bennett?" Sam said as he poured some ketchup, mustard, and pickles onto his hot dog. "How about a little wager, then? If my suspect is guilty, you buy me dinner. If your suspect is guilty, I'll buy you dinner."

Dahlia smirked at Sam as she poured the majority of the contents of the ketchup bottle onto her hot dog.

"I'll take that bet," she replied confidently. "When we get back to the precinct, I'll start looking into what restaurant I want to go to for my victory dinner."

"Keep dreaming, Bennett."

Dahlia was prepared to continue their friendly banter but was interrupted by her cell phone ringing. Shoving her lunch into Sam's hands, Dahlia pulled her phone out of the pocket of her black slacks.

"Detective Bennett," she answered the call.

Her smile faded as she listened to what the caller had to say.

"Was that my suspect calling to confess?" Sam asked with a grin when she hung up.

"I wish," Dahlia said. "It was my brother. He needs our help."

★★★

Donovan Bennett paced back and forth in an office in the administration building of the Odette Army Base. Though he was merely pacing, the combat boots he wore with his fatigues made it sound more like stomping. That, along with the sound of Donovan's dog tags tinkling against each other as he walked, caused his coworker, Roxanne Grayson, to look up from the paperwork she was working on at her desk.

"You're going to wear a hole in the floor, Dono," Roxanne said with a warm smile.

Donovan stopped mid-stride and glanced over at the thirty-something brunette.

"Sorry, Rox," he said to his longtime friend. "This whole situation has got me on edge."

"I can see that."

Donovan headed over to the window behind Roxanne's desk and looked around outside.

"I wish she would get here," he said, fingers drumming against the wood of the sill.

Roxanne's intercom beeped.

"There are two detectives here to see you and Sergeant Bennett," a man's voice filtered through the intercom speaker.

"Thank you," Roxanne replied. "Please send them in."

Sam and Dahlia were escorted to the office. Roxanne rose from her seat. The women saluted each other before smiling and embracing.

"Thanks for coming, Dahlia," Roxanne said to her friend. "Donovan and I are both relieved to have you here to assist us."

Donovan came over from the window and shook hands with Sam. He made a slight movement as if going to hug his sister, but stopped when she took a step back. Donovan let his arms fall to his sides.

"Donovan, Roxanne, this is my partner, Detective Sam Marlowe," Dahlia motioned toward Sam. "And, Sam, this is Sergeant Roxanne Grayson, an old friend of mine, and this is Sergeant Donovan Bennett, my brother."

Roxanne smiled to herself at seeing the two siblings standing next to each other. Even after all these years, they still look so much alike. Curly black hair and forest green eyes; despite one being in an army uniform and the other wearing a police badge, both carried themselves with the same air of confidence, standing tall and proud. Dahlia and Donovan were undeniably siblings, with the only discernible difference being the fact that Donovan towered over his little sister.

"What's going on, Rox?" Dahlia asked.

"There's been an incident at the base," Roxanne began to explain.

"Our commanding officer was found dead yesterday morning," Donovan said.

"Murder?" Dahlia asked.

"He was found in his bed with his throat sliced from ear to ear," Roxanne said. "It was a bloody mess, needless to say."

"Don't you guys have your own military police and justice system?" Sam asked. "I have no problem helping out my country's finest, don't get me wrong, but where do we fit in?"

"The First Sergeant put Roxanne and me in charge of the investigation," Donovan said. "We were hoping, Dahlia, that you and your partner could assist us in the investigation since you two have had more experience in working this kind of case than we've had."

Dahlia looked at Sam and sighed. There was a gleam in Sam's mercury colored eyes, Roxanne noted, following Dahlia's gaze over to her partner.

"We're in," Dahlia said.

★★★

Donovan and Dahlia began delving into the crime scene reports while Roxanne and Sam visited the crime scene to ensure that nothing was overlooked. The siblings sat quietly in Roxanne's office as they perused the images of the scene taken yesterday.

"Everything seems to still be very organized and in place, and there doesn't appear to be much blood spatter around the room, except for the area around the victim's bed, which tells me that there wasn't much of a struggle," Dahlia mused aloud.

The victim, Kent Scarpino, was discovered by his personal assistant in the morning on the day prior in his bed, drenched in blood.

"Scarpino wasn't the biggest guy height-wise, but, after being in the military for so long, he was in good shape," Donovan said. "It's reasonable to believe that he would have fought off his attacker."

"Exactly," Dahlia said. "Yet there is absolutely no sign of a struggle. I would have expected there to be blood all over the place."

She looked up from the photo she was examining and glanced at her brother.

"Donovan may have been drugged."

"Our Medical Examiners finished the autopsy last night," he said. "I'll make sure they get the toxicology report to us ASAP."

Donovan placed the call while Dahlia continued combing through the crime scene report.

★★★

Latex gloves on, Sam and Roxanne carefully entered the crime scene. The CO's barrack was small, with enough furniture and possessions to be livable. There was a pool of dried blood on the wooden floor near the bed. The mattress on the bed frame had been stripped of all its bedding which, blood-soaked, had been taken into evidence. The bedroom area was the only part of the barrack that appeared to have been disturbed. The chairs were perfectly square with the small dining table, the books on the bookshelves were all aligned and in order, and the desk was immaculate with all the papers neatly stacked and the pens, pencils, and highlighters arranged in the pen holder.

"Donovan and I already went through the place," Roxanne said. "But we would appreciate some experienced eyes to look things over to make sure we didn't miss anything."

"Sure," Sam said.

Sam progressed forward, still examining the barrack.

"Sergeant Grayson—"

"Roxanne, please," she replied. "Any friend of Dahlia's is a friend of mine."

"You two go way back?"

"We were both the only daughters in military families," Roxanne said. "I may be a few years older than Dahlia, but we became great friends anyway. We grew up together, since both our families lived on the base. We stayed friends after Major Bennett retired from the service and took over as Dean of Hammett College and Dahlia left to go to school out of state."

"And how long have you been in love with her brother?"

Roxanne blushed.

"Is it that obvious?" she asked, looking down at her combat boots.

"Hey, I'm not the top cop in Odette for the hell of it," Sam said.

"A title well deserved, for sure."

"Why haven't you done anything about it?"

"I guess there are two reasons," Roxanne said. "The biggest reason is the fact that I'm still mad at Donovan for siding with some random jerk and agreeing with him that Dahlia wasn't cut out for law enforcement and also that that career path wasn't safe for a girl. Hello? I'm a girl and I'm doing fine in this male-dominated field, so I've no doubt Dahlia can kick ass as a cop."

"Yeah, Dahlia told me about that and also what Alistair did to her best friend, Iris. Alistair Kinney, what a bastard. I'm happy to say that Alistair is in prison where he belongs. That was our first case together, and since then, Dahlia has become a kickass cop," Sam said. "What's the second reason?"

"There's also the fact that Donovan kind of already has a girlfriend—"

"That would do it."

Sam's attention was snared by a sliver of neon green sticking out from beneath a book on the nightstand. He lifted the book and withdrew a condom wrapper.

"Hey, Roxanne, what kind of man was your CO?" he asked, his back to the Sergeant.

"Good guy, straight shooter," Roxanne replied. "Dedicated quite a few years to the military. Good rapport with most of the soldiers."

"Womanizer?"

"No. He's had a few girlfriends in the time I've known him but never more than one at a time."

"Was he in a relationship before he died?"

"No, he ended it with his last girlfriend when she took a job out of state a few months ago."

Sam held up his find for Roxanne to see.

"Well, my friend here says otherwise."

"Let's show this to Donovan and Dahlia and see if we can figure out who the CO may have been spending time with."

Sam and Roxanne rejoined Dahlia and Donovan in the administration building.

"If he had a visitor from off the base, the name would be recorded in the visitor's log," Donovan said after Sam and Roxanne showed him the evidence they located. "As you two saw when you got here, all visitors are ID'd and logged before being allowed to enter the base."

"Yes, security was, as expected, thorough," Dahlia said.

"Great; Donovan, you and Sam check out the security logs," Roxanne said. "Dahlia and I will swing by the Army Hospital and see if the Medical Examiners discovered any new details."

Sam and Donovan left the office to check out the security logs. Dahlia and Roxanne, meanwhile, chatted as they made their way to the Army Hospital.

"Sergeant Grayson!" a woman called out.

Dahlia caught the brief grimace on Roxanne's face before it was instantly replaced by her usual pleasant expression.

"Sergeant LeClare," Roxanne said politely as she turned around.

A tall and lanky blonde soldier approached Dahlia and Roxanne. She eyed Dahlia curiously for a moment with her cold, gray eyes.

"Who's this?" she asked.

Dahlia extended her hand.

"Detective Dahlia Bennett, Odette PD."

"Bennett?" the woman repeated.

She grinned, her smile quickly lighting up her face.

"You're Donovan's sister," she said. "It's so good to finally meet you!" the woman embraced Dahlia, catching her off-guard. "I'm Bonnie LeClare; I'm Donovan's fiancée."

"Fiancée?" Dahlia and Roxanne repeated in unison.

Bonnie gave a melodic chuckle.

"Okay, I'm not technically his fiancée, but it's pretty much an assured thing," she said. "Anyway, what brings you to the military base?"

"Sergeant Grayson and Sergeant Bennett requested the assistance of my partner and me," Dahlia said.

"For Staff Sergeant Scarpino's murder," Bonnie said. "It's still so unbelievable that he was murdered. To have your throat slit while sleeping in your own bed ..."

"How much do people know?" Roxanne asked, fiddling with her dog tags.

"Don't worry, Rox," Bonnie reassured the brunette. "They only know what you said in your statement last night: SSG. Scarpino was found dead in his barrack."

"That's a relief."

"Speaking of which, do you have any updates on the investigation?"

"This is an ongoing investigation, so Sergeant Grayson is not at liberty to discuss it," Dahlia said.

"Oh, right, of course," Bonnie said. "I guess I'll let you two get back to it."

After a salute, Bonnie gave Dahlia and Roxanne a little wave before strolling past them. Once she was safely out of earshot, Dahlia spoke.

"Is she seriously dating my brother?"

Roxanne folded her arms across her chest and nibbled on her bottom lip.

"It's the truth," she said.

Under her breath, she added, "Unfortunately."

★★★

Donovan and Sam got the list of visitors from the day before and the day of the murder and began tracking down the individuals on the list for their alibis. When Dahlia and Roxanne rejoined them, they split the list and assisted in tracking down the visitors.

"Hey Dono," Roxanne said, skimming through the list. "Did you realize Bruce Tanner was on this list?"

Donovan peered over his partner's shoulders.

"Who's Bruce Tanner?" Dahlia asked.

"Bruce Tanner's son, Ian, was a soldier that used to be stationed here," Donovan said.

"Used to be?" Sam asked.

"He was transferred out of Odette and deployed overseas shortly afterward," Roxanne said. "Ian was killed in a roadside bombing not long after his deployment."

"I take it Bruce blamed Scarpino?" Sam asked.

"Scarpino was his recruiting officer, so Bruce blamed him for Ian joining the armed forces and his subsequent death while on active duty," Donovan said.

"Do you think he would resort to murder?" Roxanne asked.

"If he views Scarpino as the person who-indirectly-murdered his son, it's possible," Sam said.

"Stabbings usually indicate crimes of passion," Dahlia said. "And, if what you're saying is true, it seems Bruce would be quite passionate about Scarpino's alleged guilt."

"Wow, Dahlia, you sound like a regular old criminal profiler from the FBI," Roxanne said with a smile, nudging Dahlia with her elbow.

Dahlia smiled back at her. Out of the corner of her eye, she could see Donovan watching her with a proud gleam in his eye. Dahlia turned away, instead dedicating all her attention to the papers on the table in front of her.

★★★

When informed of Scarpino's death, Bruce Tanner's stern, tight-lipped expression transformed first into a smile and then into a broad grin with hearty laughter. Dahlia and Donovan's faces remained professional.

"Well how about that! There is such thing as karma!" Bruce said, slapping his knee.

Only in his mid-fifties, Bruce's appearance made him seem much older. His tired blue eyes and deep wrinkles spoke volumes about his grief.

"Our records indicate you were at the base shortly before SSG. Scarpino was murdered," Donovan said. "What was your business there?"

"Wait, do you think I killed Kent?" Bruce asked. "Hold your horses; as much as I'd like to take credit for offing the guy, I didn't. Kent sent a message to me, asking me to meet him at eight that night, but the jerk never showed."

"Do you have the note?" Dahlia asked.

"I'm sure I got it somewhere."

He got up from his lumpy blue couch and shuffled over to the adjoining kitchen. After a few moments, Bruce returned, paper in hand. He gave it to Dahlia and Donovan to review.

Dahlia snapped a picture and sent it to Sam.

"I'll need to take this for evidence," Dahlia said.

"Sure. Do whatever you want with it," Bruce said. "I have no use for it."

Dahlia took the note, and after asking Bruce for a fresh Ziploc bag, folded up the piece of paper and placed it inside the bag.

"How long did you wait for Scarpino to show up?" Dahlia asked Bruce.

"I gave him a half hour before I left, which was far more than an asshole like him deserved," Bruce said gruffly.

"Can anyone verify that?"

"Yeah, the guard at the front gate. I specifically told him that if 'his highness' ever decided to grace me with his presence, he knows where to find me," Bruce replied. "He saw me get into my truck and leave. I swear on my son's grave."

"Mr. Tanner, I am so terribly sorry for your loss," Donovan began to say. "But why do you blame SSG. Scarpino for your son's death?"

"He may not have killed my son himself," Bruce said with a sneer. "But he wanted Ian out of the way."

"What makes you say that?"

"Because that sleazebucket was screwing my son's girlfriend!"

★★★

At the army base, Sam and Roxanne cross-referenced the name that Donovan and Dahlia provided them for Ian's girlfriend, Mollie Watson, with the names of the visitors on the security log. They discovered her name on the list of visitors on the night of Scarpino's death. Donovan and Dahlia returned to the base while Sam and Roxanne went in search of Mollie.

"That's terrible," Mollie gasped when Sam and Roxanne told her the news. "Who would do such a thing?"

"That's something we were hoping you could help us with," Roxanne said.

Mollie Watson was a naturally skinny girl with bleach blond hair. She lived alone in an apartment a few miles outside the heart of Odette.

"We have reason to believe you may have been involved with the victim," Roxanne said.

Mollie let out a huff.

"Bruce told you that, didn't he?" she shook her head. "I love Bruce because he was Ian's father, but he's blowing what happened between Kent and me way out of proportion."

"Care to clarify?" Sam asked.

"Ian was so excited to join the military; he said he finally felt like he found his calling," Mollie said. "Kent was the one who recruited Ian, and they eventually became friends, or, at least, as friendly as they could become for a CO and a soldier. When Ian … passed, everyone was devastated. I was in a very dark place after Ian died. We were talking about marriage and starting a family when he returned but, suddenly, he was gone. I lost it.

"Kent was kind enough to check up on both Bruce and me. One night, I drank way too much, and Kent stopped by. We had a few more drinks together and … well, we slept together. It was an accident, but it happened, and we couldn't take it back. Bruce had stopped by to bring me some things from Ian's apartment the next day and overheard me on the phone with Kent and lost it. I tried to tell him what happened, but he wouldn't accept it."

"Have you seen Kent since that night?" Roxanne asked.

Mollie shook her head.

"No, we haven't been in contact since that night; I mean, we might occasionally see each other around town, but that's it," she replied. "I think we last saw each other a few months ago at the grocery store."

"How about two nights ago?" Sam asked. "Forget about that?"

"What are you talking about?" Mollie asked back.

"Two nights ago, we have your name listed on the Odette Army Base security log," Roxanne showed her a picture of the visitor's log.

Mollie frowned.

"That doesn't make sense. I wasn't anywhere near the base," she said.

"Really? Our records indicate otherwise," Sam said.

Mollie got up from her amber armchair and went over to the desk near the front door and grabbed some papers off of it.

"Here," she held out the receipt for Sam and Roxanne to see. "My friend's birthday was Friday night. We went out to eat. There were six of us. Plus, I'm sure my girlfriend posted some photos online too if you want to check. The restaurant was outside of Denver, so it was nowhere near the base."

Sam pulled out his cell phone and searched Mollie's name on social media while Roxanne asked some additional questions. As Mollie said, there were several photos from the birthday dinner online. Sam showed Roxanne the confirmation of the young woman's alibi, and after an extra question or two, they took their leave.

★★★

Returning to the base, Donovan and Roxanne were whisked away into a meeting with the First Sergeant, along with Bonnie. Sam and Dahlia reviewed the evidence while waiting in Roxanne's office.

"Someone used Mollie's name to make it seem like she came to the base when Kent was murdered," Dahlia said.

"Exactly," Sam said in agreement. "She would be a likely suspect based on her history with Scarpino, but, unless she took a two-hour bathroom break while at the party and none of her friends noticed, Mollie couldn't have done it. She was too far out of town for it to be feasible. Plus, did you see the outfit Mollie was wearing in those photos? In that flashy red dress, she would have stood out like a sore thumb. I'm sure at least one person would have noticed her in that little number."

"In using Mollie's name, that means someone knew about her history with Kent. Did Mollie say whether or not anyone else knew about their indiscretion?"

"She said Bruce knew. He overheard a phone conversation between the two and flipped out. It seems like Bruce thought Kent deliberately sent Ian to his death to get with Mollie."

"Bruce also claimed that Kent sent him a note requesting him to come to the base on the night of the murder," Dahlia said. "But he doesn't even show up to the meeting he supposedly set up; did someone, maybe, forge the note in Scarpino's name to make it look like he sent it to lure Bruce here?"

"It's definitely possible," Sam said. "We should send the note to the lab to be checked out and see if we can confirm if that is Scarpino's handwriting."

Donovan, Roxanne, and Bonnie joined Sam and Dahlia in Roxanne's office following their meeting with the First Sergeant.

"You guys okay?" Sam asked, an eyebrow raised as the group filtered in.

"Yes and no," Roxanne pursed her lips. "With SSG. Scarpino's death, someone needs to take over his command."

"Roxanne was nominated for the job," Donovan said.

Dahlia smiled.

"Congratulations, Rox," she said.

"And," Bonnie planted an overly dramatic kiss on Donovan's cheek. "So was my darling Donovan!"

Donovan blushed.

"It's about time they put someone worthwhile into the CO's position," Bonnie said with a huff. "Scarpino was a terrible CO and didn't deserve the post one bit!"

"What's her beef with the vic?" Sam whispered to Dahlia.

"I have no idea," she replied.

"Well, we're both going to have to appear before the Promotion Board," Roxanne said. "They can decide between us since Dono and I would probably vote for each other if given a chance."

"Congratulations to both of you," Dahlia said. "The Promotion Board has a difficult decision to make with the two of you as candidates."

"Thanks," Roxanne said.

Donovan mumbled his thanks, his eyes focused on some of Roxanne's medals and certificates hanging on the wall.

★★★

Hearing the knock on his office door, Sergeant Major Cameron Westley didn't bother to look up from the file he was reading.

"Enter," he called.

His back to the door as he stood by the filing cabinet, Westley heard the door open and close.

"Only Roxanne and Donovan are up for promotion? What the hell?"

With a grimace, Westley turned around. Bonnie had a prominent frown on her face and her arms folded across her chest.

"Both are exemplary officers," Westley said.

"I don't care!" Bonnie said.

She came around his desk, took the file folder out of his hand, and tossed it on his desk. Nearly the same height as the Sergeant Major, she closed the distance between them until their faces were inches apart. Westley tried to shrink back from the Sergeant but stopped when he felt his back hit the cabinet behind him.

"Do you think I enjoy screwing a man who is old enough to be my father?" Bonnie spat. "I'm keeping up my end of the bargain; did you forget about yours?"

Westley put his hands out to put space between them.

"I didn't forget," he said. "What I did was more of a precautionary measure."

"Oh, really?"

"Listen, Bon," Westley said. "There's only so many times that I can use the 'exceptional performers' qualification to get you promoted and up the ranks as quickly as possible. You've barely spent the required amount of time at Sergeant Rank to qualify for the Secondary Zone promotional requirement. If you suddenly jump ahead of Sergeant Grayson and Sergeant Bennett, won't it be a sign to the others that something might be amiss?"

Bonnie let out a huff.

"You listen, Wes," she said. "My grandfather is going to kick the bucket any day now; I mean, he's ancient! The condition he said I needed to meet to get his millions-and I stress 'millions'-of dollars as my inheritance, was that I need to get up as high as I can in the army to beat out the rest of his grandkids. The highest-ranking grandchild gets half of the fortune while the rest of the grandkids split the remaining fortune. There's a lot of us so the portions will be small."

"Why is he doing that again?"

"Because he was some high-ranking officer in some war that probably happened centuries ago," Bonnie said. "He thinks that the only way any of us are going to amount to anything is if we 'dedicate our lives' to the service to protect the country and its people or some shit like that. Do you honestly think this is what I want to be doing with my life? Do you?"

Westley opened his mouth to respond, but Bonnie continued speaking.

"But I guess you don't care about getting your piece of the pie, do you? And I'm sure the members of the court-martial would *love* to hear about how you've been engaged in an inappropriate relationship with one of your subordinates and all your gambling debts."

"All right, all right!" Westley said. "You've made your point."

Bonnie gave him a smile and playfully tapped his nose with her index finger.

"Good boy," she said. "I'll see you tonight."

"Yeah," Westley grumbled. "Looking forward to it."

★★★

The following day, Sam and Dahlia took a trip down to the crime lab to get the results of the handwriting analysis of the note Bruce received and the handwriting on the security log against known samples of Scarpino's writing.

"It appears that the handwriting on the note Bruce got does not match the known samples of Scarpino's writing," Dahlia read over the report.

"It was on the army letterhead paper, which I know that Scarpino had on his desk in his barrack," Sam said. "But anyone could pop in there and swipe a piece, but my question is that, if the culprit was going to go that far to make it seem like Scarpino was the one who wrote the note, why actually handwrite the note? Why not type it? I mean, the writing looks pretty similar, but the handwriting analysis could easily prove that it's not an identical match; someone was forging his signature."

"Sam, get this," Dahlia continued reading. "The handwriting on the note does match, however, with the writing on the security log. It matches the entry for Mollie Watson."

"Ian Tanner's girlfriend? You're kidding?"

"No, it's right in the report."

Sam came over to Dahlia to read the report.

"But how? It can't be Mollie," he said. "She wasn't in town during the murder. Plus, she made it seem like she and Bruce still got along, even after her little sleepover with Scarpino. Would she really want to kill Scarpino and then blame the man who was slated to be her father-in-law?"

"Weirder things have happened, Sam," Dahlia said.

"Sure, but I can't be wrong about this," Sam said. "I'm me!"

His comment caused Dahlia to put her head in her hands.

★★★

With the results from the handwriting analysis pointing toward Mollie's writing on the security log matching the note sent to Bruce, Sam and Dahlia returned to her apartment.

"That's not my writing," Mollie said.

She looked at the samples the two detectives presented her.

"Can you prove it?" Dahlia asked. "Can you write your name out a few times for us?"

Mollie got up from the kitchen table and grabbed a fresh piece of paper and a pen from the desk in the living room. She sat down and began writing her name on the paper over and over again.

"You're a lefty," Sam said as he watched Mollie write.

"Yeah," Mollie said.

"You've got a wicked backhand slant, as I'm sure you can see here," Sam said. "Also, when you cross the 't' in Watson, the line goes from right to left instead of left to right like most right handed people do and the note's writer does."

"Oh, so you're a handwriting expert now?" Dahlia asked with a smirk.

Sam's response was a grin. Looking closely at the sample Mollie produced in front of them and the examples the lab had reviewed, the differences were undeniable.

"You know," Mollie sunk down in her seat, bringing her hands down into her lap. "Ian and I used to joke about the kids we were going to have one day. We thought how hard it was going to be for them to learn how to write properly with a left-handed mom and a right-handed dad. Poor kids wouldn't know which way the letters were supposed to go ..."

Her statement was followed by a sorrowful sigh.

★★★

Roxanne and Donovan listened to the results of the handwriting analysis, as well as the follow up from Sam and Dahlia's visit with Mollie.

"That's odd," Roxanne said.

Sitting at her desk, she drummed her fingers against it as she reclined in her chair. She abruptly sat up and looked directly at the two detectives.

"But there's actually a way to confirm whether or not Mollie was telling the truth," Roxanne said. "Dono and I have certain security clearances that you two wouldn't have as civilians. We can get access to the other things that Mollie would have needed to give at the visitor's center at the front gate."

"You mean like her full name, birth date, social security number and a copy of her ID?" Dahlia asked.

"Exactly," Roxanne said.

"Good thinking," Sam said. "We can cross-check whatever information you two can find at the visitor's center with the information we can access at the police department."

"Plus, we know what Mollie looks like, so a quick check of her driver's license against the one on record at the base should be easy enough to confirm whether or not she used a fake ID or anything like that," Dahlia said.

"Dono," Roxanne turned to Donovan. "Would you mind going?"

"Sure," Donovan said.

"Why don't you go with him, Bennett?" Sam said. "You know, enjoy some quality sibling time?"

Dahlia glared at Sam, who grinned at her. She said nothing as she followed her brother out of Roxanne's office. Once they were gone, Sam turned his attention back to Roxanne.

"You didn't sound too keen on taking a trip down to the visitor's center," he said. "Who or what is down there that you want to avoid?"

Roxanne let out a small laugh.

"I have to say, Sam," she said. "You absolutely are as good of a cop as you say you are."

"All right, spill it, sister."

"Bonnie works down at the visitor's center. She supervises the soldiers there. Since you know my ... feelings about Donovan, you get why I'd rather avoid the visitor's center."

"Oh, for sure," Sam paused. "It's got to be hell having to see her all the time."

"It wasn't always that way," Roxanne said. "I mean, she actually hasn't been a Sergeant for that long ... come to think of it, she's flown through the ranks."

"Obviously, you can't fly through the ranks in the army like you would in any regular old job field."

"Right. That's odd, now that I think about it. There is an opportunity for soldiers to be considered for a promotion sooner; it's called the Secondary Zone, and it gives exceptional performers the opportunity to be promoted faster than the normal time-in-grade and time-in-service requirements. Then again, Bonnie does come from a rich and esteemed military lineage, so maybe it's in her genes."

"Rich and esteemed military lineage?" Sam asked. "Like what?"

"Command Sergeant Major George LeClare fought overseas and was injured in battle, so he was given an honorable discharge. He was given multiple medals for his actions while in the line of duty," Roxanne replied. "After his discharge, he returned to the States and returned to civilian life. CSM LeClare struck oil while hunting, sort of like a modern-day Jed Clampett, and made millions."

"Bonnie's family is loaded? Interesting," Sam said. "If the LeClares are in the oil business now, why is Bonnie in the army and not in some cushy office making six figures?"

"That's something you'd have to ask her."

Roxanne grabbed a file from her desk.

"Oh, by the way, Sam, Donovan and I got the final autopsy report from the Medical Examiner, along with the toxicology report. As it turns out, Scarpino was drugged. That's probably why he didn't fight back against his attacker."

Sam accepted the file Roxanne handed to him and read it over.

"Did they come up with a conclusive result on what Scarpino was drugged with?" he asked.

"Not yet, but the ME thinks it was probably a sleeping pill or two that Scarpino was administered. We found a bottle of over-the-counter sleeping pills on the end table next to the bed and brought it into evidence before you and Dahlia arrived, so that's likely the source of the drugs."

"Now my question is did Scarpino take the pills under his own power or did someone–my guess would be the gal he slept with since he would have been 'unarmed'–drug him to knock him unconscious, and thus, easier to kill?" Sam asked.

★★★

It was silent between the two Bennetts as they left the administration building and walked across the base to the visitor's center. Dahlia's hands slowly balled into fists. *Why the hell did Sam have to make me go with Donovan now? I could handle being with him when I had something to occupy myself with, like reviewing the crime scene reports or talking with Bruce Tanner but there's nothing to do until we get to the visitor's center. I ... can't do this. I can't keep pretending that nothing's wrong and all's well between us. Because it's not.*

"Donovan, stop," Dahlia said abruptly.

"What's wrong, Dahlia?" he asked.

"Sam and I have been at the base working with you and Roxanne for the past two days, and while I have no problem assisting you two in finding that justice is served for whoever killed SSG Scarpino, I am extremely pissed at the way you have been acting toward me," Dahlia said.

"Acting toward you?" Donovan repeated. "What are you talking about?"

"Seriously, Donovan? You seriously have to ask me what I'm talking about?"

Some soldiers who were walking by briefly glanced at the two Bennetts before returning to their conversation.

"Oh, you're referring to *that*," Donovan let out a breath. "Can we get to the visitor's center? We can talk privately in the records room."

"Why? You don't want everyone at the base to hear about what you did to your only sister?" Dahlia's volume increased.

"Please, Dahlia."

"Fine."

Falling in line behind her brother, Dahlia followed Donovan to the visitor's center. Once inside, they headed into the records room. Donovan closed the door behind them.

"Well?" Dahlia asked him, her arms folded across her chest.

"What do you want me to say, Dahlia?" he replied. "I screwed up. I listened to someone whom I shouldn't have."

"Screwed up doesn't begin to cover it, Donovan. You listened to a *killer*."

"A killer? What are you talking about?"

"Iris, Donovan. Alistair was the reason Iris, my best friend, my sister really, killed herself five years ago. I kept her secret as best I could like she wanted me to, but I think it's time you knew the truth. He raped her, and she was afraid to press charges. Being forced to see her attacker day in and day out got to her. She committed suicide, Donovan. I found her in the tub with her wrists slit." Dahlia glared up at her brother. "That son of a bitch knew I was gunning for him, to make him pay for what he did to Iris, so he targeted my family. He convinced you that I wasn't cut out to be a cop. Donovan, he got Dad to threaten to expel me from Hammett if I didn't change my major from criminal justice to something 'safe' that a girl could do."

Donovan's eyes widened, and his mouth fell open. His body tensed and his posture became rigid.

"That … that's why you transferred?"

"Yeah. That's why I transferred," Dahlia said. "I was forced to leave, and Alistar was given free rein to do whatever he wanted while I was gone. Do you know what he did during that time?"

Donovan shook his head.

"He had an affair with a prominent businesswoman, broke up her family, extorted money from her daughter and plotted a fake kidnapping. Oh, and he drugged me and attempted to make it look like we slept together, and that it was my negligence that let the crime happen," Dahlia said. "But, yeah, he's a real reliable guy, Donovan. I'm so glad you, Dad, Cody, and Ashton all listened to that fine, upstanding citizen named Alistair Kinney."

"Dahlia," Donovan said. "I … I had no idea."

Dahlia turned away from her brother. She bit her lip to keep herself from tearing up.

"This is the first time we've been together in years, and I haven't seen the tiniest bit of remorse from you. Instead, you're still acting like nothing important happened, nothing that would have impacted my life like it has. Do you think I wanted to be estranged from my family like this? Do you think that I wanted to find out that my family didn't support my dreams of becoming a cop? Do you think I enjoyed having to move across the country to leave my family behind, all while dealing with the death of my best friend and knowing that her killer was still roaming free? Oh yeah, it was a real joy, Donovan. A real joy. Did you ever once consider the fact that I missed all of you and the closeness that we used to have before Alistair poisoned our family?" Dahlia paused. "The only person who hasn't questioned my abilities is Sam. He didn't want a partner in the beginning but, when I started to doubt myself and listen to all that Alistair put in my head, he didn't give up on me. He wouldn't let me quit. Sam helped me put Alistair away in prison. Those are things that a true brother should do."

"A true brother," Donovan repeated quietly. "Yeah, you're right, Dahlia. We've screwed up big time. All of us, Dad, Cody, Ashton and me. Do you know how many times I stood by the phone, trying to get up the courage to call you and tell you how sorry I was for what we put you through and how proud I am of you? I have all of the newspaper articles documenting the cases you and Sam worked together in my office, Dahlia; believe me, Roxanne gives me hell every time I put up a new one, asking me when I was going to call you. I never had an answer for her because I didn't know. I want to reconcile with you, Dahlia, but I've never been sure if you've wanted to."

A soldier opened the door to the records room, pausing in the doorway at the sight of Donovan and Dahlia.

"Sergeant Bennett," the soldier saluted. "Am I interrupting, Sir?"

"No, it's all right," Donovan said. "Detective Bennett and I came to grab a file. We'll be on our way in a moment, and the records room will be all yours."

Donovan quickly located the file he and Dahlia needed. The two Bennetts exited the records room to return to the administration building.

★★★

"The only information that was put into the security log was the name Mollie Watson," Roxanne read through the file.

She, along with Donovan, Dahlia, and Sam, reviewed the information from the security records.

"There's no birth date, social security number, copy of her driver's license or any other required proof of identification," Donovan said. "Who approved this?"

Roxanne skimmed the records. Her finger stopped on the signature of the person who authorized Mollie's supposed visit. She looked up at Dahlia, who stood next to her at her desk.

"I guess it makes sense," Roxanne nibbled on her bottom lip. "She does supervise the visitor's center ..."

"Who is it?" Donovan asked.

Sam came around behind the desk to look at the record.

"Sorry, Dono," he said. "But your lady is in deep trouble."

"What?"

"The person who signed off on Mollie's visit was Bonnie," Roxanne said.

"Actually," Sam said. "It looks more like Bonnie put Mollie's name down on the sheet to frame her. Look at the handwriting, it's nearly the same."

"But that would mean she'd have to know about Mollie's history with Ian and SSG Scarpino for Bonnie to consider her as a viable suspect for us to look in to," Dahlia said. "Is that something she knew about, Donovan?"

"I don't know. We haven't been together for that long."

"Bonnie said you were planning to propose to her soon," she said.

"That's news to me," Donovan said. "I didn't have any plans like that."

"Donovan, can you get a sample of Bonnie's writing to confirm that she was the one who signed off on this?" Dahlia asked.

"Yeah, I should be able to do that."

"Good," Sam said. "Go do that ASAP. The three of us will hang here and see what else we can find out about Bonnie's relationship with Ian."

Without another word, Donovan left the office to find Bonnie.

"One of us should probably check in with Bruce Tanner," Roxanne said. "Ian's father would probably know if there was any connection between his son and Bonnie."

"I'll go," Dahlia popped up from her chair.

"All right," Sam said. "Have fun, Bennett."

★★★

Bruce was mowing the front lawn when Dahlia arrived at his house.

"Any news on who offed Scarpino?" he asked after he stopped the noisy mower.

"We've made some progress," Dahlia said. "But I have a few follow up questions for you."

"Shoot."

"Did Ian have any girlfriends before Mollie?"

"Yeah. He's had a few since high school, but none as serious as Mollie."

"Can you give me any of their names?"

"Sure," Bruce leaned against the startup handle of the lawnmower. "First there was Steph, then Chelsea. He met a girl in college named Bonnie, and they dated for a while until Ian went into the service-"

"Bonnie," Dahlia stopped recording the names Bruce listed to her in her notepad. "Can you tell me about her?"

"Real pretty girl. Apparently from some rich family; oil, I think they were in. She was thrilled when Ian went into the army. She said she was related to some fancy high-ranking guy in the army that served overseas and stuff like that."

"Any chance her name was Bonnie LeClare?"

Bruce thought for a moment. He snapped his fingers.

"Yep. That's her."

"Okay, they dated; how did the relationship end?" Dahlia asked.

"Well, it was right after basic training. Ian and a couple of his friends went up to Denver to celebrate, and that's where he met Mollie," Bruce said a sad smile on his face. "I remember when he came home that night. He was so overjoyed. Ian told me 'Dad, I met the girl I'm going to marry.' He ended it with Bonnie shortly afterward."

"How did she take it?"

"Pretty good, as far as I knew. They stayed friends, especially since Bonnie had enlisted right alongside Ian."

"Mr. Tanner," Dahlia began to say. "Do you know if Bonnie found out about what happened between Mollie and Scarpino after Ian's death?"

"Honestly? It wouldn't surprise me. I don't want to sound like I am a total crotchety old man, but Bonnie, I feel like she was an ass kisser," Bruce scratched his head. "Either that or a huge gossip. So, yeah, she most likely knew that Scarpino was a pile of shit who was trying to take advantage of Mollie in a dark time."

Dahlia hurriedly scribbled down all of what Bruce had told her.

Sam and Roxanne are going to love this.

★★★

Sam and Dahlia brought Bonnie's handwriting sample to the crime lab for examination after Donovan delivered it to them. The next morning, after requesting a rush on the comparison, the two detectives returned to the lab to check in on the results.

"It's a match," Dahlia summarized the findings. "Now we have Bruce's statement that Bonnie, Ian's ex-girlfriend, likely knew about the affair Mollie had with Scarpino and we have confirmation that Bonnie was the one who put Mollie's name on the visitor's log."

"Sure, but that still doesn't explain why Bonnie did all this," Sam said. "Why the hell would she target Scarpino? What did she have against him?"

"You and Roxanne found that condom wrapper in the barrack, right?"

"Yeah, we did," Sam paused. "You think she was screwing the Staff Sergeant? Isn't that against the rules, for a subordinate to be involved with a superior officer?"

"It is, but that doesn't mean it doesn't happen."

"If that's the case, maybe Scarpino came to his senses and realized that Bon-Bon was fruity in the loops and dumped her crazy ass and so she killed him in retaliation."

Dahlia considered Sam's theory.

"It's possible," she tapped the file with the end of her pen. "We should head back to the base to let Roxanne and Donovan know."

Meeting up with Donovan and Roxanne in Roxanne's office at the army base, the two detectives informed them of the results of the newest handwriting analysis.

"I guess we should inform the First Sergeant," Donovan said.

"Are you okay, Donovan?" Roxanne asked, placing a hand on his shoulder.

"Bonnie killed a man. She needs to pay for her crimes."

Roxanne phoned the First Sergeant to arrange a meeting to discuss their findings. En route to the meeting on the second floor of the administration building, the four were intercepted by another soldier. Roxanne and Donovan immediately stopped and saluted.

"Sergeant Major Westley, Sir!"

Westley saluted the two soldiers back.

"I heard from the First Sergeant that you have come to a conclusion on who killed SSG Scarpino; is that true?" he asked.

"Yes, Sir," Roxanne said. "We were on our way to meet with the First Sergeant to present our findings."

"Yes, about that ..." Westley began to say. "I need all of you to come to my office. There is something we all need to discuss first."

Once inside, Westley took a seat at his desk. He invited Sam and Dahlia to take a seat in the visitor's chairs while the two soldiers stood at ease behind them.

"All right," Westley said. "Tell me what you have."

Roxanne explained what they had found over the course of their investigation. The Sergeant Major listened quietly, his hands folded together, his extended index fingers resting against his lips.

"I see ..." Westley said thoughtfully after Roxanne finished her presentation of the facts and evidence.

The Sergeant Major got up from his chair and stood by the window behind his desk, turning away from the two detectives and two soldiers.

"Sergeant Bennett, please make sure the door to my office is locked," he said.

Donovan did as instructed, and returned to his spot next to Roxanne.

"The door is locked, Sir," he said.

"Thank you," Westley replied. "I need to make sure that no one, besides the four of you, hears this information, for now, at least."

The Sergeant Major let out a slow breath.

"I am certain that all of the information you presented to me is accurate, except for the motive. What you have told me is ... a wakeup call, and I realize that I am also at fault for what happened."

"How so?" Sam asked.

"Sergeant LeClare ... she happened to show up at the casino I was at one night a few years ago, though, now looking back, I suppose she probably followed me there ... but that doesn't matter. Regardless of how she ended up there, she found out about my little problem ... I have a gambling addiction. It's incredibly embarrassing to admit, but I need to explain everything for you to understand the whole truth. The next day, after seeing each other at the casino, Sergeant ... err, Bonnie, came to my office and confronted me about it. She threatened to tell the Sergeant Major, my superior at the time before I was promoted to this rank, about all of my gambling debts and the ... unsavory characters I owed them to. I was so close to being promoted, I panicked and asked her how much it would be to buy her silence.

"Bonnie's response was a little arrangement between us. I would assist her in climbing up the ranks in record time, and in exchange, she would not reveal my addiction or my debts and fraternization with criminals and loan sharks. She also ... seduced me and we began a sexual relationship … which I suppose was extra insurance on her part since it was something I could be court-martialed for …"

"Why would she do something like that?" Dahlia asked. "Why was it so essential for her to climb the ranks so quickly?"

"It is a part of her inheritance. I'm sure you know that Bonnie's grandfather is extremely wealthy. She told me that he didn't want his grandkids to grow up rich and spoiled rotten, instead wanting to instill the values, morals and a work ethic the army provided him during his service. The grandchild that achieved the highest rank in the army would receive a substantial sum of money when Command Sergeant Major LeClare passed away, with the rest of the grandchildren splitting the remaining fortune."

"That's pretty shitty," Sam said.

Westley glanced at Sam over his shoulder.

"I didn't make the rules," he said. "I'm only telling you what Bonnie told me."

"Okay, but how does Scarpino's death fit into this whole thing?"

"I didn't realize the lengths to which Bonnie would go to secure her fortunes until you four presented your findings now. SSG Scarpino heard Bonnie and me discussing something in our little arrangement, and he confronted me after Bonnie left. I assured him he was mistaken, but I'm not sure he believed me; he obviously didn't. I warned Bonnie about Scarpino's suspicions, and she told me that she'd take care of the situation."

"She said she'd take care of the situation, and then Scarpino ends up dead?" Sam said. "How did you not put two and two together?"

"Because that was a few months ago," Westley said. "Plus, Scarpino suddenly dropped the whole situation concerning Bonnie and me, so I figured Bonnie made good on her promise. But, with the evidence you found in the barrack, specifically the condom, I realize now that she had put Scarpino in a position where he could also be implicated and potentially court-martialed; whether it was consensual between them or she coerced him into it, Bonnie had been sleeping with Scarpino."

"If she had Scarpino under her thumb, why did she have to kill him?" Dahlia wondered aloud.

"Scarpino was going to be considered for a promotion soon," Westley said. "I have no doubt that there was no way he felt he would be able to live with the Centralized Promotion Board's decision if he was selected for promotion to First Sergeant when he was living with such a secret. Having worked with Scarpino since he was a Private, I believe that he planned on revealing what he knew about Bonnie and me, even at the risk of his own court-martial."

"Wait a second," Roxanne said. "That's how she knew!"

"Knew what, Sergeant Grayson?"

"I know for a fact that I did not reveal the details of how SSG Scarpino was killed during the press conference a few days ago. I only said that he was found dead in his barrack and that an investigation would be conducted into his death. When we first began the investigation-Dahlia, you might remember hearing this, too-Bonnie said something along the lines of how awful it must have been to have had his throat slit while sleeping in his bed."

"She *did* say that," Dahlia said. "The only way she would have known that is if she was there."

"Yes, it does seem that way," Westley said.

"Thank you for speaking with me, Sergeants. If you're ready, we'll head over to the First Sergeant's office and explain everything and get this case wrapped up."

Westley came around his desk, unlocked his door and left his office, followed by Sam, Dahlia, Roxanne, and Donovan.

★★★

After the meeting with the First Sergeant, Sam and Dahlia followed Donovan and Roxanne from the administration building to the visitor's center, where Bonnie was on duty.

"Hi, honey," Bonnie said to Donovan when he entered.

Her smile quickly faded when she saw the stoic expression on Donovan's face.

"What's wrong, Dono?" she asked.

"You killed Scarpino," Donovan said.

"What are you talking about?" Bonnie asked. "I didn't do anything of the sort. I thought you guys had your eyes on Bruce Tanner. You know, because he hated SSG Scarpino for recruiting Ian into the army."

"We did consider that," Roxanne said. "But it's funny, Sergeant LeClare, we never mentioned that lead to you. How did you know about it?"

"I supervise the visitor's center, Roxanne," Bonnie replied. "I saw his name on the list, duh. I mean, I know he hated Scarpino, so it's likely he was the one who slit the man's throat. Common sense, right?"

"And another thing," Roxanne said. "How did you know that Scarpino had his throat slit? I never mentioned that information when we announced the CO's death, yet you mentioned it to Dahlia and me. There's no way you could have known that unless you were there."

"What? No. You said Kent had his throat slit during the announcement," Bonnie put her hands on her hips.

"No, she didn't," Donovan said. "I was right there with her; Roxanne never mentioned that detail."

"She's probably making it all up because she's jealous of us," Bonnie glared at Roxanne. "She's in love with you, you know."

Sam watched as Donovan's wide eyes drifted over to Roxanne's. Seeing Roxanne turn her head away sheepishly from his intense gaze, Sam silently hoped that this was the epiphany Donovan needed to recognize what had been in front of him the whole time. *Roxanne admitted she loved Donovan; it's about freakin' time he does the same for her!*

"We already know what happened," Dahlia said. "You seduced Kent as evidenced by the condom wrapper found in his barracks. You drugged him to knock him unconscious to make things easier for you when you slit his throat."

"You sent a fake letter to Bruce Tanner, posing as Scarpino, to get him to the base, as well as added Mollie's name to the security log to cast suspicion on them based on their history with Ian," Sam said. "It was easy for you to do something like that because you're a supervisor here at the visitor's center. That grants you easy access to the security log."

"Are you truly that greedy and self-centered that you would resort to extortion, blackmail, and even murder?" Donovan asked. "And what would have happened if I found out about your little arrangement with the Sergeant Major, or even Scarpino? Would I have been next on your hit list?"

Bonnie did not reply. Donovan looked away from her.

"That's all I needed to know."

★★★

Dahlia joined her brother on the second-floor balcony of the recreation center on the base. She paused behind him, not sure of what to say. Letting out a breath, Dahlia came and stood next to Donovan.

"How are you doing?" she asked.

"I feel like a giant asshole," Donovan exhaled slowly. "How the hell could I have missed all of the signs? Bonnie had no interest in being a soldier. She was only in it for the money. Instead of dedicating herself to her country and the freedoms it provides, she was using all we stand for just for money. It wouldn't surprise me if that's the reason she wanted to be in a relationship with me; you know, Dad's prestige and money and all that."

He sighed.

"Beyond that, she destroyed the lives of numerous soldiers. Ian Tanner, SSG Scarpino, the Sergeant Major. You know, I wonder if Ian transferred out of this base to get away from Bonnie because he realized what a horrible person she was."

"I'm sorry."

"Don't be."

Donovan turned toward his sister.

"Actually, I'm the one who should be sorry," he said. "Seeing you with Sam, I realize how wrong I was for doubting your capabilities as a cop. And I needed to hear all those things you said to me when we were in the records room the other day. It may have been difficult to listen to, but I needed to hear it."

Donovan pulled a piece of paper out of his pocket and handed it to Dahlia.

"What's this?" she asked.

"When you needed a writing sample from Bonnie," he began to say. "I had a problem coming up with an excuse to tell her about why I needed it. So, I decided to tell her that I wanted to write a letter to you to get out all the things I wanted to say to you, Dahlia, but was afraid to. I had her jot down some thoughts that I listed off, which was what we gave to the examiner for the handwriting analysis. I made a copy to keep for myself, in case I ever got the nerve to say these things ... like how ashamed I am that I listened to Alistair, and how I never should have doubted you. You are an amazing cop, and the best sister any brother could ever ask for.

"Let's chalk it up to some 'bad advice,'" Dahlia replied. "Hey, at least now we both have crazies that we've dealt with."

"Can we put all that behind us? I miss my little sister."

"On one condition," Dahlia said.

"One condition?" Donovan rubbed the back of his neck. "Okay, what is it?"

"Stop denying how you feel about Roxanne. She loves you too. Any idiot can see that you have feelings for each other."

Donovan thought Dahlia's words over for a moment.

"Thanks, Dahl."

Dahlia gave her brother a long overdue hug.

★★★

Watching the exchange from a nearby window, Sam and Roxanne smiled.

"Oh, by the way, I told Dahlia to put in a good word for you with Donovan," Sam said to his new friend.

He grinned. "And I think it worked."

Roxanne punched Sam in the shoulder but smiled back nonetheless. The last part of their duty was to fix the relationship between the estranged Bennett siblings. It was mission accomplished.

THE MISSING LINK

Standing outside at the back of the Odette Police Department building, Sam took a drag of his cigarette, silently cursing his vice as a gust of chilly autumn wind slithered past. It was far too cold to be hanging around outdoors in only a slate gray shirt. The cold weather, though, was the least of his worries today.

It was his first day back at the department after the death of his mother. With the release of his stepfather, Seth Tucker, the man who put his mother in her vegetative state sixteen years ago after nearly beating her to death in a drunken rage, while on parole two years ago, Sam had been adamant with the long-term care facility staff that Seth Tucker not be allowed anywhere near his mother, Charlotte. He got the call from the facility director while he and his partner, Dahlia, were investigating a scene, that a man matching the mugshot Sam had provided the facility with was attempting to gain access to one of the patients.

Sam was sure he broke every speed limit on his way to the facility, relieved to find that Seth had fled from the property by the time he arrived. His relief was short-lived, however, when he figured that Seth would probably try again to get in to see Charlotte. Calling his beloved foster sister, Nina Hill, Sam asked her to join him at the facility to talk about what he might be able to do to protect his mother from Seth, in case the man was going to try and finish what he started sixteen years ago.

"There's only one way to protect her from him," he said to Nina.

"Sam ..." Nina was tearing up.

She placed a hand on his arm, and he turned to her, pulling her into a tight embrace.

"If she has ... to die," Sam could barely get the words out, clinging on to Nina as if she were his lifeline. "I'd rather be the one *to do it because I'm doing it because I love her and want to protect her ... not because Seth wants to ... finish the job."*

"I'll call Mom, Clarice, and Raymond," Nina murmured into his chest. "We'll all be here with you when ... it's time."

Sam let out a slow breath, resting his cheek against Nina's head.

"Nin?"

"Hmm?"

"Can you—" he started to say.

"Do you want me to call Dahlia and tell her?"

"Yeah. Please."

He had more bereavement time off but opted not to use it. The time off at his apartment, idle, would have driven him insane. Sam was back on duty at the department, but he still found that his focus was anywhere but.

"Detective Marlowe!"

Sam glanced up from the spot on the sidewalk he'd been unconsciously intently staring at and found a fellow cop headed his way.

"Peter Marsden!" he said with a smile.

Peter returned the smile.

"It's great to see you, Det—"

Sam held his hand up.

"Sam, please."

"Nice to see you again, Sam," Peter said.

"You too, Petey," Sam said. "It's been awhile. Boy, that first case we worked together, the Misty Taylor case, seems like forever ago, doesn't it? You were a rookie, fresh out of the academy, right?"

Peter chuckled.

"Yep. That was five years ago, wasn't it? Wow. Time sure flies," he said.

Another cold breeze brushed past. Peter stuffed his hands into the pockets of his sweater.

"Hey," he started to say. "I heard about your mom. I'm really sorry."

Sam shrugged.

"It was bound to happen eventually," he said. "But thanks."

"How are you doing?"

"I'll live. I'm glad to be back at the department. I prefer to keep busy than to sit around in my apartment with nothing to keep my mind from wandering."

"In that case, Sam, I need your help."

"I'm in," Sam said before the words were barely out of Peter's mouth.

"You haven't even heard what the case is about."

"Doesn't matter; I'm in."

"Thank you, Sam. I knew I could rely on you," Peter said with sincerity. "Can I meet you at your desk in a few minutes to review the details?"

"Of course. I'll meet you up there in a few."

★★★

After fixing herself a hot cup of herbal tea in the break room, Dahlia made her way back to the bullpen. Arriving at her desk, she was curious to find an unfamiliar man loitering around her partner's desk.

"Can I help you?" Dahlia asked.

The man turned around to face her.

"You must be Detective Bennett. It's a pleasure to meet you."

"And who might you be?" she asked.

"This is Detective Peter Marsden, and he's asked for our assistance on a case," Sam, who had made it up to the bullpen by this point, said. "He and I worked some cases together a few years back before Petey, here, got promoted and started doing undercover stuff. He's like a ninja; you know, you'll see him one day and then, boom, next day he's off on some super-secret mission."

With a laugh, Peter offered his hand to Dahlia, who shook it.

"I don't know if I'd necessarily say 'ninja skills,'" he said.

"I would," Sam said. "Bennett, can we get a ruling on this?"

Dahlia shook her head to bring her attention back to the conversation between Peter and Sam, causing her curly ebony hair to bounce lightly from side to side.

"Sorry, what?" she asked.

The grin on her partner's face caused Dahlia to frown.

"I think my partner's taken a fancy to you, Petey," Sam said.

He began to sing, "Peter and Dahlia sittin' in a tree! K-I-S-S-I-"

"Shut up, Sam," Dahlia replied, jabbing an elbow into his side.

Peter chuckled quietly to himself as he watched the exchange between the two detectives.

He is *pretty good looking,* Dahlia admitted to herself. Peter was taller than Sam by no more than a few inches but in as good—or, perhaps, even better—shape than the veteran detective. Beneath his gray sweater, he wore a cerulean blue dress shirt, the color of which complimented his ocean blue eyes. Peter had thick brown hair that could easily be mistaken for black under the right light. He seemed modest and hardworking, as well as honest and loyal; those attributes made Dahlia wonder how on Earth Sam hadn't strangled him during the cases they worked together. *Opposites attract, I guess.* A small smile crossed her lips. *I guess that explains Sam and me, then.*

"Immaturity aside," Dahlia said, turning to Peter. "Sam and I would be happy to help."

"Thank you both," Peter said.

He picked up a file folder from Sam's desk and handed it to Sam.

"A few weeks ago, a nineteen-year-old college student named Randy Macklin committed suicide. His parents were suspicious, though. Some way or another, his parents knew mine, so the message filtered down to me to look into Randy's death. He didn't show any signs of being depressed. He had good grades, played baseball and was out with his friends a few nights before he died. After conducting several interviews and looking into the student's background, suicide seemed unlikely," Peter said. "Digging deeper, I found a project the student volunteered for. The whole thing seemed sketchy from the moment I first read about it. I managed to secure an invite for the project, which is what I need your assistance on."

"The study of death, dying and life after death?" Sam read from Peter's report. "Sounds like a messed-up cult to me."

"That's actually a pretty apt description," Peter said. "The group is run by a professor named Oliver Nestmann. He seems paranoid to me; I mean, it took a lot of convincing to get the invitation to attend one of the group meetings."

"How does this group connect to Randy's death?" Dahlia asked.

"At first, there's no connection. But, upon further research, it appears two other young adults committed suicide after joining Dr. Nestmann's group," Peter said. "I need to go undercover to investigate the group, but I want backup. My Lieutenant isn't convinced there is enough evidence to prove Dr. Nestmann had anything to do with the two deaths, so he told me that I could investigate but on my own time. If we can come up with enough probable cause to go after the doctor, then we will. Until then, I'm on my own. That's why I came to you. I know there's something wrong here and I need your help to prove it."

"Sounds pretty sick," Sam said. "That being said, I'm game."

"Me too," Dahlia said.

"Great," Peter said. "The next meeting is scheduled for Monday."

★★★

The following Monday night, Sam and Dahlia met up with Peter at the time and location listed on Dr. Nestmann's invitation. The rectory at the Odette Memorial Gardens Cemetery was the only source of light in the cemetery at this time of night. Fog was beginning to materialize above the manicured lawn, and it swirled around Sam's legs as he walked behind Dahlia and Peter toward the rectory. If the dark, chilly atmosphere that settled over the cemetery got any colder and darker, Sam was sure that zombies were going to crawl out of their graves and start performing "Thriller."

Didn't think I'd be back here so soon, he thought to himself. It had only been a few weeks since his mother's death, and the cemetery was the last place he wanted to be right now. Hell, it was the last place he wanted to be regardless of what day or month it was; there were too many people important to him that were buried here.

Reaching the rectory, the three cops headed inside. Sam was instantly grateful to be away from the graves and also for the light and warmth that the building provided as he rubbed his hands together.

"Where are we headed?" he asked Peter.

Peter pulled the paper with Dr. Nestmann's invitation instructions on it out of his sweater pocket.

"Looks like we're going to Study #2, right past the living room and to the right," he said.

A group of young adults in their late teens to early twenties were seated casually around a simple wooden table with matching chairs, preoccupied with their cell phones. A middle-aged man with unruly brown hair scribbled notes on the whiteboard with a blood red marker. Dressed in a beige suit jacket with a cream turtleneck underneath, Dr. Oliver Nestmann appeared to be a mild-mannered and unobtrusive man.

"All right, everyone, let's get started-" he paused as he turned around and saw Peter, Sam, and Dahlia enter the conference room. "Please, come in, join us."

Oliver motioned for the three cops to join the rest of his class at the table. He addressed them again as they took their seats.

"I'm sure you are already aware, but I'm Dr. Nestmann. You must be Matthew," Oliver said to Peter.

The doctor shifted his weight, and the fingers on his right hand tapped the side of his leg repeatedly.

"Matthew," he said. "Who are these people? There was no mention of additional guests in our correspondence."

"Sorry for the surprise, Dr. Nestmann. I guess my last email didn't get to you," Peter said. "My girlfriend, Jane, and her brother, Chance, were interested in coming too. I hope that's all right."

Oliver's beady brown eyes darted back and forth between Dahlia, "Jane," and Sam, "Chance."

"I'm not sure—" he began to say.

"I could use your help, Doc," Sam said. "I ... recently lost someone important to me ... I want to hear your thoughts about death and dying and life after death. It might give me some comfort knowing that she's out there ... somewhere ..."

Clenching his fist under the table, Sam loosened his hand when he saw the doctor visibly relax. *Bingo.*

"My deepest and most sincere condolences, Chance," Oliver said. "I hope that I will be able to be of some assistance in this time."

The other participants sitting at the table offered their sympathies as well. Dahlia, sitting next to Sam, gave his hand a small tap under the table. It was a small, subtle gesture of reassurance, but it was something Sam did appreciate, though he would keep that appreciation to himself. It was still crucial for him to keep his distance from everyone, including Dahlia, if he was going to continue down his chosen path of self-destruction.

"Well," Oliver started to say, the doctor's voice bringing Sam back to the present. "Since we have new participants tonight, let's complete this questionnaire before moving on to discussing the different beliefs of various cultures throughout the world regarding death, dying and the afterlife."

He grabbed his briefcase from the corner of the room and pulled out some papers.

"I hope I'm not short on papers," Oliver said. "I wasn't expecting so many new guests tonight ..."

"It's all right, Doc," a clean-cut and athletic boy in an Odette Community College letterman jacket said. "Tatum and I can share a sheet and so can Jane and Matthew; that way, we'll only use two sheets instead of four."

"Thank you, Max," the doctor said. "That is a good suggestion."

"No problem."

Max, the jock, took the papers Oliver held out to him and passed them down the row. After grabbing a piece for himself, Sam skimmed through the questions. "What do you believe happens to us when we die?" "Do you believe in an afterlife? Heaven? Hell? Purgatory? Something else?" "What do you know about the beliefs and traditions regarding death and dying in other cultures?" "What are your own beliefs and traditions?"

Several additional questions asked similar things on the questionnaire. Strange, but not something that would likely lead to suicide, Sam considered. He grabbed a pen from the box that Max pushed down toward him before passing it along to Dahlia and Peter. After working silently on the questionnaires for some time, most of the participants completed theirs and turned them in to Oliver. Once the majority of the participants turned in their papers, the doctor began the discussion on various beliefs and traditions regarding death and dying from different areas and cultures around the world.

The discussion carried on until the meeting's conclusion. Before dismissing the group for the evening, Oliver brought up a topic of interest for the three detectives.

"Everyone, I'm sure you're aware of the untimely passing of our dear friend, Randy. As Randy was the last volunteer for our experiment, I will need a new one," Oliver said, looking around the conference table at the class. "Any takers?"

"I'll volunteer, Dr. N," Max said, raising his hand and leaning back in his chair.

"Thank you, Max," Oliver replied.

Max rotated in his chair to face the woman sitting next to him.

"And, if it's all right with you, Doc," he took the woman's hands in his. "I'd like Tatum, my gorgeous girlfriend, here, to help with the experiment. If ... no, *when* we succeed, I'd like to ask her to marry me because I know we'd be able to overcome any obstacles in our relationship because we overcame death."

Peter, Sam, and Dahlia joined the rest of the class in clapping as Tatum happily embraced her 'future' fiancé, though the three exchanged a furtive glance of suspicion with each other. Overcoming death? What the hell kind of experiment was Oliver subjecting his volunteers to?

The class was dismissed while Max and Tatum stayed behind to discuss the details of the experiment with Oliver. Peter, Sam, and Dahlia hung around in the parking lot until the two students and their professor also departed from the hospital. Max and Tatum, who came together, left in one vehicle, which Sam and Dahlia tailed. Peter did the same with Dr. Nestmann.

The young lovers drove out to the quaint little apartment they shared while Oliver returned to his single-story ranch house, where he lived alone. After keeping watch on the both residences, for a length of time, Sam, Dahlia, and Peter returned to the police department.

"There are two weeks until the next meeting, so it's reasonable to assume Dr. Nestmann will be working with Max and Tatum on the experiment during that time, as I heard him say something before we left about sharing the results with the class next meeting," Peter began pacing. "It can't be a coincidence that Randy was the previous volunteer for this experiment and he ends up dead."

"Peter, you mentioned that two other people from Dr. Nestmann's group committed suicide as well, right?" Dahlia asked. "I wonder if they volunteered for the experiment too."

Peter paused his pacing as he considered Dahlia's theory.

"That's a good point," he said. "We'll have to speak to the other students about the deaths because I feel Dr. Nestmann would clam up if we dig too deep. He's already clearly paranoid; you saw the way he reacted to the two of you dropping in on the meeting, right?"

"Maybe not, depending on how the fishing for information is presented to him," Sam said.

"What did you have in mind?" Dahlia asked.

"Unfortunately, I happen to know a thing or two about death. I might be able to gain the good doctor's trust if I become the teacher's pet."

"It's worth a shot," Peter said.

★★★

Dahlia accompanied Peter in staking out Max and Tatum while Sam followed Oliver around so they could have a "chance meeting" and Sam could strike up a conversation with the professor. Sitting in Peter's car, she struck up a conversation of her own with her fellow officer.

"How did you and Sam meet?" she asked.

Peter smiled.

"I happened to be at the right place at the right time," he said. "I started working at the department after completing the academy, and my supervising officer was out of the office one day. Sam was assigned to supervise me until Cooke came back, and well, we got a doozy of a case together. We worked a couple of other cases after that, each one was, to put it nicely, unique."

Dahlia smiled as she looked out the window.

"Yeah, Sam tends to get the interesting cases," she said.

"What about you?"

Dahlia recounted her first case with Sam, including how he wouldn't let her quit.

"I'm glad it happened," she said. "I've been able to put all that behind me thanks to Sam's, let's call it, persistence."

"I'm glad too," Peter said. "Even though I've been undercover on assignments for the past few years, I've still kept up with goings-on at the department. You've certainly made a name for yourself, Detective Bennett."

Dahlia pulled her hair back, which she had left down on this particular day, as she suddenly felt warm and flushed. She sneaked a glance at Peter, and she found him watching her with his electric blue eyes.

"Would you want to, maybe, get coffee or something sometime?" Dahlia blurted out.

Her dark spring green eyes widened and shimmered nervously as she comprehended what she said. Peter smiled sweetly at her.

"You're definitely Sam's partner; you get straight to the point," he said with a slight chuckle. "And, yes, I'd love to go out sometime. Actually, I wanted to ask you, but you beat me to it."

Dahlia smiled back at Peter.

★★★

Oliver Nestmann led a rather dull existence, Sam discovered. After waking up and dressing, he went for a cup of coffee and a breakfast wrap at the coffee shop one block over from his house. Following that, he headed to the local university to teach some classes. Oliver had lunch in his office while he graded some assignments. Another class that afternoon and then it was time to depart. Oliver stopped at a grocery store located near the college campus to do some shopping. Sam figured that would be the optimal time to "run into" the doctor.

Pushing a cart around and pretending to browse the merchandise while keeping an eye on Dr. Nestmann, Sam followed him down an aisle with no other people, which was when he made his move.

"Doctor?" he pretended to recognize the man. "Dr. Nestmann, is that you?"

Oliver put the box of pasta back on the shelf and looked over his shoulder at Sam.

"Hello there—Chance, was it?" he said.

"Good memory," Sam replied. "I gotta say, doc, that stuff you talked about the other night was fascinating. It's nice to be able to think that my loved ones are out there, somewhere, hopefully living in paradise."

"Well, thank you. It means a lot to hear you say that."

"How did you get into that field, anyway?" Sam asked. "I mean, it's not something you can usually aspire to be without someone wanting to put you in the funny farm."

"Normally yes, but not so in my case," Oliver replied. "My family ran a funeral home down in Aspen, which is where I'm originally from. I grew up around death and always found the subject intriguing. Different cultures, religions and what have you have their own beliefs on death and dying, and despite their vast differences, it is still something all people have to deal with."

"That's deep," Sam rested his elbows on the bar of the shopping cart. "I guess death is one of those things that are the same in every language, right? Like math or music?"

"It's never easy. No matter how many people we lose, it still is painful. Like you said, Chance, death is something we all experience. It is unbiased, striking anyone at any time, regardless of age, gender, wealth, religion or anything else."

"Say, Doc, have you ever lost someone important to you?"

Oliver did not respond immediately. He observed Sam quietly for a few moments.

"I have," the doctor said.

Sam waited to see if Oliver would elaborate, but the doctor did not say anything else about it.

"Well," Sam cleared his throat. "Anyway, during the meeting, Max and Tatum said something about overcoming death; can you tell me about that? I'd do anything to not feel the pain from losing two of the most important people in my life on a daily basis. I struggle with it *so* much—"

"It's something we all have in common," the doctor said. "We've all lost someone. That's what makes this study so powerful."

"Is that where the overcoming death aspect comes in? As a way to overcome the losses we've all experienced?"

"Shhh!" Oliver hushed Sam, putting one finger up to his lips and waving the other hand.

"What's wrong, Doc?"

"Until my research is confirmed, I'd prefer to keep things under wraps, you see."

"Sure, I get it," Sam said.

A modern-day Dr. Frankenstein, Sam considered; Mary Shelley would be pleased. Or appalled. He wasn't sure which, though his money was on the latter.

★★★

The three cops reconvened at Dahlia's house following their stakeouts of Max and Tatum and Oliver Nestmann.

"There has to be someone in the doctor's past that died that sparked this whole morbid interest in death and whatnot," Sam said. "If we can figure out what happened, we might be able to use that to our advantage in our investigation to help us find out how three participants in Nestmann's group ended up committing suicide."

"If there was an obituary for whoever this person was," Dahlia left her spot on the couch to grab her laptop from the desk along the west wall of her living room. "It's likely that it will still be online somewhere."

"Good thinking. And while you're at it, the Doc also said that 'we've all lost someone,' so look and see if you can find any deaths connected to Max, Tatum, Randy and the others."

Sam took a seat on the armchair across from the couch where Peter and Dahlia sat. Reclining back as he made himself comfortable, he watched both his past and present partner as they searched the internet. *Those two seem awful close already*, he noted. *I guess I wasn't hallucinating when I thought I saw sparks between them. Well, good for them. They both deserve a good person in their lives.*

"I think we've got something," Dahlia said.

"What's up, Bennett?" Sam asked.

She motioned him over to take a seat on the empty cushion to her left and Sam obliged her. Dahlia pointed to the laptop screen.

"This death notice ran in the *Odette Daily News* about eight years ago," she said. "Olivia Nestmann, nee Ashby, passed away peacefully after a short but courageous battle with cancer."

"Okay, so her last name is Nestmann; got anything more definitive than a shared name?"

Dahlia continued reading from the notice.

"She is survived by her husband, Dr. Oliver Nestmann, professor of Cultural Anthropology at Hammett College."

"Okay, I'd say that's pretty solid connection," Sam said. "Print out that notice, Bennett, and then see what you can find out about the other members of the group."

The printer on the desk behind them hummed as it spit out the printed copy of the Olivia Nestmann death notice, which Sam retrieved. He rejoined Dahlia and Peter on the couch and read over the notice.

"Sam, there's more for Olivia Nestmann," Peter said.

Sam looked up from the notice.

"Like what?" he asked.

"Each year since her death, Oliver has placed an In Memoriam in the paper," Peter said. "And I don't mean a short and sweet little insert that says something like 'always loved and never forgotten' or 'it's been years since you passed and I still love and miss you;' I mean quite extensive and expensive notices."

"And, in each notice, the doctor seems to be expressing his guilt over not being able to save her life," Dahlia said.

"But she had cancer," Sam said. "There's only so much that medicine can do, and even though Nestmann's a doctor, he's not a doctor of medicine, so there wasn't much that he could do."

"Sure, but that doesn't mean that Oliver didn't see it that way," Peter said. "Look at what he wrote in last year's In Memoriam: 'if love could have saved you, you never would have died, Olivia. I promise that I will find a way to make things right. I will do everything in my power. I will use every resource available to me. I will do whatever it takes.'"

"Find a way to make things right?" Sam repeated. "Like what? Find a cure for cancer? I'm all for that, but that doesn't seem like what the doc's after. What about Max, Tatum and the others?"

"Still working on those," Dahlia said.

She printed out the other copies of the in memoriams that the doctor had placed for his wife, which Sam and Peter perused while she searched.

"I might have found a connection to Tatum," Dahlia said after a few minutes. "There is a death notice for a ninety-year-old woman from about seven years ago. It reads: 'Antonina Christiano, age 90, passed away peacefully in her sleep a the Odette Senior Care Facility on August 1st. She was predeceased by her loving husband of 70 years, Joseph, and her infant son, Robert. Antonina is survived by her cherished children, Rosa (Frank), Gabriel (Jenni), Lola (Tyler) and Sonny (Ana). She is also survived by her beloved grandchildren … a bunch of names … Shawna, Gail, and *Tatum*.' Since Tatum is not a common name, I'm going to go out on a limb and say that it's her."

"All right, I'd say it's probably safe to say that Tatum lost her grandmother," Sam said. "How about Max? Is there someone connected to him or is he along for the ride with his lady friend?"

"I might have an idea," Peter said. "Do you guys remember the incident last year where a football player from Odette Community College died after a night of partying? He was in a coma from alcohol intoxication and passed away a few days later. During the meeting at the rectory, I remember Max was wearing a letterman jacket from OCC, and it was similar to the one that the victim wore when his picture was shown in the news for a few weeks."

"Good call, Petey," Sam said. "Max and this kid were probably teammates and possibly friends. Even if the relationship didn't extend that far, they would most likely have known each other at the very least."

"I'll see if I can find anything to confirm that theory," Dahlia said, as she continued tapping away at her laptop.

After a few minutes of digging, she was able to find some information on the student's death.

"Eric Murrell, twenty-one, pictured above with his teammates from the OCC football team," she said, pointing to the screen. "If you look at this guy, two people to the right of Eric, he looks an awful lot like Max."

Peter looked at the photo.

"Yep, that's Max, and that's Eric," he said. "I met Eric before; he was one of my sister's students from a few years ago."

"Wait, that Eric Murrell?" Sam asked. "From that case where you and I helped out your sister when she was being stalked and threatened?"

"Unfortunately, that's him. Darcy and I attended the funeral."

"Shit, man ..." the veteran cop said with a frown.

"Maybe Max feels guilty for letting his friend get drunk to the point where it killed him," Dahlia said.

"If that's true, it would be similar to how Oliver feels about his wife's death," Sam said. "Okay, lovebirds, you two have a new mission."

"Lovebirds?" Peter repeated with amusement.

Dahlia rolled her eyes and shook her head.

"What do you want us to do, Sam?" she sighed.

"Go on a double date with Max and Tatum and see what information you can find out about the doc's little 'experiment.'"

Peter and Dahlia looked at each other and shrugged.

★★★

Dahlia made arrangements with Tatum to have the four of them meet up at a restaurant downtown for, as Sam called it, a double date. Friday evening, a little after seven, Peter and Dahlia arrived at the restaurant and found Max and Tatum at a table outside on the patio. The younger couple waved the two officers over.

"Hey, Matt, Jane, nice to see you guys again," Max said as Peter and Dahlia joined them.

"It was a wonderful idea to get together like this," Tatum said to Dahlia. "It's nice to have another couple to spend time with who isn't afraid to discuss Dr. Nestmann's work."

"It's something I've never experienced before," Peter said as he unfolded his napkin and placed it on his lap. "Then again, Randy did say that it was … transcendent."

"You knew Randy?" Max asked.

"Yes. My parents knew his parents, so I guess you could say we were family friends," Peter said. "What did he say to you two about why he wanted to join the study?"

"Dr. Nestmann is the one who asked him; he asked all of us to consider joining," Tatum said.

"Right," Dahlia said. "I know he asked Matthew, here, and he passed on the information to my brother and me."

"I thought it was crucial to try and help Chance after that terrible loss he experienced," Peter said, giving Dahlia's hand a reassuring squeeze.

She reciprocated the gesture.

"That's so sweet," Tatum said. "You two must really care about each other."

"I know Chance mentioned a little something about losing someone recently during the last meeting," Max said. "What happened?"

"Chance is my stepbrother," Dahlia began to say. "Which is why we look nothing alike, as I'm sure you've noticed. We didn't like each other that much at first but, over the years, we've become like actual siblings. I was there when his mother passed away. She'd been sick for some time, and eventually, Chance realized that it was probably for the best that he remove her from life support. She lingered for a few minutes before silently drifting away."

Tatum gently brushed some tears from her eyes.

"That's so sad …" she said.

"I thought Dr. Nestmann's work could possibly help Chance with his tremendous loss," Peter said. "It was something Randy told me about that helped him."

"I'm not surprised," Max said. "I mean, even though Randy said he was too young to remember his baby brother's death all that much, it still hurt him. It had to feel like a giant hole or something in his life."

"That's how he described it," Peter said.

The conversation was put on hold when the waiter arrived to take their orders.

"Max," Dahlia said after the waiter departed. "You mentioned during the meeting that you were thinking of proposing to Tatum if all goes well with the experiment; how exciting!"

Max slung his arm over Tatum's shoulders and planted a kiss on her cheek.

"Yes, ma'am!" he said. "I believe our love is stronger than death and that, together, we can be the first ones to successfully prove Dr. N's hypothesis."

"Wow, your love is so inspirational," Dahlia said with a smile.

"Say, since we're new to this whole group thing, can you give us some information on the experiment?" Peter asked.

"Sure. What do you want to know?" Max asked.

"I guess, for starters, how does this whole," Peter lowered his voice. "'Overcoming death' thing work?"

The waiter returned to deliver their drinks and salads.

"One person," Max paused until the waiter was out of earshot again. "One person dies, and the other person brings them back to life."

"Really?" Dahlia was genuinely surprised. "Which one of you will be dying and which one of you will be bringing the other back to life?"

"I'll be letting Tatum bring me back to life," Max said with a brilliant grin. "Like I said before, I believe our love is stronger than death, and we can be the first to successfully prove Dr. N's hypothesis."

"The first?" Dahlia repeated. "How many others tried to do it?"

"Well, first there was James," Tatum picked up a crouton with her fork. "Then Kristie and then Randy."

"They all died from exsanguination after slitting their wrists," Peter said. "Are you saying that was a part of the experiment?"

"What else would it be a part of? There can't be any reanimation without any death," Max said with a laugh.

"Sorry to play the devil's advocate," Peter said. "But, if James, Kristie, and Randy couldn't survive, what makes you believe your fate won't be the same?"

"This," Max winked at Tatum. "Is why I'll make it through the experiment."

"You see," Tatum began to explain. "James, Kristie, and Randy only had Dr. Nestmann there with them when they tried to complete the experiment. Even though they desperately wanted to assist him, there was no true emotional connection there, you know? Max and I, however, have a powerful bond and emotional connection. We believe that is the missing link that will unlock the truth behind Dr. Nestmann's work."

"Dr. Nestmann was there when the other participants cut their wrists and bled out? If they were dying, why didn't he do anything to try and save them?" Dahlia asked.

"On the contrary," Tatum said. "Dr. Nestmann was very involved in trying to save James, Kristie, and Randy but, unfortunately, it didn't work. Not all experiments are guaranteed to work on the first try."

"Sure, but they're not supposed to cause death either."

"Then you literally mean 'overcoming death,'" Peter said.

"I think you've got it now, Matty."

"I'm sure Chance would love for this experiment to turn out to be a success because of his mom," Dahlia said. "But what about you guys? What are you hoping to gain from this?"

"Dr. Nestmann contacted me after my grandmother died. She was my best friend, and I miss her so much. I didn't go with my parents to the nursing home the night before she passed away because I wanted to hang out with my friends. If I'd only known that was the last day she'd be alive, I would have gone. I've felt terrible ever since I heard she passed away," Tatum said. "I thought about Dr. Nestmann's invitation and wasn't sure if I believed in all this. I was raised in a very traditional religious Italian family, so it was something new for me."

"But then, last year, one of my football buddies ... died and it was the motivation Tatum, and I needed to look into Dr. N's work," Max said. "I felt responsible for what happened to Eric. I mean, I knew he should have stopped drinking a while ago, but he kept telling me that he was okay and I believed him."

"It's not your fault, honey," Tatum placed her hand on top of Max's.

"I heard about that," Peter said. "Poor kid."

"Well, I thought that, hey, if Dr. N's on to something, maybe we could do something to fix what happened to Eric and Tatum could get a chance to say goodbye to her grandmother."

"And how about Dr. Nestmann?" Dahlia asked. "Did he ever say what happened to spark his interest in this subject?"

"He's a doctor of Cultural Anthropology, so he studies different cultures all over the world, which is interesting," Tatum said. "But we found out not too long ago that Dr. Nestmann's wife died from cancer about eight years ago. My grandma died seven years ago, so he must have started his work shortly after his wife died to be able to send out an invitation to me to join his research."

"Did he tell you what he was doing before he started his research?"

"He spent time abroad studying cultures that haven't had much contact with civilized society, I think, which is pretty cool," Max said. "You know, isolated tribes and what not that practiced things like voodoo and black magic."

"That's fascinating," Dahlia said, a hint of truth in her statement.

"I agree, Jane," Peter said. "All of this is truly amazing to think about. Do you guys think that Dr. Nestmann would mind if we sat in on and observed the experiment?"

Max looked over at Tatum.

"I don't see why not," she said. "Perhaps, when we manage to prove Dr. Nestmann's hypothesis, the two of you could put your love to the test and try the experiment as well."

Peter and Dahlia did not reply, instead turning their attention to their Caesar salads.

★★★

Max and Tatum informed Peter and Dahlia that Dr. Nestmann scheduled the experiment for the following Tuesday night. Sam followed Oliver throughout the day to keep tabs on him until the time for the test to commence that evening. *If he doesn't head over to the apartment soon, I'm going to freakin' fall asleep!* Sam thought with a yawn. *He has got to be the most boring person on the planet during the day. At night, however, it's a much different story … or so I hope.*

Shortly after nine that night, the doctor left his house and drove out to Max and Tatum's apartment, Sam right behind him. Keeping his distance to avoid being noticed, Sam followed Oliver up to the second floor of the apartment building to apartment 139, where the doctor knocked on the door with the cheery welcome mat on the floor of the hallway in front of it.

"Good evening," Oliver said as Tatum opened the door for him. "Is everyone ready? I, myself, am truly looking forward to seeing if the variable of an emotional connection will be the missing link, so to speak."

"Of course, Doctor," Tatum said. "Max and I are eager to get started."

As the doctor headed inside, Sam sent a quick text message to Peter, who excused himself from the apartment before Tatum could shut the door when his phone chimed.

"Sorry, guys," he said. "It's work. I'll be right back."

"I'll leave the door unlocked for you, Matthew," Tatum said as Peter stepped outside.

Once the door closed behind him, Peter headed down the hallway to find Sam.

"As soon as Dahlia sends me the word that everyone is occupied," Peter said. "I'll sneak you into the apartment."

"Roger that," Sam said.

The message from Dahlia came a few moments later, and Peter headed back into the apartment, discreetly directing Sam toward the bedroom to conceal himself in. Max, Tatum, Dahlia and the doctor returned to the living room where Peter was.

"Is everything all set, dear?" Dahlia asked.

"Yes, everything is good to go," Peter said.

"Glad to hear it," Oliver clapped his hands together. "Let's get started, shall we?"

The doctor placed his briefcase down on the end table in front of the deep hunter green couch and opened it up.

"As you may know, I spent time with some cultures abroad that practice various forms of ancient beliefs, voodoo, black magic, and other things that are typically frowned upon in our culture. Some witch doctors and highly regarded practitioners believed they could bring people back to life," he said. "I figured, with their primitive resources, they couldn't possibly have success but, if their knowledge, rituals, and practices were to be combined with our advanced technology, we might be able to make some progress."

"We believe in you, Dr. Nestmann," Tatum said.

"Thank you," the doctor replied.

He produced a fresh, unopened package of razor blades from his briefcase and handed it to Max, who began to open it. Max gave a shimmering silver blade to Tatum and kept one for himself.

"Are you both ready?" Oliver asked.

Tatum leaned forward to kiss Max. He pulled her into a deep embrace and reciprocated her gesture passionately.

"Your love is something magical that only a few have a chance to experience in this life," the doctor said with a sigh. "I believe that the love the two of you share may truly be the missing link."

"That's enough, doc," Sam stepped out of the bedroom. "No one is going to bleed out and then do some bullshit ritual from a quack doctor to pretend to bring them back to life."

Oliver, Max, and Tatum all whirled around to face Sam. The young couple both dropped their razors in their shock, the pieces of metal landing on the wooden floor with a tiny tink.

"What is going on, Chance?" Oliver asked.

"First of all, my name's not Chance-my first name, anyway," Sam said. "It's Detective Samuel Marlowe, and I'm from the Odette Police Department. Second of all, doc, you're under arrest."

"For what?!"

"For manslaughter. Your reckless actions and insanity caused the death of three young kids who had their whole lives ahead of them, not to mention you nearly got these two," Sam thumbed behind him at Max and Tatum, who were looking on at him in complete horror. "killed as well."

"I did no such thing!" Oliver continued to protest as Peter handcuffed him.

"Technically, Charlie Manson didn't kill anyone either," Sam said. "But both of you used some Sith Dark-Side style mind trick to convince other people to kill, only, in your case, your victims killed themselves. You used their grief against them to get your victims to do your dirty work."

"You can't arrest Dr. Nestmann," Tatum squealed, Max having to hold her back as Peter unlocked the door and then escorted Oliver out.

Sam threw his hands up, exasperated.

"You talk to them, Bennett," he said to Dahlia. "Anything I say isn't going through their frickin' thick skulls!"

"Jane, they can't do this," Max said as Sam walked away.

A grim smile crossed Dahlia's lips.

"Jane is actually my middle name," she said to them. "My name is Detective Dahlia Bennett. I'm also from the Odette Police Department. Dr. Nestmann's work is a fraud. I know … someone … who is a higher up at Hammett College, and I asked him to look into him. He has absolutely no evidence to support his work; no one would grant him the backing to perform this experiment, which is why he sought out volunteers and held meetings off campus. His work was illegal and unethical."

Max and Tatum said nothing. Dahlia let out a breath. She wasn't entirely sure they understood her, but at least they were alive and safe.

★★★

The next week, Dahlia arrived at her desk in the bullpen and was greeted with a surprise that instantly brought a smile to her lips. On her desk was a single red rose with a note attached.

"Is that from Peter?" Sam asked.

Dahlia blushed.

"Why don't you ever send me flowers, Bennett?" her partner had his devious grin on. "I know how much you love me; would it kill you to show it every once in a while?"

"Sure, Sam, if you say so."

Sam's sardonic grin relaxed into a genuine smile.

"I'm glad for you, Bennett. Truly. Peter's a great guy; you deserve someone like him."

Dahlia looked at Sam, unsure of how to respond to the sincerity in his tone. Peter's character must be better than she believed for Sam to think so highly of him; that didn't happen often.

Before she had a chance to respond, Sam's desk phone rang.

"Marlowe," he answered.

Stepping away from her desk for a moment to get a cup of water to place her flower in, Dahlia was nearly knocked over by Sam, who was racing out of the bullpen.

"Sam, what the hell?"

"No time to explain, Bennett," Sam called as he started down the stairs. "Put your stuff down and get your ass over here!"

Dahlia did as Sam requested and followed him out to his car. The passenger's side door was barely closed before Sam was flooring it out of the parking lot.

"Where are we going?" Dahlia asked, bracing herself against the dashboard as Sam sped through traffic.

She soon had her answer, but it did nothing to calm her nerves. They rushed up to the apartment and broke open the door. Entering into the apartment, Sam and Dahlia were greeted by the sight of Max and Tatum's dead bodies. They were in a pool of blood, having bled out from the deep cuts on their wrists.

"Is that who called?" Dahlia asked.

"Yeah," Sam grumbled. "They said they were going to prove Nestmann wasn't a fraud by going ahead with the experiment anyway. I thought we could save them ... I thought I could save them."

Sam turned and punched the door angrily.

"Sam, hey," Dahlia put her hand on his arm. "It's not your fault. They made their choice. You tried to help them see the light, but they wouldn't listen. You did all you could to help them. Dr. Nestmann's in jail awaiting trial and the judge refused to grant him bail in case he might try to flee. We'll get justice for them, Sam. All of them."

"Call the ME, Bennett," Sam turned and began to walk back down the hallway.

"Where are you going?" Dahlia asked as she pulled out her cell phone.

Sam ignored her and kept walking.

★★★

Sam perused the newspaper while Dahlia finished up the paperwork from their most recent case. Turning in her chair to grab something from her desk drawer, one of the headlines from the day's paper caught her eye. Dahlia's eyes darted back and forth between the paper and her partner's face. *Is that where he went yesterday after storming off from Max and Tatum's apartment?*

"Well, this paperwork is riveting," Dahlia said, rising from her chair.

Sam eyed her from over the top of his newspaper.

"I think I'm going to run to the coffee shop and grab something to drink," Dahlia said. "Want the usual?"

"Sure," Sam said. "Sounds good."

Hurrying from the bullpen, Dahlia hopped into the police cruiser and raced over to the holding center. She flashed her badge to the officer on duty.

"Detective Dahlia Bennett, Odette PD," she said. "I need to see a list of visitors for Dr. Oliver Nestmann."

"Sure thing," the officer fiddled around with some paperwork for a brief moment before handing a list to Dahlia. "Here you are. It's a shame what happened to the guy, I suppose."

Dahlia ignored the officer's comment and scanned the list of names. She could feel her heart pounding heavily in her chest as her viridian eyes came to rest on one name, in particular, that was written in a familiar handwriting. Seth Tucker.

He must have used his stepfather's name to cover his tracks, she thought. *But, so what if Sam was the last person to visit him in jail? What happened to the doctor is only a coincidence, right? It has to be.*

Snapping a picture of the list, Dahlia thanked the officer and returned the list before leaving the holding center. She took her time driving out to the coffee shop to pick up something for Sam and herself so she wouldn't return to the department empty-handed. The coffee shop wasn't overly busy, but there were a few people in line before her when she arrived. While waiting to place her order, Dahlia grabbed a newspaper from one of the tables and stared at the headline from that morning, still unable to wrap her head around it and its meaning.

`Oliver Nestmann, "Dr. Manson," found dead in jail cell.`

INNER DEMONS

It took a great deal of convincing and superhuman patience, but Nina Hill finally succeeded in getting Sam Marlowe to agree to attend their fifteen-year high school reunion.

"Nin," Sam continued to protest as Nina adjusted his scarlet tie. "If I didn't want to spend time with these people back then, what makes you think I suddenly do now?"

"Oh, hush, Sam," Nina said as she playfully swatted him on the shoulder. "We're going to see our friends and spend the evening with them. You have a lot to be proud of, with becoming a great cop and all; plus, don't you want to see if all of the bullies and assholes from high school are now poor, pathetic losers like we all hoped they'd be?"

"You drive a hard bargain, Miss Hill," Sam said with a sigh.

Nina smiled. And how could he not smile back when she looked this radiant? Her hickory brown hair had been curled and styled into a waterfall braid. The stunning sleeveless scarlet dress she wore had a flowing skirt and matched the vibrant lipstick she had chosen for the evening. Her laurel eyes were alive and shimmered with vitality and cheer. At least, that was the image she presented to the world, to the people who did not know and recognize the dramatic change that she tried to conceal with makeup and clothing.

Sam's eyes were drawn to the scars and marks on Nina's arms as she grabbed a light sweater from her closet. *She doesn't want everyone to find out the fact she's been using heroin*, Sam mused. *At least my vices don't leave physical marks.* He hated seeing what the drugs were doing to her, but he knew there was nothing he could say or do to convince her to give up her addiction; they'd had the conversation before, and Nina would challenge him right back. *You want me to quit? Then you quit too.* That usually ended up being the end of the discussion.

Sam offered Nina his arm, and the two left her apartment. The reunion was being held in the gymnasium of Odette High School. It was a place Sam hadn't been to in some years and he, though reluctant to admit, was nervous about being on campus grounds again. The place was full of bad memories.

Judging by the number of vehicles in the parking lot, the majority, if not all, of the members of their graduating class had accepted the invitation to the reunion. Sam parked his car, and he and Nina got out, making their way toward the school building arm in arm.

There was a festive blue and gold balloon archway positioned in front of the gymnasium entrance. A colorful banner welcoming them back hung above the entryway.

Sam reached the gymnasium entrance and froze. His heart was pounding so loudly that it blurred out the music coming from inside the gym. His chest hurt, and it was difficult to breathe.

"Sam, are you okay?" Nina asked.

"Y-Y-Yeah."

He tried to take a step back from the monstrous building jutting out against the darkened sky but found he couldn't; it was like the concrete below his feet had momentarily liquefied, and he had sunk down into it before it had solidified once again, trapping him in place.

"I-I-I'm hot, and kinda light headed."

He tried to pull off his tie before it strangled him, but his hands were shaking too much. Nina's hand brushed his forehead.

"You're sweating and burning up. Sam, you need to sit down. Here, give me your hand so I can lead you over to the benches. I don't want you to pass out; I don't know if I could lift you up!"

Nina led him away from the school, his body relaxing as they got further from the building. Nina walked Sam over to the school's baseball diamond and took a seat on the bleachers. She reached up and loosened his tie.

"You know," she said. "It's funny to think that my Dad used to play on this very diamond when he went to school here."

Sam wrapped his arm around Nina, and she rested her head on his shoulder. He let out a slow and shaky breath.

"Talk to me, Sam," Nina said softly. "What's going on? Please tell me so I can help you."

Sam took a few deep breaths.

"I … I can't do this, Nina."

He blinked to stop the tears from falling.

"I can't … I can't," Sam repeated, closing his eyes.

There was nothing he could do to stop the horrific scene from playing in his mind over again.

"No, no, no! Shit! No! Edwin!"

Sam collapsed onto his knees, falling forward as if he had been struck in the back with the battering ram.

Edwin lay in a pool of blood resulting from several bullet wounds to the chest. Sam grabbed Edwin's jacket from the back of the chair and used it to help apply pressure to his injuries. He checked the gray-haired man's pulse and was relieved to feel he still had one.

"Edwin, hey," Sam said. "It's Sam. Hey, come on, Ed, wake up."

There was another pop of gunfire overhead.

"S-S-Sam?" Edwin's voice was weak and hoarse.

Sam repeatedly blinked, trying to keep the tears at bay.

"I'm here, Edwin," he said, one hand applying pressure to Edwin's wounds, the other grabbing hold of the ex-cop's hand. "I'm here. We're going to get you out of here-"

Edwin shook his head in a slow, robotic movement.

"Get the shooter," he said. "Leave me here."

"I can't leave you, Edwin."

Edwin gripped Sam's arm.

"Leave me, Sam!" he repeated. "Do your job!"

"Edwin-"

"Fucking go, Sam! Don't let any kids die for me! Do your job! That's an order!"

The tears stung his eyes. Sam clenched his jaw tight enough he thought it might shatter his teeth. Another gunshot rang overhead. Edwin was right; the shooter needed to be stopped immediately.

"Sam, I'm so sorry," Nina said. "I didn't realize—"

"Neither did I," Sam sighed. "I thought I'd be fine."

"These reunion things are overrated," Nina told Sam. "Since we're all dressed up, let's go out to eat and maybe catch a movie or something, the two of us."

"It's all right, Nin," Sam said. "You go and have a great time at the reunion; I'll pick you up when it's over."

"Don't you get it, Sam? I wanted to go to the reunion *with* you, not with you as my chauffeur. I thought if you were okay with going, I'd be okay with going."

"Guess neither of us was ready to face our inner demons after all."

Sam picked at the chipped yellow paint on the bleachers.

"Sam," Nina said. "I need to ask you something, and I need you to be completely honest with me. Is this the first time you've had a flashback or panic attack since the shooting?"

"No," Sam replied in a barely audible whisper. "I haven't had anything happen in a long while-I thought I had things under control-but, no, it's not the first time."

"C'mon, Sam. Let's talk about this," Nina said. "If anyone will understand what you're going through, it will be me. Edwin was my father, too."

Being honest would only show Nina how truly fucked up he was.

"It's not going to make me think any less of you," Nina said. "You have no reason to be ashamed, either. You're not weak because of it; you're strong because you can admit that you are afraid and that you need help. Remember how I had nightmares for a while after what Scott did to me at the prom after-party our senior year? I was making good progress in counseling ... at least, up until Dad died. Please, talk to me, Sam."

"I ... I ..." Sam cleared his throat. "I've been a wreck since I found him, Nin. I ... I wanted to save him, but he told me to go. He told me to leave him there—"

"Yeah. That sounds like him ... always putting others before himself. He was a cop until the end—"

"And it's my fault he's gone."

"It is *not* your fault!"

"It is," Sam shook his head. "If I had only done more to help the shooter, Dillon, maybe ... maybe things would have been different. Maybe Edwin would still be here. Maybe the kid wouldn't have shot me in the leg, and I wouldn't have gotten hooked on painkillers. Maybe I wouldn't be as fucked up as I am. Maybe I wouldn't have done all these terrible things—"

Sam's words were drowned out by a series of pops coming from the school. Nina's head jolted up off his shoulder.

"What the hell was that?" she asked.

"I know that sound. That was a gunshot."

Sam leaped off the bleachers and ran toward the school building. Nina kicked off her heels and darted after him. Sam tugged hard at the doors to the school. They were locked.

"Check the gym doors that connect to the track field."

"Locked!" Nina called after checking the doors around the side. "What about the main entrance?"

The front would be the next best option, but Sam wanted to avoid the main entryway at all costs. *If you think I was bad at the gym entrance, Nina, you wouldn't even recognize me at the main entrance. That's where I found your father's body. That image is permanently etched in my mind, and I don't need another reminder. I don't think I could handle it.*

"There's a side entryway that the Special Ed department uses," Sam said. "Let's try there."

Heading around to the side of the school building, Sam tried the door to the special education wing. Much to his relief, it opened.

"I'll go," Nina said.

"You can't go in there, Nin! If those were gunshots like I think, you can't go in there; I can't let you get hurt!"

"What else am I supposed to do, Sam? Sit here while my friends could be getting their brains blown out? I'm not going to do anything stupid, Sam. I'm going to see what's going on and I'll come right back. Isn't it part of being a cop to assess the scene? Don't we need to confirm whether or not there *is* something bad happening before we jump to conclusions? What good would it be to have the whole Odette Police Department here for a few firecrackers or something?"

Sam did not immediately reply. His lips were set together in a firm, thin line and his eyebrows scrunched together as he gazed at Nina. *She's braver than me ... Christ, I'm a mess.*

Nina shoving her heels into his hands to hold pulled Sam from his thoughts.

"You are definitely your father's daughter," he said.

Sam pulled a cigarette out and lit it with a shaking hand as Nina made her way into the school.

"Sam!" Nina called out to him a few minutes later, breathless, as she ran back down the hallway toward him. "We have a huge problem!"

"What's going on?"

"There is a man with a gun in the gymnasium," Nina said. "He's got three people on their knees in front of him like he's going to execute them!"

Sam ran a hand through his tawny hair.

"What the hell is with this place that gives people the urge to be trigger happy?"

He ground his cigarette butt into the concrete with the sole of his shoe, his thoughts racing all over the place as he tried to decide his next step.

Sam handed his cell phone to Nina, as well as her shoes.

"Call Bennett and tell her I need back up ASAP."

"What are you going to do?"

"I'm going to try and stop this shit," repressing a shudder, he stepped through the door. "There's already been more than enough bloodshed here for one lifetime."

Staring down the hallway into the school was like staring into the lair of the beast. Sam jerked in surprise when Nina placed a hand on his arm.

"Be careful," she whispered to him, her eyes shimmering with tears.

Sam gave Nina's hand a reassuring squeeze before setting off into the building. He managed to get down the wing to the main hallway and around the corner. His skin was clammy, palms sweating and his lungs were in a vice being squeezed tighter and tighter. He steadied himself against the row of lockers and leaned his head against the cold blue metal.

Sam clenched his eyes and slammed his fists against the concrete walls surrounding the lockers. He didn't think he could go any further; he wasn't strong enough. Why wasn't he strong enough? Why was he such a pathetic failure?

Another shot rang out, and a bolt of terror surged through Sam.

His hands were on the cold steel of his service weapon. The pounding of his heart was deafening and only surpassed by the screams of the terrified students and staff trapped in the stairwell between a raging fire and the hail of gunfire from the shooter. The pain in his leg from where the kid had gotten off a shot and hit him was nothing compared to the feeling of pulling the trigger and watching the boy's body lurch forward and tumble over the railing and onto the stairs below.

That was the first time he ever shot someone, and he had killed a kid. Dillon Harris was dead, and he was hailed as a hero. But was he? Seven years later and Sam was still falling victim to the kid's tyranny. He couldn't let Dillon claim more victims simply because he was too afraid to act. He couldn't let Dillon win. Too much had already been taken from him.

Gritting his teeth and stumbling forward on shaky legs, Sam crept down the hallway toward the gym. As he approached, adrenaline started coursing through his blood. Sam was numb by the time he slipped into the stairwell that led to the smaller second-floor gym that would allow him access to the primary gym. The air in the small gym was stifling, and stank of sweat mixed with cleaning products. Hurrying across the wrestling mats, Sam headed down the stairwell to the locker room two steps at a time. When he reached the door to the gym, Sam opened it a crack. There was a man in a brown suit standing behind three other men who were down on their knees, hands behind their backs and heads down. Brown Suit Man, his back to Sam, had a gun in his hand, which he was pointing three men.

Eyes darting around the room, Sam saw a man on the gym floor, wounded, presumably having been shot by the gunman. He cursed at the sight. Sam couldn't see who the man on the floor was, his face blocked by the back of a sharply dressed golden-haired man. *Tony!* Sam was relieved to see his longtime friend.

"Psst!"

Tony looked over his shoulder. He blinked at seeing Sam in the doorway of the women's locker room. He got up from the side of the wounded man and slipped over to the locker room door. Once Tony was inside, Sam shut the door to the gym.

"What the fuck is going on?" Sam asked.

"It's Scott Farrow," Tony started to explain.

"That goddamn jock bully is going after the class *again?*"

"Yeah, but this time, it's personal. He wants you, Sam. He says he won't let any of us go until he gets you."

Sam cursed under his breath. The bad blood from their high school days apparently still coursed through Scott; fighting Sam when he tried to stop Scott from bullying other kids as sophomores. To get his revenge against his graduating class for being thrown off the football team, he poisoned the punch at the after-prom party with GHB. Even worse, Sam recalled with a shudder, Scott went after Nina at the afterparty, drugging and nearly raping her until Sam was able to stop him.

"How's the injured guy doing?"

Tony, who had become a doctor, said:

"Thankfully, he'll be all right. The bullet only grazed his arm. Rita and I managed to stop the bleeding and patched him up with the first aid kit from the gym office. I think he was more shocked by the gunshot than anything."

"He tried to be a hero, didn't he?"

"Sam, the injured guy is Wade," Tony said.

"Wade? You've got to be fucking kidding me!"

"He wanted to try and save us from Scott like you saved him when we were sophomores."

Wade, an old acquaintance from the projects where both he and Sam grew up, had been one of Scott's victims. The bully made the kid do his homework and write his papers under the threat of being beaten up. Sam stepped in when Scott threatened Wade out in the school courtyard, ultimately leading to a fist fight between them.

"Hey, Sam, where's Nina? Is she okay? Rita and I couldn't find her when Scott started going bonkers, and we're worried because she said she'd be here."

"Don't worry, she's safe," Sam said. "She's outside, calling my partner, who'll bring in the cavalry."

"Great, but what are we going to do in the meantime? We got lucky that the shot Scott fired was only a flesh wound; next time we might not be as fortunate."

Sam knew Tony was right. The next shot could seriously injure or kill someone.

"Sam, I think you should know," Tony said, pulling Sam from his thoughts. "Scott's threatening to start killing people. He said if you didn't show up by nine tonight, he was going to shoot someone every fifteen minutes … Rita and I have been trying to call you—"

"Shit," Sam ran a hand over her face. "I gave Nina my phone to call Bennett; I didn't see any of the messages."

"It doesn't matter. As long as you're here, we can hopefully get this situation under control before anything else happens."

"All right, here's the plan," Sam said. "I need to get everyone out of the gym as soon as possible. If Scott has me like he wants, I'm hoping he'll let everyone else go. You and Rita be ready to escort everyone out of here."

"Okay," Tony said. "I'm afraid to ask, but what are you going to do?"

"I'm a cop," Sam said as he slipped through the locker room door and stepped out into the gym. "It's my job to serve and protect, so I'm going to do what I have to do."

"I knew you were going to say that," Tony sighed. "Well, I'm one hundred percent behind you, man, so whatever you need, say the word."

Putting his hands up, Sam slowly began to walk forward toward Scott and his hostages.

"Scott," Sam said.

Scott whirled around to face him, the gun still trained on the three men on their knees.

"Ah! The prodigal son returns," he said with a malicious grin. "I was startin' to think you weren't gonna show up."

"Well, I'm here. Now let everyone go," Sam said.

Scott stepped closer to one of the hostages and placed a hand on his shoulder and the gun against the back of the man's head.

"Mmm ... I think not," he said. "They might come in handy."

Shit! Not good!

"Have you ever killed someone before, Scott?" Sam asked.

Scott did not respond.

"I didn't think so," Sam said. "Well, I have. I've had to kill a few people in the line of duty. In fact, the first time I ever had to end someone's life was here, a floor above us."

Sam, his hands still raised in the air, pointed toward the ceiling. Scott's eyes followed though he kept the gun trained on the hostage.

"Seven years ago, I had to kill Dillon Harris as he opened fired on a bunch of students and teachers who did nothing wrong other than report to school that morning. Everyone said I was a hero but did I feel like one? Absolutely not," Sam said. "Did you know that day still haunts me, Scott? Did you know it still affects all of the survivors and the family members and friends of the victims, too?

Dillon wanted revenge on the people whom he believed failed him like you want to get revenge on the people you blame for your failures in life; but why are you going to let all of these innocent people suffer?"

"Innocent?" Scott let out a laugh. "How the hell can you call yourself innocent? All of you!"

He lifted the gun from the hostage's head and pointed it at various people in the crowd.

"None of you cared about how *my* life was ruined!" Scott turned the gun on Sam. "Especially you, Marlowe. You are the reason my life is over!"

"I'm the reason? Dude! *You're* the reason you got thrown off the football team! *Your* stupidity caused you to miss out on that football scholarship you thought you were supposed to get. *You're* the one who got arrested for drugs and screwed up your life and your chance at a decent job. *You're* the one who tried to poison the class at the after-prom party our senior year! Not only that but *your actions*, rape, and attempted murder, are the reason you went to prison for years, not me!"

"Is now the time to be arguing with me, Marlowe?" Scott said. "Since I'm the one with the gun, I think I win the argument by default."

Sam lowered his hands.

"Okay, fine, Scott," he said. "Fine. Everything is my fault. You have me at your mercy; do with me what you will, but let everyone else go."

Scott mulled over Sam's offer for a few moments. He turned his attention back to the three hostages in front of him, yanking one up by his shoulder.

"You three, go," Scott shoved the man forward.

The three men scrambled away from Scott as fast as they could. Scott returned his focus to Sam.

"You, come over here."

Sam did as Scott asked.

"Tony, Rita, please start escorting everyone out of the gym," he called to his friends.

"All right everyone, you heard the man, the party's over," Tony clapped his hands together.

"Not yet!" Scott said.

Everyone in the gym froze in place.

"Seriously?" Sam threw his hands up and then let them fall to his sides. "What the hell is the problem now, Scott?"

"Take that jackass, Wade, out first," Scott said. "Then I want everyone to walk single file out of here. I don't want a mob of people all rushing to the door at once; I want to see you all walk out of here one by one so I know no one's gonna try anything stupid like Dorchik, there."

All of the members of the graduating class made their way toward the exit, creating one long but orderly line leading from the gym doorway. His gun to the back of Sam's head, Scott called Rita over to take the keys from him so she could unlock the doors. A few minutes later, it was Sam and Scott alone in the gymnasium.

★★★

Outside in the parking lot, Junior Detective Dahlia Bennett arrived with several other officers from the Odette Police Department. Nina rushed up to her as she exited her police cruiser.

"Dahlia!" Nina called out, breathless. "Everyone's been evacuated from the gym!"

"Good, but where's Sam?" Dahlia asked.

Nina's bottom lip trembled as she pointed toward the gym.

"Scott wanted Sam," she said. "That's why he's doing this. He has Sam in there, and I think he wants to kill him …"

"He what?"

Nina showed Dahlia the text messages and let her listen to the voicemails coming from Tony, relaying Scott's threats.

"If you don't get here by nine, I'll kill one person every fifteen minutes. Their blood will be on YOUR hands …"

"I need to get in there," Dahlia said, shoving the phone back at Nina.

Pulling her gun from her holster, Dahlia hurried toward the gym. Reaching the doors, she pulled one open a sliver to take a look inside. In the center of the gym, Scott stood facing Sam, pointing a gun at the veteran detective, though the cop was the one doing all the talking.

"You think *your* life is the only one that has been fucked up? Let me tell you, Scotty boy, things didn't work out the way I thought they would either. Seven years ago, you know the security guard that was killed in the school shooting here?" Sam asked. "Well, guess what? That man was my foster father. He saved my life and what did he get for it? His life was taken away. I was the one to find his body. Do you know how fucked up I am because of that day?"

For every step forward Sam took, Scott took one back. Despite being the one with the gun, Scott's expression and hand tremoring at his side betrayed his fear of the man he was pointing the gun at.

"Here you are, waving the gun around because you thought it would be the easy way to get revenge on the guys who you like to blame for the stupid shit *you* did and the decisions *you* made," Sam's voice was angry, but with a distinct tone of pain and hurt. "I nearly had a nervous breakdown entering the gym tonight because I am so fucking screwed up from that day! Maybe back then, when I didn't know that karma was a bunch of bullshit and it didn't matter if you were a good person or not, I would have helped you. But now, I don't feel like dealing with someone like you. I have enough inner demons to deal with to last me more than one lifetime that I don't need more demons to fight against in the real world!"

"Detective!"

Dahlia jumped when another officer addressed her, even though it was only a whisper.

"We have the building surrounded," the officer said. "We're ready to move at your command."

Dahlia's answer was cut off by the sound of a gunshot ringing out.

"Let's move!" she threw the door open and rushed inside. "Sam!"

Sam, his back facing toward his partner, slowly turned around. Moving out of the way allowed Dahlia to see the fallen body of Scott and the gun in Sam's hand.

"Are you all right?" Dahlia asked.

"Yeah."

His face was stoic, his voice, cold.

"Is he?" Dahlia began to ask, leaning to the side to look around Sam at Scott's body.

"He's dead," Sam said. "I managed to get him to release the hostages before he turned the gun on me. I had to put him down."

But how? Dahlia wondered. *A minute before the gunshot, Scott was the one holding the gun and pointing it at you. I looked away for a few seconds, but I didn't hear any sort of struggle. What the hell really happened, Sam?*

"I'm glad you're all right," she told him, pushing her thoughts aside.

Sam held the gun out for Dahlia to take into evidence. She presented it to one of the other officers to log away as she escorted Sam out of the gymnasium. Nina, who had been waiting outside, pacing as Rita tried to console and calm her, rushed toward Sam as she saw him emerge. They held each other tightly.

★★★

Sitting in the waiting room of Odette General Hospital, Nina at his side, Sam, and several other classmates anxiously awaited news on Wade's condition. Tony had rushed him to the ER right after Scott released the hostages and the injured man was taken directly into surgery. Sam glanced at the clock up on the wall across from him. As the seconds ticked past, the more nervous he became for Wade. *Don't die on me, buddy. Don't let Scott win.*

The doctor entered the waiting room, everyone immediately training their eyes on him. Tony popped up from his seat and hurried over to him. They spoke for a few minutes before shaking hands and parting ways. Tony walked over to Sam, Nina, and their classmates.

"Wade is out of surgery and should make a full recovery," he broke out into a grin.

Sam hugged Nina, and the other occupants of the waiting room cheered.

"I have to go call Bennett and let her know," he said, getting up from his chair.

Stepping out into the hallway, Sam pulled his phone out of his pocket but stopped when he saw Dahlia headed toward him.

"Good timing, Bennett," he said. "I was about to call you."

"Is there an update on Wade?" she asked.

"The doctor just told us that Wade is out of surgery. He should make a full recovery."

"Oh, thank goodness."

"You said it."

Dahlia folded her arms across her chest.

"Listen, Sam," she said. "I need to ask you a question about what happened back at the gym-"

"You want to know whether or not I killed Scott in self-defense?"

"Yes, actually," Dahlia said. "It can be off the record if need be. I need to know the truth about what happened. I mean, no one's questioning what you did to save your classmates."

"Except for you."

"Except for me."

Sam let out a slow breath and stuffed his phone back into his pants pocket.

"Do you know why Scott did what he did?" he asked.

"Not entirely," Dahlia said. "I didn't have time to look into the guy's background. When I got Nina's call, I got the SWAT team, and we headed straight to the school."

"Scott and I had a long history, Bennett, and not a good one. When we were sophomores in high school, I found out that he was threatening kids like Wade with violence unless they did what he wanted. In Wade's case, it was his homework and projects to keep his grades up to continue to play on the football team. Of course, once I found out, I couldn't let it keep happening, so I put a stop to it. Sure, the week of detentions sucked, but Scott got suspended from school and from the football team, which eventually led him to be booted from the team."

"And he blamed you for that?"

"Not only that," Sam said. "Scott turned to drugs after getting kicked off the team, and I know that he got arrested; I saw him get taken from the school in handcuffs. He was pissed that he got in trouble for drugs and that the rest of his classmates were going to get off scot-free, if you'll excuse the pun, for drinking at the after-prom party our senior year. Know how he tried to fix the problem? By poisoning the punch with GHB. Oh, and he wanted to explicitly tell me that he hated me and blamed me for what happened to him by drugging Nina and kidnapping her, nearly raping her until I managed to find him and beat the shit out of him."

"I have no words, Sam," Dahlia said.

"Yeah, I had no idea what to say when I found out what all the hubbub was about either. I completely forgot about Scott after he was sent to prison for what he did at the party. Guess he didn't forget about me, though."

"It seems that way, but you didn't answer my question. What really happened between the two of you right before SWAT and I entered the gym?"

"You really want to know?" Sam asked, an eyebrow raised.

He could see the shudder that shot through his partner from his tone of voice.

"Yes," Dahlia said, looking her partner straight in the eye.

"I took the gun from him," Sam said. "He didn't think I'd do anything like that, so I plucked it right out of his hand. I pointed the gun at him, and boom, I shot him. He had his hands up. He didn't want me to, but I had to. I had to put him down."

Sam watched with interest as Dahlia processed what he told her. She was silent for a few minutes.

"Thank you for telling me," was all she said before turning and walking away.

Sam kept his eyes on Dahlia as she headed down the hallway away from him. He stuffed his hands into his pants pockets.

I've told you the truth, Bennett. The ball's in your court now.

★★★

Dahlia stared blankly at her computer on her desk in the bullpen of the police department. Sam's words echoed in her mind. *"I pointed the gun at him, and boom, I shot him. He had his hands up. He didn't want me to, but I had to. I had to put him down."*

She ran a hand over her face, exasperated. What the hell was she supposed to say in her report? 'Suspect put hands up to surrender, but Detective Marlowe shot anyway?' Dahlia shuddered at the thought. Internal Affairs would have a field day with that one. Sam would be investigated and suspended. Worst case scenario, he could be fired for his actions.

"Dammit, Sam ..." Dahlia's fingers hovered over the keyboard. *Can I ... can I really do this? Can I really lie in the case report like this?*

Dahlia's eyes drifted over to Sam's empty desk, and she sighed. Her fingers began to move across the keys with fervor.

"Detective Samuel Marlowe shot suspect Scott Farrow in self-defense. After wrestling the gun away from the suspect, Det. Marlowe was forced to shoot Farrow when Farrow went to attack him."

Dahlia stared at the words on the screen in front of her when she finished her case report. With a shaking hand, she moved the cursor over the "send" button, and after a brief pause, clicked the button.

Report submitted.

AN EYE FOR AN EYE

Beep. Beep. The steady rhythm of the heart monitor was the most beautiful sound in the world to Sam. He'd become a permanent fixture in room 106 of Odette General Hospital over the past day, frozen in place on the deep jade green armchair at the bedside of Nina Hill. His dearly loved foster sister had been rushed to the emergency room after Sam had found her unresponsive on the couch in the living room of her apartment.

Sam was sure why she was in such a state, and the lab results from the medical tests only confirmed his fears; Nina had overdosed. Based on the number of naloxone doses needed to pull her out of her overdose, Sam and the doctors believed that it was caused by heroin laced with Fentanyl. She'd been an addict for some time now, and while he did his best to supply her with pure dope, Sam's access to the drugs had to be meticulously planned so he didn't draw too much attention to himself and put his job and freedom at risk. *She must have needed a quick fix and bought the laced heroin that nearly killed her.* He did his best to protect her since he couldn't stop her addiction, and Sam knew it was only a matter of time until her risky behavior caught up with her. Apparently, that time was now, and that realization killed him.

"Sam?"

Despite hearing the voice and recognizing it as belonging to his partner, Junior Detective Dahlia Bennett, Sam did not respond. All of his attention was absorbed by Nina's tiny pale frame as she lay unconscious in the mess of wires connected to her from the various machines surrounding her bed.

"Why are you here, Bennett?" he asked eventually.

"I was worried when you didn't show up at the police department this morning, so I called Clarice, and she told me what happened to Nina," Dahlia said as she walked over to where Sam was seated and gently placed a hand on his shoulder. "I wanted to make sure that both of you were all right."

Again, Sam said nothing. He could feel Dahlia's compassionate gaze on him, but it did nothing to detract his attention from Nina and the tight grip he had on her small hand.

They sat in silence until there was a soft knock on the door.

"Detective Marlowe," Nina's physician, Dr. Baird, said. "Ms. Hill's lab results are in."

One of the few times since his arrival at the hospital, Sam turned his attention away from Nina's bedside. Before speaking again, Dr. Baird looked over at Dahlia.

"Are you family, ma'am?" the doctor asked her.

"Yeah, she is," Sam replied for her. "She's also a cop and my partner. We're both investigating the overdose so you can give the results to both of us."

Dahlia mouthed the words "thank you" to him in response to him acknowledging her as family. *Normally I'd banter with you about this, Bennett, but, quite frankly, I'm too exhausted. Besides, I have more important things to worry about.*

Dr. Baird opened up the medical file.

"The tests confirmed the presence of heroin in Nina's system, which we believe to either have been laced or cut with Fentanyl."

"Fentanyl," Sam repeated. "That's the stuff that's used as a painkiller and also as a part of the drugs used in anesthesia to knock people out before surgeries."

"That's correct. It's an analgesic typically utilized in the medical field. However, people have found a recreational use for it on the street. On top of that, Fentanyl is mixed with other drugs like heroin to increase the euphoric effect. It is a dangerous combination, though, especially when the user does not know that the drug, heroin, for example, has been laced with the Fentanyl. The more Fentanyl one consumes, the more it suppresses respiration. Taking too much can cause drowsiness, nausea, and confusion and also decrease the ability to breathe. If the body cannot breathe, obviously, it can lead to death. Thankfully, Ms. Hill was brought in enough time so we could successfully administer the naloxone to help her overcome the overdose."

"Will she be all right?" Sam asked, intensely gazing up at the doctor.

"I can give you no guarantees," Baird said. "But, based on the progress I've seen in her tests and levels over the past twenty-four hours, I believe Ms. Hill will be able to pull through and make a full recovery."

"Thank you, doc," Sam said.

"Of course," Baird replied. "Glad to be able to help."

Dahlia came over to Sam as Dr. Baird left the room, sliding the stool across the floor to sit next to him.

"I'm so glad to hear that Nina should be able to pull through," she said.

"Me too. I don't know what I would have done if she …" Sam's voice trailed off.

He shook his head vigorously to rid himself of that morbid thought. That was not an idea he ever wanted to entertain.

"Say, Bennett," Sam glanced over his shoulder at her. "I've been here for nearly twenty-four hours straight; I could use a shower, a nap, fresh clothes, and some food."

"I can stay with Nina," Dahlia said.

"Would you? That would mean so much to me, Bennett. I mean it."

"Of course. It's no problem, Sam. Peter and I were supposed to meet for lunch today, so I'll let him know to bring lunch up here, and we can spend some time together while keeping an eye on her for you."

Before Sam realized what he was doing, he scooted forward to the edge of his seat and hugged Dahlia. Dahlia blinked, stunned.

"Thank you, Bennett," Sam said, getting up from the armchair and stretching dramatically. "I owe you one."

"Nah; it's what partners do," Dahlia replied.

"Dammit, Bennett," Sam said with a shake of his head. "Why do you have to be such a freakin' girl scout?"

"What are you talking about?" Dahlia's confusion was written plainly across her face.

Stopping in the doorway of the hospital room, Sam let out a slow breath. *Because I used your care and compassion against you, Bennett, as an excuse to go do some things that you'd kill me for if you found out what I was up to. You didn't even hesitate for a moment when I asked you to stay here and watch over Nina; not even when you remembered you had plans to go out and do something special with your boyfriend. You're too freakin' selfless, Bennett. I, on the other hand, am selfish.*

"Don't worry about it," Sam said instead. "Thanks."

He then quickly headed out of the room with no further discussion. Envisioning the little devil and angel on each shoulder vying for his attention, Sam was quick to send the latter flying as he wholeheartedly rushed into the arms of the fiendish imaginary figure.

★★★

Using his key to gain access to Nina's apartment, Sam began tearing the place apart looking for any indication of the origin of the spiked heroin his foster sister had consumed. While searching the apartment, he recalled that there had been two other cases in the recent weeks of overdoses with similar circumstances that had been handled by Vice and Narcotics. He knew, based on those two other individuals, Nina had not deliberately sought out the laced drug; the drug dealer of the three victims had doled out the spiked dope without the victims even knowing it. Now Sam needed to discover who that was.

Coming across Nina's phone, which was peeking out from underneath the couch, Sam searched through the contacts and recent messages and calls. He recognized most of the numbers or names listed in the records, save for a couple of them. Sam was prepared to call one of the numbers when his gray eyes spotted a name that he hadn't expected Nina to be familiar with: Arthur Emmons.

Arthur Emmons was a regular street urchin, having a long rap sheet consisting of offenses like burglary, drug possession, and assault. He'd been in and out of prison a few times, and save for the drunken brawl that led to his assault charge, he was a harmless guy. As a frequent flyer at the police department for drug possession and intent to distribute, Sam knew who the man was, though he didn't know him on a personal level.

Putting a name and a face to the person who sent Nina to the hospital, Sam's hands began to tremble as he clenched them tightly, leaving nail marks in his palms, though he didn't feel it. *Arthur Emmons ... you fucking son of a bitch! I knew you were a dealer who was splitting the profits with that pompous quack of a doctor,*

Trenton, when we broke up his drug ring three years ago. Your name was in his little book of clients. The only reason your ass isn't sitting in prison with the others whose names were written in it is because your name was on the page I tore out because it had Nina's name on it.

Gnashing his teeth together so tightly that his jaw started to ache, Sam slowly opened and closed his mouth. Running a hand through his hair, he let out a breath. He needed a fix, something to calm the swirling storm inside of him. Sam headed into Nina's bedroom and rummaged through the drawers of her vanity until he found her stash of joints. Grabbing one, and stuffing a couple into his pockets for later, he returned to the living room and sunk down onto the couch. He lit up the joint and exhaled a puff of smoke before closing his eyes and resting his head against the back of the sofa.

I gave you a chance to clean up your act by letting you stay out on the streets for the past few years, but you blew your chance. Now I'm coming for you, you stupid bastard. Now you have to pay the consequences. It's an eye for an eye, after all.

★★★

Standing outside the interrogation room at the Odette Police Department, Sam finished up his phone call with Dahlia.

"Okay, Sam," Dahlia said. "As soon as Gloria, Clarice or Raymond get here, I'll head out to the address and see what I can find."

"Great," Sam said before ending the call.

Stuffing his cell phone into his pants pocket, he made his way into Interrogation Room 3.

"What's going on?" Arthur Emmons asked as he pushed his thick glasses back into place with his middle finger when Sam entered the room. "What's so important that I get dragged away from my job by a bunch of cops and then thrown into an interrogation room at the police department?"

Sam took a seat at the table across from him.

"We need to have a little chat, Artie," he said.

"About what?"

"About the newest item up for sale at your little drug emporium: Fentanyl-laced heroin."

Arthur's mouth flew open, and he gave Sam and incredulous stare.

"What the hell are you talking about?" he asked.

"Don't play dumb with me, Emmons!" Sam slammed the table with his fist. "You knew that shit was spiked and you deliberately distributed it, without a single concern about what it could do to the people you sold it to!"

"But I didn't! I know Fentanyl is supposed to give you a killer high, but it's also dangerous. I steer clear of that shit, though the money for sellin' it is tempting."

"Gee, how about that? A drug-dealing criminal with a moral code," Sam said. "You say you stay away from it, Artie, yet three buyers of yours end up in the hospital after overdosing on Fentanyl and heroin! That's an awfully big coincidence, don't you think?"

"I swear it's not mine!"

"Then where pray tell, did you get it from?"

Arthur slumped down in his chair, his chipped and dirt-stained fingers tapping the table.

"I'm not sayin' anything else until I have a lawyer," he said.

"What do you need a lawyer for? You're not under arrest or anything. We're having a friendly chat down at the police department, right?"

"You have an interesting definition of what a 'friendly chat' is."

"Fine," Sam said. "Here's the deal. If you don't want to go to prison and face a lot—and I stress a *lot*—of jail time, you'll tell me all I want to know about the Fentanyl-laced heroin. You do that, and you can walk out of here without any drug-related charges against you."

"And if I don't?" Arthur asked.

"Then I would suggest giving your wife a kiss goodbye because you'll be spending the next twenty years or so in the penitentiary being called 'wifey' by your cellmate 'Bubba.' I know you've been to prison for a few years before but this time would be different. You're a repeat offender, Artie, so you'd be looking at a lot of time in the pen."

"Fine," Arthur said with a huff. "I won it in a card game. The guy running the thing didn't have enough cash on him, so he made me a deal. He gave me the dope and said I could sell it for a pretty penny, even more than I won in the game."

"Does this budding entrepreneur have a name?"

"He goes by 'Lucky Louini.'"

"And where did 'Lucky Louini' get his stash from?" Sam asked.

"I know he used to get it from Dr. Trenton, that celeb doctor guy that I was, um, also acquainted with," Arthur looked away from Sam for a brief moment. "But now I don't know. All I know is that he had it on him during the card game and gave it to me as a reward for winning the hand."

Sam's next question was interrupted by his cell phone vibrating in his pocket.

"I'll be right back," he grumbled to Arthur before stepping out into the hallway.

Checking the caller ID on his phone, Sam found that it was Dahlia.

"This better be important, Bennett," he snapped.

"We have a huge problem at the Emmons house," Dahlia started to say.

"What kind of problem?"

"We found a body."

"No shit," Sam's golden-brown eyebrows went up in surprise.

"I'll send you a picture of the victim."

A few seconds later, a soft ding chimed in his ear, and Sam checked the message Dahlia had sent him. The victim was a woman who appeared to be in her late thirties. She wore her chocolate chip colored hair in two pigtails, which barely reached the tops of her shoulders. Her eyes were closed, and she looked rather serene, which was quite the opposite of the area above her eyes, her forehead, which had a bloody gunshot wound in it.

"I guess the Fentanyl-heroin issue is the least of Artie's worries now," Sam said. "Good work, Bennett."

"We're still working to ID her."

"No need. This is Kelsey Emmons, Artie's wife," Sam said. "I've seen her when she's come to bail his sorry ass out of holding a time or ten."

Sam stepped back into the interrogation room after ending the call.

"So, Artie," Sam slid back into his chair at the table. "How's your wife?"

Artie seemed puzzled by the question, but answered nonetheless.

"Kelsey's fine," he said. "Why do you want to know?"

"How about your relationship? Was it solid or were you two fighting a lot recently?"

"We're happy," Artie frowned. "What does this have to do with anything?"

Sam clapped his hands together slowly a few times, applauding the man across from him.

"Bravo, Artie. Truly, your feigned ignorance is almost believable," he said. "Almost."

"Seriously, I have no idea what you're talking about!"

"Your wife, Artie; Kelsey's dead."

"She's ... dead?" Artie's strangled voice came out as barely a whisper. "No; I don't believe you."

Sam pulled up the photo Dahlia had sent to him and showed it to Artie. The shock of seeing his wife's body in the picture caused all of the blood run out of his face.

"Wh–what happened?" Artie choked the words out. "Who did this to her?"

"You tell me," Sam said, unflinchingly staring at Artie.

"You think I did this?" Artie gasped, tears beginning to cascade down his face. "You're insane!"

"Is it really insane to think so? I mean, there are so many things that could explain why you murdered your wife, Artie," Sam said. "Perhaps Kelsey got tired of having a low life criminal as a husband and wanted to leave, but you wouldn't let her. Maybe Kelsey knew you spiked the heroin and was going to rat you out, so you had to silence her. Maybe Kelsey–"

"Enough! I didn't do it! I swear! I did not murder my wife!"

Sam got up from the table and headed toward the door. Hand on the doorknob, he paused, glancing back over his shoulder at a broken-down Artie.

"You can say that all you want, Artie," Sam said. "But the evidence will trump your pathetic sob story. You are going to be spending the rest of your life in prison, where monsters like you belong."

★★★

Pausing in the doorway of Nina's hospital room at the sight of Sam so sweetly and tenderly doting on his sister, Dahlia watched the scene with a smile on her face. She enjoyed seeing this side of him; it was a rare occurrence like a comet or a blue moon, but it was still there nonetheless. Dahlia waited patiently in the doorway until Sam took his usual seat in the armchair next to Nina's bed, not wanting to frighten her usually guarded partner from letting down his walls again. Once a sufficient amount of time had passed, she continued forward into the hospital room.

"Hi Sam," Dahlia said. "How's Nina doing?"

"Much better, Bennett. Thanks for asking," Sam replied. "She was awake for a bit earlier, so she's coming around, thankfully."

"That's wonderful, Sam," Dahlia said.

She reached into her purse and produced a file folder, which she handed to Sam.

"Oh, here's the ballistics report, fresh from the lab, by the way."

Sam eagerly opened up the file and quickly began to devour the report. The Medical Examiner was able to recover the bullet from Kelsey Emmon's body during the autopsy. The ballistics markings were examined and compared to the guns found at the crime scene, which belonged to Arthur Emmons. The comparison yielded a positive identification to a Colt .45 registered to Arthur.

"A positive match," Sam read the report. "We got the bastard. The jury will convict him without hesitation."

"I can't believe he used his own gun and then returned it to his safe without any attempt to conceal his crime," Dahlia said. "It doesn't make any sense."

"My foster father, Edwin, used to tell me 'we don't catch the smart ones,'" Sam said.

"None of this seems strange to you? I mean, Arthur adamantly denied murdering his wife when you interrogated him at the police department the other day, yet he didn't bother to conceal the evidence connecting him to the crime at his house. That whole situation seems odd. Why bother to deny it when you leave all of the evidence out in the open for anyone to find?"

"It could be denial," Sam said. "Arthur could have killed his wife in a fit of rage or something and then was stunned that he did it, truly not believing that he was responsible for her death. I'm sure the shock of seeing his wife murdered scrambled his little gray cells."

Dahlia acquiesced, figuring that her partner was correct, though the whole situation still didn't sit right with her. She decided to change the subject.

"I'm relieved to see Nina's doing better," Dahlia said to Sam.

"You and me both, Bennett," Sam replied, turning his attention to her sleeping figure. "She should be able to leave the hospital in a day or so."

"That's great news, Sam," Dahlia smiled at her partner. "I have no doubt she'll make a full recovery at home because you'll be there at her side taking excellent care of her; she's very lucky to have you."

Sam merely shrugged in response. When it came to his family, Dahlia found, Sam's usual arrogant and self-assured nature melted away into a modest humility.

"I'm lucky to have her," Sam said. "I'm lucky to have all three of them, Gloria, Clarice, and Nina. These last few days have been torture for all of us, worrying about Nina, but it's helped that we've had each other during this whole ordeal."

Dahlia quietly studied Sam for a few moments. There was genuine emotion in her partner's voice in the rare instances in which he discussed his family. It was no secret in those moments how deeply he cared about and was protective of his mother and sisters. But when it came to Nina, Dahlia had an inkling that there was more than familial love and affection between the two.

Her suspicions had been confirmed at Clarice and Raymond's wedding a few months ago. At the reception, Nina had successfully dragged Sam out onto the dance floor with her. More than once. Including a dance to a slow song. Together.

Dahlia knew that if anyone else had asked him to dance, Sam would have laughed and responded with one of his trademark snarky remarks. Peter, her boyfriend, and date to the wedding, recognized the difference in behavior in his old friend and colleague too. If it weren't for the fact that Nina was wearing a bridesmaid's dress instead of a wedding gown, with the manner in which she and Sam acted around each other, it would have been easy to assume she and Sam were the ones who had tied the knot instead of Clarice and Raymond.

Sure, Sam could try to dismiss it and blame it on the alcohol, but he didn't consume much that evening. She and Peter were seated near the head table where Sam, who was in the wedding party, was seated. He only had a glass or two of champagne and then a rum and coke later in the evening. She'd seen him pound them back after particularly emotionally taxing cases when they'd gone out after work with some of their fellow officers or the just two of them and it took much more than that little bit to get him truly drunk enough to lose his inhibitions.

No; he did it because he wanted to. He did it because he was in love with Nina.

Why doesn't he tell Nina how he feels about her? Dahlia wondered. *Does he think that it's taboo or something because they were foster siblings? No, that can't be it; Sam doesn't give a shit about what other people think. Does he honestly not know how he feels about her? How could he not? If this wasn't a wakeup call, I don't know what is.*

"Sam," Dahlia began slowly, not sure how to proceed. "You can say that Nina's recovery from this whole ordeal is a miracle and she now has a new chance at life. Why don't you take advantage of the fact that she is still here, alive and well, and tell her how much she means to you?"

"What are you talking about, Bennett?" Sam asked.

"Do you need me to smack you upside the head to get it through your thick skull? It's obvious to anyone who knows you that you are in love with Nina. I have no doubt that she feels the same way about you. Why are you denying yourself this happiness?"

"Because I don't deserve it," Sam said more to himself than to her.

"Of course, you do, Sam," Dahlia placed a hand on his shoulder.

"Who are you? My mom?"

Dahlia let out a soft chuckle.

"Your 'cop mom,' maybe," she said. "I mean, I do keep an eye on you at all times to make sure that you don't get in too much trouble or hurt yourself or anything like that. Plus, I have to make sure you behave properly and mind your manners and-"

"I get it," Sam said.

Though his voice sounded grumpy, Dahlia could see that the edges of his lips had curled up in a smile.

"Seriously, Sam," she said. "I've been stuck with you day in, and day out for the last few years-lucky me-and I know that you are a good cop because you want to help people and make a difference in the lives of others. You deserve a chance to be happy."

"You have no idea what I've done, Bennett," Sam said. "If only you knew, I don't think you'd be feeling the same way about me."

What I've done? The words echoed in Dahlia's mind. *Is he talking about what happened to that fraud of a doctor, Oliver Nestmann?*

"Are you talking about Dr. Nestmann?" she asked.

That seemed to capture Sam's attention. He turned his head to look at her.

"You mean 'Dr. Manson?' The professor who was obsessed with death and convinced a bunch of grief-stricken kids to kill themselves all in the name of 'research?'" he asked.

"Thanks for the history lesson," Dahlia said with a small laugh. "Yeah, that doctor."

"What about him?"

Dahlia brought a hand up to her necklace and began shifting the pendant back and forth.

"Well," she started to say. "I think you at least know more than you're letting on about what happened to him."

"Know more than I'm letting on? How so?"

"When I saw the headline in the paper that talked about how Dr. Nestmann was found dead in his cell shortly after we arrested him, I went to the holding cell to check the visitor's log. Your name was on there, Sam."

The tiny smile that had formed on Sam's face disappeared as quickly as it appeared.

"I can assure you that my name was *not* on there," he said. "What the hell makes you think that I'd go and visit that whackjob?"

"Okay, it wasn't actually your name, per se, but I know it was you, Sam, because I know your handwriting; I've seen it on enough reports and files to be able to identify it," Dahlia said. "Does the name 'Seth Tucker' ring a bell?"

"If hell's bells can ring, then yeah, it's familiar."

"There's practically no way that your stepfather would know Dr. Nestmann, so why would he visit him in prison?"

"Maybe to see if the quack actually *could* bring people back from the dead?" Sam said with a shrug. "You know, since I had to pull the plug on my mother's life support, I kind of ruined it for him to be able to finish what he started over sixteen years ago. The case involving Dr. Nutjob was all over the news, Bennett. Unless the man lives under a rock somewhere, I'm pretty sure he heard of the guy the news dubbed 'Dr. Manson.'"

"Okay, I'll give you that," Dahlia said. "But I think that you used your stepfather's name to hide your identity when you went to visit Dr. Nestmann."

"And why pray tell, would I do that?"

"You tell me," Dahlia paused. "The only thing I can say is that I know, based on the visitor's log, that you were the last person to see the doctor before he died. That seems to be an awfully big coincidence."

Her statement drew a reaction out of Sam, much to her surprise. He completely turned in his chair to face her, his silver eyes boring deeply into her green ones.

"Are you suggesting that I had something to do with Nestmann's death?" Sam asked.

"Did you?" Dahlia asked in response.

"What do you think? Do you believe that I am truly capable of something like that?"

Dahlia opened her mouth to respond but found herself unable to speak. *Is he capable of killing someone in cold blood? I mean, sure, he's had to kill while in the line of duty before, but killing Nestmann like that would be an entirely different situation. Sure, his blatant disregard for the rules can be a pain in the ass and some of the things he does or says I want to smack him for, but those things are trivial compared to something as monumental as murder. My gut says yes, but my heart says no. What do I believe?*

"I ... I ..." Dahlia began to say. "I guess I'm being paranoid."

Sam's hard expression seemed to soften.

"Be careful, Bennett," he said. "If you keep saying shit like that out loud, you might get thrown into the funny farm."

"Haha," Dahlia lightly punched him in the shoulder.

"Why don't you go home and rest, Bennett? It seems like you could use some time away from the department."

"Only if you promise to do the same."

"Now that I know Nina is going to be okay, I guess I could do that," Sam said.

The two detectives walked in silence from the hospital room.

★★★

Sam took a necessary detour after parting ways with Dahlia at the hospital. His car was barely in park when he hopped out in front of the automotive garage owned by Benedict Stoner.

"Where is he?" Sam growled at the legs in the gray jumpsuit sticking out from beneath a red car.

Getting no response, Sam kicked the legs in the shins.

"Goddamn it!" the owner of the legs grumbled.

Stoner slid out from underneath the car and sat up to rub his shin.

"What do you want, Marlowe?" he asked.

Sam's eyes went directly to the gray-haired man's nose, which was noticeably crooked. *Guess it never healed straight after I broke it three years ago. Well, at least it can serve as a reminder to keep your mouth shut as a drug dealer when you have a cop as a client.*

"Where is he?" Sam repeated.

"Who?"

"Luke Skywalker; who the hell do you think? Seth!"

Stoner thumbed up toward the ceiling.

"Upstairs, in the apartment," he said.

Sam turned and headed through the archway toward the door labeled "employees only."

"Fucking bastard ..." Stoner grumbled to himself, though Sam was still able to hear him.

"Hey," he called down to the older man. "If you don't have anything nice to say, don't say anything at all."

"Fuck off."

Sam opened the door and headed up the stairs toward the small apartment where Stoner resided above the garage. He pounded on the apartment door.

"Seth! Open up, you worthless piece of shit!"

Sam barely had enough time to stop himself from knocking to not hit Seth Tucker in the face.

"Nice to see you too," Seth said. "What do you want?"

Sam said nothing as he headed into the apartment.

"Shut the door," he said.

Seth shut the door and locked it.

"What do you want?" Seth repeated.

"I've come to warn you," Sam said.

"Of what?"

Sam turned around to face his stepfather.

"My partner," he said. "You're going to have to lay low for a while. My partner is starting to wonder if something's wrong with some of the cases we've worked on."

"Is your partner asking about the Emmons chick?" Seth asked. "I did her in like you asked me to."

"I know you did and no, thankfully not. She wasn't entirely sure what to make of all the evidence pointing toward Arthur, but I have no doubt that we'll be able to get a conviction with the way we staged the scene," he said. "Emmons is going to pay for nearly killing Nina."

"What about the other two guys that you talked about? That 'Louie' guy and 'Adam' something-or-other; I thought you said they need to be 'eliminated?'"

"I did and don't worry, that's still part of the plan. However, if you jump too soon, Bennett is going to start putting two and two together, and then we'll be in a pickle."

"Why don't you just off her?" Seth asked.

Sam's eyes narrowed until they were barely more than slits.

"Did you just suggest what I think you did?" his voice was no more than a whisper.

Seth folded his arms across his chest.

"You heard me. Kill your partner."

Sam's sight went red as the words registered in his mind. He charged at Seth, grabbing two fistfuls of the older man's shirt and shoving him back against the nearest wall.

"What the fuck are you doing?" Seth coughed, sounding like the wind had been knocked out of him from the impact with the wall.

"Don't you ever think about hurting her," Sam said through gritted teeth.

Seth tried to shove him back and break free from his hold, but Sam held firm.

"I ain't gonna kill her!" Seth raised his hands in surrender as much as Sam's grip allowed.

Sam loosened his grip enough for Seth to slap his hands away.

"Listen, we have a job to do," Sam said. "You're either with me or against me. And if you're against me, I will do everything in my power to make your life a living hell, got it?"

"I paid my debt to society-"

"To society, maybe, but not to me. It's my mother you took away from me at fourteen. It's my mother that I had to visit in a care facility for years and see her lifeless body connected to a zillion wires and tubes that kept her alive. It's my mother that I had to decide to pull the plug on to protect her from you."

"Yeah, yeah," Seth grumbled in response.

"There's not much work out there for violent offenders with felonies on their records," Sam said. "Not many other people are going to put your special skills of violence and murder to use like I will. You want to earn a living? You do what I say."

Sam made his way toward the door, his shoulder deliberately knocking into Seth.

"I'll send word when it's time to move on the next target," he said.

Sam said nothing further before exiting the apartment. On his way out, he heard Seth mutter under his breath:

"Fine. Whatever, you little bastard."

Wait until this is all over, Seth, Sam thought as he made his way down the stairs and out of the garage. *Once you've done what I need you to, your life will be in my hands, Seth. I promise you that. I will get justice for what you did to my mother and how you destroyed my life. You have my word.*

GOOD COP, BAD COP

Detective Samuel Marlowe hooked his thumbs into his belt loops and leaned up against the brick wall as he watched from the second story window the reporters on the ground below pushing and shoving each other to get to the front of the crowd.

"They're a bunch of damned vultures," he said, a prominent frown on his face.

Junior Detective Dahlia Bennett glanced up from the paperwork she had been completing.

"But I thought you liked the press, Sam," she said as she tucked a stray piece of curly black hair back behind her ear. "You know, bask in the glory of how you singlehandedly kept the city safe from evildoers."

Sam watched the scrum of reporters part as four police officers quickly escorted a man in handcuffs and with police jackets draped over his head into the Odette Police Department.

"They're not here to see me," Sam said. "They're here for Louie Donato."

Dahlia raised a manicured eyebrow at Sam.

"You mean The Louie Donato?" she asked. "The same one that you've been trying to nail since the Fentanyl-laced heroin epidemic last year?"

Sam strolled over to his desk. Compared to Dahlia's, his desk appeared cluttered and disorganized, but Sam knew where everything was. He shoved some stray papers aside and grabbed his hair comb, stuffing it in the back pocket of his navy trousers.

"Yeah, that Louie Donato," Sam said. "He's been laying low and trying to stay out of trouble ever since his buddy, Arthur Emmons, was put in the slammer for killing his wife, but now, he's finally slipped up. It's our job to put him in jail where he belongs. So, grab your things, Bennett. If you want to become a full-fledged detective soon, you're going to need to learn from the best, so you're going to sit in on this one."

Dahlia popped out of her chair, nearly knocking over her neatly stacked books and papers. She gathered everything she deemed necessary to bring to the interrogation room and skipped over to Sam, who was straightening his shirt collar in the tiny oval mirror that hung on the wall of the bullpen.

"Christ, Bennett, this is a murder investigation, not the first day of school," he said. "Put that shit back; you're only going to need a pen, paper and the case file, Bennett, not the entire stock of Office Depot. You should know this by now."

"Sorry, Sam," Dahlia said as she returned some of her things to her desk. "I'm excited. This is a big case; I want to make sure that everything goes perfectly."

Pleased with his appearance, Sam said, "I'm gonna have a smoke before this all goes down. Meet me outside the interrogation room in about twenty minutes."

"Yes, sir!" Dahlia saluted.

★★★

Standing outside the interrogation room, Dahlia impatiently glanced down at her watch. Annoyed at his tardiness, she searched for any sight of her partner, finally spotting him walking toward her from the south hallway.

"You're late, Sam," Dahlia said.

"Nah, you're early, Bennett."

Sam opened the door to the interrogation room. As he crossed the threshold, Dahlia heard him mutter:

"You're going down, Donato."

He seems to have a personal agenda against this guy. I'm concerned about what might happen in here ... once Sam sets his mind to something, there's no stopping him ... even if it means doing something illegal.

Seated at the lone table in the interrogation room was the man who had suddenly been thrust into the spotlight, Louie Donato. He slumped in the chair, his rusty hair disheveled. Exhaustion and defeat carved dark circles under his yellow eyes.

"Oh no, not you," Louie moaned at the sight of Sam. "Anyone but you."

"Nice to see you too," Sam said as he sat down across from Louie.

Dahlia listened with interest as she grabbed a spare chair from the table and positioned it in the corner of the room to watch the interrogation.

"Can't you take over?" Louie asked Dahlia.

"Sorry, but I can't," Dahlia shook her head. "The chief asked for Detective Marlowe personally."

"So, Louie, long time, no see," Sam said. "As I recall, the last time you were here, you were a two-bit criminal being brought up on illegal gambling charges. Now you've graduated to murder, congrats."

"I didn't do it!" Louie said. "I loved Honey; I would never hurt her!"

"Yeah, that's the same thing Arthur Emmons said before he blew his wife's brains out last year. You know, one of your drug dealing buddies that you gave the Fentanyl-laced heroin to?"

"Just because one guy killed his wife, it doesn't mean I did."

"You're right," Sam said. "That can't make the charges stick, but evidence can."

"Wait, what?"

Sam leaned back in his chair.

"Oh, we have plenty of evidence to convict you," he said.

Louie tapped his fingers against the table.

"I ... I want my lawyer," he said.

"What do you need a lawyer for?" Sam asked. "We haven't read you your rights yet. You should know that, with you being a frequent flyer at the police department and all."

"I can contact your lawyer—" Dahlia started to say.

Her statement was interrupted by Sam raising a hand to stop her. Dahlia frowned. *The jerk just shushed me!*

"Let's chat, Louie; why don't you start by telling me what you were doing on the night of June 20th?"

"Why should I?" Louie said. "You've already made your mind up that I'm guilty."

"Humor me."

"Fine," Louie sighed. "I was working at the casino during my regular shift, which ended at five. I called Honey before I left to see what she wanted for dinner. I picked up takeout before heading home. We had dinner and then split a bottle of wine. Honey said she wanted to discuss something over a glass of wine. We talked and then went to bed."

"What did you talk about?" Sam asked.

"Nothing in particular."

"That wasn't an ordinary chat, Louie. It sounds like Honey needed some liquid courage first."

Louie put his arms on the table in front of him, resting his head in his hands for a moment before looking back up at Sam.

"We argued."

"About what?"

"I plead the fifth."

Sam, who had been twirling his pen around, stopped abruptly and straightened up in his chair.

"Louis," he said. "You're only going to hurt yourself by not telling me everything."

"But that's the thing," Louie said. "Telling you what we argued about will only make me seem guiltier than you already think I am."

"I can't help you if you don't help me."

Louie closed his eyes tightly. Dahlia shifted in her seat. She could practically feel the pain and despair emanating from him.

"She told me she was cheating on me," he said.

"I see," Sam said. "Did she say who she was cheating with?"

"Believe me, if she did, I would be guilty of murder because I would have killed that bastard."

"Has Honey ever cheated on you before?"

"No, never."

"Did she give you any indication why?" Sam asked.

"No. This was completely out of left field," Louie said. "I mean, we had our fights like any other couple, but our relationship was solid, at least I thought so."

"Did it, perhaps, have anything to do with your criminal history?"

"You had to bring that up, didn't you, Marlowe?"

"I'm a detective, Louie. I have to explore every avenue in an investigation."

"That's funny. I don't recall you ever being so thorough before."

A faint smile crossed Sam's lips, which Dahlia could see clearly in the reflection of the one-way glass behind Louie.

"You're a criminal, and I'm a cop; you do something wrong, and it's my job to arrest you," Sam paused. "But I'm sure you're well aware of how that works."

"Yes, I've done some stupid things-"

"You got caught running an illegal betting and gambling ring. Twice. Oh, and did I forget to mention sometimes drugs would be used to bet or payout instead of cash? Including a potentially deadly combo of heroin and Fentanyl?"

"Yeah, I know, but I've cleaned up my act. I've got a legitimate job at the casino now. I'm going straight."

"I guess Lucky Louini's services are officially closed?"

"I have put the name 'Lucky Louini' behind me," Louie said.

"Tell me, Louie, what inspired your change of heart?" Sam asked. "Did it have anything to do with the fact that you were one strike away from a one-way ticket to a permanent residence at the Odette Penitentiary?"

Louie let out a breath.

"Yeah, I admit that was part of it-especially since I knew you were gunning for me to get that last strike-but that was not the only reason," Louie replied. "I also wanted to clean up my act for Honey. She stuck with me through every stupid thing I've done, and she deserved better than the two-bit criminal that she agreed to marry ten years ago."

"You're right, Louie. Honey did deserve better," Sam said. "Instead, this is what she got."

Sam held his hand out to Dahlia.

"Are you sure this is a good idea, Sam?" Dahlia whispered.

"Give me the damn picture, Bennett," he said.

"Sam-"

"That's an order."

Dahlia pressed her lips together in a firm, thin line. Sam liked to pull the 'that's an order card' when he wanted her to do something but didn't want her to protest it. He knew she wouldn't disobey the rules or an order from a superior officer; though, in moments like these, Dahlia thought, he wasn't a superior officer, merely a higher ranking one.

"Here you are, Your Highness," she grumbled as she placed the photo in Sam's outstretched hand.

"You see what she gets, Louie?" Sam slammed the picture down on the table.

Louie immediately closed his eyes and turned away.

"I don't want to look at it!" Louie said. "I can't see her like that!"

"Open your eyes, Louie. You need to take a good, hard look at how you repay your wife for all the years she stood behind your sorry ass. You repaid Honey with a bullet to the head!"

The pressure from Sam got to Louie, and he reluctantly opened one eye. Honey had been found on her bedroom floor with a single gunshot wound between her sapphire blue eyes. Her golden locks were splayed around her head like an angel's halo stained with blood. Louie turned in his chair and leaned forward, dry heaving.

"I'm gonna be sick," Louie gasped.

"Grab the trash bin, Bennett," Sam said. "I'll get some ginger ale and paper towels."

Sam left the room while Dahlia grabbed the trash bin. She managed to place it in front of Louie and jump back before the handcuffed man lost his lunch.

"Here," Sam said when he returned moments later.

He placed a can of ginger ale and a roll of paper towels on the table. "I'm gonna step out while Louini, here, composes himself."

Dahlia threw a glare at Sam, but he ignored her displeasure and left. She grabbed the paper towels and handed them to Louie before opening the soda can with a loud click.

"Sorry about this," he said to Dahlia as he wiped his sweaty brow with a fresh paper towel.

Dahlia snuck a glance at the door and saw that Sam was nowhere near them.

"Louie-off the record-did you murder your wife?" she asked.

"No," Louie choked out. "I could never hurt her like that. You have to believe me …"

Louie looked into Dahlia's eyes. Working as a cop over the years, she learned to read people's body language, and everything Louie was silently telling her was that he was innocent. *I think he's telling the truth … Louie didn't kill his wife.*

The silence in the room was soon broken when the interrogation room door flew open, and Sam strolled in.

"Feeling better?" he asked.

"Yeah," Louie said wiping his mouth, not breaking eye contact with Dahlia.

"Good," Sam plopped back down in his chair. "Where's your gun, Louie?"

Louie shifted uncomfortably in his chair.

"I can't find it."

"That's awfully convenient."

"Seriously, detective, my gun is missing. It wasn't in my gun case. I honestly have no idea where my gun disappeared to."

"Did you report it missing?" Sam asked.

"No."

"Any reason?"

"I've been in enough legal trouble, and I didn't want to get the police involved," Louie said.

"Or did you want to pretend it was missing so you could have an alibi after you killed your wife with it?"

"Someone used my gun to murder Honey?" Louie asked, eyes wide.

"Ballistics report matches a .32 FN Browning registered to a 'Louis Donato,'" Sam said.

"It can't be! My gun is missing; whoever's got my gun shot my wife!"

Sam said nothing as he stood up from his seat.

"Sure, Louie, it's a conspiracy against you. Tell that to the judge; maybe they'll let you go by reason of insanity."

Sam turned to face Dahlia, who was still rooted to her spot in the corner. *This is unbelievable. All of the evidence Sam presented points to Louie, but I don't believe he did it. What the hell is going on?*

"You can call his lawyer now, Bennett," Sam said to her. "Because now, Louie Donato, you are under arrest for the murder of your wife."

"I didn't kill Honey!" Louie said, tears welling up in his eyes. "I thought you were going to help me!"

Sam, who had been primping his appearance in the reflection of the one-way glass, said matter-of-factly:

"Yeah, well, I decided to help myself instead."

"You bastard," Louie sneered. "You'll never get away with this."

Sam winked at Louie.

"I already did. Now, if you'll excuse me, I need to give the media what they want. Me."

★★★

Reclining back in his chair with his feet on his desk, Sam didn't bother to open his eyes as the clack of heels against the wooden floor approached him.

"Congrats, Sam, you made the front page," Dahlia said as she tossed something onto his chest. "Wife killer guilty, gets life."

Sam opened his eyes and picked up the newspaper.

"I look pretty damn good," he said.

Dahlia rolled her eyes and walked back to her desk.

"What's with you, Bennett?" Sam asked as he folded up the newspaper and threw it aside on his desk. "You should be happy; we got a murderer off the streets."

"If you say so," Dahlia replied, eyes glued to the paperwork Sam knew she was only pretending to fill out.

"What, you think he's innocent?" Sam asked.

Dahlia shrugged in response. Annoyed, Sam swung his feet off the desk and faced his partner.

"Listen, Bennett," he said. "Louie Donato was guilty and where do guilty people end up? Prison. It's as simple as that."

"So, you never once considered that Louie could have been innocent?" Dahlia blurted out. "Not a single time since Honey's body was found last year?"

"I don't know what he said to you to brainwash that mind of yours, but, whatever it is, I want you to forget it. Now," Sam said, his voice stern. "He killed his wife with his gun in his house after arguing with her when she revealed she had an affair. With that amount of evidence, Louie should have called the police on himself after he was done murdering Honey."

The expression on Dahlia's face revealed to Sam that she was not convinced by his argument.

"I will repeat what my foster father used to say until the end of time: we don't catch the smart ones. There was so much evidence pointing to Louie, how could he not have done it? If he were a smart criminal, he wouldn't have been arrested twice before he murdered his wife."

"If you say so," Dahlia replied with her infamous last words.

★★★

With a quick flick, Sam ignited his trusty blue lighter. He held the flame up to the edge of his fresh cigarette until it glowed. Sam offered a light to his companion on this particular evening, and she held her cigarette out to oblige the offer. Layla Young let out a puff of smoke as she laid back on the pillow. She nervously bit her bottom lip, effectively removing the last remnants of her lipstick.

"Listen, Sam," Layla started to say. "We need to talk."

"Sure. What's on your mind?" Sam replied as he tucked a stray piece of Layla's fiery red hair back behind her ear.

"I appreciate you allowing me to help Adam in this way," Layla said, her chocolate eyes peering deeply into Sam's gray ones. "But he's turning his life around."

"So, what?"

"So, we're going to need to break this off."

"Oh, I see how it is," Sam threw back the covers and got out of bed and began to pick up his clothing that was scattered throughout the cramped bedroom of Layla's house. "The moment your husband decides to finally keep his sorry ass out of the slammer and stop cooking up heroin, you toss me aside like yesterday's news."

"Don't you dare try to play that card with me! You're the one that came up with this stupid ass scheme! I only agreed to it to keep Adam out of prison!"

"Layla—"

"No, don't 'Layla' me," Layla stammered.

She tossed the bed sheets back angrily, smashed her cigarette in the crystal ashtray on the nightstand next to her bed and threw on a t-shirt before storming over to Sam.

"I have done every single thing you have asked of me, no matter how disgusting or vile it was. Hell, I even agreed to sleep with you! And do you know why I did that? To help my husband stay out of jail!" Layla said, poking Sam's bare chest with her finger for emphasis. "But I'm done. I am done with you, Sam, and your stupid games. And you know what? I'm going to tell Adam. I'm going to tell him all about what you made me do to keep him out of prison. Then, you'll be sorry."

Sam grabbed Layla's hand as she went to poke his chest yet again and gripped her wrist tightly. Layla winced.

"You say anything, and you will regret it," Sam growled.

Layla yanked her hand away.

"Oh yeah? Whatcha gonna do, big man? Kill me?"

Sam pulled his shirt over his head. He grabbed his things and headed toward the bedroom doorway.

"You got my payment?" Sam asked coldly.

Layla begrudgingly went over to the dilapidated dresser, rummaged through a drawer for a moment before pulling out a little bag.

"Here," she said, tossing the bag to Sam.

Sam took a quick look at the bag of heroin and Fentanyl. Turning, he threw a seething glance over his shoulder at Layla and stepped out of the room.

"I'll see myself out," he said.

Under his breath, he added, "But only after I take care of your darling husband's prized possession first."

★★★

He waited until night had blanketed the city before driving out to the automotive garage owned by Benedict Stoner. The drug-dealing mechanic was passed out in a chair in his office, so Sam ignored him as he made his way up to the second-floor apartment. He let himself inside.

Seth Tucker was reclined on the couch, empty beer cans littering the floor next to him. He was asleep, one arm lying on the arm of the couch above his head, the other clutching a mostly empty bottle of scotch. Sam stood in the doorway and looked at the spectacle. He shook his head before heading over to Seth and kicking the couch.

"Get up," he said.

Seth grumbled and opened his eyes.

"What do you want?" he snapped.

Sam's frown deepened when he found Seth's eyes roving up and down his body, a smile forming on his lips.

"How'd your night go?" Seth grinned.

Sam took a couple steps back to catch sight of himself in the mirror hanging on the wall near the doorway. *Shit.* There were still some faint traces of Layla's blood red lipstick still on his cheeks and neck. *Christ ... the things I don't do to make things easier for this piece of shit.* Sam grabbed a handful of tissues from the bathroom and began scrubbing away the remnants of his earlier activities. When he finished, he turned back to Seth, who was sitting up and watching him, still clutching the bottle of scotch.

"Here," Sam pulled a gun from out of his holster with one of the tissues. "You have what you need to finish the job."

Seth accepted the gun, looking it over.

"Smith & Wesson," he mumbled. "Nice piece."

Sam said nothing as he headed for the door and exited the apartment.

★★★

Dahlia tapped the end of her pen against her cheek thoughtfully as she carefully skimmed through the case report that Sam had given her to review.

"Victim Layla Young was shot twice in the heart with a Smith & Wesson revolver, which was discovered to belong to the victim's spouse, Adam Young. According to Mr. Young, the gun was a family heirloom that was passed down from the grandfather of Mr. Young to his father, and is now in Mr. Young's possession," Dahlia read aloud.

She looked up from the report on her desk and glanced a few feet across the bullpen at Sam. He was in his usual laid-back position, with his feet on his desk, and was sipping a fresh cup of coffee from a Styrofoam cup. Once he finished his drink, Sam crushed the cup in his hands and shot it like a basketball into the trash bin next to his desk.

"Doesn't this seem awfully familiar to you?" Dahlia asked. "You know, Kelsey Emmons was shot and killed two years ago, then Honey Donato was shot and killed last year and now this?"

Sam did not respond immediately.

"Hey, Larry Bird, get your head out of the court and focus," she said sternly. "This is the third woman in three years to be murdered, all having been shot to death by their husbands, all of whom claimed that their guns were missing shortly before their wives were killed."

"I'm sorry, Bennett. What were you saying? I tune out conspiracy theories."

"Must you be such an asshole, Sam?"

"My personality is one of my best features." Sam grinned at his partner.

"I'm serious, Sam. I think there's more to this and that the husbands were innocent. I want to speak to the Captain and see if he'll let me reopen these investigations."

Dahlia stood up from her chair, pausing when she heard Sam utter a "tsk, tsk," noise.

"I wouldn't do that if I were you."

Dahlia put her hands on her hips.

"And why not?"

"Because if you go sticking that pretty little nose of yours in places it doesn't belong, you might end up getting in trouble."

"Gee, Sam, that almost makes it sound like you killed these three women and then framed their husbands for their murder."

"You need to lay off the Agatha Christie and Georgette Heyer books, Bennett, because that is awfully absurd. Seriously, that is a more intricate revenge plot than the one in 'The Count of Monte Cristo.' I do appreciate you giving me that much credit, though, to be able to come up with such a scheme."

Dahlia was quiet for a moment, mulling over what Sam had told her in his ill attempt at humor to make light of a humorless subject.

"I still want to talk to the Captain about these cases," she said. "They're not sitting right with me."

"Bennett, you need to take a break. Why don't you go grab me a pop from the vending machine in the cafeteria?"

Dahlia opened her mouth to protest, but Sam spoke before she had the chance to, "That's an order, Bennett."

"Yes, sir," Dahlia grumbled before turning and stomping out of the bullpen.

Once the coast was clear, Sam rummaged around in his desk, sticking his hand back to the furthest recess of his bottom desk drawer. His fingers closed around the bag of drugs, which he pulled out and hurriedly stuffed into his briefcase as Dahlia came back into the bullpen, soda in hand.

"Your pop, your highness," she said to him.

"Thanks, Bennett," Sam said as he accepted the can with a wink. "I don't know how I'd manage without you."

"Good thing because you're going to be stuck with me for a long time," Dahlia replied as she sat down at her desk once again. "Even after I'm promoted to full detective, you'll still be stuck with me."

"Sure, Dahlia, if you say so," he said, borrowing the phrase she had used many a time against him.

"Yeah, I do say so," Dahlia said.

★★★

Dahlia waited until Sam left for the evening to speak to the Captain. Once she saw Sam pull away in his car, she rushed from the window and toward the Captain's office.

"Cap, do you have a minute?" Dahlia asked, poking her head through the door.

Captain Buchanan looked up from the report he was perusing and motioned for Dahlia to enter.

"What's up, Detective Bennett?" he asked.

Dahlia entered the office, closing the door behind her. She stood in front of the Captain's desk, ready to discuss her suspicions on the cases, but found herself unable to speak. *Can I ... Can I really do this?*

"Are you okay, Dahlia?" the Captain asked, jarring Dahlia from her thoughts. "You look a little pale."

Great.

"Yes," Dahlia started to say. "Well, no, actually."

She paused, letting out a breath to calm her nerves.

"I need to talk to you about some of the cases that Detective Marlowe and I worked on."

The Captain closed the report and tossed it aside on his desk.

"Which cases?" he asked.

"There are three cases I know for sure that I want to review," Dahlia said. "But ... there may be others, too."

"Three cases?"

"Yes. The Arthur Emmons, Louie Donato and Adam Young cases."

The Captain frowned.

"Adam Young?" he repeated. "Isn't that the case you're working on right now?"

"It is," Dahlia said. "And the characteristics of this case are almost identical to what happened in the Emmons and Donato cases. I don't believe that Arthur and Louie were guilty; I am convinced someone else is the culprit."

The Captain motioned for Dahlia to explain.

"Go ahead, Detective Bennett," he said. "I'm listening."

★★★

After stopping in Benedict Stoner's office for a 'little chat,' Sam entered the second-floor apartment, practically pushing past Seth when his stepfather opened the door.

"Nice to see you too," Seth grumbled as he shut the door. "What was going on downstairs? It sounded like a car backfiring."

I was taking care of a loose end by the name of Benedict Stoner, Sam thought. To Seth he said, "It's over. Your work is finished."

Seth walked over to Sam.

"What now?" he asked. "I did everything you asked. I killed everyone on your hit list. Give me what I want. Give me what I earned."

"You should consider the fact that I haven't killed your ass as your payment," Sam fished around in his pocket.

He pulled out the packet of drugs he lifted from the Young house when he and Dahlia investigated the crime scene earlier and tossed it to Seth. His stepfather greedily snatched up the heroin and plopped on the couch to immediately shoot up. Sam watched with disgust. He sat quietly in an armchair across from Seth as the man shot up and rode out his high, eventually becoming mellow and lethargic.

Seth leaned back against the couch, slowly sliding off to the side until he was held upright by the arm of the sofa. Sam could tell from the fluttering of the man's eyelids that he was on the brink of passing out and falling into a deep slumber. He got up from the armchair and headed over to the couch, stopping in front of Seth.

"It's funny," Sam began to say. "For the longest time, I was afraid of you."

Seth let out something that resembled a laugh but may have actually been a sleepy snort.

"Ever since you stepped into my life, you've been nothing but trouble," Sam said. "You hurt my mom. Over and over and over again. You hurt me, too, but my bruises were nothing in comparison to seeing the torture my mother went through at your hands. You were always the embodiment of evil."

Sam squatted down, so he was at Seth's level.

"But you know what? I'm not afraid of you anymore," he said. "All you are is a hedonistic addict who is good at nothing else but hurting others. I'm not afraid of you because I know I can control you. And that's what I did. I made you kill the three men that nearly destroyed one of the few good things in my life. Arthur Emmons; he was the one who supplied the Fentanyl-laced heroin to Nina that almost killed her. Louie Donato; he gave the spiked dope to Arthur. Adam Young; he's the one who cooked up the heroin and cut it with Fentanyl. All of those men are right where they belong, in prison and forced to live with the knowledge that their loved ones are dead, like how my loved one was nearly killed at their hands.

"You see, letting them go to prison wouldn't solve the problem. They could still get out or take a plea bargain for a smaller sentence. Plus, if someone in Vice and Narcotics decided to stick their nose where it didn't belong, they could have found out that Nina was purchasing her drugs from them and then she'd be arrested too. I couldn't have that. I made a promise years ago to protect Nina, and so far, I've done a shit job at it.

"But do you want to know what the real kicker in the whole situation is? Remember that celebrity doctor guy that was running the illegal drug ring out of his wife's pharmacy? Well, he had a little black book of all his clients who bought from him and all of the suppliers he split the profits with. Nina's name was in that book. Yep, it was right there next to Arthur Emmons, Louie Donato, and Adam Young. So was Benedict Stoner's, but that's a whole other story."

Sam paused when Seth shifted his position slightly. The man was still out cold.

"I couldn't let Nina go down with the doctor, so I took the page with her name right out of the book. But, in doing that, Emmons, Donato, and Young were removed from the book too. You'd think that, after the whole spectacle of taking Trenton's drug ring down and the subsequent arrests of all of his clients and suppliers, those three would have turned their lives around and dropped out of the drug game. But no. They kept going, and it nearly got Nina killed and almost got me in trouble. I couldn't go after those three for what they did to Nina through legal means because then it would implicate me too; I mean, I did tamper with evidence, but I did it because I needed to do it," he said. "Besides, I learned long ago that being a good, law-abiding person didn't amount to much in this world. All you get is a tragic ending like Edwin did with three bullets into the chest from some kid who decided to shoot up his school. My foster father deserved far more than that. They say you fight fire with fire, right? So, I knew I had to fight those who break the law by breaking the law myself. Though, I couldn't break the law as a cop. That's where you come in, 'dad.'"

The name was said with venom and contempt. *If anyone deserved to be called Dad, it would have been Edwin, not this fucking waste of human life.*

"It didn't matter what you did; you were bound to end up in prison again," Sam said. "I figured why not use that to my advantage? You're a natural brute who likes violence. Might as well put those strengths, I guess you could call them, to good use. I blackmailed the wives of the three men into having an affair with me so I could gain access to their belongings and get their guns. Once I had the gun, all I had to do was hand it over to you and let you do the easy part. Staging the crime scene, planting the evidence and getting the hubbies to go to prison for what you did was all me."

Sam pulled his police badge out of his pocket and ran his thumb over the shield.

"With this badge, I can play the role of both good cop and bad cop," he let out a small laugh that held no humor in it. "But, now that all three men are behind bars, I can stop this charade. For now, at least. And do you know what that means, Seth? It means you've outlived your usefulness."

He stuffed the shield back in his pocket and stood up, stretching his legs and cracking his neck. Sam withdrew a gun from his holster and stared down at the weapon for a few moments.

"Do you know how long I've been waiting for this moment?" he asked, though Seth was well into unconsciousness after coming down from his high and couldn't answer. "Ever since the first time I found out you hurt my mom, I've wanted to hurt you. As I grew older, simply hurting you wouldn't be enough anymore. I started to dream about killing you, punishing you for the hell you put us through."

Sam took the gun and wrapped Seth's hand around it. Maneuvering his stepfather's hand so that the muzzle touched his temple, Sam held Seth's hand that gripped the gun.

"De …" Seth mumbled.

The sudden sound startled Sam, causing a shockwave to course through his body.

"What?" he asked.

"De ..." Seth repeated. "De ... mar ... a ..."

"De ... mar ... a? De-mar-a ... Demara? What's that supposed to mean, Seth?"

"Hide ... away ... De ... mar ... a ... go there ..."

Hideaway? Demara? What the hell was Seth talking about?

Sam shook his head, bringing his focus back to the present. He felt Seth's grip on the gun tighten. Taking one last good look at his stepfather, Sam put his finger over Seth's on the trigger.

"This is for my mother," Sam whispered. "This is for Charlotte."

He pulled the trigger. Sam had enough time to let go of Seth's hand and jump back to avoid the spray of blood and brains from his stepfather. Breathing heavily, Sam's knees buckled, and he collapsed to the floor, silver eyes still locked on Seth.

He expected to feel relieved. He expected to feel happy. He expected to feel triumphant for finally destroying the monster that murdered his mother and destroyed his life.

Sam blinked. He didn't feel anything. He was ... numb. No anger. No sadness. No happiness. No peace. Just silence.

Forcing himself up, Sam stumbled toward the bathroom, turning on the faucet by nudging it with his elbow and washing the blood from his hands. It took some scrubbing and nearly the entire bottle of soap for the veteran cop to feel sufficiently clean. Turning the water off with his elbow again, Sam stared down at his hands. He then lifted his head to gaze at himself in the mirror.

What am I doing? Is this really what I've become? Am I really no better than Seth? A monster that hurts and kills people to get what he wants?

The words Dahlia said to him while he was sitting at Nina's bedside while she was recovering from her overdose in the hospital rang in his ears.

"I know you better than anyone, stating I've been stuck with you day in and day out for the last few years—lucky me—and I know that you are a good cop because you want to help people and make a difference in the lives of others. You deserve a chance to be happy," she had told him.

Of course, he didn't believe her. Why should he be happy? He was a killer.

No. Everything was over with. He was done. He was no longer going down that road. He couldn't.

Taking one last glance at Seth's body, Sam headed downstairs and left the garage.

It was all over. He was done with that path. Completely done.

LIFELINE

Dahlia let out an annoyed huff as the call she placed went straight to voicemail yet again.

"Sam, it's Dahlia," she said as she started to get out of the police cruiser. "Where the hell are you? I've been trying to get a hold of you for nearly a half hour! We have a scene to investigate. A customer showed up at Stoner's Automotive and found the owner, Benedict Stoner, dead. I'm at the garage now, so you need to get your ass here ASAP."

Ending her call and stuffing her cell phone into her pocket, Dahlia made her way up the chipped and faded blacktop toward the garage. She passed by an officer standing next to a pale woman sitting on a folding chair, shaking hands holding onto a Styrofoam cup of tea, the contents of which were dangerously close to spilling over the edges from her constant shivering.

"Detective Caldwell," she said to the older cop, who was standing in the office when she entered.

Rusty Caldwell gave her a handshake.

"Officer Nabil is outside with Billie Putnam," he said. "She was coming in for an inspection scheduled for eleven this morning but didn't see Stoner anywhere when she got here. She said she tried the office and that's where she found our friend here."

Dahlia put on a fresh pair of latex gloves as Rusty spoke, moving past the older cop to get closer to the body. Stoner was seated in his chair at the lone desk in the office. His head was thrown back against the back of the chair, his eyes closed.

"Looks like a single gunshot wound to the head," Dahlia said to herself. "No gunshot residue, stippling or powder burns around the wound, so the shooter was probably standing somewhere around the office doorway to be far enough to fire a distant shot."

"Guy's no stranger to firearms, though," Rusty said.

"What makes you say that?"

"This was a single shot to the forehead from a few feet away; I'm not gonna say the shooter was a sniper, but he had pretty solid and confident aim."

Dahlia glanced between the body and the doorway and back again.

"Good point," she said.

"Detectives!" A crime scene tech rushed into the room. "We found another one!"

"Another what?" Dahlia asked.

"Another body."

"Where?"

"Upstairs on the second floor. There's an apartment up there."

Dahlia and Rusty followed the tech from the office to the stairwell leading to the second floor. The door was open; Dahlia's eyes were immediately drawn to the slumped figure on the couch. There was a gun on the floor near the figure's hand.

"Another body," Rusty let out a breath. "What the hell happened here?"

He looked over his shoulder at Dahlia.

"Murder-suicide?"

"It's a possibility," Dahlia said.

She headed toward the body, pausing when a flicker of blue from beneath the couch caught her eye.

"Rusty," Dahlia turned to the veteran cop. "Why don't you take the witness's statement while I look around up here?"

"Sure," Rusty said with a shrug.

Dahlia addressed the crime scene tech as Rusty left the apartment.

"Could you give me a moment?" she asked.

The tech stepped out of the apartment, closing the door after exiting. Dahlia hurried over to the door to lock it. It took a few attempts to turn the lock in the handle, she found, as a result of her shaking hands. *Please don't be what I think*, Dahlia nibbled on her bottom lip as she headed back toward the couch. She carefully got down on all fours and felt beneath the sofa, taking care to not disturb any of the evidence from the body or the weapon. Her fingers tightened around the small, thin object.

"No, no, no," Dahlia whispered as she looked at the object.

It was a blue cigarette lighter. *Please don't have anything on the bottom*, she clenched her eyes shut as she turned the lighter over to take a peek at the silver bottom. Opening one viridian eye, Dahlia was greeted by the sight of a smiley face etched in permanent marker on the bottom.

I knew it ... this is Sam's lighter. This is the smiley face he drew when he was bored during the budget meeting we were required to attend last year.

Dahlia looked up from the lighter, turning her attention toward the body on the couch.

"Who are you?" she whispered to the dead man.

Dahlia jumped at the sound of footsteps coming up the stairs. Sticking the lighter in her back pocket, she raced back to the door to unlock it. She had enough time to return to the couch and strike a casual pose as Rusty poked his head into the room.

"I got the lady's statement," he said. "I had Nabil take her to get checked out after we finished. I don't want her passing out and have to deal with an unconscious broad on top of two bodies."

Dahlia was only half-listening, every few words of Rusty's drowned out by the pounding of her heart in her ears.

"That's fine, Rusty," she said. "Thank you. My partner should be here any time now so you can head out if you'd like."

"Sure. I'll send you the report when I get back to the station."

Dahlia did not respond. Her thoughts were somewhere else entirely.

★★★

Nursing a drink at the bar, Sam wanted to get completely and utterly wasted. The bartender was eyeing him each time he walked by, so Sam figured he'd probably have to move along to another bar before he was cut off. He wondered how many other bars in the area would be open to serving him more booze if he came in already wreaking of alcohol. He downed his drink quickly, doing his best to ignore the rowdy, over-served patrons shoving each other around behind him.

"De ... " Seth mumbled.

The sudden sound startled Sam, causing a shockwave to course through his body.

"What?" he asked.

"De ..." Seth repeated. *"De ... mar ... a."*

"De ... mar ... a? De-mar-a ... Demara? What's that supposed to mean, Seth?"

"Hide ... away ... De ... mar ... a ... go there ..."

Hideaway? Demara? What the hell was Seth talking about?

Sam didn't know if it was a coherent thought or the ramblings of a man high out of his mind and it bothered him. He wanted to know what it meant. He *needed* to know what it meant.

"Ay! Watch it!" Sam growled indignantly as someone bumped into him, pulling him from his thoughts.

"You wanna say that to my face?"

A mirthless grin crept onto Sam's face. He pushed up his shirt sleeves and faced the man behind him, a beefy looking Goliath whom Sam figured probably spent the majority of his days either at the bar drinking or at the gym working out.

"Say it to your face?" Sam repeated. "If you insist."

★★★

Two victims, both shot with a single bullet to the head, Dahlia reviewed her notes at her desk in the bullpen of the Odette Police Department. Murder-suicide, Rusty had mentioned; it appeared to be the case. But, Dahlia knew that the identity of the second victim threw a huge wrench into that theory. The man found dead on the couch in the upstairs apartment was Seth Tucker, Sam's stepfather and the man who was responsible for putting his mother into the hospital in a vegetative state after nearly beating her to death almost twenty years ago.

Dahlia opened the top right drawer of her desk and shoved some papers aside to get a glimpse of the blue lighter she found at the crime scene. *Sam ... you were there for Seth, weren't you?* She wondered. *But why? I thought you hated the man for what he did to your mother.*

A chill shot through her body, diving down her spine. Of course, there was a logical explanation as to why Sam would be visiting someone like Seth, but it was the answer Dahlia least wanted to be true. It was likely that both Benedict Stoner and Seth Tucker were killed by the same person, based on the circumstances of their deaths; if Sam murdered Seth, then it was likely he killed Stoner as well.

Dahlia groaned softly and put her head on her desk. She could taste her breakfast sandwich again.

"Are you okay, Dahlia?"

She lifted her head at the sound of a man's voice. It was Peter Marsden.

"I just got back from a crime scene with two bodies," she told her boyfriend and fellow detective. "And Sam has decided today was the perfect day to pull a disappearing act."

"Yikes," he said. "Rough morning; want some tea?"

Words were failing her by this point so the only response Dahlia could muster was a dip of her chin. Peter gave her a soft smile before stepping out of the bullpen. Once he was out of sight, Dahlia used a piece of paper to pick up the lighter from the drawer and stuffed it inside her briefcase. *No one needs to know about this ... not yet, at least.*

Peter returned a few moments later, carrying a mug of hot tea in his hands, which he set down on her desk.

"Herbal green tea, with lemon and one packet of sugar," he said. "Like you like it."

"Thanks," Dahlia said, taking the cup and taking a sip gratefully.

Peter took a seat at Sam's desk and began rummaging around in the mess. Dahlia watched him quietly as she sipped her tea.

"Did he give you an idea of where he might have gone?" Peter asked.

"That's funny," Dahlia said dryly. "You know Sam, Peter; if he doesn't want you to know something, he'll do whatever he can to keep you from finding it out."

"I know," Peter said with a sigh. "Wishful thinking, I guess."

He peeked through Sam's desk drawers before giving up and turning to face Dahlia.

"Want me to swing by his apartment?"

Dahlia thought things over for a moment. *The lighter ... if I can find Sam, I can ask him about the lighter, and we can maybe figure this out ... before any other evidence points the finger at him and he gets in serious trouble.*

"That's okay," Dahlia put the tea aside. "I could use a drive to clear my head. I'll see if he's there. Plus, if he is at his apartment, I can beat the snot out of him, and there won't be any witnesses."

Peter chuckled.

★★★

While the drive cleared her head, the search of Sam's apartment only made Dahlia's head hurt again. *Dammit, Sam!* She put her hands on her head, exasperated. *You're making yourself seem guiltier and guiltier! Why don't you walk into the department with a tee-shirt that has 'guilty' written across it in big, bold letters at this rate?*

The flurry of thoughts storming her mind caused Dahlia to nearly miss her ringing cell phone until it was about a ring or two away from going to voicemail.

"Hi Peter," she answered the call.

"Any luck locating our fugitive?" Peter asked.

"Fugitive?" Dahlia's voice cracked.

Peter laughed on the other end of the line.

"I meant Sam," he said. "Are you sure you're okay, Dahl? You're awfully jumpy today; I'm worried about you."

"Oh, sorry," Dahlia said. "Sam's being an asshole and complicating an already complicated situation. It's giving me a lot to think about and sort through, I guess."

"Any sign of Sam?"

"His phone is here with the battery removed, along with his badge and his service weapon. He's gone, and I have a feeling he doesn't want to be found."

"You're going to go after him, right?"

"Of course. If I tried to pull a stunt like this, Sam would be right there looking for me, through hell or high water, to read me the riot act when he found me. He always said the rules were merely a suggestion, so, if vanishing without a trace is how he wants to play the game, then he's going to get a taste of his own medicine."

"I'll put out an APB," Peter said.

"Thanks," Dahlia said before ending the call.

She spun on her heels and marched out of the apartment.

★★★

Driving around Odette, and checking all of Sam's usual haunts, Dahlia was growing increasingly worried and frustrated. His foster mother, Gloria, had not seen or heard from him, nor did his foster sister, Clarice. What concerned Dahlia was that Nina, Sam's foster sister and the person to whom he was closest, did not know where he was. He had vanished. Gripping the steering wheel tightly, she jumped at the sound of the police radio calling for her.

"Detective Bennett," the receiver crackled. "Please respond."

Still speeding down the highway, Dahlia kept one hand on the wheel as she reached for the radio receiver.

"This is Detective Bennett," she replied.

"Detective, this is dispatch. We received a hit on your APB. An individual matching the description was brought in to the Colorado Springs Police Department."

"Colorado Springs?" Dahlia said to herself, eyebrows furrowed. *Colorado Springs? What the hell was he doing there?*

"Roger, dispatch. Heading to the CSPD right now."

Odette was located an hour outside of Colorado Springs. Courtesy of the cruiser's lights and sirens, Dahlia made record time to the big city. Unfamiliar with the area, it took some navigating, but she was able to find her way to the department.

"Detective Dahlia Bennett, Odette PD," Dahlia flashed her badge to the desk sergeant upon entering the building. "I received word from dispatch that you had an individual matching the description we issued in our APB."

The desk sergeant checked her notes.

"Yes, ma'am," she said. "We brought him into holding."

"Holding? On what charges?"

"It says here ... assault, public intoxication, and disorderly conduct."

Dahlia pursed her lips. *Really, Sam? Assault? Public intoxication and disorderly conduct?*

"Yeah, that sounds like him," she said. "Can you take me to him?"

"Sure. It's this way."

Dahlia followed the officer down a hallway, through a set of double doors and into the holding area in the back of the building.

"Lieutenant Poole, this is Detective Bennett from the Odette PD," the desk sergeant said to the middle-aged blond-haired man in charge of holding. "She's here about the guy who matched the APB issued a few hours ago."

"Ah, yes, our drunk and disorderly," Lieutenant Poole said.

"Got a name?" Dahlia asked.

"Drunky McGee wouldn't give us his name at first," Lieutenant Poole grabbed a clipboard off the desk next to him. "But we ran his prints and got a hit shortly before you arrived. Guess he forgot his prints would be in the system since he was a cop."

"Well, if it is who I'm looking for," Dahlia replied. "It wouldn't be because he forgot; it would be because he's an obstreperous jackass."

"Samuel Marlowe?" Poole asked, eyebrow raised.

"Yes, unfortunately, that ass is my partner."

That nugget of info surprised Poole, his eyebrows shot upward, but his expression quickly sobered back to professionalism.

"The charges weren't going to stick, as he and his rumble partners were all equally at fault for the incident at the bar," he said. "We were going to let him and his new 'friends' sober up in the drunk tank unless you'd like to take Mr. Marlowe home?"

"Yeah, that would probably be best," Dahlia replied. "I can take him off your hands."

"I guess, though, he'd probably feel safer staying in the drunk tank," Poole said with a laugh.

"Oh, absolutely."

Poole chuckled as he pulled a full ring of keys from off his belt. He walked over to holding cell three and proceeded to unlock it.

"Let's go, sunshine," Poole said to Sam. "Your carriage awaits you, your highness."

Sam, sporting a fresh black eye and a few scratches, sauntered out of the holding cell. He saw Dahlia standing there and abruptly did an about face and returned to the holding cell.

"I'm not going with her," Sam said to Poole.

Poole glanced behind him at Dahlia.

"Samuel Chance Marlowe," Dahlia said. "Get out here. Now."

If anyone else had issued the command, Sam would have laughed in their face and told them to fuck off. But not Dahlia. He couldn't do that with Dahlia. It was because of Dahlia that he was in this predicament in the first place.

Reluctantly, Sam shuffled out of the holding cell. He said nothing and avoided any and all eye contact with his partner. Instead, Dahlia filled out the paperwork for his release while Sam silently watched her from his spot on the bench.

★★★

It wasn't until they left the Colorado Springs PD, were in Dahlia's cruiser and speeding down the highway did Dahlia finally address him.

"Are you going to tell me what's going on or am I going to have to beat it out of you?" she asked, eyes still focused on the road ahead.

Sam stared out the passenger's seat window.

"Don't pull this shit with me, Sam," Dahlia said. "First, you're a no-show at work today. Then, I see you left behind your badge, gun and cell phone, which had the battery removed, by the way, as an extra precaution. And now, I had to drive all the way out to Colorado Springs to get your drunk ass out of holding because your stupidity got you arrested. Sam, what the hell?"

What was he supposed to say? *Well, Dahlia, you and I have been partners for years now, and I'd like to even consider us friends, though we're probably close enough to consider each other honorary siblings. I've been hiding a dark secret this whole time. I'm a murderer, Dahlia. I'm a murderer. I coerced Dr. Nestmann into killing himself. I took the gun from Scott Farrow when he was holding up the high school reunion, and instead of arresting him, I chose to kill him. But what's even worse was that I enlisted my stepfather's help to get revenge on the people who nearly killed Nina. I had affairs with the women to get close enough to them to get the evidence to frame their husbands for their deaths after Seth killed them. When Seth outlived his usefulness, I finally killed him like I always wanted to. I also killed Benedict Stoner, my former drug dealer, because he was a loose end. Do you know why I had to do all that? Because of you, Dahlia. You've been digging into my crimes, and it scares me because I know you're capable of discovering the truth ... Seth told me that I should kill you to keep you from finding out the truth, but I couldn't do it, Dahlia. I couldn't kill you ... that's why I ran ... I couldn't do it.*

Sam jerked forward, wrapping his arms around his middle.

"Pull over," he gasped.

"Why? So, you can ditch me again?" Dahlia replied.

"Pull over, or I'm gonna fucking puke on you!"

Dahlia flipped on the cruiser's lights and veered off to the side of the highway. Sam flung the car door open and fell out of the car. On his hands and knees, he barely made it off the pavement and into the field of grass and overgrown foliage a few feet away before projectile vomiting. Dahlia, who had been racing after him in case he was feigning illness and was going to attempt to escape, immediately slowed her walk and winced and turned away as Sam continued to empty the contents of his stomach.

Exhausted and covered in a fine sheen of sweat, Sam closed his eyes and sat back on his heels.

"Here."

Sam looked up and saw Dahlia holding out the towel she kept in the trunk for emergency purposes. He accepted it and buried his face in it. Towel still on his head, Sam let himself be guided by Dahlia a few feet away to a clean patch of grass. She helped him sit and then took a seat next to him.

"I think it was our first case together," Dahlia said as she pulled her knees up to her chest and wrapped her arms around them. "You told me if we're going to make our partnership work, not to bullshit you. Well, Sam, same goes for you."

Sam gave no response. Dahlia lifted the towel off his face. A visible shiver shot through her body, Sam noticed, when she discovered his face was stained with tears. Without another word, Dahlia's hand fell to her side, and she turned her attention back toward the traffic whirring past the two of them. After a few minutes of silence, Sam looked over at Dahlia.

"What are you doing?" His voice was hoarse.

"Waiting," Dahlia replied simply. "I'll be right here waiting when you're ready to talk."

Of course, her natural goodness was going to make this more difficult. But he had to tell her.

"I," Sam's voice cracked. "I'm a monster."

"What do you mean?" Dahlia asked calmly.

"I've done terrible, horrendous things, Dahlia, things for which amends cannot be made."

"What if I helped you?" Dahlia asked sincerely.

"No," Sam shouted, causing Dahlia to jump. "I've fucked up so badly. I … I'm a murderer."

Dahlia said nothing. Sam searched her eyes for any flicker of emotion.

"Can you … can you tell me what happened?" she asked, pausing to clear her throat when her voice cracked.

With a shaky breath exhaled, Sam's tale commenced. He could tell by the way her hands balled into little fists and her intense focus on some random spot on the ground, that it took every ounce of Dahlia's willpower to not run, burst into tears or take her gun out of her holster and shoot him.

"Last night," he lowered his head, staring down at the ends of his askew and wrinkled white shirt. "I ... I went to Stoner's Automotive and—"

"I know," Dahlia said.

Sam's head jerked up, and he immediately stared at his partner.

"You know?" he repeated.

Dahlia kept her eyes elsewhere as she dipped her hand into her pants pocket for a second. She pulled something out and held it out for Sam to see.

"My lighter ..." he whispered.

"When I went upstairs to the apartment, the light hit it in the right way that it was able to catch my eye. I found it under the couch," Dahlia said.

Sam shook his head, bringing his focus back to the present. He felt Seth's grip on the gun tighten. Taking one last good look at his stepfather, Sam put his finger over Seth's on the trigger.

"This is for my mother," Sam whispered. "This is for Charlotte."

The trigger was pulled, and Sam had just enough time to let go of Seth's hand and jump back to avoid the spray of blood and brains from his stepfather. Breathing heavily, Sam's knees buckled, and he collapsed to the floor, silver eyes still locked on Seth.

That's when it must have fallen out of my pocket, Sam figured.

"You murdered Stoner and Seth, setting up the scene to look like Seth killed Stoner before taking his own life," Dahlia said. "Didn't you?"

"Yes ..."

"Why?"

"Because ..." Sam wasn't sure what to say. "Because they were criminals ..."

"Sam, that's the damn pot calling the kettle black!" Dahlia said. "And what do you think you are, after doing all those things? A hero? A vigilante of justice?"

"No, I—"

"You're a cop, Sam; what the hell were you thinking? Why didn't you ask me for help?" Dahlia rambled on, not giving Sam a chance to answer.

Not that he would know how to answer her questions if he had the chance to.

"I guess …" Sam said. "I guess it's because I know that walking the straight and narrow wouldn't amount to shit."

"What's that supposed to mean?"

Sam fell back into the soft, fragrant grass behind him. He stared up at the sky, watching the billowy white clouds as they floated by at a snail's pace.

"I tried to do the right thing. I used to be a good little boy scout, following the rules, and you know, doing my part to keep the city safe from evildoers."

"What changed?"

"I learned the hard way that there's a gray area to justice. I had a chance to give back and try to pay forward the kindness and good fortune that Edwin and the Hills gave me when I was at my lowest point. Dillon Harris; that kid was in a similar situation to what I was in, so I wanted to help him like Edwin helped me. His mother was abusive and neglectful like my stepfather was with my mother and me. For a minute there, I thought I might be making some progress; Dillon was starting to come out of his shell for a bit, but then his mother intervened and prevented me from having any contact with her son. I followed all the rules to try and overcome this. I contacted the Department of Family and Child Services to do welfare checks, and I tried contacting the family myself to show Dillon that someone out there cared for him and wanted to help him. The only thing that got me was a threat from Dillon's mom that, if we didn't stop bugging her, she would sue the department for harassment. You know what I did? I listened to the rules and stopped bothering them. Do you know what happened because of that? Dillon killed his mother and then went and shot up the school right afterward. I was done following the rules after that day. If following the rules and 'doing the right thing' got Edwin killed, then I was going to take justice into my own hands."

"But that community outreach program you started with Edwin has done a lot of good, Sam."

"Yeah, now that I'm not a part of it."

Sam winced when Dahlia smacked his chest.

"Must you be so irritating?" she said.

"Do you think I enjoy being this way? Hurt and angry at the world all the time for the constant string of misfortunes that it keeps foisting on me day in and day out? Having a self-imposed exile from anyone that I care about because I'm afraid anyone who gets close to me might get hurt? Being forced to numb my pain with drugs to get through the day? Sorry, Bennett, but that's nowhere near as fun as it sounds, trust me."

"Sam ..."

He heard her sniff but kept his focus on the sky above.

"I couldn't risk Arthur Emmons, Louie Donato or Adam Young not paying for their crimes. They nearly killed someone whom I care about deeply, someone I promised Edwin I'd watch over and protect. When she nearly died, I realized I broke my promise. I had to fix the things I fucked up, even if it meant framing them for the murders of their wives. I had to make sure that they were going to go to prison for the rest of their lives and not have a chance to get out and do the same thing to someone else. If they got out of prison or were found not guilty in court, how many other people would be at risk of dying from those three drug dealers?"

"But why Seth? Why work with a man that you hated beyond all reason?" Dahlia asked.

Sam shrugged.

"I ... I thought about doing it myself, but I couldn't imagine killing innocent women like that," he let out a laugh that was full of disdain and not humor. "Who better for the job than the man who killed my mother and left me to find her bloodied body in our apartment?"

"And why did Seth agree to help you? What did he get out of all this?"

"Seth's been a drunk and an addict for as long as I can remember, so I found that I could control him by supplying him with drugs and alcohol. When I was at one of their houses, the Emmons, Donato or Young place, I had easy access to their stashes. Plus, I was able to gather whatever evidence I needed to give to Seth to kill the women and then frame the husbands for it."

"I was right. Arthur Emmons, Louie Donato and Adam Young were all innocent."

"Of killing their wives? Yes," Sam said. "But of other crimes? Guilty as hell."

"And when you finished the … your … hit list, you killed Seth?"

Sam closed his eyes and brought an arm over his face. *He didn't outlive his usefulness, and it wasn't out of revenge that I killed Seth,* Sam thought. *There's another reason I had to do it.*

"Yeah …"

"Nice to see you too," Seth said. "What do you want?"

Sam said nothing as he headed into the apartment.

"Shut the door," he said.

Seth shut the door and locked it.

"What do you want?" Seth repeated.

"I've come to warn you," Sam said.

"Of what?"

Sam turned around to face his stepfather.

"My partner," he said. "You're going to have to lay low for a while. My partner is starting to wonder if something's wrong with some cases we've worked on."

"Is your partner asking about the Emmons chick?" Seth asked. "I did her in like you asked me to."

"I know you did and no, thankfully not. She wasn't entirely sure what to make of all the evidence pointing toward Arthur, but I have no doubt that we'll be able to get a conviction with the way we staged the scene," he said. "Emmons is going to pay for nearly killing Nina."

"What about the other two guys that you talked about? That 'Louie' guy and 'Adam' something-or-other; I thought you said they need to be 'eliminated?'"

"I did and don't worry, that's still part of the plan. However, if you jump too soon, Bennett is going to start putting two and two together, and then we'll be in a pickle."

"Why don't you just off her?" Seth asked.

Sam's eyes narrowed until they were barely more than slits.

"Did you just suggest what I think you did?" his voice was no more than a whisper.

Seth folded his arms across his chest.

"You heard me. Kill your partner."

Sam's sight went red as the words registered in his mind. He charged at Seth, grabbing two fistfuls of the older man's shirt and shoving him back against the nearest wall.

"What the fuck are you doing?" Seth coughed, sounding like the wind had been knocked out of him from the impact with the wall.

"Don't you ever think about hurting her," Sam said through gritted teeth.

Seth tried to shove him back and break free from his hold, but Sam held firm.

"I ain't gonna kill her!" Seth raised his hands in surrender as much as Sam's grip allowed.

Sam loosened his grip enough for Seth to slap his hands away.

Even though Seth claimed he wasn't going to hurt Dahlia, Sam knew that he couldn't trust his stepfather's word. As soon as everything was over, he had to kill Seth to protect Dahlia.

"When ..." Sam started to say. "When you started asking questions ... Seth suggested that I ... I kill you, Bennett ..."

"He what?" Dahlia gasped.

"He wanted me to kill you, but there was no way in hell that I could ever do that. I made him promise that he wasn't going to do something to you and he did, but I knew I couldn't trust him," Sam let out a shaky breath and squeezed his eyes shut to keep himself from tearing up again. "He already killed one person I loved, so what was going to stop him from taking away another?"

"Sam, look at me."

He didn't move.

"Sam, look at me," Dahlia repeated.

Sam still didn't move. He felt Dahlia's hands grab his arms and remove it from covering his face.

"Open your eyes!"

He obeyed, finding Dahlia staring intently down at him. Under her intense gaze, Sam felt the words he never wanted to say bubbling up in his throat, threatening to spill out of his mouth.

"I couldn't let Seth kill you, Dahlia because you're my best friend," Sam said.

He hated mushy, sentimental stuff.

"I like working with you," he said. "I've even grown to love you like you were my kid sister or something. I couldn't let anything happen to you because I need you in my life, Dahlia. You're my conscience, my lifeline. The only problem is that I realized that way too late. If only I had opened myself up to that realization earlier, maybe, I wouldn't be in this position. But I'm glad that I was able to come to that understanding before anything ... you know ... happened ... to you ..."

Sam saw Dahlia avert her gaze, blinking rapidly in an attempt to keep the tears at bay.

"You've been a giant pain in the ass for years now, Sam," she said. "When I transferred home to Odette, I was excited to start my career as a cop. I thought I could change the world. And then, I find out that I'm going to be paired up with the top detective at the department; I was ecstatic. At least, I was ecstatic until I found out that this detective wanted nothing to do with me. You know, it's funny, after our first case together, when you refused to let me quit, I made it my personal mission to do whatever it took to get you to let me inside those damned walls that you built up. It wasn't easy, I'll give you that. I may not always agree with your methods or beliefs, but I know that I've learned a lot from you about the law, justice, the world and even myself. If I'm completely honest with myself, I know deep down that I love you too. Before you pretty much made me fix things with my estranged brothers, I started to consider you to be like a brother to me. And after, I definitely viewed you as my brother."

Dahila got up from where she had been sitting, dusting some stray blades of grass and dirt from off her pants. She stood in front of him, holding her hand out.

"Stand up."

Sam eyed her hand for a moment before reaching up and taking her hand. Once he was standing up again, Dahlia brushed off some of the debris that collected on his clothes as well. She adjusted his shirt and then placed a gentle peck on Sam's cheek.

"That's for having the balls to admit what you did and doing everything you could to protect me. And this," Sam didn't have time to register what Dahlia was doing when her fist collided forcefully with his face. "Is for all the stupid shit you did and for making me have to clean it all up!"

Sam stood there holding his burning cheek. The punch was probably going to leave a second colorful black eye in a few days. He wasn't sure what stung more, the punch or the kiss. Regardless, he figured he deserved both.

"So, um, now what?" Sam asked with uncertainty.

Her back to him, Dahlia turned around slowly. Sam's eyes were immediately drawn to the lighter in her hands. Dahlia was flicking the ignition with her thumb. Tears were welling up in her eyes.

"You were in Colorado Springs all night," she said softly.

"What?"

"You were in Colorado Springs. Do you hear me? You were nowhere near Stoner's Automotive last night. Seth Tucker wanted drugs from Benedict Stoner, and when Stoner wouldn't give him anything, Seth shot him, stole his drugs and went upstairs to shoot up before shooting himself."

"Dahlia, don't …" Sam started to say.

She held a hand up to stop him.

"You've done enough talking," Dahlia said.

She tossed the lighter up and down in her hand lightly. Sam could only watch as Dahlia took the lighter and threw it into the field where it was swallowed up by the long blades of grass and overgrowth. They stood silently next to each other, staring out at the place where the lighter may have landed.

"When we get back to Odette," Dahlia stared forward at the field. "You are going to go to Nina, and the two of you are going to leave for a while until this whole thing blows over; do you hear me?"

"Yes," Sam said just as quietly. "And after that?"

"After that … I don't know. You've left me with quite a mess. I am not going to let your stupid decisions fuck up my career. I've worked too hard to build a name and reputation for myself, and you are *not* going to destroy that. Like I said, you've left me with quite a mess, Samuel Marlowe."

The edges of his lips curled up into a small smile.

"Well, if it helps, I know there's no one better to clean up my messes than you, Dahlia," Sam said.

With a shake of her head and a sigh, Dahlia headed back to the police cruiser.

★★★

It was bittersweet to not have Sam around, especially after the Captain designated her as his new lead detective during what she told him was an 'extended leave of absence' for Sam. Sitting at her desk in the bullpen, Dahlia's thoughts began to wander. She hated seeing Sam's usually cluttered desk empty and vacant.

"Hey."

Dahlia shook her head to rein her thoughts back in. She looked up to see Peter standing in front of her, a bouquet of flowers in his hands.

"Thought you could use some cheering up," he said.

Dahlia gave him a small smile as she got up to accept the flowers. She placed a peck on his cheek, rising up on her tiptoes to do so.

"You have no idea."

She stepped away to grab a mug and water to put the flowers in. When she returned, Dahlia found Peter standing at her desk, looking down at an envelope.

"What's that?" she asked.

"The mailroom attendant stopped by," Peter said. "I don't know what it is. All he said that he had a special delivery for Detective Dahlia Bennett."

Dahlia's brows furrowed in confusion as she accepted the letter from Peter. It was a plain white envelope, she noted, with no remarkable features, save for her name written across it in a familiar handwriting. There was no return address, however, to confirm her suspicions.

"It couldn't have come through the regular mail," she said. "There's no stamp or address for either the sender or the recipient."

"I don't know," Peter said with a shrug. "The attendant only said that whoever dropped it off stated it was urgent this letter be delivered directly to you, Detective."

Dahlia opened the letter and discovered the writing inside was familiar too. It was as she surmised; the writing belonged to Sam.

Hey Bennett,

I've been doing a lot of thinking ever since our little chat on the side of the highway. I've come to the conclusion that me just sitting around, waiting for things to blow over is a waste of my time. I could be doing so much good somewhere out there. So, that's what I've decided to do. I'm going to take your advice and start fresh someplace new and try to make amends for all the shit I've done. I think it'll balance out my negative karma crap, right? Ah, hell. Whatever. If it does, it does. If it doesn't, well, then I'm in for a hell of a life in my next lifetime. Either way, thanks, Bennett. Yin and yang; Thing 1 and Thing 2; Bonnie and Clyde; whatever you want to call it, you're my better half. I owe my new life to you, and I will make you truly proud of me. I'll miss you, Bennett. Take care of Gloria, Clarice, and Raymond for me. Oh, and Peter, too.

Do what you need to do to make things right, Bennett. I'm ready to pay for my crimes, but ONLY on one condition: YOU have to be the one to bring me in. I owe you at least that much for all you've done for me. Until then, I'll be Hiding Away somewhere over the rainbow (or some shit like that).

Catch me if you can,

SM

"Make amends?" Peter asked, having read the letter over her shoulder. "'Catch me if you can? Pay for my crimes?' What's that supposed to mean?"

Dahlia folded up the letter and held it in her hands.

"It's a very long, and quite frankly, unbelievable story," she said. "Something that would only make sense if you know Sam Marlowe."

"Well, I do happen to know the man, so, let's hear it."

"Let's go somewhere quiet," Dahlia said. "So, we can talk."

"Sure," Peter said, offering her his hand.

Catch me if you can, Dahlia reflected as she and Peter walked out of the bullpen together. *Well, challenge accepted, Sam. Challenge accepted.*

SALLIE MOPPERT

A New York native, Sallie has a Master's degree in Criminal Justice, with a Specialization in Forensic Science. A lifelong mystery fan, she has combined her love and passion for writing with her interests in criminal justice, law, and forensic science.

Sallie currently resides in New York with her family and two dogs, and works as a freelance writer/editor.

READER'S GUIDE

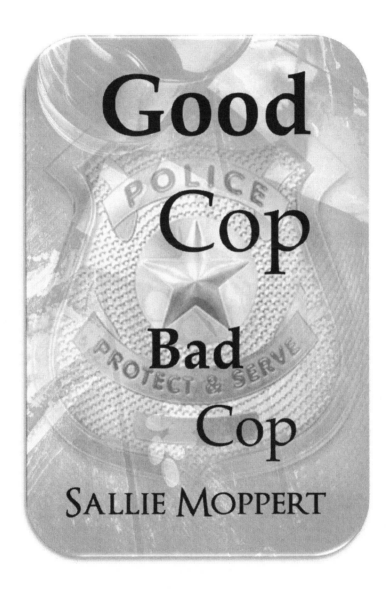

Good
Cop

Bad
Cop

SALLIE MOPPERT

1. How did Seth's attack on Charlotte set the stage for Sam's downfall?

2. How did Edwin's influence affect Sam? Why didn't it prevent Sam from going down the path to vigilante justice?

3. What was Nina's role in Sam's life? How did she influence him? Was that influence positive or negative?

4. What were the other major events in Sam's life and how did they contribute to his downfall?

5. Why did Captain Buchanan think Sam needed a partner? What did he hope to accomplish?

6. Did Dahlia influence Sam? What about the reverse? What effect did they have on each other?

7. Why did Sam turn to Seth as a tool for vigilante justice?

8. What is Sam's motivation to leave Odette? Do you think he will truly change?

9. How do you think Dahlia changed over the course of the stories?

10. Sam believed that 'the means justify the end.' Do you agree?

A Note from the Publisher

Dear Reader,

Thank you for reading Sallie Moppert's debut novel *Good Cop Bad Cop*.

We feel the best way to show appreciation for an author is by leaving a review. You may do so on any of the following sites:

www.ZimbellHousePublishing.com
Goodreads.com
Amazon.com
or Kindle.com

Join our mailing list to receive updates on new releases, discounts, bonus content, and other great books from

Or visit us online to sign up at:

http://www.ZimbellHousePublishing.com